HELL HOUNDS

ANDREW P. WESTON

Perseid Press
P.O. Box 584
Centerville MA 02632

HELL HOUNDS

Cover art and cover design by Roy Mauritsen.

Cover design © Perseid Press
A Perseid Press Original

First Perseid Press Kindle edition October 2017
First Perseid Press Trade edition October 2017
First Perseid Press Electronic Edition October 2017

Hard cover ISBN 13: 978-0-9982687-9-8, ISBN 10: 09982687-9-8
Trade version: ISBN-13: 978-0-9982687-8-1, ISBN 10: 09982687-8-X
Kindle version, ISBN-13: 978-0-9982687-7-4, ISBN-10: 09982687-7-1
ePub version: ISBN-13: 978-0-9982687-6-7, ISBN-10: 09982687-6-3

Published in the United States of America

10 9 8 7 6 5 4 3 2 1

To Janet,
who continues to let me play in the best playground — ever!

And to all those who know that dreams are both the

journey and the destination:

"But only in their dreams can men be truly free,

'Twas always thus, and always thus will be . . ."

John Keating (Robin Williams' character in the motion

picture *Dead Poets Society*)

Contents

The misery of that sight of souls in Hell
Condemned and constant is their loss
Groveling, to howl like dogs, beneath the flail
That flattens to the foul soaked ground, and try
Vainly for ease by turning. And the whale
Above them roams and ravens the loathsome hound
Cerberus, and feeds upon them

– Dante Alighieri 1265–1321, *The Divine Comedy*

Prologue

Hidden amongst the ziggurat spires adorning the north-western corner of the Palace of Westmonster, I had a commanding view of a midnight skyline that could only belong to Olde London Town. As usual, the rainbow-haloed blush of the streetlights far below twinkled into the distance, distinguishing those parts of the city anchored in the modern day from the remnants scattered throughout the broad spectrum of other eras known to saturate this, the topsy-turviest existence in all of latter-day hell; otherwise known as the Juxtapose level.

From my vantage point, a patchwork quilt of simple open fires, gas streetlamps, and brilliant neon beacons spread in all directions. Whatever the period, it made no difference; everything remained veiled beneath the stain of original sin.

I inhaled deeply, my phantom nostrils flaring in pleasure as a pungent blend of brimstone and exhaust fumes filled my nonexistent lungs.

Home: the perfect place for me, Daemon Grim, the Reaper, Satan's personal enforcer.

This was my kind of place, and I loved it here. But I suppose that was understandable, as I was top of the food chain.

Movement down below and on the opposite bank of the River Tombs caught my attention. I phased, and in the blink of an eye materialized among the crenels of the highest buttresses on the far side of Westmonster Bridge. Safe amongst the shadows, I adjusted my perspective and zeroed in on Phosphate Magnum Square in the district of Lambsdeath, a place synonymous with hellegal weapons trafficking. Not that you could call it a square anymore. Ruptured gas mains, shattered cobbles, and a veritable no man's land of debris from semi-demolished buildings littered the Victorian thoroughfare, all courtesy of our Sibitti friends and the latest tremors they had engendered over the past several months.

Vegetation, taking advantage of the unexpected reprieve from all-enveloping brickwork, had exploded from every available crack and fissure, adding a tangled maze of roots and foliage to the already treacherous minefield that remained. Along with it came cloying swarms of insects. Freed at last from the confines of centuries-old pipe work, they wove their droning spell through the air like chitinous starlings; worrying people and animals alike under a relentless assault of gnashing mandibles and venomous stings.

If that wasn't distracting enough, an endless drizzle of oily black rain fell from leaden clouds, making the going treacherous underfoot. But not for the assassin I'd espied.

Dressed from head to toe in a figure-hugging flaytex catsuit and soft-soled boots, she looked completely at home in this environment, and every inch the femme fatale she clearly was. In fact, so innocuous was her presence that she was able to pierce the legion of hearse flies swarming about the crown of debris without attracting the slightest curiosity.

An exceptional achievement. And part of the reason for my interest.

On Satan's orders, I had increased my efforts to uncover the extent of the cancer eating its way through the heart of our society. A difficult task. And yet, indirectly, I'd had the help of the late—and not so great—Dr. Thomas Neill Cream, for his antics alerted me to the existence of the problem in the first place.

Now reassigned to the Cirque du Freak, Cream would be out of the way for millennia, enjoying the torments lavished upon our lobotomized, mutant novelty acts. That still left Chopin and Tesla, though, along with Erra and his Sibitti ass-wipes. And, of course, we now had our very own psychopathic angel on the loose.

A devil's cauldron of a mix if ever there was one.

Bearing in mind what had happened to us the last time out, Satan wanted me to expand my team to ensure we were never too thin on the ground again. Easier said than done. For while the underworld was full of murderous cutthroats and rogues, it hadn't been easy finding that special someone with skill set that marked them out from all the other cattle.

In fact, out of the dozen or so candidates I had considered during the past four months, only one had made a lasting impression: the young lady below me now.

Tonight would be the fifth assignment I'd tagged along on (without her knowledge, of course) and I had to admit, I was impressed with her work. Over the past several weeks she had managed to take out a Low Court judge, midsession, as he summed up a case in the primary courtroom of the Olde Bully; a high-value inmate under witness protection in the isolation wing of Wormblood Scrubs maximum security prison; and her last job involved one of the most clinical demonstrations I had ever witnessed of how to dispatch an entire coven of Dread-Locks while armed with nothing but a pair of combat knives blessed in the flames of the Bālefire.

Not bad for someone who doesn't appear augmented apart from a preternatural ability to move stealthily. It must be down to training and focus. I wonder what she'll be like once she receives her enhancements.

I had already made up my mind, but I wanted this final opportunity to make sure I had settled on the right choice.

I noticed she had nestled amongst the undergrowth and creepy-crawlies to wait for her target to appear, most likely from one of the derelict buildings opposite, so I seized the opportunity to scan through her hellographic-profile to help pass the time.

Okay . . .

Marie-Anne Charlotte de Corday d'Armont, known simply as Charlotte Corday, or l'ange de l'assassinat, the angel of the assassination. Born 1768 in France to a minor aristocratic family, she was executed by guillotine when only twenty-four years old for the murder of Jacobin leader, Jean-Paul Marat, a person whom history calls the instigator of the radicalized course undertaken by insurgents during the initial stages of the French revolution.

I flicked across to an addendum.

From what it says here, Marat was responsible for the political purge of the prisons. He believed France was under the threat of invasion, and that those held in custody would rise up on their release and fight against the people. So he ordered them slain. I glanced at the death toll and my eyes widened in pleasure: *over fourteen hundred killed in Paris alone, including a goodly number of priests. Nice work. Unfortunately, that led to a split amongst the factions, and especially with those against such an aggressive stance. Ah, I see, Marat singled out the Girondins in particular. Although they were a minor group, they played a leading role in the legislative assembly and promoted a more tempered course through which to engender nationalism. Hmm. Evidently, Charlotte sympathized with the Girondin movement, and became so concerned by Marat's witch-hunt against his own people that she took it upon herself to visit his home on the pretext of providing valuable information regarding a supposed Girondin uprising. Once alone, she stabbed him whilst he was in the bath* . . . I did a double take. *In the bath! How embarrassing.*

I glanced down at my would-be recruit.

At least it explains her preference for daggers.

Then I flipped back to the bullet points regarding her trial:

At her sentencing, she declared, "I have killed one man to save thousands." Oh dear, oh dear. Yet another principled idealist, eh?

Next, I took a closer look at the more pertinent details. They made interesting reading:

After arriving in hell, Charlotte went through the inevitable period of trauma and maladjustment. Like most of the condemned, she couldn't believe her "righteous" act had resulted in damnation and an eternity of judgment. Her outrage led to a number of ill-advised run-ins with injustice. Needless to say, she pissed off the wrong people, and the Boss ordered the Undertaker to permanently disfigure her as an incentive to shut up and switch on.

And switch on she did, for once she resigned herself to her lot, Charlotte made the nature of her infinite punishment the subject of a whole new vocation and, after changing her name to reflect the character of her deformity, abandoned the land of her birth and set about acquiring the expertise that would put Charlotte Corday—aka Lady Gemini—on the map as one of the underworld's most accomplished assassins.

I brought up a hellographic representation of Lady Gem-ini's latest persona and took a moment to study the ravaged countenance slowly spinning in the air before me.

The right side of her face embodied the rest of her lithe and athletic form. It was flawless. As pale as alabaster, her skin was so smooth and blemish free that I thought at first she must be wearing a mask molded from liquid porcelain, an ef-fect only heightened by the shimmering luster of raven-blue hair cascading down over her shoulders.

Her face separated by a livid puckered scar running down the center of her skull, her left side marred by flaking contusions and gaping lesions, she reminded me of a parch-ment that had been left out in the sun to crack and dry. The two halves of her face attached to each other with a series of jagged surgical staples that showed clearly through gothic makeup and Ombre lipstick. I could only imagine the pain she would experience every time she tried to make any facial expression.

Fortunately, I completed my run-through just in time.

Across the street, a small crowd of mobsters had just ex-ited an old style ale house, and Lady Gemini came even more alert. Hunkering down into a small depression created by the collapse of a major sewer tunnel, she removed a long cylin-drical pipe from one of her elongated thigh-flaps, and rum-maged around in her breast pocket with the other hand.

I watched her movements with professional curiosity.

She hasn't taken her eyes off them once. Now that's the kind of attitude I want to see.

The group comprised two boss types: one a Gomez Ad-ams wannabe; the other a startlingly accurate representation of what you would get if you stuffed a bulldog inside human flesh; a statutory retinue of muscle-bound, knuckle-drag-ging, brain-dead hoods; and a hulking great lawyer dripping mucus and blood with every step. His steaming name badge gleamed dully in the twilight, and identified him as *Othello*.

Scanning their auras, I doubted the combined IQs of the thugs would challenge the slime Othello left in his wake, so they were obviously there to look mean, grunt in single syllables, and take bullets for their masters.

Which is what they'll probably be doing a few seconds from now . . .

I adjusted the sensitivity of my sweeps and glanced back and forth between the two parties. The Godfather wake was oblivious to the danger. Gemini merely studied them from her place of concealment and slowly raised the tube to her lips.

So who's the mark?

Gemini's heartbeat never wavered. Nor was there any discernible peak of excitement. If anything, her esoteric presence diminished until next to nothing.

She's the proverbial ice queen: detached, focused, professional.

Without warning, the air shimmered and Gemini winked out of sight.

A chameleon mesh? This should get interes–

No sooner had she disappeared than the undulating mass of hearse flies orbiting her proximity swooped away and descended en masse upon the unfortunate gangsters. In moments, they were twisting and turning and waving their arms so furiously it looked as if they had suddenly decided to engage in a hip-hop dance off.

Is she *doing that?*

Strangled curses turned the air blue as overzealous insects began to bite.

One voice cried out louder than the others.

"Ow!"

Othello slapped the side of his filthy reptilian neck. He coughed, staggered, and reached out to support himself on the nearest boss. Mr. Gomez flinched from contact with a lawyer: he swatted Othello's hand away as if his illustrious hellegally-qualified acquaintance had the plague. Seconds later, Othello's knees gave way and he crashed to the floor, whereupon his essence started to fade almost immediately.

The rest of the entourage took one look at the dissipating mist and starburst away from the scene in terror, closely followed by an inquisitive cloud of hungry buzzing friends.

Oh, very clever. She made it look like a simple acci– Eh?

By the time I looked back, Gemini had already slithered down from the mound and was halfway toward Westmonster Causeway.

Unholy shit but she's fast. I had never seen her run before. *I wonder how long she can keep it up.*

I never found out. Reaching the banks of the river, Gemini kept going—straight as a die—leaped the shattered balustrade and jumped straight into the filthy waters of the Tombs without creating so much as a splash.

Content to remain submerged, she allowed the current to carry her south, toward Davy Jones' Locker, a place I was familiar with. The world of the living knew that area as Battersea Station—a decommissioned power plant—but here in hell, the Locker served as the main port for the whole of Juxtapose and was under the control of the Pirate Lords, a fierce band of brigands who catered to the needs of those voyagers and traders mad enough to brave the worst stretch of interdimensionhell water in the underworld: the Bitter Sea. A crazy undertaking to even contemplate now the Sibitti had stirred things up.

The pirates were a savage lot, and I owed them a debt of gratitude. Nevertheless, I didn't want to mix business with pleasure. Not tonight.

I tracked Gemini as she slowly drifted along. By the time she reached the ruined environs of St Thomas' Hospital, I decided it would be best to act.

Descending sharply, I morphed into a tangible form, scooped her out from the murky depths, and deposited her before the shattered doors of the main building itself.

Once again, her tenacity and resolve impressed me.

Despite the surprise, Gemini didn't panic; she landed lightly on the balls of her feet, knives drawn, and her posture combat ready.

The essence of her blades sang to me and caused my eyes to ignite deep in the folds of my cowl.

When she finally registered who had interrupted her private sojourn along the capital's most infamous waterway, her deformed brow twitched upward but she didn't relax her guard.

Oh, I think I'm going to like you.

I thought it best to reciprocate.

Removing my scythe from within the folds of my cloak, I held it before me and, with a commanding thought, expanded it into its combat configuration. Only then did I discern the slightest flare of alarm skittering along the outer edge of her aura.

"What did you use back there?" I asked by way of introduction. "Was it hemlock, oleander, or Deadly Nightshade?"

"My own special concoction," she replied, "formulated to blend the fungal properties of a natural bite with the toxic effects of monkshood. My culture can cause fatal reactions within five to ten seconds of reaching the bloodstream."

"I noticed. And it mimicked hearse fly symptoms perfectly: nausea, dizziness and almost instantaneous asphyxiation. Ingenious."

"Not ingenious enough though, was it?" Her gaze never wavered. "But why don't we dispense with the act and idle pleasantries and jump straight to the part where you reap my sorry ass for being a naughty girl? It'll be interesting to experience how the Undertaker will screw me over this time around."

Yes. I'm going to like you a lot. You've a spine of steel, and you're not afraid to cut to the chase.

"Well, down here your life *is* a stage, and under normal circumstances I would be your curtain call. But fortunately for you, I like your ass the way it is."

Gemini didn't seem amused by my teasing. Her eyebrow arched even higher, and I had to fight the impulse not to laugh out loud.

"What do you mean?" she spat.

"It just so happens that I'm on the hunt for a *naughty* girl—one who wants to expand her repertoire to include a more unsophisticated audience." I stepped closer. "Interested?"

"For real?"

"Yes. I've been monitoring your activities rather closely over the past several weeks. Not only can you handle yourself in a fight, but you seem to have a predisposition toward stealth and speed and an uncanny knack with insects. Tell me, are you limited to small fry or can you influence other things in a useful way?"

"You mean can I control animals . . . or something even larger?" She shrugged. "If I must. Although with humans I tend to stick to pushing impulses or ideas into their heads. It takes far too much concentration to try anything more. And

I tend to shy away from demons unless they're distracted. It wouldn't do for one of them to catch me snooping around inside their tiny little one-track alien minds."

Humans and demons? Without augmentation? Outstanding.

"Impressive. Then why not take what you do to a whole other level?"

"To another level?"

I could tell by the way she kept echoing my questions that Gemini hadn't cottoned on to what I was offering.

It's time to be direct. "I've been following you for a reason, Gemini. I'd like to offer you a job."

"A job?" My statement only seemed to confuse her more. "What? You want *me* to take someone out for *you*? But why, you're the Reap–" Then she put the pieces together. "Jesus Christ!" she blasphemed, and the ground beneath our feet trembled at the sound of her words as, wide-eyed, Gemini stared into the depths of my hood and mumbled, "Is this a joke?"

I raised my scythe toward her, business end first, and dipped into the vast reservoir of power within me. In moments, the glyphs adorning my armor blazed to life and steaming tendrils of sulfur wafted off into the night.

"Why don't you find out? Hold on tight to *this* with both hands."

Gemini's gaze dropped to the razor sheen of the finely crafted medusanite. I studied her closely as she took in every detail of the wave frost—the distinctive pattern created from its forging amongst the flames of the Bãlefire, and subsequent cooling in the glacial ice flows of Niflheim—and then looked back to me.

"Seriously?"

"Trust me. It never cuts or causes harm unless I want it to. In a way, this weapon is also my staff of office. It does more, much more, than most people realize."

I waited.

But not for long. Apparently, Gemini wasn't one to ever beat about the bush.

"Fuck it!" Grimacing, she clenched her teeth, scrunched her eyes tight, and reached out to seize the blade in both hands.

No sooner had her skin made contact than I channeled the waiting energy down along the shaft and into her fragile flesh.

A coruscating skein of power surrounded Gemini as if she were inside a bubble. She gasped, tensed, and her back arched as the sizzling penumbra lifted her nearly a foot into the air.

Now transfixed, I had her complete attention.

"Marie-Anne Charlotte de Corday d'Armont, be advised: You are about to be anointed into the Ancient Disorder of Hell Hounds, a fraternity whose history is as malevolent as it is abominable. Few are considered and even fewer chosen. Do you understand the gravitas of what you now face?"

She nodded for me to continue.

"And do you gravely swear that you will unfaithfully adhere to the debased tenets of our creed, that you will do your utmost to be guided by the Laws of Lucifer, to protect and defend the most despicable of the Doctrines of the Devil? Will you endeavor to pursue all enemies of the state throughout the length and breadth of the Sheolspace continuum and do your damnedest to execute both them and your duty without fear of favor, or hope of reprieve?"

"I, Marie-Anne Charlotte de Corday d'Armont, do so swear."

As she spoke, Gemini ran one hand along the razor's edge of my weapon. Blood flowed, only to evaporate instantly in a sputtering rush as the genetic key was accepted.

I imbibed her scent, and reverted to ancient Hellanese:

"*Mar-sin troh a' lùthseain mi sealbġhetoman a' Satanasaínim* (Then by the power invested in me and in the name of Satan), *Thu ar thoir* ŭghdrash *do ruaígfeadháte uile a' ríghachdes measg ilfrinn* (You are empowered to hunt throughout all the realms of hell)."

Uttered aloud, the timbre of our most primal and archaic language drew forth the full dominion of the Bãlefire. It took effect almost immediately, so I placed my free hand upon the crown of Gemini's head to complete the indoctrination ceremony:

"*Fritheille a-níse etom gu suthain. Cho cobhair mi, Drôch-Fhear báirig* (Serve now and forevermore. So says the everlasting Dark Lord)."

I exerted my will, and the nimbus encompassing Gemini bloomed with amber and scarlet mastery. It began to pulsate, and concentric waves of dreadful potency radiated inward, infusing her skin in the rose gold vitality of the fires of Hades.

As the spectacle diminished, Gemini slowly descended to the ground.

Wonder etched her features in a sweet lopsided smile and she kept turning her hands back and forth, over and over, as if she expected them to burst into flames at any moment. Eventually, she looked up at me, eyes still aglow from the inner furnace.

"So what now?"

"Now your life changes: over the next twelve hours or so, the Bãlefire will bond with your DNHA and trigger the full range of your occult enhancements. Don't be fooled. While we've had a taste of what they might be, prepare yourself for one or two surprises.

"If I were you, I'd use my remaining time wisely. Finish whatever it is you were doing. See your client and get your pay, tonight. Oh, and ensure you take your name off the lists. As skilled and infamous as you've become, you're not a simple assassin for hire anymore. Then get some rest; you're going to need everything you've got for tomorrow."

"Tomorrow?"

"When you report for duty." I paused, raised my hand and spoke a single word in the divine language. "*A-hôt* (Sister)."

Gemini jumped as if she had received an electric shock.

"The encryption I've just given you will allow you access through our own private entrance, Traitors Gate. If you survive the tests, the cipher will permanently bond to your essence—"

"Hang on! Survive the tests . . . What bloody tests?"

Gemini had the decency to appear genuinely outraged.

I phased without bothering to answer. A moment later I traversed the festering midnight pall that shrouded Juxtapose, on my way back toward the Den of Iniquity. When I glanced behind, it was obvious Gemini was a bit panicky. I thought it might be nice to exacerbate the problem, just to see how she handled the unexpected.

Projecting a death's-head grin through the ether, I crooned: *Funny you should mention 'bloody tests.' I hope for your sake you're as good as I think you are. Still, I suppose we'll all find out tomorrow, won't we?*

I cut the signal as a blistering tirade fried the atmosphere. *Oh yes, she'll do.*

Chapter 1: Made to Measure

Fresh from his latest spending spree, the Angel Grislington — now known to a select few as Angelus Giseldone — carried a brace of bespite suits, jackets, trousers and neckties in a garment-bag over one shoulder as he made his merry way along Bondage Street toward his next appointment.

The fluttering radiance of Paradise did little to lift the gloom from a sky pregnant with clouds and rush-hour traffic fumes. Angelus didn't mind. He was managing to create quite a stir all by himself and he reveled in it.

The *click* of his well-shod heels and the rhythmic *tap–tap–tap* of the spiked umbrella tip signaled to other denizens that he was approaching; his arrogant gait and unnervingly confident demeanor indicated they should get out of the way. And indeed, most did.

For those few who didn't, the tune he dared to whistle aloud — Irving Berlin's *I'm in Heaven* — soon removed any doubt that he was an entity not to be underestimated. He might present the austere image of one of His Infernal Majesty's Blue Suits, and a high-ranking one at that, but there was something unhinged within the depths of his gaze that caused those final few stragglers to scramble aside at the last second.

The fugitive from injustice couldn't have cared less. He was in an exuberant mood, and still delighted at the novelty of being free to walk amongst crowds, where emotions ran riot and a deluge of sights, sounds, and other sensations washed across him at every turn.

And soon, I'll be taking the experience to a whole new level.

Without breaking stride, Angelus stepped off the main street and into a broad and spacious arcade. His gaze drank in every detail that the baroque furnishings and glitzy displays had to offer, and soon he reached his destination: a chic Victorian-style shoe shop sporting a large wooden framed floor-to-ceiling window.

Highlighted by concealed neon tubes, elegant gold lettering declared:

Cleaver & Lee
Our Soles Are a Feet of Design
Hellforleather Cloisters
Bondage Street, Olde London Town
Bespite Shoemakers
Cleaver.Lee.co.jux.doom
(As worn by the Arch Deceiver Himself)

Angelus paused for a moment to sample the smorgasbord of foul temperaments emanating from the rabble as they passed by, and used the opportunity to glance nonchalantly up and down the walkway.

Yes, I've cooped myself up for too long. It's time to experience the full range of what this ancient city has to offer. He peeked furtively about him once more. *Especially as my shadows appear to have given up the ghost at long last.* Then he snorted. *As if I'd be in the least bit interested in helping now they've served their purpose. Imbeciles, what do . . .* Hell-*oo?*

On impulse, Angelus raised his brolly and tipped his hat to a voluptuous blonde wearing a tight roll neck sweater who sighed past him in a breeze of pheromones and feminine allure. She held his gaze for a few paces and smiled, but then dismissed him from her sight. Nonetheless, her hips continued to weave their spell until she arrived at a pink VW-style convertible illegally parked at the far end of the mall.

Mesmerized, Grislington stared as she opened the door and slunk with feline grace into the driver's seat. Only then did she deign to turn and smile once more. Then she winked, blew him a kiss, and with a jaunty wave bade him farewell before hitting the accelerator and gunning out into traffic without looking.

A screech of brakes on all sides provided a shrill accompaniment to the cacophony of horns, yells, and cursing that echoed back from enraged motorists along the arcade.

Angelus discovered he was grinning, and made a point of memorizing the license plate: *NORMA J.*

Hmm. Of course, once I've started to broaden my horizons, I might have to expand my schedule to include the rest of Satan's little fiefdom. After all, there's so much to see and do . . . and experience.

As one in a daydream, he turned to mount highly polished brass steps and push on the shop's door.

Ting!

The bell sounded loudly a second time as he entered, and the heady smell of polished leather, cured hides added an ambiance that Angelus found soothing. Photographs and framed newspaper clips lined the walls, indicating such notables as Shakespeare, Wellington, and Napoleon as previous customers. Among these hung a recent snap of the Father of Lies himself, stylishly attired in his chief-executive chalk-stripe guise.

Well, would you look at that. He does *shop here, after all? Ha. Although I'm betting he doesn't pay a diablo for anything.*

"I'll be with you in a moment," a voice called.

Surveying the rest of the interior, Angelus espied only one other person present — Gregory Cleaver, the younger of the two proprietors — and waited as the tradesman busied himself, tidying away the item he was currently working on.

Poor fool. I guess in this case, Royal patronage *means endless handouts . . . or else!*

At last, Gregory stepped out from behind the island counter situated toward the rear of the shop floor and smiled over the top of his half-moon glasses.

"Mister Angelus, welcome." Gregory gestured toward a worn and inviting tan leather couch positioned in the exact center of the room. "Please, take the weight off your feet and relax. Do lay your bag on the seat. I'll be with you in a moment. As always, your timing is impeccable. I'm just this second putting the finishing touches on your opening commission." He made a tight, circular motion in the air with his hand. "Your shoes will soon be shining like the coals of Phoenix Falls in Crematoria."

"Thank you, I'm sure everything will be just perfect." Angelus eased himself into his seat and patted the bag beside him. "If there's one thing I've discovered about Juxtapose since my posting here, it's that you can't beat the efficiency of the more disreputable establishments. You certainly are a cut above the rest when it comes to quality and service."

Gregory beamed at the compliment and chuckled, "Alas, that byline belongs to the esteemed Dirge and Skinners. Still, ours is catchy enough."

"And deserved, believe me. I have suffered the idiosyncrasies of our Dark Father in one capacity or another for millennia. If only your level of proficiency reflected throughout the other circles, or even reached my own beloved bureau, then perhaps His Infernal Majesty wouldn't have to suffer the aggravating machinations of Erra and his minions so often. Machinations, I might stress, that are a cancer to the foundation of good order." Lowering his voice, Angelus inclined his head and added, "Remember, we Blue Suits collect the taxes. If you only knew how badly commerce is affected in those realms harder hit by disruptions, you'd turn in your grave."

"Don't we anyway?" Gregory responded, clearly wary of straying onto a subject that might earn him an untimely visit to the Undertaker.

Sensing the lackey's anxiety, Angelus deigned to redirect the conversation. He clucked in mock empathy, shook his head, and made a placating gesture. "Fear not, good sir. Nothing we say or do within these walls will ever tickle the ears of those who would see your ruin as a stepping stone to fouler achievements. After all, I am a shining light within the ranks of the devil's brightest bureaucrats, and even I must guard against those who would subvert my authority in an effort to make my job — and me — redundant. How could I ever succeed without the underworld's preeminent shoemakers to help me watch my step — literally — and look smart while I'm doing it?

"Speaking of which, didn't you say my commission is about ready?"

"Why, yes I did." Gregory turned back to his work desk and picked up a hide-bound ledger sporting a thick crimson ribbon. As he thumbed through the pages, he explained, "I was giving everything a final once-over before collection. Where the process calls for it, we pride ourselves on providing a product coated with no less than thirteen seared layers of polish. It produces a finish with a deep, penetrating shine you won: two burgundy, two mid-brown; four hexford standards in black; two pairs of curt shoes, one standard, one patent; a single pair of deck shoes, navy blue; and finally, three sets of open-toed scandals. Correct?"

"Precisely so. And all these items are now complete?"

"Indeed they are, but as I mentioned, I'm just adding the final layer of polish to the last pair of rogues. We strive to be careful around the perforations, you see, to avoid an overabundance of wax, but it shouldn't take more than a quarter of an hour to remedy . . . if you don't mind the inconvenience, that is?"

"Not at all. You've been kind enough to rush my order through, so I'll happily wait a few minutes until you finish."

Gregory smiled, but continued to hover.

"Was there anything else, Mister Gregory?"

"Just one thing. As you requested, I've added your woodlast templates to our repeating roster. Did you decide on replacements every four months, or six?"

"Four, I think. Now that His Foul Majesty has appointed me his Commissioner to the Hexchequer, I have to look my best at all times. It will entail a lot of traveling over the next year or so, but it'll be well worth it in the end . . . as it will to those whom I grace with my continuing patronage."

Angelus could see that his unsubtle inference was not lost on the budding entrepreneur before him.

Trying to adopt an unconcerned air, Gregory asked, "And would you like me to make an immediate start on the next consignment? Remember, traditional construct for a project of this size will take up to twenty weeks to complete . . . upon receipt of the appropriate deposit."

It always comes down to money in the end. Dead or alive, their miniscule minds and limited talents can never get past the materialistic craving that has plagued the race since the moment of its creation.

Angelus concentrated and made a fist. He sensed himself diminish slightly as something hot and sharp materialized in his palm. When he held out his hand again, he rolled the mystery object back and forth between his thumb and forefinger, whereupon it glittered fiercely as if illuminated from within by starlight.

"I take it *this* will be sufficient to cover the work already completed?"

Gregory's eyes flared as his gaze fell on pure seraphinite.

At that Angelus smiled, for he could see the telltale gleam of the gem's many facets reflected in the shoemaker's glasses, along with a gnawing hunger that simmered just beneath the surface of his aplomb.

This one tries to hide his selfish longing, but it's there if you know how to look.

"More than sufficient, Mister Angelus," Gregory gushed, "and for a great many years in advance, I fear." He looked suddenly awkward. "But, *ahem*, will you be requiring a receipt for a down-payment of this size?"

Angelus made a show of pondering his decision.

After a good long while he leaned forward and, in a conspiratorial tone, whispered, "As I emphasized to Mister Crispin over at Dirge and Skinners, I'm a fiercely private individual and outside of work, I like to keep myself to myself." He shrugged. "However, I seem to have a knack at playing the murkets. It makes me very good at what I do, and my acumen has fattened our Dark Father's personal portfolio considerably. Now, while he has rewarded me amply over the years by making me a very wealthy man in my own right, he's still the devil, and Satan being Satan, doesn't allow me to spend anywhere near as much as I'd like." Angelus tapped the side of his nose with one finger and winked. "So, what say we keep this little transaction between us? Just ensure to balance your books by declaring sufficient revenue to cover the cost of materials used and think of an inventive way to keep the rest for yourself . . . as a sign of bad faith."

Gregory's face broke into a wide grin, and he rubbed his hands together. "I think this visit calls for a celebration, don't you? Would you care to join me in a little something I keep for my most prestigious clients?"

"If it's a quality tipple, certainly."

"Then you'll be pleased to know that, as with our shoes, I only stock the best." Gregory stooped to retrieve an ornate bottle containing a lustrous topaz-brown liquid from behind the counter. Along with it came two richly engraved goblets. "Ta-dah! Diabhalvulin 18, as approved by His Infernal Majesty's Reaper himself."

"Diabhalvulin 18?" Angelus was pleasantly surprised. "Then I think you'd better make mine a double."

"Indeed I will. In fact, with what you've put down as a deposit, I'll order in a case, just for you, along with your own decanter. That way, you may imbibe on every occasion you visit, fittings or no."

He poured two generous measures into the glasses, and handed one to Angelus.

They toasted, and after taking a sip, Angelus turned toward the window to savor the sensation as the fiery spirit went down. Of blessed origins, there were very few foods or beverages outside of heaven that could trigger any form of response from his taste buds. Fortunately, Diabhalvulin 18 was one of those rare treasures. It not only hit the spot, but kept going until it had burnt the lining of the esophagus away too.

The drink put Angelus in a reflective mood, and made him think of the Reaper.

How can he not know what he is? I felt it as soon as he entered the chamber, and yet, he seemed hardly aware of his own capabilities. It's hard to believe that one of such might and mastery would willingly . . . ?

Movement in an alley on the far side of the arcade caught his eye. As he focused on that area, a familiar face winked away.

Tesla?

Angelus smiled.

So, it seems my shadows are still intent on flitting hither and thither.

He raised his glass in another salute.

Very well. Like you, I needn't rely on a stable hydraspace environment to move about swiftly. So, let us see if you can keep up.

*

Bathed in the sweat of hard-earned rapture, Frédéric Chopin threw caution to the wind and increased the tempo. As smooth as satin sliding over highly polished glass, the notes flowed one after the other, faster and faster, until the cadence storming out from the deepest recesses of his imagination threatened to flood against the gates of heaven itself.

But there was a price to pay for such exertions, and sure enough, a familiar ache started burning its way through his wrists and knuckles.

He glanced toward the clock on the far side of the room.

Almost five minutes this time? Nikola was right. I must be building up some form of resilience against the effects of my personalized bane.

Encouraged, Chopin tried to distract himself by letting the music gain its own momentum and thinking of other things.

Why does the Reaper continue to plot against me? I am no threat to him, or his despicable master. All I want is the opportunity to hold my one true love in my arms again.

A fleeting glimpse of dark eyes and a smiling profile framed by long flowing hair graced the outer veneer of his memories. Then his mood soured.

I'll never give up, ungrateful swine. His bloodthirsty compatriots would still be rotting in a Sibitti enforcer's dungeon if not for me.

Chopin poured ever more effort into his task, and for a moment, the purity of the composition managed to soothe the frustrations still gnawing their way through the pit of his stomach. Ultimately, the diversion couldn't last, and all too soon the spasms intensified enough to cause an outright seizure.

His bones fractured and venomous needles shot along the tendons and muscles in his arms. Piercing his brain, anguish shattered the gulf between sanity and madness.

The sweet music faltered, his perceptions expanded; and once again, the bittersweet embrace of his curse made manifest enfolded Chopin.

A confusing maelstrom of images assailed him from every quarter, filling an alien vista with icons and places and situations he had never seen before. Thrown together in a haphazard fashion, they mingled freely with all the obstacles and oppressive resentment he'd endured during the eternity that had been his penance, here in latter-day hell. Even so,

Chopin refused to be daunted, and somehow managed to find the fortitude to relax and let his mind wander back to the one memory that always anchored his spirit.

George . . . I swear, one day we will *meet again.*

No sooner had he stopped struggling than the Elysian current powering his vision pulled him under. In an instant he felt himself sinking into an inky, silent oblivion and was content.

Unable to see, he nevertheless perceived a growing sensation of pressure. It intruded at the edge of his awareness and became more invasive with each passing second. Presently, spots appeared before his eyes. They swelled and multiplied, jumping across his plane of existence until they solidified into something tangible; something that speckled with golden highlights.

What is *that?*

Its nature remained elusive, ever beyond his reach. But it called to him in ways that promised to fulfill all his dreams and answer all his prayers, if only he'd make the effort to swim that little bit deeper and reach out to grasp —

Without warning, an undertow gripped Chopin's ankles and yanked him away. Before he realized what was happening, another vortex caught him, and sent him spiraling back into the close confines of his skull.

Pain distorted his vision, and this time, the flashes of light accompanied a sickening sense of dislocation. When at last the room stopped spinning, Chopin blinked his eyes open to find he had fallen to the floor in front of his stool.

With the utmost care, he cradled his arms to his chest and rolled gingerly onto his knees. Once in position, he prepared himself, bit his bottom lip and began snapping each of his finger bones back into place, one after the other. Soon, he was bathed in sweat and panting from his exertions.

It'll be worth it in the end, it'll be worth it in the end, it'll be . . .

Feeling faint, Chopin climbed unsteadily to his feet. His hands clasped, he braced himself against the piano. Relying on his mantra to anchor his resolve, he pulled:

Crack!

A bolt of lightning seared his soul as a multitude of tiny bones repositioned simultaneously. But Chopin dared not dwell on the misery. He still had his other wrist to do:

Crack!

Catching his reflection in the mirror, Chopin wasn't surprised to find his skin had blanched a pasty shade of gray. Through clenched teeth, he hissed, "A pox upon you, Undertaker, for willing this blight upon me. You couldn't have fashioned a more appropriate form of punishment."

Then he grinned slyly and bent to lift a sophisticated Wash & Burn miniature sound recorder from its cradle.

"But I've found a way to circumvent your little gift, allowing me to reclaim what I once was . . . even if the road is a long and arduous one."

He pressed the *play* button and rocked from side to side as sonorous tones resonated throughout the room.

That's nearly thirty minutes toward a new concerto now. Sighing heavily at what the achievement had cost him, he stared back at the sunken visage of his mirror image. *If only the Reaper was that easy to sway. Still, if he's unwilling to compromise, we always have plan B to fall back on, along with a* personal *message. And our preparations are all but complete.*

Chopin reached out for the iced wine he'd left to chill before the exercise began. With trembling fingers, he poured himself a large helping. Squeezing the glass as firmly as he dared, he surrendered to the relief brought by such contact.

Swilling the cubes until they tinkled, he downed the contents in one gulp.

Gods, but that's a blessing . . . even if it does taste like cold vomit.

He was just about to pour another helping when the air distorted in front of him, and his partner in crime appeared.

"Well met. How did — ?"

Chopin's greeting died on his lips, for Nikola Tesla's expression made his face look as though he'd slept on piss-soaked nettles.

"He spotted me," Tesla mumbled, throwing himself into the nearest chair.

"So the game's up at last?"

"I suspect Grislington has known all along and just hasn't shown it." Tugging at one end of his finely manicured mustache, Tesla added, "We sometimes forget we're not dealing with an ordinary denizen of hell; or even an extraordinary one, for that matter. He's a bloody cherub for Azazel's sake, an honest to God, out of this world, angel." At the sound of the deific name, trembling shook the floor, the ceiling, and recanted pictures on the walls. "I know it doesn't help that he's half crazy and walks around with that 'part vacant/part axe murderer' stare, but I think that's how he's fooled us. He might pretend he's not all there — but in reality, he's so switched on that we might as well decorate him in baubles and lights, stick a star on his head, call him a Christmas tree, and be done with him."

Hmm, like someone else I know.

"I can now admit I've suspected for some time now, which is why I had us hang back and observe. I'd hoped his newfound freedom might make him careless. But all it's done is emphasize that he's a cosmic time bomb waiting to explode. That angel is patient, cunning, and chock full of abilities we've not even seen yet."

"And we're still no closer to discovering the location of the *Sword of Celestial Arches* than we were at the beginning."

"Welcome to my world, old friend," Chopin chided, "endless doom and gloom. Unless you're prepared to work your ass off to overcome each and every hurdle this godforsaken hellhole puts in your way."

Tesla raised his arm and waggled his fingers. "At least I know the transporter signets work perfectly."

"They do?"

"Yes. That's how I got away. When I realized Grislington had seen me, I didn't have time to activate the orb. I just thought . . . *shit!* Next thing I knew, I materialized back here."

"So the mental interface performed as you anticipated it would?"

"It appears that way." Tesla held out his hand before him and studied the strange blue gems embedded into the band of the ring he wore. "I was worried the inclusion of my DNHA might trigger my particular curse, but my eternal prohibition doesn't trigger punishment unless I personally try to build what I've designed in my head."

"Edison is proving his worth after all, then?"

Tesla chuckled and smirked. "Yes. How fortuitous he stole so many of my ideas when we were alive. He knows my work so well that, once I explained what to do, he produced the wherewithal to expedite our needs. These new toys not only function, but they eliminate the crackling sound and the smell of ozone that so often betrayed our presence. And they're a damned sight faster now, too. As I say, I'd barely had time to register the fact that my cover had been blown and I needed to get out of there, when — *poof* — I found myself here."

"You see, some good was gained from today's venture. At least we know we can accelerate our schedule a bit. The sooner we obtain more totems to replace those lost at Cog Isle, the better."

Tesla's smirk broadened. "Maybe so, but you haven't heard the best part yet. Because of the layout of the arcade, I had to get closer to Grislington than ever before. That's probably why he spotted me. Nevertheless, I think my faux pas might have been worth it."

"Why do you say that?"

"Because I saw *how* he's been paying for everything." Tesla edged forward in his seat. "Contrary to what we thought, he hasn't been coercing people, or using his heavenly wiles to get his own way. Oh no. He's been sacrificing fragments of his tincture."

Chopin stared, at first uncomprehending. "What do you mean, sacrificing fragments of his . . . ?" Then he realized what Tesla meant: *Seraphinite!* All thoughts of pain forgotten, his jaw dropped open. "Do you know what this means?"

"I do, but I advise you to exercise caution. Olde London Town is the Reaper's home turf. We are fugitives from injustice. And while we've managed to establish a new base of operations free from prying eyes, and gotten away with keeping tabs on our angelic counterpart by means of an odd visit here and there, we'd be fools to contemplate anything more likely to draw Grim's attention. Especially now we're so close to resuming our hunt."

Frustrated by the logic in his friend's words, Chopin verged on tantrum, but chose a new idea instead, one which had never occurred to him in all this time:

Who's to say Tesla and I must do this deed?

His mental world quaking as if he'd spoken the Almighty name, he mused aloud:

"Nikola, do you still have a contact in MI13?"

"The Satanic Intelligence Service? Yes, I do. Why?"

Chopin poured his belated second drink, and a first one for his friend. "Come join me in a toast; I think you'll like what I have to say."

Chapter 2: Sold Down the River

The banks of the River Inseine became darker and more ominous the closer we got to Perish. But that was to be expected. On this side of the English Charnel, Perish was known as a center of hellish vindication; a place where Gallic charm had been replaced by deep and premeditated ghoulish harm. The people were as cruel and sinister as their capital, and just as gross as my Inquisitors. You never had to worry whether someone might stab you in the back; they would quite happily do it to your face whilst kissing your cheek.

I loved the place; it represented everything the underworld should be, and the mere sight of it spreading off into the distance like a slumbering cancer did much to relieve the growing unease I felt over our reason for being here.

We had set out from Olde London Town just over four hours ago by boat — a necessary hindrance while Erra's minions continued to run amok — for while I was confident in my own ability to navigate the hazards of destabilized hydraspace alone, I'd had to bring my team with me and wasn't going to take the risk of spreading their atoms across infernity.

To minimize travel delays, I'd reenlisted the services of one of the most infamous buccaneers ever to pollute the seven seas of hell, one Captain Charles — 'Allweather' — Vane.

Hung for piracy in 1721, he'd been condemned to everlasting torment the moment the noose broke his neck. Unabashed, he had continued his reign of terror and torture in perdition, the only difference being that here he gathered kudos for it.

He became an acquaintance of mine last year, when he proved himself loyal and dependable during the fiasco involving Dr. Thomas Neill Cream. The thing I found most endearing about Vane was that he refused to remain chained to his era, and was one of the few corsairs who continually modernized his fleet to include the very latest vessels and equipment.

The *Lone Ranger III* was the name of the craft they sailed, and the name reflected Vane's ethic. She was a pressurized, hermetically sealed Hellhound H13 patrol boat. Powered by six Cerberus aqua-jet diesels, she possessed a cruising range of nine hundred and seventy nautical miles and an average cruising speed of fifty-nine knots. A nifty extra was the addition of armor plating and two Dragondance .50 millimeter cannons.

Just the ticket when you needed to punch through troubled waters.

What made it even better was the fact that Vane was the true and rightful owner of the Moral Compass, an esoteric totem that allowed its possessor to navigate any course, through any medium, whilst remaining true. So, it didn't matter what those Sibitti tosspots did to the Sheolspace continuum: Vane would be able to get us in one piece to whatever destination we desired.

Just as well, since we'd gotten underway secretly and with all haste.

Late last night, there had been a breakout from the Brass-Steel prison, and my contacts within the Fiendish Bureau of Investigation, Bella and Donna Nightshade, had intercepted a message passed over the Hell Data Net between the Brass-Steel's governor, the marquis de Launay, and local gend-harmes from the Ministry of Injustice.

The communiqué contained some interesting terms, in particular, those relating to: *appeared out of nowhere*; *artifacts*; *move like phantoms*; *disappeared without a trace*; and *extremely powerful in spite of heavy resistance*.

Bella and Donna had alerted me immediately by way of telepathic hail, and also took steps to sanitize the area by dispatching trusted agents from Perish's secret service — *the Directon Générale de la Satinique Intérieure* — to hold the area until our arrival.

As soon as I heard, I knew what this jailbreak must signify.

Perdition had been quiet for far too long. Grislington had gone to ground since his escape, doing whatever it was that lunatic angels liked to do in hell once freed from an eternity of captive boredom. Chopin and Tesla had obviously grown tired of sucking up to my ass and trying to win me over. One or the other — or both — were up to their old tricks, so I realized I would have to be very careful.

Last time out, I had allowed myself to become distracted and had ended up chasing my own tail. I had been screwed — twice — and members of my own personal retinue captured and hurt.

His Infernal Majesty had seen fit to empathize by augmenting my powers far beyond what they were, but at the same time, he had blocked my ability to return to corporeal form. That's why Satan's Reaper now had to slink around everywhere without a face and encased within a living suit of palladinium armor. I might possess a huge pair of golden balls in the sight of all and sundry, but I wasn't exempt from the satanic consequences of failure.

That lesson extended to the only other person I had ever grown close to: Strawberry. She could no longer touch me intimately without suffering the fate of every other denizen . . . Instant ruination and a one-way trip to Slab A.

Our Dark Father hadn't told me yet what penalty he intended to impose upon the Hounds for the ignominy of capture or death at enemy hands. Whatever it was, it would be inventive and just the thing to remind the masses — and us — who was boss.

Hence my determination to protect my team at all costs. This episode would be the first of many, all interconnected and wound up tighter than a ball of twine. At times, even I might be at pains to distinguish who was who and what was where. But as I'd learned the hard way, if I refused to be distracted and remained focused on my mission goals, my enemies' schemes would slowly unravel, until I could tie all threads together at a time and place of my choosing.

And when I do, heaven won't be able to help those who've pissed me off.

I studied my team as they prepared themselves for disembarkation.

Nimrod stood nearest. One of my closest confidants and our lead Hell Hound, he embodied a mighty hunter hiding his deep and bitter hatred of those Above behind a façade of utter tranquility. Despite his stoic air, he exemplified the sort of person who could only express himself through extreme violence; and as such, Nimrod found his true happiness whenever rending lawbreakers limb from limb.

Prince Ōsu, known to us as Yamato Takeru, stood beside him. In life, Yamato had been a legendary ninja and elemental champion from first-century Japan. Protected by his fabled weapon, the *Sword of the Gathering Clouds of Heaven*, he had been undefeated in battle and had taken thousands of heads. In death, only a mob of Sibitti scumbags could get the better of him. An experience I could relate to, as three of the crafty bastards had managed to catch me with my pants down when I was at my weakest.

A truly educational chapter of my netherlife I shall always treasure.

My best tracker, Champ Ferguson, sat opposite them with his legs dangling over the gunwale. An infamous Confederate guerilla fighter from the American Civil War, Champ was exactly the kind of person a Hound should be: cruel, sadistic, and relentless. And that was *before* he earned eternal damnation. He had a hundred-percent record when it came to tracking down Satan's enemies, which included Erra's personified weapons. His manner didn't ingratiate him to many people. But I didn't give a shit. He was here to catch *bad* bad guys, not win popularity contests.

And there, leaning against the bow rails with her arms folded and watching everyone closely, was the very latest puppy to join our pack. Charlotte Corday, aka Lady Gemini, assassin extraordinaire. Someone who had not only surprised us all just two days ago by the ease with which she had aced the trials, but also by the manner in which she had done so . . . Without recourse to her newly-emerging enhancements.

We all carried the bruises of that encounter and Champ more than most. *He* still walked with a limp. But then again, she had tap-danced on his head and gone flamenco on his testicles before kicking him unconscious with a resounding *Olé!*

I winced in testosterone-laced sympathy and noticed with interest how often Champ glanced her way when he thought she wasn't watching. She was, of course, and every now and then the corner of her mouth on the good side would lift a little.

I altered my perspective to read their auras.

Hades help me, the idiots are smitten. Thank purgatory they'll soon be on different continents of the netherworlds.

The last thing I needed was an added distraction within the ranks, but as luck would have it, I had decided on the strategy we would follow prior to departure and before I realized the possibility that a budding romance might raise its ugly head. What's more, I'd based that stratagem on simple necessity.

The circumstances of Grislington's flight from the Black Keep involved the loss of the *Sword of Celestial Arches*, a weapon bestowed upon him by none other than He Who Cannot Be Named.

But that sword was more than a mere blade — much more. The weapon acted as an artfully contrived talisman which could open a portal to nearly any location in manifold levels of reality. A relic missing since the time of Grislington's escape, I had the unenviable task of tracking it down before its existence became common knowledge, since such power in the wrong hands would wreak untold havoc throughout all the hells. The trouble was nobody had the slightest idea where it might be. I did have my suspicions, though. If this fabled sword was anything like my scythe, it linked in some arcane fashion to its perfect wielder — in this case, Grislington. That truth boded ill for us, for there was no telling what mischief a deranged angel with that mighty weapon might get up to, should he choose to go on the rampage.

As if the situation weren't already dire enough, reliable intelligence from the Devil's Children on Chopin and Tesla suggested they'd amassed an unspecified variety of divine trophies, along with an indefinite number of multi-phasic rift generators, otherwise known as teleport orbs. In themselves, the orbs ranked as sophisticated devices able to facilitate entrance to any level of hell. Before the last upheaval, it was rumored the generators had also been capable of linking every circle of the underverse simultaneously via a network of artificial wormholes, though that aspect of their functionality had never been proven. In any event, such a feat remained highly unlikely now that the Sibitti had screwed things up. Sadly, that didn't alter the fact that Chopin and Tesla would nevertheless be able to employ a tool that would grant them speedy access to a variety of cities on single planes in quick succession.

Yet another advantage our enemies possessed that I had to counter.

Vane was hellacious sailor and the Lone Ranger III was fast, but there was no way he would stand a chance of keeping up with my targets when they started to flit about from metropolis to metropolis and realm to realm. I'd decided to bring the Hounds with me so I could drop them off at strategic locations throughout the underworld. Not only would it spread my resources, but it would allow me to respond that little bit faster when incidents occurred, safe in the knowledge that I had backup nearby.

Gemini wasn't too happy when she realized where we were coming on this, her first assignment, but as I emphasized to her; this was not the Paris nor were these the people she remembered from life. If anything, Perish would make her feel right at home for the first time in a long, long while.

From what I could see, watching her reaction, my hunch was right.

Notre-Damned came fully into view, and the crew turned to stare at one of the thirteen wonders of the underverse.

Gemini followed suit, and was captivated the moment she laid eyes on it.

Not that I could blame her, for this beacon was a herald advertizing the fact that here, as nowhere else, the stark clarity of eternal damnation had been encapsulated by a shrine that loudly declared the transcendent beauty of evil.

Fluted spires and belfries stretched upward, reaching so far and so high that they threatened to puncture the clouds blanketing the sky from horizon to horizon. On every corner, wide eyed gargoyles stared down, their pigeon-shit-encrusted tongues flicking lewd suggestions to the crowds passing below. Captured in stone, intertwined angels and demons cavorted across open cut friezes. And in that display a blasphemy of errors was revealed, declaring the reality of the factual rapport between heaven and hell: that they were infatuated; locked in the eternal discord of love and hate, good and bad; a relationship where one simply couldn't exist without the other.

Everyone fell silent and savored this testimony to corruption's sweet entanglement at its insidious best.

Then I noticed that the grand old lady of Perish wasn't the only thing attracting attention from passersby: A growing number of pedestrians up on the Boulevard de la Brass-Steel had stopped to watch as we headed toward the jetty.

That's it then. Surprise over. By the time we set foot on shore, half the city will know the Hell Hounds have arrived, and the Reaper with them.

I turned to my team: "Champ, Yamato. I want you two to split up and do a circuit of the commercial district. Keep your eyes and ears open and find out what the word is on the street. Reconnoiter for an hour or so and then rendezvous at Bistro Noir. That's François de UnBorn's place, situated on the corner of Rue de l'Hôtel de E'ville and Rue Geoffroy l'Asinîne.

You can't miss it, especially with the Hanging Gardens of Babylon feature he has festooned all over the outside. He's on the payroll, remember, so even if you come up blank after checking with him, send what you discover to me telepathically. Once you're done, get yourselves back here and prepare for the journey across to New Hell."

They nodded in reply, and I beckoned to Nimrod and Gemini.

"You two are coming with me to the Brass-Steel. However, before you join me inside, I want to know if the locals picked up on anything over the past week or so. You know the score — unusual comings and goings by strangers, out of place guests booking in at slummy hotels. Concentrate on the Porte Saint-Antoine area. Gemini, you'll understand more of the vibe around that place than Nimrod so take the lead and find out what you can before joining me inside. I don't think it'll be difficult to find me. I'll be with the marquis, so just follow the sound of bleating excuses." I projected the image of a grin toward them. "If I'm right, the circumstances of the breakout would have been impossible for him to prevent. But I'm not telling him that."

Gemini snorted with ill-concealed mirth, doing her best to hold the ravaged side of her face still. As usual, Nimrod's stoic demeanor didn't change, but I knew he was figuratively wetting himself.

"Would ye mind, Reaper, if I seize the opportunity t' send some o' my lads ashore?"

I turned to find Charles Vane emerging from the main bridge.

He continued, "We set off at short notice, so we'll need t' ensure we're fully stocked before we attempt the crossing. Compass or no, the Bitter Sea/Frantic Ocean divide can be a mite troublesome, especially now the anchors have come adrift. We might pierce the veil and find ourselves smack bang in the middle o' New Hell harbor itself, or we could get dropped a thousand leagues out t' sea. It'll be best t' be prepared."

"I agree. But if your men can get that done within the hour, I'd be grateful." I cocked a thumb over my shoulder toward the Brass-Steel. "Just in case we uncover anything in there that requires a speedy response."

As Vane turned away and started bellowing orders, I looked above the growing press of onlookers toward our goal.

Right, let's go and see what's waiting for us.

Chapter 3: Balls of Brass and Steel

Built over an extended period between 1357 and the mid 1380s, the Bastille was a fortress originally constructed to protect the eastern approaches of the city of Paris from the English threat during the Hundred Years' War. Indeed, as time passed, her eight strong towers did prove to be a formidable barrier to the strategic gateway of Porte Saint-Antoine.

Nevertheless, because she figured prominently in France's domestic conflicts—including the fighting between rival factions of the Burgundians and the Armagnacs, and the Wars of Religion, in the15th and16th centuries respectively—the nature of the citadel was gradually changed, and by 1417 the Bastille served as a state prison.

Stormed on July 14th, 1789 by a crowd during one of the most turbulent periods of the French Revolution, the Bastille became an important symbol to the republican movement.

Although demolished and rebuilt in the land of the living, sufficient suffering and despair had been absorbed into the original framework of her bricks and mortar to ensure this exquisite establishment would survive. Metamorphosing down into latter-day hell, she manifested her old soul in Perish, where she earned renown as the Brass-Steel; an overcrowded, metal-plated pressure cooker of an institution in which prisoners suffered searing torture.

I had personally consigned more than twenty thousand souls here over the centuries, and considered its dedicated cells the perfect place for prolonged and harrowing distress.

Each of the towers came equipped with calottes—special shell rooms on different levels in which prisoners hung and roasted over open flames. Down in the dungeons they had cachots—steel-floored and water-filled oubliettes, heated from below by the raw tincture of the Bãlefire itself. This was a place where thermophilic nightmares manifested. And true to form, the screams emanating from this hellhole every night put Dante's vision to shame and always seemed to make denizens living in the vicinity hanker for lobster.

I thought it rather apt too, that its governor at the time of the storming, Bernard-René Jourdan—the marquis de Launay—had been sentenced to eternal servitude here.

History states he did his best to placate a mob intent on raiding his storerooms on the hunt for gunpowder. But we knew better, for Satan has always been able to read the hearts of men.

Supported by eighty invalid war veterans and some thirty Swiss grenadiers, he proposed a peaceful resolution by inviting a limited number of citizens inside to select what they wanted. Once within the confines of the courtyard, however, de Launay ordered them used for target practice to send a message to the protestors remaining outside.

It sent a message, all right. The crowd rioted. And when the gates were eventually breached, the unfortunate marquis was lynched (repeatedly stabbed and shot), and then suffered the further disgrace of having his head sawn off by Mathieu Jouve Jourdan, a local butcher; whereupon it was impaled on a pike and paraded around the city for all to see.

Despite the fact that I am one of the most sadistic and creatively brutal creatures you could ever stumble across, I had always found such actions by humans confusing.

I mean, what's the point in doing that? Dead is dead. It's not like they could wake him up and hurt him all over again . . . unlike here, where torment waxes eternal, oblivion is transient, and only obliteration offers surcease.

Standing within the confines of the head warden's office in the second tower—the Tower of Traitors—I listened to the governor prattle on and on as to why he wasn't at fault for this, the only breakout ever to have occurred since the prison's inception, and did my best not to stare at the evidence of that ignominious death without laughing.

But it was hard; for once again the Undertaker had been keen to display the seemingly limitless scope of his halitosis-ridden sense of humor.

Unlike Bertran de Born, de Launay kept his head here. But there was a catch: a huge zipper sewn into the circumference of his neck. Livid, pink, and permanently swollen, it looked painful to endure. But nowhere near as painful as the double pull tabs *Ol' Bad-Breath* had created to hold together those rows of brass teeth. *That* meant using the governor's own scrotum, cunningly fashioned and twisted into a rather stylish (if somewhat hairy) cravat.

It carried a sense of karma that appealed, for the crowd had wanted to cut this guy's 'nads off and serve them to him on a plate.

I peeked at the blue-veined arrangement for the umpteenth time and chewed on my nonexistent bottom lip.

Close enough.

". . . can see why I'd prefer you to actually examine the scene of the crime yourself, Reaper," de Launay insisted. "My staff reacted extremely well, given that they were taken by surprise, fighting off both intruders with proficiency and determination. Why, if . . ."

Two? Let me guess.

". . . have ensured the evidence we recovered remained here for your inspection. But this imbecile—" he gestured toward the only other person in the room—"had the audacity to inter me within my own watch commander's office. Insufferable! To be treated this way within my own prison, it's . . . it's . . ." He stamped his foot and his ball-sack flopped about, tightening the skin on his throat. "Well, I'm at a loss for words."

About bloody time.

Taking advantage of the unexpected break, Pascal Fléau, section head of the local branch of the GDSI—the *Directon Générale de la Satinique Intérieure*—Perish's special intelligence division of the Devil's Children, stepped forward and nodded.

"Reaper. As requested, we closed the Brass-Steel to all traffic, both occult and mundane, and remains quarantined until further notice. We sealed the cell in which the infraction took place, and isolated the prisoners in a separate chamber within this tower. Of course, all of the items recovered within the cachot have been left in situ for sulforensic examination"—I didn't miss the icy *'you are a fucking retard'* glare he threw de Launay's way—"to avoid cross-contamination. Due to the nature of the intelligence gained from our initial enquiries, those staff on duty, including those taking part in warding off the intruders, were ripcorded." He held out a Hexar master memory stick. "You'll see why when you peruse the contents of *this*. It contains information our Master will want restricted."

"Thank you, Pascal. One moment, please."

Breaking the seal, I imbued myself with the stored recollections of every guard who had witnessed the incident.
Their collective essence was most revealing.

*Aha! Definitely Chopin and Tesla! And what's this, some-
thing that might be a proscribed artifact? Shattered, by the
look of it. How in Hades did that happen?*

I regarded Pascal with newfound respect. He obviously
knew his stuff, even the stuff he shouldn't know about.

"Well done. You appreciate that all your operatives, yourself included, will have to undergo the same cleansing process when we're finished here?"

"Of course, Reaper," Pascal inclined his head, "but it is
a small price to pay. All those *owned* by His Dark Majesty
forgo much to retain the dishonor of pure service. My time
on the slab will be brief, my reward eternal."

The subtle inference was clear. While most of his staff
might be Devil's Children, Pascal was someone different,
someone who belonged to a very select group: the Devil's
Own, a secret service within a Secret Service.

Then I remembered what *fléau* meant in Standard English: *scourge.*

*That's rather apt. Bella and Donna must have said some-
thing to him about me. Okay, he's the kind of professional I
can work with, let's see where this leads.*

Extending my presence out across the city, I summoned
my closest aides.

*Nimrod, Gemini. Round off what you're doing and get
your asses in here, on the double.*

Then I turned back to Pascal.

"I take it the dungeon in question also forms part of this
tower?"

"Yes, it does, Reaper," de Launay cut in rudely, "and I took the liberty of having it drained and the Bãlefire diverted so you could inspect the interior as soon as you arrived."

"And the water?"

"I'm sorry, the water?"

Seriously?

"Yes, the runny liquid stuff you pour in the cachots to boil the inmates. Did you think to save it so we could examine it?"

"No. No, I didn't. It was flushed down the— so you . . . I mean, I didn't think . . ."

Pascal's eyes glazed over. He cursed in French and slapped his head before transforming the move into a graceful, if somewhat obscene, gesture.

With what remained of my face obscured behind a cloud of dense vapors, I couldn't escape the feeling de Launay would probably know exactly where I was staring. So, when his rising anxiety caused his testicles to start jiggling about again, it took all my will power not to stare.

Somehow, the theatrics of the spectacle helped rein back my growing impatience.

"Right," I snapped, "you'd better take me to the scene of the breakout and pray there's something left that hasn't been screwed up — yet."

Glad to regain his liberty, the governor leaped for the door. Outside, we passed a checkpoint consisting of two GDSI agents, and started to negotiate a series of narrow stone steps lit every so often by braziers set into recesses along the wall.

En route, I whispered to Pascal, "Would you mind waiting in the courtyard for my people?" I projected an image of Nimrod and Gemini directly into his psyche. "I don't imagine they'll be more than ten minutes. They both have level thirteen access, so you can give them a full update before escorting them to me. By then, I hope to have sorted the wheat from the chaff."

"That's a relief to hear." His gaze bored into de Launay's back. "Please include that idiot in your harvest. I don't know how much more I can take before I shoot myself."

Join the queue.

"I'll see what I can do. In the meantime, compile what we know on the escaped prisoner and pass it to me mentally."

"I already have a report prepared but just in case I've missed something pertinent, I'll check the prison's archives before I send it. I'll also notify my staff you are on the way."

Oh yes, I think we're going to get along.

We reached the ground-level vestibule where a small contingent of Secret Service personnel awaited us. As Pascal peeled away, he took several along with him, leaving de Launay free to lead me toward a large door guarded by two of the most inconspicuous people I have ever seen.

Male and female, they were of a similar height and totally unremarkable build. Neither possessed the distinguishing features one might expect from a bodyguard or highly trained agent of injustice; not even a bear trap gaze or statutory dark glasses.

Regardless of how ordinary they seemed, each radiated a suppressed air of quiet confidence—and nothing else. I wouldn't have given them a second glance when passing in the street.

That, I believe, is exactly the point.

De Launay swept past without a glance and continued on down a separate spiraling staircase. I followed close behind. No sooner had I crossed the threshold than a tingling sensation manifested in the sole of my boots. It intensified with every step I took and wormed its way up my body.

This is a considerable barrier.

After a dozen yards, I could understand why it was so thick. It shielded the presence of pure harmbrosia from the outside world: the Bãlefire. Its glorious essence permeated the floors and walls of this place, and even its atmosphere.

I inhaled and felt the heady rush of rapture darken my rancid heart. My eyes ignited and the sigils adorning my armor flared to life. As my lifeblood sang in response to the resonance of its soul mate, the foundations of the entire fortress rocked.

De Launay had come to a stop on an intervening landing. Face blanched with terror, he backed away until he pressed against bare stone and could go no farther.

"Where . . . Where do you want to go fi– first?"

"The cell from which the escape took place"—I had to fight the inclination to unzip his head with my scythe there and then—"after which, I'll speak with the prisoners who witnessed the actual escape itself. And Governor, it might be best to hurry. In a place like this, I find it difficult to control my . . . *urges.*"

He got the hint.

In moments, de Launay was skipping down the stairs toward the dungeon so fast, I felt sure he'd sprout wings and fly. Thus we completed our descent in record time, and as we rounded a final bend I saw another pair of Devil's Children awaiting our arrival. They had heard the commotion of our approach and moved aside in anticipation.

Sure enough, de Launay hurtled right past them. No sooner did he gain refuge in the hallway than he collapsed in a gonad-shaking heap, gasping for breath.

A glance was all it took to explain why:

The flight had shrunk the skin of his scrotum so much that it was now pulling the zip sliders tighter and tighter. Quite simply, he was on the verge of choking on his own balls.

What a way to go.

The GDSI agents and I stood mesmerized by the sight. But, true to form, none of us offered to render last aid.

Could you imagine trying to clear his airway? quipped one agent to the other telepathically, but loud enough for me to hear.

We all burst out laughing.

The hilarity didn't last long. I stepped across de Launay's shuddering body and came up short. More than twelve hours had passed since the breakout, and yet a disconcerting timbre still laced the air. It smacked of what I expected—the incongruous enchantment of the divine and deviltry—and yet, the slightest trace of something else also tainted the ether.

The first thing I noticed was a shattered weapon on the floor. Looking much like the remnants of a small sword or an overlarge anlace, its dull and lifeless fragments appeared scorched, and in one instance had actually melted around the junction between pommel and grip.

Something about it seemed familiar. Then it hit me:

That's a Dagger of Damocles!

The odd cryptic aftertaste originated at a point where a gem had once adorned the hilt. Now, all that remained was a gaping lesion from which wisps of sickly green smoke ascended in dissipating spirals.

Altering my sensitivity, I zoomed in to take a closer look.

The wound stank of wild sorcery.

But how is this possible? That thing is supposed to be able to negate any power, no matter what the source. Even benighted angels have to watch out, so . . . ?

Thereupon I remembered certain aspects of the way Cream had used his particular weapon inside Grislington's cell back at the Black Keep.

Ah, that's right. The user must focus it on a particular target. Even so, it's of divine origin. It surely has a built-in safeguard to prevent this kind of thing from happening?

With the utmost caution, I paced around the fizzling remnants of one of heaven's most iconic vessels and squatted down beside it so I could better study what remained of its ruined nature. I was shocked to discover the chemical bonds maintaining its cohesive integrity were slowly rotting away.

This power doesn't originate from anywhere in the underverse. Nor is it celestial in nature. Sooo . . . ?

Whatever this ensorcelled contagion was, it was alien, it was still active, and if left unchecked, it would totally consume the composition of the blessed metal before me.

I wonder?

Throughout the length and breadth of hell, there were only a handful of denizens who would be able to even attempt what I was about to do. Fortunately, my current location helped, as it was supercharging my core way beyond what was normal.

Here goes nothing.

Standing, I spread my arms wide and summoned the two opposing poles of my disparate soul simultaneously.

A clean white light erupted from my left palm, a rich scarlet ambiance from the right. Bringing my gauntlets together, I interlaced my fingers and spoke rapidly, repeating a similar sentence twice: first in the divine language, and second in ancient Hellanese.

"*Tav yey qa-fé Eló-him, a-mad ha-pâ-tah* (In the name of the One, stand revealed).

"*Etoman a' Satanasaínim, bi comharr* (And in the name of Satan, stand revealed)."

A corona of argent-ruby light pulsed away from me. Where it washed across the shards, flickering particles became visible. Similar in appearance to charged globules of protoplasm, they seemed to froth and fester as they devoured the fabric of the dagger.

Unholy shit! No wonder Pascal ripcorded the guards. This is a proscribed item, yet something . . . or someone has rendered it inert.

Whatever *this* was needed further examination and I wracked my brains trying to think of a solution. Only one possible course came to mind.

Squeezing my fists even tighter together, I conjured a fresh compulsion. As before, I repeated the command in both tongues:

"*Te-hareth—Cuir caísigh.* (Be frozen in time)."

Here's hoping I can at least slow this process down.

Sparks ignited along the length and breadth of each remnant, and within seconds, all shared a rosy cream envelope of eldritch theurgy.

The aggravating reverberation cut off.

Satisfied that the virus couldn't spread, I moved forward to examine the torture chamber.

The cachot measured some twenty feet in circumference and was the same again tall. From what I could see, the ceiling was fashioned from large brass plates, while the walls and floor were all made of pressed steel. An industrial-sized faucet in the roof pumped in the putrid waters of the Inseine on a nightly basis. A slight adjustment of my perspective showed me the series of pipes beneath the grille decking, strengthened to withstand the flow of more than ten tons of pure Bãlefire essence per minute. A considerable volume for such a tiny room, and more than enough to peel the skin from the fifty people customarily squeezed inside.

A most inventive method of punishment. And I know of two additional candidates, when I catch up with them.

Doing my best to dismiss the call of my particular brand of opiate, I turned to examine the remains of the door, and called de Launay to my side.

"Governor, do you notice what's attracted my attention?" I pointed to the shape of the hole, halfway up the frame. "That was not caused by explosives. If it was, the metal would be blackened, shredded, and jagged around the edges. This is a perfect circle and has a glassy texture around the border. Have you any idea what could have caused it?"

Eager to help, de Launay was quick to answer.

"My men say they saw a small device roll away from the door and get caught by the water that came pouring through. It won't be far. Everything is sealed down here."

I closed my eyes.

The Bãlefire called to me immediately, its esoteric blueprint as familiar as the rhythm of my own heart. Ignoring it, I pushed ahead and listened for patterns that weren't a natural part of this environment.

There!

A subtle buzz, almost indistinguishable from the background thrum of idling pumps and high-pressure valves caught my attention. I followed it toward its source.

Although we were belowground, the structure of the outer wall of the dungeon appeared identical in layout to the rooms above. Therefore, the foundations still incorporated a small vestibule in which could hold a window frame. Here, stonework and intervening earth barred the way, so the portico served as an ad hoc weapons rack. The humming sound came from that area.

When I peeked inside, I saw a small gray baseball-sized object embedded into the masonry, high up in a corner where the plaster had crumbled. Reaching out, I prized it loose from its resting place and found it was still warm to the touch.

Well, would you believe it, a multi-phasic portal generator?

The casing had a small dent running along one side. Nevertheless, whenever my fingers strayed too close to any of the buttons set within an indented triangular area on the top of the device, it emitted a high pitched whine.

And it looks as if it's still working.

At that moment, I felt a tingle behind my eyes.

Reaper? came Pascal's thought.

Here's a précis of your escaped prisoner. He sent a data package. *Oh, and your Hounds have arrived. I'll escort them down now.*

Excellent timing, Pascal, I'll see you in a few minutes.

I opened the file and glanced through its contents.

Isabella I Queen of Castile–22 April 1451–26 November 1504.

Married to Ferdinand II of Aragon, their union became the basis for political and religious reforms in Spain under their grandson, Holy Roman Emperor Charles V, although her reforms extended well beyond the borders of her kingdom. She was the main instigator of the *"Reconquista,"* ordering the conversion or exile of Muslim and Jewish subjects in the Spanish Inquisition. Through her, *La Santa Hermandas*—the Holy Brotherhood—gained wide-ranging power to bring to trial all those suspected of heresy against the church, no matter how flimsy the evidence.

Oh yes, I remember her. She never knew it but she was one of our greatest advocates, especially as she secretly got off on the fact she had the power of life and death over others . . . like someone else I know?

A fleeting image of Strawberry teased me from the shadows. I did my best to dismiss it and flipped to the summary highlighting Isabella's achievements.

It says here she was directly responsible for the demise of more than two thousand people, and carried that addiction with her when she was condemned to hell. Aha! That's why she's in the Brass-Steel.

I skimmed through her rap sheet and my eyes widened at the tally.

Irrespective of the fact that it's our number one pastime, she couldn't stop killing. After arriving here, her need to murder increased, and she would slay nearly anyone she encountered. Bummer.

This raised a question: *So why would Chopin and Tesla choose to free her? Are they nuts? And how would they have met?*

I decided I needed more information. Clearing my mind, I filed the report away and turned back to de Launay.

"I want to see the prisoners. Now."

"Come with me," he squeaked, "we moved them to a room above this one to await interrogation."

At last, something he did right.

We filed back up one flight of stairs and less than a minute later arrived outside a similar looking cell door. Two more GDSI agents awaited us, and the older one addressed me as I approached.

"Reaper, we've been expecting you."

"Anything to report?"

"No. On Pascal's orders we have kept the vermin segregated and their cognitive functions muted. They have not
been allowed to communicate with one another since the incident and are ready for your interrogation."

"Thank you. For your own safety it will be best if you
leave this area and wait in the reception above. Further instructions will be issued shortly."

They both nodded and made their way upstairs.

Once they had gone, I threw back the bolts and opened
the door. More than four dozen naked inmates waited inside, strung upside-down like pig carcasses, fit for nothing
but further butchery. A psychic fuzzer lay on the floor in the
exact center of the room, positioned there to scramble their
sensibilities . . .

With a wave of my hand I switched off the device and let
the power of my will sweep across them like a laser.

"*Coid dean thu tuíg* (What do you know)?"

The compulsive element interwoven within the nucleus
of my question had them spilling their guts before they realized what was happening. They didn't even need to open
their mouths. I simply readied my mind, changed my perspective, and the myriad thoughts jumbling and tumbling my
way morphed into a blow-by-blow recount; except that this
time, I could relive the moment of the escape as if I were one
of them:

Helpless, impotent endurance . . .

A flash of light, a tang of metal as experienced through
senses dulled by repeated atrocities.

What now?

Enforced detachment impeached.

I am helpless to influence what is coming.

Concussive pain as an explosion multiplies its shockwave in the aqueous nature of our confinement.

Denial . . .

What new torment do they seek to inflict on us?

The abrupt release of both heat and pressure as the irresistible tug of water pulls us toward an unexpected breach.

Confusion . . .

Distant sounds reverberate: of gunfire and ricochets, of shouting and cursing; of people gagging and retching in an effort to clear lungs clogged by vomit and filthy water.

Anxiety . . .

The dislocating smell of flesh charred from bone.

Fear . . .

Am I next?

Unidentified assailants wielding unknown devices and an obscenely large pair of bolt croppers.

Terror . . .

Leave me be.

Someone crumples to a cell floor; someone else drags him away.

It's not me?

Relief . . .

Thank Satan for that.

Overwhelming power coalescing.

Stronger than all those around it, a thought (both lucid and self-assured) clarifies in a shocked room.

A Dagger of Damocles? Here?

As potential builds in the ether, a reflexive gesture creates the perfect contradiction: Antithetical energies stitch the air as barely-contained potential releases in a cataclysmic rush, obliterating all restraint.

Objects splash and metal clatters to the floor.

Feet pound the stones as reinforcements rush to intercede.

Too late, an alarm sounds in the background.

Gotcha!

Dismissing the rabble, I released my hold upon them and zeroed in on someone who, up until now, had remained remarkably inconspicuous.

Who are you?

Shocked, I realized that my 'mystery witness' continued to register as a blank slate although I stared directly at him.

In the blink of an eye, my scythe jumped into my hands. I phased and, in a whirling blur, set about dispatching each and every occupant. Five seconds later, the cell filled with dissipating essences — except for the one with my blade a hairsbreadth from his throat.

He didn't even flinch.

This guy has nerve, alright. "I asked you a question. Who are you?"

A pair of piercing green eyes regarded me through swollen eyelids. For some reason, I found his calmness disconcerting.

Then he smiled. "Heinrich Cornelius Agrippa Von Nettesheim at your service, Reaper." He inclined his head toward his nakedness and somehow managed to make the gesture appear graceful. "Please excuse my state of undress. I wasn't expecting such"—his gaze flicked past me and his grin widened—"distinguished company."

I glanced over my shoulder to find Gemini, Nimrod and Pascal watching from the corridor. De Launay was still there, but cowering against the far wall behind them.

Ah, good!

"Nimrod, Gemini. The breakout occurred on the floor below. I've given it a cursory going over, but I'd like you two to conduct a more thorough search. You'll note there are certain items that will require sulforensic examination. If you take the governor with you, he'll show you where they are. Please

ensure everything is prepared for sterile transport and wait
for me there. I'll see you shortly."

They left without a word and I turned back to what I suspected might be my only reliable source of truth. Just for fun,
I set him swinging with the flat of my blade.

"How are you connected?"

"May I at least be granted a modicum of decency before
I answer your questions?"

"That sounds fair enough. But this is hell, and things
aren't fair."

With a flick of my wrist, I severed the chains binding
Nettesheim's ankles together. He dropped like the proverbial
stone and I braced myself for the thud.

It never came. Instead, he tucked, rolled, and came to his
feet in one fluid motion.

Hello?

"How long have you been here?"

"I've been enjoying the facilities now for, ooh, the past
eighteen months." He paused to stretch, and cracked the
bones in his neck and shoulders. "I'd give the place four or
maybe five skulls in the Bad Hothell Guide. You really ought
to try it, Reaper. The food is shit, but the sauna is to die for."

I didn't want to, but I found his dry humor impressive,
in the face of such adversity—and infectious. Studying him
more closely, certain anomalies became apparent: his skin
had regained its normal elasticity, the edema and discolor-
ation associated with prolonged and repeated immersions
quickly fading; neither his body nor mind bore any evidence
whatsoever of endless cycles of scalding and burning.

*It's like I'm looking at someone who's never seen the in-
side of a torture chamber.*

"You don't seem in the least bit put out by your, ah,
circumstances?"

"As you said, this is hell. It's not supposed to be a picnic, but since my condemnation, I've so often found the opposite to be the case." He sneered. "I find that disappointing. So, if I can avoid eradication for long enough, I'm determined to savor the underworld's eternal torments to the full. And I do mean every deviance, every vile inducement, and every foul chastisement there is. This shit-tip"—he made a dismissive gesture—"is quite low on my fuck-it list, but at least I'll be able to cross it off once—"

"Hang on," I interrupted, "are you saying you deliberately got yourself thrown in here just so you could tick off an activity or location from some homemade catalog or sick comedy of errors?"

He bowed and replied with a flourish, "One of my easier accomplishments."

"That? As easy as screwing with the Dagger of Damocles downstairs?"

"Pah, Chopin and Tesla are assholes. They don't fully understand the metaphysical aspects of what they're dealing with."

"And you do?"

"To a certain extent. At least I don't want to see the natural balance of the underverse upset in order to achieve my goals."

"How do you know Chopin and Tesla? Are you affiliated with them or our escaped prisoner in any way?'

"No, we've never met. But I see . . . *things*. Understand things. That's how I knew what to do to unravel the bond protecting the talisman." A pained expression crossed his face. "It . . . it's difficult for me to elucidate without sounding like I desperately need the comfort of a custom-made padded cell."

Nettesheim didn't have to explain. I was scanning the shit out of him as we spoke and his aura testified he was telling the truth. Or at least he believed he was.

When I didn't say anything, he took it as a cue to continue:

"You might say I'm widely traveled, Reaper. I've dabbled in all sorts of nonsense over the years, both when I was alive and after my death." He tapped the side of his head. "You never know when something you've learned might come in useful." Then he wiggled his fingers. "Abracadabra and all that."

I suddenly realized why he was so reticent to explain himself fully.

"Are you telling me you used magic to destroy the Damocles Dagger?"

"Magic, sorcery, hocus-pocus. Call it what you will. It is but a tiny aspect of the various states of energy connecting everything together. A source that, for the most part, lies dormant and beyond our reach. But for those who possess sufficient awareness and strength of will . . ." He rubbed his fingers together and gold and emerald sparks crackled through the air. "Well, such exuberance may be exploited in the most ingenious of ways."

"But there's no such thing as . . ." I thought of the angelic weapon lying shattered on the floor beneath us and the vehemence of the alien corruption eating its way through its composition, "*that* kind of airy-fairy magic."

That's supposed to be bullshit. A smokescreen designed to fool the unwary in the world above into thinking the dark arts are just a bit of harmless fun. It's not real . . . is it?

I decided this man's background warranted further scrutiny.

"Pascal? I think you understand better than most the danger Mister Nettesheim represents. Use whatever resources you need to move him into a facility suited to his . . . peculiarities."

Stepping quickly forward, Pascal clicked his fingers twice, and then removed a set of blandcuffs from inside his jacket. After fitting the braces about Nettesheim's wrists, Pascal activated them.

A discordant hum saturated our environment, immediately setting my teeth on edge.

The prisoner's eyes went blank, and I felt his cognitive presence diminish somewhat.

Several more agents materialized from thin air, presumably in response to their boss' summons, and emplaced a control collar and chains around Nettesheim's neck and ankles.

Once suitably restrained, they led Nettesheim from the cell.

Something in the back of my still niggled at me. "Pascal, I want to know exactly who this soul is, why he's here, and what his relationship may be to the other damned who're involved. Once he's in a secure place, test his limits. Be as inventive as you like. I'm particularly interested in discovering how he does what he does and why. Nobody has access to such enhancements unless sanctioned by our Dark Father. So where's his power coming from? Compile an "eyes-only" report for His Satanic Majesty and myself, including a thorough rundown and your recommendations. Understood?"

"I'll get right on it."

As he passed, Nettesheim somehow managed to lock eyes with me. He murmured, "Thank. You. Reaper. This. Wasn't. On. My. List. It. Should. Be. Fun."

How the . . . ?

"And get some stronger restraints," I called out.

Un-be-fucking-lievable. Talk about a will of iron.

I watched them go and once they had disappeared around the curve of the stairs decided it might be best to check in with Nimrod and Gemini in case they had uncovered anything I had missed.

Upon returning to the basement, I found Nimrod kneeling by the remains of the angelic weapon. De Launay was over to one side, doing his thing: being absolutely useless.

"Report."

Nimrod stood and peered about him. "Well, we've got everything squared away and ready for transport. But this . . . ?" He jutted his chin toward the anlace. "In all my thousands of years of service, I've never seen anything like it."

I noticed how Nimrod rubbed his chest as he spoke. And no wonder. When one of those blades had run him through, Satan had tasked the Undertaker to plague Nimrod with a phantom ache ever after, to remind him of his lapse in service. The mere presence of the dagger would be exacerbating Nimrod's discomfort.

"Anyway," he continued, "who was the clown you were interrogating upstairs?"

"That's what I'm hoping Pascal will find out. He gave a name, Nettesheim, but there's something about him I can't quite put my finger on."

"Do you think he's tied to Chopin and Tesla in any respect?"

I pondered my conversation with Nettesheim and the distinct feelings he had radiated as we talked, then transferred a précis of the incident directly into Nimrod's mind.

"No. If anything, he hates them and anyone like them who would, in his opinion, upset the *natural* balance and order of things."

"Really?" Nimrod gestured toward the icon for a second time. "Well, if he feels like that and can do *this* to a Damocles Dagger, get him on the bloody team. With the way things are going lately, I've a sneaking suspicion we're going to need all the help we can get."

Nimrod's suggestion struck a chord.

Ha! You never know. Stranger things have happened.

Only then did I realize it was unusually quiet.

"By the way, where's Gemini?"

"I don't know," Nimrod confessed, "I asked her to check the oubliette for clues, but she's been in there for quite a while now."

Together, we went to find our newest Hound.

Head down and with her ass high in the air, Gemini's nose pressed against a large drainage grille in the floor. It was hard to tell from this angle, for such a position emphasized how tight her figure-hugging flaytex catsuit was, and how perfectly it complemented her extraordinary physique.

Needless to say, Nimrod and I halted in the doorway and stopped to admire the view.

I really must get her to wear something a little less distracting now she's on the team. Mind you, it could work to our advantage in certain circ–

"I can hear what you're thinking, you know?" she growled.

Pulled from what could have been a delightfully provocative daydream, I mumbled, "Are you all right?"

"Of course I am. Now hush, I'm trying to listen."

Listen?

Intrigued, I tiptoed across the cell and squatted by her side.

Eyes wide, Gemini's face held a look of rapt concentration. Her lips moved from time to time, and I got the distinct impression she was conversing with someone.

I adjusted my senses, but all I could hear was water gurgling somewhere down in the depths of the drainage system, and the resonant throb of the Bãlefire just below that in the storage vats.

What's going on? Nimrod pantomimed from the threshold, not daring to disturb her by using mental speech.

Damned if I know. I shrugged, putting a finger to my lips.

Evidently, we weren't stealthy enough.

"If you must know, I'm talking to the rockcoaches down in the sewer," she replied. "They say they have something for me."

Eh? "So?"

"To tell the truth, it's a bit freaky," she explained. "Before you boosted me, I received only impressions and feelings from creatures around me. And while I could interact and even influence them, I experienced nothing like this. Now I can actually discern how different species communicate. It was distracting at first, but I'm starting to zero-in on specifics."

This was news to me. Rockcoaches were hell's equivalent of cockroaches. Armored and endowed with oversized, razor sharp mandibles, they were a blessing in a place like this that tended to accumulate waste, dead skin, and severed body parts too inconsequential for reassignment. It was obvious that several colonies had gathered in strength to dine upon the banquet laid on for them every evening.

And it would appear some of them had a gift for my latest recruit.

"So what are they saying?" I whispered.

Gemini turned her head from side to side for a moment, and then abruptly sat back on her heels.

"They told me something got flushed down the vent the other night, something that feels dread . . . or maybe they mean . . . 'chill.' Whichever, it got snagged at one of the lower junctions, forcing a few colonies to abandon their nests."

"Are they saying what this *something* is?"

"They can't; they don't have a word for it. But that doesn't matter. One of them is bringing the item to me as we speak." She pointed to the main drain in the center of the floor. "Over there."

As one, we held our breath.

Distant at first, the skirr of bony, rhythmic feet drew near, bringing with it a cadence that sounded as if someone tiny was tap-dancing across a metal stage. It got closer, and I heard a rustling of paper. Something began bobbing up and down near the outer edge of the grille. Ivory-colored, it reminded me of compacted cardboard or scrunched tissue. Moments later, the mystery article popped through the hole and lay still, closely followed by a pair of long antennae that waggled furiously to and fro in the air.

Then the rockcoach appeared: a lucent bronze apparition of scurrying legs and scissoring mandibles. After circling in place a few times to get its bearings, it lifted the soggy mass up in its jaws with great care and came scampering toward us without the slightest sign of fear.

Depositing its treasure between Gemini's feet, it started to chitter excitedly and flutter coppery wings.

"What does it want?" I hissed, mesmerized by such unusual behavior.

"Payment," Gemini replied. "Hang on a moment."

Unperturbed, she took out one of her knives and pricked the end of her thumb. A speck of thick dark blood appeared.

She squeezed until a larger droplet had formed and then allowed it to drip to the floor.

The rockcoach leaped on the morsel and danced round and round it until it had consumed the offering. Then it was off, disappearing down the nearest vent without as much as a thank you or good-bye.

Retrieving the mystery gift, I discerned an echo of power still resonating through its texture.

It's vellum. A bit damp, but I can soon fix that.

With the utmost care, I used the subtle nuance of the Bălefire to heat our prize through until it was dry enough to unfold. As I did so, I could see that one side of the parchment bore writing. I didn't need two guesses to know what I would find.

Here we go again. "Well, shall we see what our friends have to say?"

Nimrod and Gemini shuffled closer. I held the message in front of me so they could follow along. It read:

Didn't you see me waiting patiently in the corner for our game to resume?

Painting by numbers is a shocking form of therapy, you know,

So I was the one eating crayons and using colorful language,

Especially those metaphors that lobotomize all forms of hope.

No longer isolated, I now have more than time to kill,

And as I await the dissolution of my sanity

I look deep inside toward that puckered concept of self,

Only to discover it's a monument to the fallacy

Of hanging on by the skin of my teeth.

As I've lately discovered,

The only true way to peace is to bite off more than I can chew,

Otherwise, my dreams will end up like my severed tongue,

A cadaver, lying dead in the corner,

Decaying, along with all hopes of leaving here

This side of a mortician's bag.

As expected, the perfectly-crafted cursive handwriting deteriorated as the verse went on, and at the end resembled a doctors' scrawl:

Although we'd provided Gemini with a rundown of our current targets, she was still learning the specifics of their modus operandi.

"Is this what usually happens?" she asked, clearly confused by the note's contents.

"Yes. Chopin in particular enjoys the theatrics of the chase. As you saw from his file, he likes to have a little dig at me whilst leaving a clue as to where he and Tesla will strike next. He's confident because he knows he'll have the advantage of speed and mobility, while we'll be hampered by the continued instability of the Sheolspace continuum."

"Isn't that a dangerous game to play?"

"Yes, but that's why he baits us. He's hoping to goad us into chasing him recklessly so we'll make mistakes. Why do you think I'm spreading the Hounds between the various circles he frequents? I can still travel the hydraspace boundaries very swiftly, but he knows I won't risk you. So he thinks to slow me down. Well, guess what, I'll have you all in place before we start to tighten the screws. And when we do, Satan help him."

"And this rhyme will tell you where he'll go?"

I glanced through the contents again and smiled.

"Yup! It's surprisingly informative." I waved the parchment in the air. "If I'm reading this right, it's telling me I have to haul my ass all the way over to New Hell. That's where I'll discover who his latest recruit is, and where I'll get the next clue."

"Recruit?"

"Oh yes. As I say, if this location is correct, there's little doubt."

"Pity we can't surprise him, then." Gemini looked thoughtful for a moment. "Isn't there any way you can teach us how to phase?"

"I'm afraid not. Like your ability with animals and insects, it's either inherent or it isn't. It's a pity Tesla's inventions are so ingenious. We've tried a hundred times to replicate the finesse . . ."

Of course! Inspiration struck me speechless.

"What?" they both chorused.

"You've given me a fresh perspective. Excuse me for one moment while I go and dispose of the useless sack of skin in the corridor outside. The fewer who overhear what I've got to say next, the better . . ."

Chapter 4: From Little Acorns

As his ministers of mayhem gathered before him, Erra slouched back upon his throne and brooded in silence.

Hastily constructed from the bloody residue of broken dreams and fallen empires, his court was an attestation to his character and reflected his mood perfectly. Indeed, at this very moment his sovereignty pulsed with a sickly green light that leached into the Corinthian columns and marble floors of his palace like an infection; one that seemed intent on eating its way through to the very heart of the universe itself.

As was his wont here, Erra had erected his pavilion atop a barrow of rancid corpses. The decaying flesh festered, and every now and then, the entire mound flexed and shifted as the legion of insects and rodents burrowing their way among the twisted torsos and lopped limbs fought over the choicest remains to be found within their putrid prize.

Erra considered his surroundings the perfect balm to soothe his agitation; for while certain aspects of his enforcers' ministrations had gratified him over the past months, one or two areas yet vexed him beyond measure.

"Do you bring me glad tidings?" he asked, as the Seven gathered together at last.

"Alas, my liege, no." As spokesman, the First came forth from the others. "As I have been at pains to stress, Grim appears to have fully habituated to his modified condition and continues to be a thorn in our side. We are fortunate his master is distracted by threats of rebellion, for if the Reaper's efforts were directed solely toward us, I fear our commission here would be beset by unacceptable peril."

The skulls adorning the crests and rails of Erra's throne steamed with a vile mélange of vapor and dread, and the lord of pestilence made no attempt to hide his scorn.

"You are personified weapons all, sons of heaven and earth, champions without peer . . . or so I thought. It shames me to think that you fear to face one you previously vanquished so easily."

"Sire, while we long to fight a worthy enemy, none of us here are under any illusions as to the extent of our dominion. That we are powerful is an understatement evidenced by our achievements to date . . ." And then, without any hint of contrition, the entity added, "Nevertheless, we were fortunate in our first direct encounter with Lucifer's minion, for though greatly weakened, the Reaper proved a most resilient foe, one capable of inflicting trauma upon us before being overwhelmed. And even when he lay bested, we were unable to undo his nature, for his essence is bound to the fabric of hell in a way that defies explanation."

"Your point being?"

"My point is that both Lucifer and his pawn adapt swiftly, as the Sixth nearly found out to his cost at Skull Isle. Remember how effortlessly Grim collapsed the wards throughout the island and dropped the mantle surrounding the prison chamber? Those enchantments took more than two days for all seven of us in our elemental majesty to erect. With the

Reaper in such an augmented condition, I doubt that three of us together would now prevail over him."

The weight of truth in his enforcer's words gave Erra pause.

"Then how do you suggest you best proceed?"

"Our accomplishments regarding the cosmic anchors have proven an unprecedented success. Fatalities have increased a thousandfold, while trade, travel, and everyday commerce remain severely disrupted. Yet we must beware playing into Lucifer's hands."

"How so?"

The personified weapon glanced toward his brothers before continuing:

"It is something we have discussed amongst ourselves at length, sire. Our mission here is to expose His Satanic Travesty as a charlatan, to prove him incapable of exacting the torment of the unjust, no matter how richly deserved. And while our manipulations of the Sheolspace continuum compound suffering and discontent throughout every level of hell, it would appear we might be aiding Lucifer through our labors. Have you noted how quick he is to claim credit for our pains? Perhaps it is time to revise our tactics and adopt a new strategy?"

"A new strategy?" Erra queried his servant's line of reasoning. "What do you propose?"

"Nothing definite, as yet. We cannot rush forward without further contemplation. However, several points remain clear. Brute strength and overwhelming power are nowhere near as effective as we'd anticipated. You've seen how the rabble absorb punishment and adjust to compensate. Perhaps our aims might be achieved not by strength, but by guile?"

Erra liked the sound of what he was hearing. "Yes, yes. Some of our greatest victories have been achieved by insidious means: virulent outbreaks, invisible to the eye, that spread pandemonium at the slightest touch; viruses that foment death in secret . . . until outward symptoms advertise the fact that it is already too late." He warmed to his subject. "True to say, if your foes do not realize they are under attack, they cannot defend themselves."

"Or why not choose sleight of hand and deliver what they expect, to divert attention away from what really will be happening?"

"Which is?"

"Undermining the very foundation of Lucifer's arrogance." The First drew himself up to his full height. "Sire, you've seen how the masses look upon the Reaper. He is Satan's poster boy. The devil views any affront to Grim's authority as a direct challenge to the Adversary himself. Why not sow the seeds of His Infernal Failure's downfall in a way that exposes the Reaper as being as susceptible to our artifices as the rest of the minions?"

"And have you the slightest inkling how such a thing might be achieved?"

An animated buzz broke out amongst six of the seven. Throwing back their hoods, they gathered together in a tight knot.

"Not yet," admitted the First, "as I said, we must ensure Grim never realizes he actually is under attack initially; otherwise our efforts will be in vain. One option might be to make use of the humans. Now Chopin and Tesla have resumed their game, Grim will be duty bound to take the field once more."

Erra paused, pensive for a time, before asking, "Have you considered the angel? Grislington seems content to revel in his newfound freedom, albeit from behind the scenes. Might circumstances be manufactured to highlight to the masses the fact that Altos is not the only heavenly messenger who deigns to walk the roads of hell?"

All seven fell silent as they absorbed the implications of this fresh suggestion.

The First turned to his companions, and Erra watched as their auras flickered with excitement. Their mental exchange resumed and grew more animated.

Aloud, Erra continued, "We were all impressed by the way Grislington orchestrated his release. Even for us, it was a master class in manipulation and misdirection. If you could somehow motivate him to—I don't know—set his designs on things counter to infernal policy, which would keep Grim more than occupied."

Eventually, they reached a consensus. The Seven parted and formed a fulgurous arc of intent before their liege, whereupon the First bowed low:

"As always, your wisdom transcends our own. We will make this matter a priority. We chose two of us: one will shadow Chopin and Tesla; the other, Grislington. While remaining alert to opportunities we can exploit, the rest of us will scour the length and breadth of the underworld for a suitable medium through which to insert our viral intent. Rest assured that we feel confident; the next phase of our operation will reap a rich harvest."

Without further ado, the champions departed, leaving Erra in a reflective mood.

An artful stratagem, it seems. For while we must be patient and wait for the fruits of our labors to ripen, I feel the long-term results will be worth it in the end.

Erra recalled a human proverb he had once heard.

What was it again? Ah yes, 'Mighty oaks from . . . '

*

The Angel Grislington settled in to wait for the second half of the show to begin and had to admit, Icepiccadilly Circus—with its stalls and its tents and pavilions, each bedecked in constellations of twinkling lights—was an amazing experience, and by far the best place he had visited all week.

St Flames Park had quickly become boring after the novelty of the magma fountains and open-air brimstone flumes wore off. And while the living ice sculptures of the Chilsea Embankment offered much in the way of uncultured sophistication, he soon tired of it. Such things might be rarities and therefore all the rage in the underverse but, where he was from, social restraint and eclectic savoir were the mind-numbing norm and something he desperately wished to avoid.

And avoid it he had, for the carnivoral atmosphere of the Cirque du Freak had more than made up for the monotonous start to his vacation.

As Grislington tucked into his third clawberry iscream, he cast his eye over the program, reviewing the earlier performances.

"I have to say that out of all the acts so far, the Dwarf Dart Deluge was simplicity itself. How anyone could fail to find it funny, I don't know. What a recipe for disaster."

Grislington glanced at the entry advertizing the performance:

Roll up, roll up, roll up.
Test your skills in our Dwarf Dart Deluge challenge.
Have YOU got what it takes to hit the mark?

Take one target with a large hole where the bull's-eye should be.

Add a pit of ravenous reavers below.

Select a bound and gagged imp of your choice from our bevy of aspirants keen to regain His Infernal Majesty's favor.

Stuff 'em in a cannon, and off you go.

Yes! It's their lives in your hands.

You hit the mark; they sail through the hole to safety.

You miss—they die!

What could possibly go wrong?

. . . Only 10 Ds a pop . . .

As advertized in the Sinday Times entertainment supplement

(Don't forget your cutout coupon for a guaranteed 10% discount)

"Yes, that was definitely my favorite . . . with the limbless trapeze act a close second." He skimmed down the second half of the listings. "Although it mentions the *Inside Out Man* isn't to be missed?"

Intrigued, Grislington flipped to the bibliography on the inside back page.

"Hmm. It says here that old *Blood 'n' Guts* is the stuff of myth and legend. A veteran of more than seventy-five thousand performances, nobody knows his real name, or the true reason as to why Satan has made him appear every night for more than two hundred years. All they do know for certain is that *his* is the act to beat."

As quickly as he could, the angel reviewed the outline explaining the basis of the routine.

"Oh, I see. So it's not a play on words? All of his internal organs are literally on the outside and taped to his torso in some obscene fashion?"

He glanced at a promo banner included in the advert.

Yuck!

"And what's more, they only give him thirty seconds grace to negotiate a barbed wire and razorblade filled maze and assault course. If he doesn't manage to find the exit in time, he's forced to contend with an entire pack of hellhounds."

The image of what three hundred pounds of muscled flames, fur and fangs could do to an armored knight made Grislington wince.

So what they'll do to old Blood 'n' Guts is . . . is . . . ?

Grislington let his imagination run riot.

Messy . . . Now that I have to see.

"Oh yes. This is exactly what a holiday should be all about."

The lights began to dim and Grislington couldn't help but notice the expectant hush that fell across the entire audience almost at once.

He sat up. And on cue, everyone else craned forward in anticipation.

Grislington turned to study his fellow spectators, and a sudden realization hit him.

They're hooked, and they don't even know it?

He clapped his hands in delight, causing a ripple of sympathetic applause to radiate away around him, as other patrons (thinking he was praising the show) joined in.

Oh, very clever. Fabricated on the pretext of entertaining his precious Blue Suits, this charade of a parade of the grotesque and mutated has nothing to do with benevolence and everything to do with narcissistic vanity. And if what I have learned is correct, attendance is compulsory, even for the masses. He smacked a hand against his forehead. *And that would explain why this event sits on the site of a temporal node. I can't think of a better way to ensure that vassals from every era attend the lesson in the here and now.*

He chuckled in appreciation at the scale of the deception.

An audacious plan.

In his mind's eye, Grislington imagined Satan standing on an ornate balcony overlooking the teeming hordes below. *"Witness My dominion, my majesty—and the stranglehold I exert over every facet of your lives."* Adopting a despotic stance, his voice boomed. *"Behold . . . Am I not the greatest con artist in history?"*

That aspect raised a sobering point.

And what a masterstroke of duplicity he managed with the Reaper. It's not only the wool pulled over the fool's eyes, but the entire herd of bleating sheep. Why, Satan must have planted those seeds at the . . . Ooh!

At that moment, everything went dark and a swarm of searchlights stabbed down from multiple points around the eaves. Within the cone of each beam, a team of warm-up clowns cavorted out into the arena, flowers squirting and buckets slopping over with foul-looking liquids. Gamboling and cartwheeling, they acted the fools and doused themselves and each other with gusto. And it was plain to see why:

Each had been strapped into a radio-controlled explosive vest with a huge painted number for easy identification. Unwilling dupes, they knew only too well the consequences of failing to please the crowd.

All thoughts of plots and intrigue forgotten, Grislington hefted his remote control and eyed a likely candidate: some poor soul without hands and feet and sporting a large scar bisecting his scalp, a soul who didn't appear as enthusiastic as the rest of his brightly painted fellows.

I know that face from . . . Cream?

A thrill of recognition fluttered along his spine.

It is! It's the unworthy doctor himself. Aha! He's wearing unlucky number seven.

An evil leer turned Grislington's face into that of a specter.

So, you can't handle the punishment eh . . . ? And then, before he realized what he was doing, Grislington had depressed the button. *Then let's see how you handle this!*

In the ring, a sickening retort split the air. The sawdust turned red, and gore sprayed onlookers seated in the front rows. A heartbeat later, a telltale pitter-patter accompanied the lumps of meat, intestines and other bodily appendages now raining down.

A silence ensued as the multitude caught their breath in surprise. Then a deafening roar raised the canvas.

Caught up in the moment, Grislington's voice rang the loudest of all.

Chapter 5: Slay'em

As luck would have it, we passed the Bitter Sea/Frantic Ocean divide without a hitch and found ourselves a mere ten nautical miles off the coast of New Hell Harbor, well within those territorial waters. Once again, the Moral Compass had proven its worth in the face of Sibitti meddling, and I for one was glad to get on with our investigation.

Paradise was already setting, so I sent Yamato and Champ on ahead in the *Lone Ranger III* with orders to commandeer a suite at the Hexcalibur Hotel. It would provide a solid base of operations for anything that might occur over here, whilst allowing us direct access to the jailers from the Brass-Steel as and when the Undertaker revived them. As much as we all hated his halitosis-ridden guts, old Bad Breath had proven his worth during our last mission, proving that nobody else could match his finesse when it came to extracting information from the minds of those freshly transposed onto his slab.

Mind you, I was one of the few denizens outside the Undertaker's staff to know what is was, deep in the bowels of the Mortuary, which allowed him to do that.

Just thinking about it brought back memories of a huge cloud of ectoplasmic gas hovering in midair within a vast cavern. Measuring more than two hundred yards in diameter, the invocation represented the necromantic agglomeration of New Dead souls arriving in hell, as well as those awaiting reanimation. An incredible achievement when you realized it included the unadulterated sum of everything about them: Who they were, what they did, and every single memory collected during their lives—and un-lives. Such intelligence constituted a powerful tool in the arsenal of one who would search out your deepest darkest secrets and then use them as a basis for Satan's everlasting judgment.

And, hopefully, the Undertaker will soon be using his aptitude to provide us with an edge in this latest pursuit.

Glad to see my Hounds busily organizing our base camp, I set off with all haste, using the transporter device we had seized from the prison to teleport directly to the location so skillfully woven into the text of our first clue. While I could have phased, I was made of sterner stuff and wanted to test the generator myself before leaving it in the care of my team. Unlike them, I was sure I could handle any unexpected booby-traps our *friends* might have left for us.

Landing only moments later, I could testify that the orb seemed glitch-free, apart from the whirl of residual vertigo-inducing sensations it induced in me.

Phew, what a rush. Thank Satan for no mercies. This will give us a clear advantage in days to come. As soon as I'm finished here, I'll send it back for Nimrod and Gemini to use. I'm sure they'll enjoy the ride.

Satisfied, I tucked the generator away and unfolded the note again. Although its contents had spoken clearly on first reading, I wanted to reassure myself I remained on the right track:

Didn't you see me waiting patiently in the corner for our game to resume?

Painting by numbers is a shocking form of therapy you know,

So I was the one eating crayons and using colorful language,

Especially those metaphors that lobotomize all forms of hope.

No longer isolated, I now have more than time to kill,

And as I await the dissolution of my sanity

I look deep inside toward that puckered concept of self,

Only to discover it's a monument to the fallacy

Of hanging on by the skin of my teeth.

As I've lately learned,

The only true way to peace is to bite off more than I can chew,

Otherwise, my dreams will end up like my severed tongue,

A cadaver, lying dead in the corner,

Decaying, along with all hopes of leaving here

This side of a mortician's bag.

Yes, this entire verse is like a compass needle pointing to one place. I glanced up and read the sign across the top of the gates: 'Cadavers Lunatic Asylum.'

In my mind, several of the lines clinched the deal. In particular, the references to:

'*Shocking form of therapy; metaphors that lobotomize all forms of hope; no longer isolated; I now have more than time to kill; the only true way to peace,*' and of course; '*a cadaver, lying dead in the corner . . .* '

Topside, this institution and the land upon which it sat had been interwoven with superstition, torment and suffering for centuries. Known by a variety of names—The Danvers State Hospital and the State Lunatic Hospital at Danvers, to

name a few—it had opened in 1874 as a one-of-a-kind psy-
chiatric facility situated on Hathorne Hill in Essex County,
Massachusetts. Unfortunately for them, it also gained notoriety as the home of the Neanderthal-inducing effects of pre-
frontal lobotomy treatment and electroshock therapy.

I grunted. It always made me smile how humans tried
to hide all manner of sins behind the labels *treatment* and
therapy.

Ha! Well, it didn't fool us.

Designed to cater to as many as five hundred patients,
its needs soon outstripped resources: by the 1940s, more
than two thousand people jammed the hallways, wards and
basements of this former jewel of psychological care. Out
of necessity, doctors adopted extreme measures to keep so
many inmates pacified. Some had lobotomies. Others received shock conditioning. Many more wore straightjackets
or other specialized restrictive garments. Doctors drugged all
patients.

Hand in hand with neglectful malpractice, abject misery
reigned supreme.

Really, it was no surprise that a number of dark-hearted
souls therein came to our attention. As did Danvers itself, for
its foundations sat upon historic grounds that the underworld
found especially alluring: a history involving hardship, sup-
pression and prejudice.

What many people topside—and especially those living
outside of North America—didn't realize was that *Danvers*
wasn't this area's original name. No, when settled, this entire
district went by an epithet that nowadays seemed to invoke
alarm and trepidation. *Salem*.

And while Salem was a derivative of the Hebrew word
for peace, its early history was anything but harmonious, for

old world beliefs and notions soon clashed with new world rigidity.

Times were different then, and in seventeenth-century North America, the supernatural was part of everyday life. Not in a bad way, of course, nor would it have earned citizens an automatic condemnation to hell, for peasants of that era used charms and a diluted form of witchcraft to invoke blessings on a productive crop as often as saying prayers or going to church on Sunday.

After the arrival of English Protestants, however, things soon changed. Seeking to purify the Church of England of what they considered to be *un*acceptable Roman Catholic practices, they adopted a critical form of worship, as invasive as it was uncompromising.

We loved it, for nothing carried more fear to the puritan community than people who appeared to be possessed by demons. It had only taken a single operative from the Devil's Children to stir up the population. In no time at all, everyday decent folk were displaying all the symptoms of mass hysteria.

History came to know that period as the Salem witch trials. We savored it as a chapter wherein twenty innocent souls unjustly met their deaths at their neighbors' hands.

No wonder, then, that after Danvers had been reduced to rubble, the tainted pedigree of its dark past percolated down into latter-day hell, where it manifested anew as Cadavers Lunatic Asylum, Slay'em, Black Massachusetts—an institution where the underworld's worst sociopaths were sent to endure a most insidious form of personalized anguish.

I can only imagine . . . ?

No sooner had I started to walk toward the main perimeter entrance than I felt the telltale prickle of mundane sensors and all manner of arcane scans wash across my body.

Wow! They're on the ball.

"Welcome, Reaper," intoned a voice from a nearby speaker; "sorry for the invasive nature of the greeting, but we're still in lockdown. We've been expecting you."

"Expecting me, eh?" *Here we go again.*

"Yes, although I must say, given the fragility of hydraspace, we didn't realize you'd arrive so quickly. Nonetheless, we look forward to your insights. I'll notify the warden you are here."

I knew it. Chopin and Tesla must have started their shenanigans from the word go.

The background hum of electrified fencing ceased, and the whine of hydraulics indicated which of the closest TLCs (Track & Lock Cannons) had cut out. I let the matter drop.

I'm sure I'll find out soon enough.

As the double gates swung open, a telescopic bridge began to extend across a lava-filled moat. Beyond it, a half-mile cinder roadway bordered on both sides by acres of manicured lawns led toward the front of the facility; lawns which, so far as I could see, appeared devoid of all life.

At the terminus of the drive, stood a pyro-fountain fashioned into a life-sized statue of His Infernal Majesty relaxing upon his diamond throne, spewing molten iron from horned ridges into an ornate pool. Behind it, the once-châteauesque features of the main building and its four sprawling wings hulked, suitably hellish. Ornate spires and graceful towers had morphed into flying buttresses adorned with cruel edges and spiked pinnacles. Its formerly airy gables and sweeping eaves had become razored peaks and Stygian troughs trimmed by gothic brimstone guttering and pipework.

The overall effect resembled a charred and blackened edifice highlighted along its edges with liquid fire.

I thought the place rather comely, and when the dulcet cries of those currently being tortured wafted toward me on the simmering breeze, I felt right at home.

"Just stick to the path and you won't get hassled," the same voice advised. "See you in a few minutes."

Sounds interesting. Spinning about, I gazed back into the surrounding forest and out across the deserted grounds. *Hassled by what?*

Suitably warned, I continued along the path, headed toward the dark doors of the reception area. Even at this distance, I noticed how the lights twinkling through the barred windows of the west wing flickered on and off intermittently. The volume of the shrieks emanating from that area rose and fell in tandem with the surges.

Aha! I see the therapy sessions here must place a heavy burden on the local hellectricity supplier. I wonder what the monthly bill totals. I passed the time by pondering the mathematical answer to that question, and soon heard a baying from somewhere behind me.

Turning, I scanned the distant tree line to the east in time to see a group of large animals emerging from the undergrowth. I zoomed in on them and grinned.

Hellhounds.

Now I understood why the campus was deserted.

They must let them run free during lockdown. What an excellent deterrent.

Famous throughout the underworld, hellhounds looked like a flaming, rabid cross of wolf, hyena and panther, and averaged three hundred pounds in weight. They possessed the speed of a cheetah, the power of a bull, and the stamina of a horse. Not the creature you wanted hunting you, especially when you considered that they also had better eyesight than a hawk and a more acute sense of smell than a grizzly bear.

Once they were on your tail, you'd had it.

Like another pack I know well.

In mere seconds, the beasts had closed the distance be-tween us and came to a slavering stop on the fringes of the grass. Shedding sparks and circling on the spot, they snarled incessantly and pawed the ground.

I glanced up and down the driveway.

Well trained guard dogs. No doubt conditioned from pups not to engage anyone on the road unless otherwise instructed.

The alpha raised its snout and sniffed the air.

It took me a moment to realize he could sense the glori-ous energy that ran through my veins, for we shared that en-ergy in common.

"So, you recognize another brute, do you?" I crooned.

Raising my arm, I walked slowly toward the alpha dog and very carefully offered him the back of my hand.

A large wet snout drizzled up and down my sleeve, leav-ing a trail of acidic mucus and snot. Black lips curled to re-veal dagger-sized ivory teeth and scarlet gums. Questioning growls scoured the ether in warning.

"Who's a good boy, then? You can taste it, can't you? Probably wondering why I'm not running along on all fours like the rest of you, eh?"

I scratched his snout and the action sent a rush of Bãlefire through my fingers.

"Is this what you want?"

A yip of pleasure pierced the air. I repeated my gesture and his tail sprang up and started to wag.

Friend. Fiend. Hot. Good.

The pictures associated with his thoughts were feral and primitive. What's more, they didn't so much appear in my mind as punch their way inside.

Flames ignited in the depths of the alpha's eyes, drawing a response from mine. He barked an acknowledgment, wheeled on the spot, and led his pack away in a blistering rush.

"I love you too," I called after them.

After watching them run for a few moments, I turned back toward the hospital to find a few concerned faces observing me from the safety of the reception steps. Consisting of two men in bloodstained coveralls and a stern-looking woman in a crisp white lab coat, they seemed genuinely astonished at what they'd witnessed.

I suppose I'd better go and see what shit Chopin and Tesla have left me to wade through this time. For some reason, my brush with the hellhounds had left me feeling frisky. *But not before I've had a bit of fun.*

Within the blink of an eye, I phased and appeared right in front of them.

"*Boo!*"

They all stumbled back in alarm.

"Christ on a stick!" the female gasped. The turf under their feet rocked irritably, then subsided. Steadying herself, she slapped away offers of assistance from the orderlies and struck a conciliatory note: "My apologies for swearing out of turn, Reaper. But you caught me by surprise."

A gleaming gold pin affixed to her breast identified her as Dr. Luna Freeman. For some reason, the name rang a bell.

"Relax . . . Luna. I have that effect on everyone." I flashed my most winning smile, forgetting once again that the cowl and all-enveloping miasma surrounding my face would never allow her to see it. "Let's start again. You obviously know who I am and why I'm here. I understand the warden is expecting me?"

She graced me with a withering glance before gesturing me to follow. Over her shoulder, she replied, "Yes, that's right. But you must forgive him. Because of the condition of most of our patients, the security measures here are topnotch, including those that aren't readily apparent. So, for this to happen now . . . well, it's knocked the wind out of our sails. Warden Livingstone is down in the sickbay receiving treatment: a tincture to soothe his nerves."

From the look she threw me, there was obviously more to that statement than was apparent. I let it ride. As I was rapidly beginning to suspect, like everything else in this place, he'd find those truths eventually.

Nevertheless, the governor's name was too good an opportunity to simply dismiss.

Livingstone? Damn, what a shame he isn't a psychiatrist or something. I'd have loved to use the line.

Somehow, I resisted the urge to ask the inevitable question.

In no time, the welcoming committee had ushered me along a sumptuous lobby area, past a grandiose reception desk, and through a tiered set of three airlock-style armored doors, cleverly disguised with steel embellishments and bulletproof glass.

Beyond them, the hallway became more austere and businesslike; free of any loose fittings or sharp objects that might be chewed, swallowed, or inserted where they shouldn't be by Freaky Friday candidates for the next space mission to Insanityville.

To be honest, what I saw put my mind at rest.

They've obviously paid attention to detail here. That's indicative of a tight ship and a switched-on staff. It'll be interesting to see what stunts Chopin and Tesla managed to get away with.

The hallway led to a central hub incorporating a broad winding staircase, an encircling walkway, and four ancillary corridors branching toward the main wings. Several hospital-bed elevators sat at regular intervals around the outer circumference of the gallery itself.

Without bothering to ask, Luna elected to use the stairway, and we descended in silence: one, two, and then three levels.

Once we reached the bottom, she pointed toward a set of double swing-doors adjacent to the eastern sub passage. These were made of brass-edged wood. Originally painted white, they had tarnished brown over the years. Each door bore a patchwork of dents, teeth marks, chips and boot scuffs.

There, if anywhere, the history of this place is clear for all to see.

The sign above the entrance read Medi-Bay, although some bright spark had used a permanent marker to alter the letter *e* to *a*.

As if they needed to emphasize anything.

Muffled screams echoed out into the corridor from inside.

I rest my case.

I glanced back toward Luna for conformation.

"And Warden Livingstone's in there?"

"Oh yes . . . you'll see."

Without any further explanation, she turned on her heel and stalked back the way we had come, her ever-present flunkies in tow.

Well, good-bye, Luna Free– Hang on: Luna Freeman?

My surroundings blessed me with a moment's inspiration.

Hey! I wonder if she's a relation of Walter 'Ice pick' Freeman, the lobotomy butcher. I laughed aloud. *Talk about carrying on the family business. Well I nev–*

Shrieks issuing from the sickbay suddenly squelched.

Duty calls. I'd better get in there and see what's going on.

*

Situated on the corner of Boil Street and So'vile Row, Alchemy's Black & Tan Coffee Shop was one of the better refreshment houses to be found anywhere in Olde London Town. Not only did the establishment serve the finest arab-cadabra beans, but its cream never curdled and its staff feigned politeness to a superlative degree of servility.

No wonder, then, that its clientele comprised some of the wealthiest and most gregarious denizens found in the underworld. Everyone who was anyone came here to see and socialize.

Nevertheless, the striking middle-aged woman seated by herself at the window table drew hardly a second glance from other patrons, which was odd since her long blonde hair and sun-kissed skin were marvels to behold.

Wearing a tailored knee-length dress in complementary black and white hues and belted at the waist by a contrasting scarlet sash, her outfit accentuated her figure perfectly and oozed a quality few would be able to match.

Ideal attire for those seeking companionship.

Nevertheless, something about her bearing suggested clearly that she preferred her own company. That and the bottomless pit of a gaze which, when it latched onto anyone straying too close, made them visibly quake in their boots.

Left to herself, she seemed content to stare out of the window whilst taking an occasional sip of her drink.

Pedestrians passing by in the street were oblivious to her existence. Just as well, for her predatory air made it obvious she was waiting for someone.

Now and again she stiffened in her seat, and then her lips would move as though she was arguing with herself. Eventually, each episode would pass and she would relax once more and withdraw into a self-induced fugue.

A long-case clock on the mantelpiece chimed once, marking 6:55 p.m. GMT—Gehenna Mean Time—whereupon she immediately vacated her chair and made her way toward the exit.

"Miss? Excuse me, miss?" the waiter called. "You've not paid for your drink."

The woman paused in the doorway but didn't look back.

"Young sir, you'll find I've left more than enough to cover the cost of my beverage on the table." She spoke quietly, and with a distinctive Mediterranean accent. "If you're quick, you'll make quite a killing . . ."

And then she was lost to the crowds outside where nobody was in a position to witness the evil grin that marred her beautiful face, or overhear the rest of her statement. "As will I, this night."

Chapter 6: Shock Therapy

I swept across the landing and kicked the medi-bay doors open. They crashed apart with a bang. A single glance was all it took me to confirm I had stepped into another time zone.

Gone was the modern-day sterility reflected throughout the rest of the hospital. In its place I discovered a room akin to the tunnels of the London Underground during the Blitz.

Is Cadavers situated on the fringes of a temporal pocket?

A single light bulb hung by frayed wiring from the ceiling, but its wan light barely reflected from the ivory tiled walls. To my left, a broken mirror overlooked a filthy, chipped porcelain sink, its bowl covered in scum, courtesy of the dirty water dripping incessantly from a faulty tap. On my right, a series of crooked, over-laden shelves supported a selection of soiled bandages and rusted surgical instruments of varying shapes and sizes. A battered medical trolley graced the far wall. Complete with worn straps, it perched precariously upon three wheels.

As mesmerizing as this was, however, my attention fixed on the center of the room where four burly male nurses labored to hold someone captive in what looked like a turn-of-the-century dentist's chair. Sweating profusely and obviously distracted by their efforts, they ignored an extra pair of flailing legs protruded from the mass, punctuated by a constant barrage of cursing.

It would seem someone's putting up a spot of resistance?

Regardless of the racket, a series of rhythmic crackling sounds predominated. With each sizzling retort, a spray of sparks spat high into the air. The solitary bulb dimmed in sympathy on every occasion, as if acknowledging the gravity of the situation.

The restrained unfortunate panted harshly and intermittently uttered another stream of obscenities that fried the ether blue.

And this is for their staff? Hells bells, I'd love to see what they do with the inmates.

One of the struggling attendants happened to peek over his shoulder. His gaze met mine. A pregnant pause followed as it slowly dawned on him who was standing there, and then his expression turned to one of alarm.

"Shit! The Reaper's here already, doctor. You'd better wind this up."

Did he say 'doctor'? Who . . . ?

As the attendants jumped away from the figure on the chair, I tried to make out whom they were addressing. My scrutiny fell upon the patient, the only one present dressed in surgical scrubs. Then I noticed: *he* was the one holding an antiquated set of jump leads to his own temples.

Hang on. That's the warden? So he's the one they . . . ?

Slow off the mark, my intuition finally kicked in. *He's medically qualified?*

The compulsion to deliver the immortal line proved irresistible:

"Doctor Livingstone, I presume?"

The worthy doctor grinned, shook his head vigorously from side to side, and sat bolt upright.

"Yes, that's me." He lingered to run his tongue along one of the exposed electrodes. That final jolt seemed to do the trick. "Aah, that's better."

Jackknifing erect with no sign of discomfort, he strode toward me and extended his hand.

I did a double take.

Rarely did I meet anyone who had actually done their homework on me, and who would understand that, under these circumstances, it would be safe to exchange a handshake.

About bloody time . . .

Then my double take did a double take.

Looking directly at Livingstone, I noticed that his eyes appeared to be out of sync. One stared right through me as though I didn't exist. The other rotated round and around in its socket, as if pursuing imaginary flies.

Fortunately, he didn't appear to notice my gaffe and breezed on: "I'm glad you could get here so promptly. It's not often that a Category-A inmate gets out of his cell, and it's a relief to see how seriously the Administration takes our missing patients. Although I must say, I'm somewhat surprised. What with the disruptions and such, I didn't think you'd be able to get here while we were still in the initial lockdown."

"Hang on . . ." *That didn't sound right.* "Missing patient? Don't you mean 'escaped'?"

Livingstone seemed genuinely shocked by my statement. For the briefest instant, both of his eyes focused together.

"I'm sorry, Reaper, but we can't say for sure just yet. It's only been three hours since we discovered his cage was empty; and with a building this size, there are many places they can hide in, especially down here in the sublevels. As you've no doubt noted, it's a maze of tunnels. When his exit raised the alarm, we triggered his subdermal tag and completed an initial sweep, as per protocol, but came up blank. So I ordered the lockdown and called for help, they sent you." Livingstone scratched his head. The gesture set his roving eye in motion again. "We're only now finishing off the last of the room searches. Of course, if he escaped onto the grounds outside, he's fucked anyway. If the TLCs don't get him, the hounds eat first and bark about it later. Hopefully, we— Are you all right, Reaper?"

The fact of the matter was that I didn't feel right. Apparently, I was still a little wonky from side effects of the orb, for I could have sworn Livingstone had just said the security breach occurred only three hours ago.

I glanced at the holographic time-keeper on the back of my gauntlet. It flared and the numbers *19:10GMT—11:10 NHT* appeared.

But that's impossible. There hasn't been enough . . . ?

The sense of disorientation intensified, and for a moment I got the impression that the ground beneath my feet had turned to quicksand and was trying to suck me down.

Livingstone froze in place, and a shadow copy of his form stretched backward like an elastic band. The wraith Livingstone appeared to be saying something, something that filtered through to me in snatches, as if contending against gusts of wind. Whatever the words, they didn't clarify until the paradox reversed itself, and Livingstone's phantom aspect started to catch up to the rest of his body.

". . . we can't say . . . only been three hours . . . all sorts of places they can sneak off and . . . sublevels. As you've . . . maze of tunnels. When the . . . subdermal tag . . . as per protocol, but . . . ordered the lockdown and called . . . get outside, he's fucked any . . . TLCs . . . hounds are con . . . eat first, and bark abo . . . Hopefully, we—Are you all right, Reaper?"

Everything snapped back into place.

What the hell?

A recent memory sprang to mind. In it, I was prizing a gray baseball-sized object out of the wall back at the Brass-Steel.

The generator did have a dent in its side. Perhaps the blow damaged some of the internal components? I'd better have it checked out before anyone else tries to use it.

"I said, 'are you all right, Reaper?'" Livingstone repeated. He cocked his head toward the contraption next to the dentist chair. "I can give you a little zap of something that'll settle your nerves if you'd like?"

"That won't be necessary," I replied, "I'm just a little fatigued from all the running around. If you'd excuse me for one minute, there's something I need to do."

Turning away, I removed the orb from within the folds of my robe, altered my perspective, and sent out a long-distance hail.

Nimrod, can you hear?

Nimrod's reply was instantaneous. *Loud and clear, Daemon. Problems?*

I hope not. I paused to send a compressed telepathic data bundle regarding my experience of only moments ago streaming his way. *Now, it might simply be down to the fact that Cadavers sits close to a temporal nexus. We've all seen how the creation of a teleport bridge can sometimes produce gravity ripples that screw with people's balance for a while.*

Like human ears cause vertigo in pressurized jets?

Precisely. However, don't forget the damage to generator's casing during the breakout. Something inside probably shook loose. I'm going to send it to you in a moment. Have Pascal get one of his boffins to check it out. And Nimrod, make it a priority. Even with the dizziness, this device will be one hell of an ace up our collective sleeve. I don't want to miss the opportunity to use it if one presents itself. Here it comes . . .

Understood.

Summoning my power, I conjured an image of Nimrod's face in my mind, and then uttered a single word in ancient Hellanese.

"*Dorash* (Portal)."

A miniature black helix peeled open in the air before me. Surrounded by an electrum of scarlet and gray lightning, it brought with it a welcoming exhalation of rotten eggs and a deep sub-harmonic reverberation I found soothing. I placed the orb inside it, and then relaxed my psychic grip. The void condensed almost immediately and winked out of sight.

Nimrod?

Got it! his thoughts declared. *I'll get right on this and update you when we have something.*

Likewise, I replied, *expect something from me soon.*

The ether went dead.

Turning back to my host, I found him alone and waiting patiently with a modern d'Hell Tablet in his hand. The front page was open, displaying the gaunt visage of someone possessing closely trimmed hair and a neat mustache. For all that, his beard was unruly and portrayed a wild and disheveled look. One glance told me this was a person who knew he would never experience happiness again.

"And this is?"

"The man of the hour. It's a bit of a trek over to the isolation wards, so I thought you'd like to swot up on him as we walk. We can chat further when you're finished."

As I suspected. Regardless of the fact he would probably make a fascinating case study himself, Livingstone is more switched-on than he looks and runs a tight ship.

"Thank you, doctor. Please, lead the way."

I followed him out from the medi-bay and the two of us set off along one of the subterranean corridors. As we walked, I swiped through the screens before me:

Charles Julius Guiteau. 8 September1841–30 June 1882:
Born as the fourth of six children in Freeport, Illinois, Guiteau was an American preacher, writer, lawyer and would-be politician who never lived up to the potential he believed he possessed. Infamous for the assassination of the twentieth President of the United States, James A. Garner.

I wasn't in the least surprised to find we had another assassin on our hands. However, try as I might, I couldn't remember the specifics on this guy from memory alone, and decided to peruse his record in more detail.
Okay, what does it say here?

After failing to get into university, Guiteau joined a utopian sect—The Oneida Community—only to fall short in his devotions. He left the order twice, and ended up filing spurious charges against the community's founder, John Humphrey Noyes. Guiteau's behavior during this period became so erratic that his own father disowned him, and declared him irresponsibly insane.

Guiteau then moved to Chicago where he somehow managed to obtain a license to practice law. Once again, his ineptitude proved his undoing and most of his cases resulted in enraged clients and judicial criticism. Next, he tried theology and published a book—The Truth—which was almost entirely plagiarized from the work of the aforementioned John Humphrey Noyes.

On 11 June 1880, he was a passenger on the SS Stonington when it collided with the SS Narragansett in Long Island

Sound, at night, in heavy fog. The accident resulted in significant loss of life aboard the Narragansett, and although nobody from the Stonington had been hurt, Guiteau felt spared to serve a higher purpose. As such, he turned to politics to better serve his fellow man.

He wrote a speech in support of Ulysses S. Grant which he revised when Garfield won the Republican nomination in the 1880 Presidential campaign. He delivered that speech only twice. Regardless, Guiteau believed himself responsible for Garfield's victory and insisted on an ambassadorship for his services.

His demand unmet, Guiteau's cries for reward waxed ever more frequent and outlandish, until he lost access to Garfield and his cabinet members.

Incensed, Guiteau borrowed fifteen dollars to buy a .442 caliber Webley British Bulldog revolver with ivory handles, establishing a clear intent to kill. Evidently, he selected such an embellishment as he felt it would look better as a museum exhibit after the assassination.

On 2 July 1881, Guiteau located Garner at the Baltimore & Potomac Railroad Station, Washington, D.C. and shot him twice in the back.

My sense of injustice flared.

What a dick! A loser, with a capital yellow streak down his back. Murder is murder, and the more the merrier. But have the guts to take someone out face to face.

I skimmed down to the details regarding his trial:

Blind to the overwhelming evidence against him, Guiteau pleaded not guilty, and continued to display increasingly bizarre and violent behavior toward all in the courtroom including the judge, prosecution, jury, and even his own defense team. Everyone was subjected to long and laborious outbursts, and especially those who tried to brand him insane; a condition that might have worked in his favor. Alas for him, it seemed to onlookers that no one worked harder to convict Guiteau than Guiteau himself.

On the way to the gallows, he smiled to spectators and reporters alike and appeared happy to be the center of attention. Indeed, he milked the occasion for all it was worth, and insisted on reciting a poem, "I am going to the Lordy," before he died.

I had to bite back a laugh.

He certainly did go to the Lordy, though not the one he might have wanted.

Flicking through the rest of the crap, I concentrated instead on what mattered most; his Infernal Rap Sheet. In moments, I was summarizing his activities here in hell:

So, having been condemned, the Undertaker addressed Guiteau's penchant for verbalized self-aggrandizement by removing his larynx and replacing it with razor-blades. Clever. Any time the fool tries to talk or even eat food, he cuts himself. And from what it says here, Bad Breath also compounded Guiteau's craving for the one thing he managed to get right in life: Death. He is now blighted with an overwhelming compulsion to ice anyone he takes a liking to, or those he feels might be able to help him advance. Nearly three thousand confirmed hits in—what?—less than a hundred and fifty years. Not bad, and in some ways, he's similar to Isabella Castile.

Something about this situation struck me as odd.

So how will Chopin and Tesla manage the appetites of these freaks? They'll not sit quiet, awaiting tasking between assignments.

Unbidden, I received Strawberry's memory of confinement, her will neutralized by powers beyond her ken. Her
vacant, helpless eyes still called out to me . . .

Fucking angelic artifacts. That's how.

"As long as they exist, we're all in danger," I mumbled
to myself.

"Sorry, Reaper," Livingstone looked back "Were you
speaking to me?"

I waved the tablet at him.

"I was just wondering what you can tell me about Guiteau that's not in here."

"Not a great deal, I'm afraid." Even from behind, I could
see that the subject annoyed Livingstone. "Guiteau's one of
those patients we're not allowed to . . . *interact* with." He
added an obscene hand gesture. "Orders from on low."

"So what *are* you allowed to do?"

"Why, make him suffer, of course. As you've no doubt
read, in life, Guiteau was an attention-seeking butterfly who
flitted from one situation to the next in an attempt to feed off
the success of others. It's our job to ram his inadequacies
down his throat by micro-managing everything he does."

"Sounds fun."

"Oh it is, believe me. We grafted his flesh to a chair bolted
to the floor before a widescreen TV. It plays the National Gehennagrapic History channel, twenty-four hours a day, sev-
en days a week. The shows basically highlight the achievements and accolades of hell's darkest and worst denizens. As
you can imagine, their successes pour endless amounts of
salt on an ever open wound."

"Ouch. And was that your idea?"

"A team effort. Although I did come up with the suggestion of keeping Guiteau medicated around the clock," he

chuckled, "you know, just to stimulate the cognitive areas of his brain so he doesn't keep dropping off to sleep."

I could get to like this guy.

Then a practicality of the arrangement raised a question.

"Isn't it messy keeping him in a chair all the time? I mean, doesn't that generate a lot of work for your staff?"

"Not at all. We used a commode instead of a normal seat, and positioned it above an open drain with a direct flue to the main sewer. Needless to say, it smells rank in there, and the fumes will blister your skin if you stay too long. But, as we only feed him once a day and the staff wear gas masks anyway, nobody minds. It's worth the hassle just to watch his reaction."

"So your methods are effective?"

Livingstone stopped in his tracks and turned to face me squarely.

"Reaper, I'm a psychiatrist in one of the most notorious nut houses in hell. I've seen some strange things in my time, believe me. But watching someone chew their own fingers off on a regular basis just so they can stuff them in their ears in a vain attempt not to hear what's being broadcast . . ." Both of Livingstone's eyes snapped into focus, and reflected a faraway look that I could only describe as pure elation. "Ah, that's priceless."

"What happens when he runs out of fingers?"

"That's just it, Reaper. He doesn't. The Undertaker cursed Guiteau with superior regenerative faculties. They grow back in a matter of hours. And the fun thing about it is, when they do, the nerve endings will have been tweaked so his sense of touch becomes even more sensitive to physical stimuli than before." His gaze intensified into one of deepest fascination. "Can you imagine the level of suffering?" He sniffed. "Still, it doesn't seem to make any difference. Every day is the same, and bloody digits end up all over the floor. You'll see, we're just about there."

Livingstone gestured toward the passage ahead of us and pressed on.

Sure enough, in the space of a few strides we turned a corner, and the endless rows of armored doors sporting port-hole windows disappeared. In their place, a line of special-ized chambers stretched off into the distance.

Situated side by side, the placement of the chambers de-nied their occupants any opportunity to interact. Each pos-sessed a floor-to-ceiling window almost as wide as the room itself. On closer examination, I saw they were molded from persphex, a diabolical blend of occult polymers that were soundproof and immune to most forms of esoteric interfer-ence, edged or ballistic weapons, and good old-fashioned re-peated head-butting.

The walls had likewise been adapted, lined with seam-less sheets of damage-resistant memory foam. From what I could feel, the floor construction made use of a harder ther-moflex-rubber blend. Chew retardant, it offered a high de-gree of *give* to unsteady inmates, which was just as well if what I was looking at was indicative of the mental state of everybody down here.

Appearing more like an enclosure at a zoo, the first cell was unadorned except for a single wide shelf, positioned against the far wall at waist height. A layer of filthy straw had been scattered across it, most of which had fallen to the floor, creating a cowpat-encrusted halo of muck and flies.

Well, that's the sleeping arrangements sorted.

A huge tractor tire dangled from the center of the ceil-ing on a thick chain. The straightjacketed occupant could sit astride the inner rim of his makeshift ride and swinging back and forth for all he was worth. This went on for a few minutes until, inevitably, he lost his balance. Crashing face first into the deck, he bounced once, twitched, and then lay still.

"Not that I give a shit," I mumbled, "but is that normal?"

"For him it is. When alive, he was part of a trapeze act with the circus. Found out his wife was *performing* elsewhere with a fellow artiste, so he arranged for a convenient accident, one which killed both the spouse and her lover when the supports tragically snapped. Unfortunately, it also collapsed the entire tent. Scores perished. The authorities couldn't pin anything on him—swinging does bring its own particular hazards, after all—but he didn't fool His Satanic Majesty, who earmarked him for a position within the Blue Suits."

"Seriously?"

"Deadly. This is part of a mental conditioning program we enforce. Our subject has been on it for fifty years now, since his death. Next month, we enter a new phase, which will continue until he's ready for work."

"I see. And where is Guiteau kept?"

"Oh, his room is just along here, several units down."

Livingstone set off again and quickened the pace. In no time at all we passed a lobotomized freak licking his way through the window; a bearded monstrosity dressed in a tutu, dancing with a naked, life-sized decapitated Barbie doll; and more worryingly, a demure-looking woman sporting an outrageous mustache who simply studied us quietly as we traversed the horizon of her tiny, self-contained world.

At last, I arrived outside the scene of the crime; for a crime I was sure it was.

Guiteau's chamber was much like the others I had seen. Spartan and completely devoid of any creature comforts except for an LCD TV and separate commode.

This is exactly as Livingstone described it.

I noted certain aspects of the interior.

So, we have an electrical socket up on the ceiling, and the extension cord won't support the weight of a man. The sewer grille seems to be welded shut and doesn't look tampered with. What's more, the walls don't bear any signs of concealed damage.

I ran my armored fingers across the persphex barrier.

It's without blemish and completely intact.

That left the airlock, over on the far side of the room.

Although I doubt very much he ever made it that far.

Aloud, I asked, "I'm particularly interested in the details surrounding Guiteau's actual disappearance. What can you tell me about it?"

"Quite a bit and not a lot," Livingstone snapped. "Let me explain and you'll see why I'm pissed."

Retrieving his pad, he brought up a different image. As he did so, he gestured to the gallery wall behind us. "Did you notice the cameras on the way in?"

I looked, and lo and behold, a series of small blemishes ran the length of the darkened corridor. Positioned adjacent to each cell, my heightened senses indicated they housed miniature surveillance units, which seemed to allow for overlapping fields of view.

"No, I must admit, I wasn't looking and completely missed them."

"Well, it's no surprise. They are designed to be inconspicuous . . ."He then pointed up toward the two opposite corners of the ceiling within Guiteau's cell. "As are the ones we have planted inside each cubicle. They grant us total coverage of what takes place inside. Which makes what I'm about to show you particularly irritating."

Livingstone shuffled around to stand beside me and held the pad up to my cowl.

"Note the time, Reaper. Sixteen thirty-two hours, today. Now watch what happens when I press play—"

He did so, treating me to an overhead view of Guiteau on his specialized commode. Guiteau rocked violently from side to side, obviously upset by what he must watch. His protestations continued for a while, and then, without warning, a wash of static burst across the screen and everything went blank.

Livingstone continued, "And before you ask, yes, the same thing happened to each of the other cameras covering his chamber. Interesting, when you consider they run on completely independent circuits. Keep watching."

The timer counted past fifteen seconds, and suddenly, normal services resumed, albeit with one less person in view.

"Now do you appreciate why I'm so annoyed? I had my head of security run a full diagnostic on our systems. There were no power outages or energy spikes, and yet all three cameras suffered the same malfunction. The hatchway logs showed no open access doors on this level within an hour on either side of the anomaly. We also have dedicated surveillance in the service corridor running behind the cells. Nobody went in. Nobody came out. And yet, the elusive Mr. Guiteau vanished with a subdermal implant that coincidentally decided to go on the fritz at the same time." He edged closer and lowered his voice. "That's why I sealed the place and was so keen that only you and I come here, for I suspect he may have been in league with a member of my staff. I'd like you to—"

This guy is loyal to Satan? Now that *I will remember.*

"So nobody's been inside this cell?" I interrupted. "Not even to check?"

"No. I knew you'd want to keep it sanitized and free from cross contamination, so I ensured to keep it clear of snoopers."

You've just earned yourself a black mark, my friend.

I placed a consoling hand on his shoulder. "Don't worry about it, Warden. I can assure you, none of your staff let you down. Far from it."

He looked confused.

"Let's just say, I strongly suspect Guiteau might have been sprung by members of a small group of anarchists I've been pursuing. Unfortunately, these fugitives from injustice have access to certain devices that can circumvent all manner of security protocols—"

"Do you mean the Tesla orbs?"

"You've heard of them?"

"Who hasn't? They're all the rage amongst rebel militia groups. But that's by the by. Why are these fuckers breaking into my asylum and making off with Category-A patients? Not only does it make me look incompetent, but it could have ramifications across—"

"Rest assured," I cut in, "if what I suspect is true, you're just another casualty on their growing list of felonies. Felonies for which I intend to make them pay dearly. What say we check out my theory?"

Before he could respond, I tightened my grip and phased us through the intervening barrier and into the cell.

Livingstone was appalled.

"How in Hades' name did you do that? The persphex is supposed to be impervious to manipulation. Does nothing work the way it's suppo– Unholy shit!" He started choking. "The—the smell . . ." Then he doubled over, gagging and retching.

In the blink of an eye, I erected a courtesy shield about us.

"Better?"

Eyes streaming, Livingstone tried desperately to clear his lungs.

"Does . . . doesn't the ste– the stench bother you?"

"When you've visited the Mortuary as often as I have, this isn't so bad . . ." I stepped away and cast my awareness out into the room about us, "and to be honest, I don't have time to notice. Now, let's see if we can get to the bottom of this little charade."

I concentrated and allowed my essence to blend into the constitution of the floor, walls and ceiling. Finding nothing, I collapsed the bubble in toward me, smaller and smaller, until I was skittering amongst the molecules in the air and the fibers in the wiring, and even the grains running through the wood used in the chair and its frame.

Still nothing?

Finally, I turned my astral attention upon the only other item within the chamber.

There!

Opening my eyes, I spun to face the TV and peered intently at the screen.

Something impinged on the edge of my perception. It barely had time to register before it was gone again.

I stopped staring and allowed my eyes to relax. For the briefest instant, I saw it again.

"Ha, did you spot that?"

"What?" Livingstone's gaze flicked between me and the latest presentation from National Gehennagrapic. "What have you seen?"

I strode toward the set and raised my hand.

"*Birúiste* (Be revealed)."

The power of the hex settled over the TV and the picture froze, revealing a subliminal message transposed into its electronic matrix by an ingenious addition to the main circuit board.

Thanks to Tesla's ingenuity, no doubt.

It read:

It won't take an Einstein to work this one out,
Especially as its name is worth repeating.
$E = mc\ X^2 - (d)$
Caught here, my resolve would dissolve.
Hell, I'd even be forced to look up and plead the Fifth
And throw myself upon the dark panorama of your mercy.
I've given you enough . . .
Now it's up to you.

Pointing to it, I explained, "This confirms that nobody on your staff is culpable of treason."

"How?"

"It's bait. The ones I'm after try to goad me with little snippets like this."

"They try to wind you up. The Reaper. Are they mad?"

"Far from it. By giving a clue as to where they'll strike next, they're hoping I'll go charging off after them before I'm ready. Evidently, they must think there's some way to take advantage of me." I shrugged. "It won't work, but it doesn't stop them trying."

Livingstone turned back to the screen and read through the passage again.

"And that is going to tell you where they'll be?"

"Yep. I've just got to fathom it out and get my Hounds there ahead of them." I invited him closer. "Shall we?"

Together, we began to pick our way through the puzzle, line by line.

One thing struck me immediately. "See there? That's Einstein's theory of relativity mixed in with a formula I've never seen before."

"But, Reaper," Livingstone tugged on the sleeve of my robe, "the first passage specifically says you won't need Einstein to decipher the clue. Might that mean you have to ignore the 'E = mc' part?"

Hey, that's a good idea.

I studied the equation again.

"So that means I have an X or the multiplication symbol squared, minus whatever the d is meant to represent."

Livingstone was insistent. "If you don't mind my saying so, I have a sneaking suspicion you're not supposed to look on it as a mathematical sequence at all. Stop approaching this from a scientific angle, and treat it more like—"

"A word picture?" I completed his thought for him.

Does it even paint a picture?

I compared the characters again.

Okay then. I've got an X, or a multiplication emblem. Then a 2, minus a D. Or what about, X squared . . . Multiply squared . . . Times squared . . . Hang on! Times squared minus a D?

Tiny trumpet-wielding demons blew a fanfare to victory in the playground of my mind.

"Times Square?" I mumbled.

Livingstone leaped onto my idea.

"So *that's* why it ends with an odd phrase and refers to a name worth repeating." I turned to look at him, and he explained, "I'm a Frank Sinatra fan. 'It's up to you, New York, New York.' The home of Limes Square, or Times Square as they still call it topside."

I caught his point immediately. Here, in the underworld, Limes Square was a huge open cesspit where they disposed of rotting limbs and other organic materials until they had decayed enough to . . . *Dissolve and return to the slab for recycling. Oh, very clever.*

I read from the fourth line on, again.

"So, from Limes Square, I'd be able to look up and . . ." *plead the Fifth, and throw myself upon a dark panorama of . . ."*Does that refer to the Empire Stake Building, do you think? It's on Fifth, or as we say here, Filth Avenue."

"And everybody knows it's the place many new arrivals run to, thinking they'll be able to end the misery of their unjust consignment to hell." Livingstone snickered. "What a delightfully romantic notion, imagining for one moment that throwing themselves from the eighty-sixth floor observation deck of an infernal skyscraper will miraculously turn back the clock and make everything all right." On this occasion, his roving eye spun like a roulette wheel. "Oh look! I committed technical suicide, and now I'm in heaven. Fools!"

Bingo! I've got the next location. Time to go.

As I gathered my power for the side to side hop, I decided it might be best to get this man on the payroll.

"Doc, I've got to be going, but rest assured I'll be putting a word in for you with His Infernal Majesty. When your assignment here ends, give me a call. I have a feeling your talents might be put to better use back at the Den of Iniquity."

"Really?" His jaw dropped and a wide smile erupted across his face. "But that would be f—"

I phased, and was surprised to catch an unexpected change in his demeanor.

"—uuuck me!"

For some reason, his expression of joy had crumbled into one of pure disgust.

And then I remembered.

Bugger! I left him inside the cell without a gas mask.

*

The pulse beneath her fingertips quivered and stuttered.

Aroused beyond measure, the assassin merely tightened her grip, for each desperate palpitation only served to feed the gnawing ache between her legs.

That's it, that's it. Just let go. Let the inevitability of this moment take us and transform us both into something new.

As if obedient to her command, the erratic rhythm weakened by the second.

Sensing that the moment of rapture had finally arrived, the femme fatale allowed her senses to bore deep into her victim, and held her breath in anticipation.

Go on, take the step . . .

Butterflies danced inside her stomach.

A final shiver . . . and then all tension faded from the supine form below her.

She trembled and, just in time, glanced down to capture the image in his eyes as they focused beyond the veil. Mouth agape and tongue protruding, his blushing corpse ached for the inhalation that would never come, this side of the Undertaker's ministrations.

His body faded. Only then did his killer relinquish her hold upon his livid neck.

Satisfied, she knelt to one side and licked the blood from her hands, reveling in the static wash of its vitality and the metallic undertones of the memories imbued within its viscous ruby depths.

Well, well, well. Someone's been a naughty boy. Consorting with—with . . .

The intimacy of her actions wrought unavoidable consequences.

A seizure claimed her and she stiffened. Free at last, the wellspring of her pent-up ardor erupted in a flood that coursed through her synapses and gushed along her nerves, followed by a secondary and even stronger surge of excitement. Broaching the walls of her self-control with ease, it brought with it the heady rush of orgasmic release.

Biting down a howl of pleasure, she shuddered, threw her arms wide and fell back. In such a position, her spine arched over at an impossible angle. She cared not. Thus transfixed, the hit-woman was content to remain crucified upon a rack of her own devising while receding waves of dark fulfillment filtered all memory of recent frustrations from her soul.

Time passed, and eventually, the grandfather clock situated near the main entrance struck the half hour.

Stirring, she glanced at her watch. It read: *19.30.*

I am reborn. An angel of release on a mission of mercy.

Standing, Isabella Castile climbed nimbly down from the table, smoothed the lines of her exquisitely cut   dress back into place and, for the first time, looked carefully around the interior of the premises.

The desk beside her dominated the shop floor. Surrounding it, rack upon rack of clothes and dozens of suits in various stages of construction made the space look much smaller than it actually was. Higher up, shelves bowed under the weight of shaped fabrics and bales of cloth, and threatened to spill their contents to onto floor.

It was harder to pin him down than I imagined it would be, she pouted. *Though I must admit, it took me by surprise, a gentleman of his age and stature running round and around whilst screaming at the top of his lungs.* Then she giggled.

Still, it's difficult to maintain such a pace with a pair of scissors embedded in your neck.

As if that thought reminded her of the earlier ruckus, she peered down and studied the crimson stain now soaking into the weave of the sumptuous carpet.

Someone's going to have a difficult job clearing that up in the morning.

From there, Isabella's gaze strayed to the fitting rooms—where two customers had met a quick if grisly end, stabbed through the heart with message spikes—and on to the photographs festooning every open space along the back wall. She didn't appear to be paying much attention until she happened upon the one depicting His Infernal Majesty in a brand new bespite suit from this very institution.

Aha!

Suddenly awake, Isabella sidled across to the picture. After studying it for a moment, she pressed the wooden frame in the bottom right-hand corner, and heard a barely audible *tick-tick.*

The mount had been set on a hinge that swung silently open. Behind it, a robust Insurgent and Greenleaf 666 wall safe lay exposed.

She smiled, and for once her face held a bloom of genuine warmth.

Crispin, Crispin, Crispin. What a pathetic attempt at security. Not that I'd have required your help for this part. She inhaled deeply. *This place reeks of divinity. Narrow-minded fool. Did you not realize such a prize could never hide from those of finer talents?*

Pausing to sort through those recollections she did need, Isabella quickly located what she was looking for—the combination. The dial was soon spinning rapidly back and forth until a loud *click* announced she had been successful.

With a turn of the handle, the reinforced door yawned wide.

Inside, a number of documents and an assortment of diablos, gold bars, blood bags and other currencies lay piled together in assorted heaps. Beneath them, lost amongst the press of larger items, sat a small plum-colored velvet pouch, held fast at the top by a stout golden cord.

Ignoring everything else, Isabella reached in and plucked her prize from its hiding place. With a reverential air, she loosened the knot and tipped the contents into her hand.

A tiny lucent gem shone back, infusing her palm with the radiance of the Milky Way and filling the air with the chimes of a crystal midnight on distant shores.

Such dominion. Here, I hold a mastery of the rarest stripe.

She listened for a moment and its song filled her with a sense of urgency.

And I must be away, for its twin lies nearby and calls to it.

As quickly as she could, Isabella replaced the seraphinite back within its bag, and then deposited her stash inside her purse. Everything else she left as it was.

Although there was no need, she tiptoed theatrically to the window, caressed the blinds apart and peeped outside. Despite the glare from the neon sidelights, she was able to discern a steady ebb and flow of pedestrians.

Good, time to make my second call.

Retrieving the keys, Isabella slipped the catch and stepped out into the rancid night air without making any effort to conceal herself. Then, with a great deal of pomp and ceremony, she made a point of locking the door, whereupon she tested its latch over and over again, as if concerned for the security of the establishment in which she had so recently committed bloody murder.

Her charade worked. By making it look as if she belonged there, no one paid her the slightest heed.

Descending the steps, Isabella set out for Bondage Street and cast a final glance over her shoulder, where golden letters shone from the display:

Dirge & Skinners—Suits to die for
So 'vile Row
Bespite Tailors & Shirt makers
Dirge.Skinners.co.jux.doom

How prophetic. Though, unless the Undertaker is feeling benevolent, I suppose Mr. Skinner will soon have to change the sign.

She hadn't taken more than a dozen steps when two young women turned the corner ahead of her and started to approach.

Isabella glanced about. Nobody else strolled nearby.

She began to salivate as a familiar itch teased its way into the pit of her belly. Before she realized what was happening, a subliminal compunction overwhelmed the anagogic desire budding within her.

Her eyes glazed over and she let the girls pass without incident.

Only after a full minute had elapsed did Isabella regain full control of her senses.

It seems I must content myself with the task at hand.

She looked at the faint scar running along the inside of her wrist.

So be it. I'll play along with their restrictions . . . for now.

Chapter 7: That's Show Business

Engines snarled and horns blared.

Although the rush-hour traffic was gridlocked, it didn't prevent drivers from stamping their feet to the floor whenever the rare opportunity arose. Braking harshly only moments later, they were quick to lean from windows and vent their frustrations at being caught, yet again, on one of the busiest roads in the underworld.

Stepping out into the din, the Angel Grislington seemed oblivious to the clot.

"What an ingenious form of entertainment," he mumbled to himself, "so simple, and yet so profoundly indicative of what latter-day hell is all about."

In a daze, he turned back to stare at the very latest venue in this, his *Things to do and places to go* itinerary, and scratched his head.

"Brilliant."

Strolling across to the nearest bench, he shooed a flock of hell-pigeons away and laid a newspaper across the feces-coated rungs. After taking a seat, he flipped to the front inside pages of an elaborate pamphlet detailing a brief history of the origins and development of the establishment he had just left:

Based firmly on a concept devised by Marie Tussaud (nee Grosholts), "Madame Two-Swords & Terrorium" is unique amongst the infinite layers of the underverse in its approach to correctional castigation and public entertainment.

In life, Marie Tussaud learned her craft from Dr. Philippe Curtius, a Swiss physician skilled in the art of wax modeling. She came to fame during the French Revolution, where she would search through corpses to find the severed heads of executed citizens from which to make her death masks. Those masks acted as revolutionary flags, paraded through the streets of Paris on a regular basis.

Tussaud's notoriety spread and she traveled to London to exhibit her works in the Lyceum Theatre. Because of the Napoleonic Wars, she was unable to return home, and settled in Baker Street, where she opened her first independent exhibition. Tussaud's death masks attracted a lot of interest, and she expanded her concept to include life-sized models of celebrities and renowned characters from history, both dead and alive.

Nevertheless, the public's fascination with death continued to manifest. Tussaud began to concentrate on the more sinister and macabre, guaranteeing her success as a worldwide phenomenon. Following her death in 1850, His Satanic Majesty acknowledged the value of her work by graciously sponsoring the rejuvenation of her main center of business here, in Olde London Town.

But don't forget, this is hell after all, and we couldn't just leave the most infamous museum ever dedicated to the damned to its own devices. Oh no . . .

Therefore, Old Nick saw fit to add a most delicious development. Not only does Madame Two-Swords incorporate the foulest of specimens from the underworld's past, but it also houses unliving malefactors from the present day too. Yes, in a diabolical twist, our dark father has seen to it that this is the only place in all infernity where you will be able to witness live waxwork exhibits who have incurred his wrath engaging in combat to the death.

Wait!

Did we say Live. Waxwork. Exhibits?

We surely did.

Genetically altered by the Undertaker, the cells in the bodies of our fiendish fighting felons no longer metabolize energy in the way they used to. Instead, they produce lipids, marvelous little molecules that gradually turn the anatomy of our decrepit lawbreakers into wax.

Once deemed ready for combat, they are kept in refrigerated rooms where they await the dishonor of being called forth to entertain you, our most unwelcome guests.

Armed with nothing but sword and shield, and forced into the steaming jungle heat of the Terrorium, how will they fare?

Will they quickly dispatch their foes and live to fight another day, or will their timidity amidst humidity result in a slow and wilting death?

Will they prove their mettle, or will their resolve dissolve?

One thing's for sure, if they can't stand the heat, they won't last long in this devil's kitchen of an arena, where the only way out is in the bottom of a bucket.

But don't take our word for it, come witness the debacle for yourself.

Price: Only 20:00 Ðs

Madame Two-Swords & Terrorium, 13–26, Gnarlybones Road, OLT, NW1 13LR.

Mme. Two-Swords.co.jux.doom

As sponsored in "Flaw & Disorder"

The monthly magazine of your unfriendly Ministry of Infernal Affairs

(Intimidating you to help us make the underworld a bitter place)

In a reflective mood, Grislington thought back on the oppressive environment of the huge, greenhouse-like bowl of the Terrorium.

"What a truly amazing experience. The contenders started to liquefy the moment they stepped inside. No wonder they were so keen to get down to business. Out of the three bouts I witnessed, the only pair foolish enough to remain overly cautious literally melted away before my eyes. And once they were nothing but greasy smuts on the floor, they were ignominiously scooped into piss-pots and carted off like refuse. If what the compère said is true, they won't be in for an easy ride. They've either earned themselves a one-way ticket to the Cirque du Freak, or Tussaud's will sell their plasticized asses on to Santa's Sex Emporium down in Soho-Ho."

Indifferent to the suffering of others, Grislington found himself captivated by the inventiveness and scope of the relentless and invasive retribution he had witnessed so far.

"How humiliating, being remolded into a doll whose only reason for existence is to satisfy the perverted lusts of someone else. And a denizen of hell at that. Oh my."

His celestial mind boggled.

I guess that's show business.

Grislington's vocalizations were drawing the attention of a growing crowd.

True to form, he didn't give two hoots. Egocentric to a tee, he paused to grace his transient audience with a jaunty wave and a direct *'fuck off or die'* stare before continuing as if oblivious to their existence.

"If my recent experiences have taught me anything, it's that hell is as diverse as it is innovative." He had a sudden idea. "I know. Perhaps I should try my luck farther afield and see what the other realms have to offer. After all, the under-verse embraces each culture's foibles and idiosyncrasies as if they were a wellspring of debased inspiration. Perhaps I might gain further stimulation by embracing the full spectrum of what *they* have to offer?"

But I'll need suitable attire.

He glanced at his watch: 8:20 p.m.

"Thank badness for late night shopping. If I'm quick, I'll be able to walk there before he shuts."

*

By traveling under my own steam, I didn't suffer any of the disorienting side effects I had experienced when using the rift generator. Materializing within the main lobby of the Hexcalibur Hotel, I quickly found my bearings and sent out a telepathic hail for Yamato and Champ to join me on the double.

Cups and saucers clattered to the floor as denizens fell back in alarm.

A pocket-sized battleaxe of a woman stepped out from behind the main reception desk. Endowed with thick-rimmed spectacles and flagstone-sized front teeth, she radiated fastidiousness through every belittling gesture and patronizing glance she possessed.

And she possessed plenty.

In spite of her diminutive height, the crowd parted before her like the Red Sea, and by the time she had crossed the intervening space, I had counted at least fourteen ingenious little ways in which she bluntly conveyed the fact that this was her domain and woe betide me if I didn't toe the line.

Unfortunately for her, I was in no mood to play Pharaoh and Moses.

Nora Woods. We meet again.

As she jackbooted her way into my personal space, I raised a single finger in greeting.

"*Ablach* (Cripple)."

The power of the hex dropped her to her knees, and the gathered throng fell silent.

Stunned by the abrupt change in her circumstances, Nora struggled to retain her dignity and peered up from the floor in pained surprise.

That look said it all. I now had her complete attention.

"Good evening. While I appreciate I look a little different from our last encounter, it doesn't alter the fact that you still seem to have a stick up your ass about your own self-importance. Not a wise thing to do with someone whose presence signifies the authority of the Dark Sovereign himself." I squatted down beside her, and continued. "And while I gave you the benefit of the doubt and put up with your dissention the last time I was here, be under no illusions. Such things don't happen twice."

I extended my hand.

Nora's magnified eyes flared and she scrabbled backward across the floor. To her credit, she didn't whimper. Not once.

The nearest patrons edged away.

Her predicament struck a chord, and I almost showed leniency.

But where's the fun in that?

I clenched my fist, jerking her aloft.

"*Cuirlauìs hetom loìsh* (Ignite and burn)."

Flickering flames encompassed Nora in a nimbus of gold and scarlet light. The halo flared and her hair and clothes combusted, consumed within the blink of an eye by an inferno of blazing intensity that quickly ate its way into her flesh.

Blisters erupted across her body, pulling the rest of her skin tight. Within seconds, Nora's features locked in a rictus of terrified horror. For the briefest instant, a skeleton hung in midair, bright, whole and clean. Then it too blackened and crumbled, falling in on itself to join a small mound of carbonized ash back on the floor.

The conflagration snuffed itself out. In all, the process had taken less than ten seconds from beginning to end.

Something shiny peeked out from the embers.

I looked closer.

Two ridiculously large front teeth had refused to burn.

I grinned.

Difficult to the end . . . This time around, anyway.

At that moment, Yamato and Champ came bounding down the stairs and into the foyer, weapons drawn, ready to play.

"Shoot, boss," Champ called out, "what's with the indoor grill-fest? I'd have brought a couple of chilled Ping Paos to knock back while we waited for the ribs to cool."

"Just sending a message"—I glanced at the oily black smoke lingering amongst the chandeliers and back to the sea of worried faces trying desperately to look anywhere else but at us now that the show was over—"that I think has been received loud and clear. Talking of which . . ." I stood and motioned for my Hounds to step closer, "we have our next target venue."

I paused to transfer the details of the latest clue directly into their minds.

"That was fast," Yamato stated. "You've been away less than an hour and we've only just this minute finished checking out the penthouse suite."

I didn't let my concerns show.

Less than an hour? Hellfire, the Sibitti's tampering must be screwing with the temporal flux between circles more than I realized. They've always been confusing at the best of times, but at least there was a warped consistency we'd come to know and hate. Still . . . we can't complain, especially while it seems to be working in our favor.

Aloud, I continued, "What can I say; greased lightning and superlative efficiency are my middle names. However . . ." I made a pass in the air and a privacy shield bloomed to life about us. A second flourish caused two trench coats to appear. "Put these on. We don't know what Chopin or Tesla's interest might be at that location yet, or how they'll employ Castile or Guiteau's talents. So you'll be traveling incognito and going in ahead of me. Use the Azazel gate to get you there. It's just around the corner from here and will take you directly to the Queens Boulevard of Broken Dreams travel hub. Check out the lay of the land and report back."

"And where will you be?" Yamato asked.

"Close by, observing. My new form makes it difficult to blend in unless I use a glamour and I don't want to risk doing that, as the—"

Daemon?

A voice I knew intimately bypassed my barriers and resounded loudly within the confines of my skull.

Strawberry? Are you okay?

Not really. In your absence I've been keeping an eye out for anything that might be labeled as unusual. A difficult task, as you can imagine. And . . .

I could taste the conflict in her emotions.

Tell me. Just spit it out.

I think it'd be better if you came home quickly.

Home? Strawberry, I'm all the way over in New Hell. Yamato and Champ and I are just about to follow up on a lead that might help us close the gap on Chopin and Tesla. Can't it wait?

This is more important.

An otherworldly projection materialized before me, containing a single dazzling construct of pristine brilliance and unfathomable obscurity. Hauntingly beautiful, it somehow managed to absorb all light about it as it shimmered through every color imaginable.

Seraphinite!

The implications of this intelligence tingled down my spine, and for a heartbeat, I saw only overlapping vistas and contrasting vanities. Above me, celestial energies flared in a chaotic rush of polymorphic majesty that all but fried the heavens. Below, crimson expressions boiled within an unholy maelstrom of malevolence that threatened to shatter the very foundations of reality.

I stood between them; a dimorphic fulcrum upon which the future of creation itself might be decided.

A sense of self, hidden away for so very long, intruded.

What? I am . . . I feel . . . How long has passed since . . . ?

And then it was over, and the vision shattered into myriad tinkling fragments that swept all comprehension away.

Daemon?

"Boss. Daemon. Are you all right?"

Barely a heartbeat had passed.

"I'm fine," I muttered, annoyed by the unexpected but necessary intrusion. "It looks like something has come up back in Olde London Town. Something only I can deal with."

I shared my concerns with them and expanded my consciousness so they could sense Strawberry's presence.

Addressing Yamato and Champ, I added, "Look, you guys go on ahead as planned. But remember, blend in. If Chopin or Tesla show their faces, or either of the escapees, come to that, don't piss about. Take them down. Hard."

"That's more like it!" Champ chortled. He rubbed his hands together with evident glee. "A simple cut 'n' shut. My favorite."

Yamato was more reserved.

"And what about intelligence?"

"We're in the right place for that. If you need to ghost them, just do it and get your asses straight back here and over the road. I'm sure the Undertaker will be only too pleased to assist in peeling open their minds . . . along with other parts of their anatomy."

Both nodded, and without a further word, took their coats and walked from the hotel.

I decided it would be best to make my way back to Juxtapose using the Bālefire.

Strawberry, where are you now?

A crystal-clear image appeared of an up-market shopping arcade.

I've had the area cordoned off while MI13 investigators and sulforensic teams give the place the once-over.

Good. Clear a space for me, I'm on my way.

*

Satisfied that he had at last managed to reestablish contact with their target, Chopin relaxed and allowed the cryptic process to begin. Telltale eddies signaled gravity's claim upon his consciousness, and in moments his will descended through the energy lattices toward the anchor of his corporeal shell.

A distinctive glimmer out of the corner of one ethereal eye caught his attention.

Again? But what are you . . . exactly?

Instinctively, Chopin groped toward it. But as had happened before, no sooner did he reach out than the object of his scrutiny sank deeper within the bore of confusing currents surrounding him.

He followed, determined this time to discover as much as he could regarding the elusive apparition. However, within the space of a few strokes, Chopin was dismayed to realize his curse had followed him onto the astral plane. Excruciating pain exploded along his fingers as his joints dislocated, effectively crippling his efforts to swim against the tide.

Not now!

A burst of anger focused his resolve into a white-hot needle of intent. Beyond worry of failure or concern of loss, Chopin struck out and felt himself course forward like a marlin through choppy seas.

His hands brushed against something; something that was at once fibrous and smooth.

Vacant eye sockets flared, and golden effervescence gurgled up all around him.

Chopin gasped, for the momentary contact brought with it the most amazing contradictory feeling. Pins and needles pierced his flesh with barbs that burned like acid along the nerves of his wrists. The sensation spread into his arms and shoulders in an agonizing rush that left only ecstasy in its wake.

His head spun, and before he knew it, Chopin was back within the confines of his sumptuous drawing room with a concerned Nikola Tesla rushing to his aid, chilled wine at the ready.

"Is everything all right? Did you find him?"

"Yes, yes. Stop fussing." Chopin was quick to put Tesla's mind at ease. "Whatever it was that hid the Reaper from my sight was obviously temporary. He's at the Hexcalibur Hotel as we speak, causing a scene with two of his lapdogs."

"So what happened, do you think?"

Chopin took the proffered glass.

"I honestly can't say. Within minutes of his manifestation off the coast of New Hell Harbor, he simply disappeared. I don't know whether that's down to some new strategy he's only now decided to press, or a side effect of the Sibitti's meddling with the Sheolspace continuum."

An aficionado of all things metaphysical, Tesla seemed fascinated by the possibilities such a concept presented.

"I'm betting it was just a fluke."

"A fluke?"

In reply to Chopin's look of consternation, Tesla continued, "Think about it. If this were some new strategy the Reaper had developed, would he show himself again so soon? No, he'd be off sharpening his dexterity so he could arrive unannounced at our door. So, logic dictates it was either a coincidence or he slipped into some kind of dead-zone. Think of it as an astral pocket caused by the unraveling of the hydraspace lanes."

He has a point, I suppose.

Nevertheless, Chopin still felt ill at ease.

"It would be best to remain cautious. My talents may be sibylline in nature, but they are not omniscient." He raised a toast and smiled. "That's why we work so well together. Our strengths play to the other's weaknesses."

The two men took seats opposite each other and sipped their drinks.

"So what was all the panic about?" Tesla enquired. "It looked as if you were in a great deal of distress. I thought for a moment you were being pursued."

Chopin waved down his companion's concerns.

"That, my friend, was due to something else entirely . . ." He stared at his fingers and flexed them repeatedly. They were free of pain for the first time in an age. "Something wonderful."

Astute as ever, Tesla was on his statement like a rash.

"Not the new vision you've been blessed with?" He leaned forward in his chair. "It was, wasn't it? What did you see? Is it a totem? A weapon, perhaps? Or a periapt?"

"Patience, patience. You know the way this works. Details either come in a rush or they take their own good time. Whatever the outcome, I get the sense this latest development might be something we would prize above all others."

Chopin glanced at his hands again. After placing his glass on the table, he cracked his knuckles by way of demonstration.

Not a twinge.

Tesla caught the inference and fell quiet.

Eventually, he asked, "So, what do you suggest we do now?"

"Now?" Chopin looked across Tesla's shoulder and allowed his gaze to focus on the Awful Tower in the far distance. "Why, I'd have thought that was obvious. The stage is set and we have ringside seats . . ." He lifted his drink high in the air and proposed a toast. "As the saying goes, the show must go on."

Chapter 8: Tempus Fugit

Nimrod exited the stronghold and paced out onto the observation deck.

The flickering lights of Perish stretched away on all sides like a fretwork of lava-filled veins, making the city appear both salient and vital. Nevertheless, he didn't have time to savor either the scale or the view, for while Don Pérignone had been hospitable and eager to please, neither he—as Perish's premier crime boss—nor his elusive partner, François de UnBorn, had been able to unearth the information Nimrod required.

I suppose I should have expected it really. They may have a finger in every pie, but this is Perish and that finger still likes to stick it to the man if the opportunity presents itself.

Most denizens were aware of the fact that the Don's influence was absolute between the twelfth and sixteenth horrondissements, which basically covered everything south of the river. They also knew that de UnBorn ran the city's white market, along with the movement of rare commodities and information. What people didn't realize was that both hoods owed their unparalleled success to the discreet benevolence of Nimrod's pack leader, Daemon Grim; someone who had gone to great lengths to remain hidden behind the scenes while surreptitiously neutralizing any threat to their dominance in this region.

Needless to say, business had been good and the relationship had paid dividends since its inception. On this occasion, however, the coffers were empty.

I can't believe that people as notorious as Chopin and Tesla can stay submerged in the mire for so long without coming up for air. Someone, somewhere, must be willing to talk?

Word on the street was clear.

Chopin and Tesla had returned to Perish less than a month ago. Chopin looked on the city as the only bastion of uncultured *savoir-vivre* which truly deserved his patronage. Tesla's interests were far more mercenary. As one of the major staging areas for the large-scale deployment of guerrillas and their myriad rival factions, Perish attracted a lot of interest from revolutionary leaders and financiers alike. The safe transportation of troops and equipment was big business and Tesla was only too willing to provide the toys to help them achieve their aims, *if* the price was right.

But knowing they were here was one thing. Pinning down precisely where was another. Nimrod had felt as if he were trying to piss-write his name in sand on a windy day in the desert. Information had simply drained away or dried up.

This tends to confirm the truth of Daemon's suspicions of a leak within the Blue Suits. Some bastard is cutting off the flow and Hades help them when we find them.

Don Pérignone had even gone so far as to make his erstwhile deposer—and onetime second—Al Catraz the spurious offer of a reprieve on the Reaper's behalf, just to see what the phantoms of the Inseine might know.

While the ruse had worked, what had come back was puzzling at best.

"He has the balls to want what he cannot have, and lives beyond the opus ring in sight of Dante's hangout."

*

The only portion Nimrod could fathom was the obvious reference to Dante's hangout—Inferno's nightclub—situated atop the structure he was currently visiting: the Awful Tower.

This isn't exactly helpful. He turned slowly on the spot. *Seeing as nearly three million other denizens live in sight of the same bloody thing, and that's just within the city environs.*

He tried to calculate how distant a person would have to be *not* to notice this, one of the most iconic structures in the whole of Perish.

Hell, this fucker's got so many lights on it you could see the damned thing from orbit . . . From orbit? His astral sight punched up through the all-enveloping shroud of clouds. *Nah, he wouldn't go to such extremes, especially with the current instability of the Sheolspace continuum . . . though I wouldn't put it past Tesla.*

Strangling down his frustrations, Nimrod stomped toward his new partner.

Gemini was leaning on the outer balustrade, head in hands. He had left her there nearly an hour previously while he went to chew through some final details with Pérignone in the Don's office. Nimrod had hoped that, as a former Parisian native, she might have some insight as to where a fugitive would gravitate in the hope of remaining inconspicuous.

From what he could see, she was either deep in thought or studying the glowing trails of firefries and lightning-jacks as they flew lazy circuits over the lantern-strewn walkways of the Chomp-de-Marsh just over a mile away. Regardless of

the distance, the constant drone of so many nighttime, mutant, flesh-eating insects was enough to counter the sound of
the endless streams of nearby traffic.

"Anything?" he asked.

"I'm sorry, no." She straightened and jutted her chin toward the marsh. "The last time I walked those gardens, I did
it for real during the Revolution, topside, so I don't really
have a clue where to begin. As I mentioned before; after my
damnation and revival here in hell, I avoided this place like
the plague and spent most of my time scouring the different
eras of Olde London Town. A pity"—Gemini's ravaged face
softened and she got a faraway look in her eyes—"because
the Reap-Daemon said this city was very different from the
Paris I knew." She inhaled deeply. "And I understand now
what he meant."

Nimrod took a moment to survey the fire-lined arteries of
the sprawling edifice below them.

"Yes, I appreciate what you mean. Whether you want it to
or not, Perish does tend to get under your skin. Who knows,
one day you might even want to get a place here."

"One day, perhaps," she murmured, "but not yet."

"Anyway, enough of the romantic shite." Nimrod gestured, and they started to make their way across to the Victorian elevator. "Time is pressing and we're no closer to our
prey than we were at the beginning." They entered the cage,
and he slammed shut the door. "Let's get on over to the Ministry of Injustice and see if they have anything for us."

Gemini looked uncomfortable at the mere mention of
Perish's injustice headquarters.

"What, more bad memories of your death?"

"Not really. It's just that Daemon mentioned there was a
possible leak among the Blue Suits or even Devil's Children.
Is it wise to let them in on the nature of our enquiries?"

Sharp girl.

"We should be all right. Remember, we have Pascal working with us now. He's something different, and if what I heard is correct, our Dark Master has seen to it that the Devil's Own are as loyal as we are."

Nimrod was pleased to see that Gemini looked unconvinced.

Excellent, that suspicious streak will serve us well.

"In any event," he continued, "while we're there, we can at least get our hands on that travel orb. Wait until you see what it can do, Gemini. I tell you—"

A loud thrumming sound alerted Nimrod to the fact that a squadron of lightning-jacks was buzzing toward the carriage.

He lashed out.

"Fuck off, you buggers!"

"Hey," Gemini interceded, "leave them alone. They're not bothering you. They sensed I was here and have come to check me out."

Eh?

Nimrod's hand froze mid-swipe.

Zzzzzt!

A radiant orange and brown body alighted on his fingertips, wings abuzz, fang-sized stinger aglow and dripping with iridescent green venom.

Nimrod could see his astonished face reflected in the huge black eyes that regarded him from beneath six-inch long feelers. The lightning-jack clacked its mandibles, and then skipped the short distance to land on Gemini's head, where it danced round and round.

He couldn't help but notice how the pitch of its hum changed.

It almost sounds . . . happy?

Gemini giggled, held her arms out in the air, suddenly swamped by an inquisitive swarm of insects, all seemingly intent on making her acquaintance.

The sight graced Nimrod with a moment's inspiration.

"Hang on, you say they sensed you?" He glanced toward the Chomp-de-Marsh. "From that distance?"

Gemini shrugged, and her movements left a series of lurid bioluminescent streaks in her wake. "Yes, why?"

"Can they identify faces? If you were to project someone's profile into their minds, would they be able to remember it and look for those specific features as they went about their business?"

"I doubt it." Gemini appeared thoughtful for a moment. "Insects tend to detect and home in on pheromones as opposed to physical features . . . but I suppose I could always try that with the birds? Not that they'd be much good, of course, unless Chopin and Tesla ventured out in plain sight on a regular basis."

The seeds of an idea began to germinate in Nimrod's mind.

Then Gemini surprised him.

"It's a shame you don't have any of their clothing or other personal belongings. Sweat tends to linger if garments haven't been washed right. Do you understand what I mean? If you'd had such items, there might have been enough residual triggers left to give the insects something to go on . . ." Her face brightened. "Mind you, if you did have stuff like that, we'd be able to ask the sewer rats for help. Their sense of smell is second-to-none, especially in the tunnels underground where they can reach all sorts of out of the way places people wouldn't dream of ever venturing."

Nimrod grinned.

A certain boarded up address in Place Venôme came to mind.

*

People who didn't have the ability to travel the interdimensionhell highways connecting one realm to another tended to forget that time didn't exist within the hydraspace environment. And that was before the Sibitti added a roller-coaster ride factor into the equation. So my supposedly instantaneous crossing between New Hell and Juxtapose stretched into a soul-wracking eternity, where diabolically warped conduits flashed and flared like neural pathways all around me for what seemed like hours. Ubiquitous in nature, they made me feel as if I was part of the frenzied synaptic process of a crazy intergalactic brain. But at last my journey came to an end.

The superficies ahead thinned abruptly and peeled back. Moments later, I emerged onto the sidewalk in a head-ringing exhalation of supercharged particles and foul vapors.

People jumped away in surprise. All but one.

Dressed in a similar over-cowl to mine, she looked like an adept from some obscure ancient order. Or she would have, were it not for the shawl of Venetian blonde hair cascading down across her shoulders.

Strawberry.

She rushed forward as if to embrace me, eyes bright with anticipation and suppressed emotion. A warning gesture from me brought her up short.

The light faded and her arms dropped to her sides.

A knife twisted inside my heart.

Patience, not in front of the others, I cautioned mentally. *We have all eternity before us. This situation cannot last forever, so take comfort. When it ends—and it will, I promise you—we'll make up for lost time.*

Strawberry acknowledged my counsel with a barely perceptible nod. Nevertheless, the pain etched across her features was hard to bear. For once, I was glad she couldn't see my face.

Get a grip, Daemon.

I covered the moment of awkwardness by scanning our immediate environment.

We were in what appeared to be a small covered shopping plaza. Comprising a number of well appointed businesses, the walkways and shop fronts were festooned in black and yellow "do not cross" tape; and an unsightly number of sulforensic examiners in bright orange hexmat suits and helmets.

I wondered why they were taking so many precautions. Then my equilibrium returned, and an acute tang assailed my rarified senses.

Seraphinite.

The air reeked of it. And one place more than most.

A sign in the window of a Victorian-style shoe shop piqued my interest:

Cleaver & Lee
Our Soles Are a Feet of Design
Hellforleather Cloisters, Bondage Street
Olde London Town
Bespite Shoemakers
Cleaver.Lee.co.jux.doom
(As worn by the Arch Deceiver Himself)

"'Cleaver and Lee.' Why does that name ring a bell?"

"The Boss gets his shoes here from time to time," Strawberry replied dispassionately. "Obviously, he liked their work enough to grant them his disloyal patronage."

The Boss? Is that why the killer selected this place?

Then I thought better of it.

But he never pays for anything he can simply take. And especially not with something as precious as seraphinite.

Then it hit me.

Grislington. Of course, who else would have such currency on tap?

I turned back to Strawberry.

"So what do we have exactly?"

"This is the second place to be paid a visit tonight." She started to lead me toward the premises and transferred a mental picture of a similar scene at a bespite tailor's establishment only a mile away in So'vile Row. "As you will note, both were exclusive gentlemen's retailers, and both exhibit the same M.O."

We paused at the threshold and Strawberry pointed out a worn leather couch occupying the center of the room. The upholstery was drenched in what looked and smelled like fresh blood. In itself, that seemed impossible, for the stain spread from the cushions, across the floor, and all the way back to an island-style work desk situated at the rear of the shop.

She explained, "Whoever is responsible is skilled and professional. We can deduce this from the fact that each of the outfitters had customers at the time of the hit. However, there are no signs of further struggles. We ran a search on various bits of property we recovered, which included a driver's license or two. Guess what? The clients are missing. There's absolutely no physical or esoteric trace of them. Someone dispatched them swiftly and professionally. It'll

be some time before their empyreal remains coalesce sufficiently for reassignment, so until then, we're in the dark.
However, it's not all doom and gloom." Indicating the blood-
bath before us, Strawberry continued. "The carnage you see
before us was reserved for the partner working late tonight,
in this case, a Mister Gregory Cleaver. Our assassin did the
same with Crispin Dirge over at Dirge and Skinners. It would
seem she made a point of butchering both men before bleed-
ing them dry."

"She?"

"Oh yes. Our hitwoman got off on making them suffer . . ." Strawberry inhaled and her eyes glazed over with
pleasure. "I can still taste a hint of her in the air."

Knowing Strawberry and her kinks as I did, I appreciated
she would know exactly what she was talking about.

She concluded, "From what I've been able to ascertain
from the ledgers, both businesses had a shared clientele. But
one in particular stands out: a Mister Angelus Giseldone. No
prizes for guessing who that really is. Giseldone requested
sizable commissions not truly reflected by receipts and pa-
perwork. Not surprising, this is hell after all. I haven't had the
sulforensic accountants do their number yet but from what I
can ascertain, each of the businesses banked a few shavings
whilst keeping the bulk of the seraphinite in hidden safes."
She shrugged. "Not hidden or safe enough, evidently."

"So you think they tried to conceal what they had?"

"I'm positive. I know you have to be careful around this
stuff, but step inside and take a quick whiff. *Saturated* doesn't
begin to describe it."

I did as Strawberry suggested.

Big mistake.

As before, an otherworldly existence that somehow molded itself across the deepest contours of my mind, eclipsing my sensibilities.

Above me, the heavens blazed bright in a chilling demonstration of omnipotent mastery. Below, the abyss beckoned, mocking the spectacle with an unrelenting display of might that left no doubt of its intentions. It hungered, and if left unchecked, such craving would consume everything that was pure and righteous.

I hovered between them both; a living conduit amidst opposing forces capable of eliminating all life in the universe.

A challenge rang forth, and my reply thundered across the expanse. Two blazing swords clashed. Anathema to each other's existence, light cancelled dark and evil, good. Galaxies trembled; stars sundered.

Arcane energies threaded the fabric of spacetime with plasmic eruptions. Insidious in nature, their potential swelled until the plane of reality fractured in a paroxysm of limitless might.

Daemon?

Engulfed within a storm of disparate rage, I felt the moment of death and rebirth, and was lost to the precipitous expanse that opened wide to swallow me whole.

Daemon, can you hear me?

One moment I was plummeting toward certain calamity, and the next I was back inside the shop. Surprised by the jarring change in perspective, I lost my balance.

Strawberry rushed to assist.

Alarmed by her willingness to put herself in peril, I reeled away and back out of the door.

"No, wait!" *Something is different?* "Just wait a moment."

Investigators and scientists alike stopped what they were doing and stared. I ignored them, for my hypercharged senses alerted me to the fact that a mystery presence lingered nearby. Whoever or whatever it was brooded, ancient and cold, content to watch from the shadows. Something about it evoked feelings of barely restrained potential and danger. Bãlefire embers stirred to life in the pit of my stomach.

That's all the confirmation I need.

The seals adorning my armor flashed and my eyes ignited the ever-present brume within the confines of my cowl. The conflagration bloomed, encompassing me in ribbons of fervid flame. I caught my reflection in a window and realized that, to passersby, I must have looked like the raging fires of hell in personalized form.

Good. This should create the right impression.

The Ministry teams scattered. Most ran. Some dived for cover. A few simply cowered on the floor. I paid them scant heed, for whatever had attracted my attention reacted by flitting from side to side through the structure of the adjoining premises in an obvious effort to avoid my scrutiny.

I ramped up the power and my pursuing gaze seared paint, shattered windows and left scorch marks in its wake.

A distinct impression of alarm coalesced at a point near the end of the arcade. By the time I had concentrated on it, the apparition wasn't there anymore.

It seems other parties have an interest in events?

"What the fuck was that?" Strawberry growled in my ear.

I didn't reply.

To be honest, I wasn't sure yet. Nor did I have time to dwell on the matter, for at that precise moment a tall and rather distinguished-looking gentleman rounded the corner, encountered the tape, and stopped dead in his tracks.

Dressed in a pinstripe suit and navy overcoat, I thought at first he must be one of the Boss's Blue Suits. But as his gaze met mine, the look of astonishment faded from his fine-ly wrought features, and he winked.

Who the . . . ?

His features rippled, only to reform in a perfect balance of masculinity and femininity. His eyes glittered, lost to a brand of insanity of his own making.

"You!" my voice boomed along the colonnade.

The calm façade of an abomination locked onto me, and when he smiled, he actually sent chills down my spine.

Strawberry snarled.

Two knives hissed through the air.

I could understand her prejudice. This fucker had slaugh-tered her without a second thought back on the Isle of Cogs.

And you've still got to answer for that.

My reactions were blindingly swift. Drawing my weap-on, I phased and attempted to cleave his head from his body. Nonetheless, the angel was deceptively alert and by the time I materialized a split second later, he was already gone, and my blade scythed impotently through empty air.

Thud! Thud!

Strawberry's daggers embedded up to their hilts in the wall beside me an instant later.

A cauldron of hatred frothed inside me.

Was he the phantom presence?

Struggling to contain my rising anger, I stepped out into the street and replayed the incident in my head.

No, that was separate and distinct. Sharp and restrained. What's more, Grislington looked genuinely surprised to find us here.

I extended my senses further into the crowds, searching for a target on which to vent my growing wrath.

Nothing . . .

So we do *have another player to deal with? Fantastic. As if I wasn't busy enough.*

The shock of this new discovery and irritation at the ease with which Strawberry's former attacker had gotten away took its toll.

Frustrated beyond measure, I slammed the heel of my staff into the ground and released a blistering wall of fire. The shockwave seethed the length and breadth of Bondage Street. As it passed, hundreds of denizens ignited, expiring instantly in a shower of sparks and dust. Now-driverless vehicles crashed, one into the other, or mounted the sidewalk to career through shop windows. Horns blared. Streetlights toppled. Sirens rang.

I didn't give a rat's ass.

It's because of that supercilious prick that Strawberry's genetics so drastically altered. To her, my slightest touch means death.

"Yes, run, you wanker!" I barked. "When I catch up with you, you'll find out . . ."

My voice faltered.

Grislington reappeared not thirty yards in front of me.

Cool as a cucumber, he was making a point of inspecting his nails, as if *now* was the perfect moment for him to be checking on his personal grooming.

"Good evening, Reaper," he glanced past me and pulled a face, "up to your old tricks I see, taking out your frustrations and failures on those who are innocent."

"This is hell. No one is innocent."

Grislington ignored me, and carried on as if reading my mind.

"And really, why do you blame me for this current predicament? If you couldn't see your personal relationship was interfering with your effectiveness . . . well. You're more of a fool than I realized. Is not what you covet proscribed here in the underworld? I did you a favor, for now the teeming masses bear witness to the fact that Satan's pet leads by his own celibate example."

What? I slammed my mental barriers into place. "You motherfucker!"

I called, and the dreadful vitality of the underverse flooded my system, enhancing my potential with the darkest bane in existence.

Then the penny dropped.

He's the most powerful adversary I've ever faced. And yet, instead of simply getting down to it, he's baiting me into unleashing my hell-spawned capabilities. Why? What is he trying to hide?

Only with the greatest difficulty was I able to fight back the desire to fry him where he stood. But I did.

Restraint added a crystalline sheen to my fury.

Grislington appeared to notice and stopped examining his nails.

Gotcha!

"What's the matter? Frightened to put your money where your mouth is?"

I had an idea, and maneuvered farther into the center of the road.

My ghostly watcher chose that moment to return.

And now we have an audience. Good . . . let whatever it is get an eyeful of this.

So quietly it was almost a whisper, I said, "Tell me, while you were stitching mailbags and hanging around in showers—or doing whatever it is you do in prison all day—did you ever hear of the saying, 'you reap what you sow?'"

"Yes," Grislington replied, "I do believe I did."

"Excellent." I collapsed my scythe and replaced it within its holster. "You see, every time we've met, you've either managed to catch me off guard or you've gone to a lot of trouble to provoke me into letting rip without thought or consequence. Well, guess what?" I balled my fists. "This time it's not going to work. You're about to experience what happens when you sow so much crap it comes back to haunt you."

Grislington's eyes narrowed in confusion, so I decided to get to the point.

"I'm going to literally beat the shit out of you."

In a demonstration of supreme control, I swallowed down the entire sum of all the rage seething inside me and stepped toward him.

It felt like skating on a crust of lava. The road glazed over, and I could hear the asphalt sizzling and crackling underneath me.

As I closed the gap, Grislington's hands inched toward the buttons of his coat. A silver gleam peeped out from within its folds.

He's worried I've got . . . A Vidium Sword. So he did manage to recover it.

I couldn't back down now, and decided to press the advantage of his uncertainty.

"Concerned? I've always wondered how well you'd do in a physical confrontation." I checked my stride to look him up and down. "Because from what I can see, you'd probably snap in two if you sneezed too hard. But let's check that theory out."

Jumping forward, I broke into a run.

"Oh, I'm sure you'd love to express your animalistic nature," Grislington crooned, "however, this is neither the time nor the place for such a confrontation . . ." He blinked away, only to reappear several yards behind me. "But don't worry, time flies, and that day will soon be upon us. Until then . . ."

I took a swing.

Argent mastery trilled in the ether, and then he was gone.

"Until then," I echoed. "Coward."

Live cables from a downed power line danced through a growing pool of fuel, spitting sparks and igniting promises of further mayhem. I gazed into the flames and by their light, noticed the dazzling reflections thrown off by my watcher out of the corner of one eye.

For some reason, I had no problem spotting it this time around and could see it observing me from within the ruins of a nearby burnt-out bus.

"And what about you, my sharp-edged soul-auditing friend? Do *you* want to play?"

The slightest flex within the prism of reality signified it didn't. Moments later, it too had vanished.

Billy no-mates or what? I'm gonna start getting a complex.

"Daemon?"Strawberry emerged from the shelter of the arcade. "I can sense the turmoil within you from here, are you okay?"

"Not really," I shouted back. "It'd be best if you kept your distance for a while." I replaced my hood and started making for nearby Hexford Street. "As you've rightly concluded, I'm feeling a little vexed and need to . . . express myself. Don't worry. Once I've wreaked havoc, I'm sure I'll be all right. I'll meet you back at the Den in half an hour."

Unable to contain myself any longer, I phased the rest of the way and got down to business.

Moments later, the screaming began.

Chapter 9: The Enemy of My Enemy

Although voluminous and black, each cloud possessed a bright yellow interior, creating the illusion that the entire billowing swathe that blanketed the sky from horizon to horizon was suffused with hot neon light. Because of this, today's visitors to the Empire Stake Building wore protective glasses and paradise-block, something unnecessary for more than a century.

From what Yamato could surmise, most people didn't appear to mind, for Paradise's close proximity afforded them a relatively clear and unobstructed view of the Frantic Ocean to the south and the shifting Tectonic Mountains to the north; vistas rarely seen in Madhatten because of the all-pervasive gloom.

Aware of the need for discretion, Yamato began another circuit of the eighty-sixth floor observation deck, maintaining a discreet distance from other patrons whilst pretending to enjoy the sights.

Most were here by themselves, or had come in ones and twos. But not all.

To his left, a small knot of well-dressed denizens clustered beneath the shade of a porcupine dome of black umbrellas. Blue Suits all, freshly appointed to New Hell, for their guide droned on and on regarding the benefits of serving His Satanic Majesty here, in the throbbing heart of one of the greatest cities of the underverse.

Opposite them, a group of demons and Dread-Locks huddled together by the doors, deep in conversation. Yamato was surprised, as his experience tended to show such creatures rarely mixed or shared anything in common.

Still, this is hell and stranger things happen every day. He glanced across to the corner on his right where the largest crowd had congregated. *I rest my case.*

There, a shore party from the *HSMS Titanic* created a more colorful spectacle. It appeared that this evening's "I've Got That Sinking Feeling" theme was *1920s Gangster v Drag*, for a flock of ostrich feather-bearded molls (squeezed into a stunning variety of ill-fitting flapper shifts) circulated amongst wafer thin suited females sporting stenciled mustaches, fedoras, and white shirts and braces.

Champagne glasses clinked; art deco necklaces chinked; and as the illegal hooch took its toll, their muted conversation gradually became louder and louder.

Yamato looked on disdainfully. It never ceased to amaze him how willing certain denizens were to face the consequences of their debauchery. Nevertheless, flesh-eating arachnids aside, the nightly dunking debacle was one of the most popular attractions in New Hell, and tickets were sold-out more than six months in advance.

A fresh batch of frightseers trooped out onto the deck and Yamato was amused to see that Champ had attached himself to the rear of the file, where he was failing miserably to make the acquaintance of a willowy brunette. From the face she was pulling, she found him about as appealing as a case of bubonic plague. Unabashed, Champ continued to press his luck for a few minutes longer, until he tired of his sport and began to make his way toward Yamato's position.

"Anything?" Yamato asked, without turning to face his partner directly.

Inured to public sentiment, Champ hawked the contents of his nose onto the floor.

"Jack shit! I checked the upper observation area three times. So far as I could see, there aren't any VIDs, visitin' dignitaries, or anyone else for that matter who might present a viable target." He paused to wink at the woman who had spurned his advances. She promptly sniffed and turned her nose up. "Are you sure this ain't some turkey shoot? I thought we'd get to cut some flesh for sure."

"Patience, my friend. The day is young and we are in one of the most volatile hotspots in all the underverse. The opportunity for some degree of violence will surely present itself."

As if on cue, a scuffle broke out amongst the gangster throng.

From the look of it, some bright spark had set one of the molls' beards on fire. In an effort to douse the offending flames, the panicking reveler snatched a drink out of the hands of the lady-man next to him. That person reacted graciously by kicking the injured party in the nuts. Tit-for-tat blows multiplied; bystanders crowded in, cheering the contenders. Eventually, the moll with a now-singed and disfigured face returned the glass by thrusting it as hard as he could into the eye socket of his aggressor.

The spat ended abruptly when the concierge assigned to escort the group around the building grabbed both men by their necklaces, dragged them to the precipitous edge of the deck, and threw them off.

A moment of shocked silence ensued. Then—amid a hullabaloo of whooping and cackling—everyone rushed to the edge to watch the poor unfortunates plunge toward the stakes below.

Someone began to holler. Others joined in, and in moments, a rising clamor kept pace with the deadly descent. Eight seconds later, the moment of impact was announced by a loud "Hurrah!" whereupon everyone turned away, clapping and toasting and slapping each other on the back.

The Hounds glanced at each other and shrugged. Such disagreements were commonplace and not worth the hassle of breaking cover.

As order returned, Yamato noticed a rather tall individual wearing a suit and navy mackintosh stroll out onto the gallery. He wore his hair slicked back in what the fashionistas called *Satanic chic*; under his arm he tucked a still-sizzling copy of the New Hell Times.

Something about him didn't add up and Yamato narrowed his eyes.

For one, the waterproof looked oddly out of place on such a balmy day. Something Yamato could testify to, for his own trench coat, though lighter, was proving uncomfortably warm. Second, the Blue Suit appeared to be positively glowing in the presence of Paradise.

Yamato decided to investigate.

The slightest gesture was all it took for his partner to grasp the gravity of the situation. They moved as one, away from each other, and homed in on their target from opposite sides.

The bureaucrat strolled nonchalantly toward his colleagues, giving no indication that he was aware of the Hounds' scrutiny. However, Yamato knew only too well that looks could be deceiving. As he walked, he made sure to unbutton his coat so he could rest his hand on the hilt of his sword.

Less than a minute later, Yamato had circled the deck and taken up a position behind one of the viewfinders. Using its bulk, he adjusted his posture to get a better look. Unfortunately, the party from the Titanic chose that moment to intervene, sweeping between him and his target in a swathe of headbands, suspenders and over-painted glitz.

One of the molls near the back stumbled, losing his wig and spilling the contents of his glass and purse all over the floor. The Blue Suits shuffled away from the commotion and turned their backs, disdainful of those they considered beneath them.

Cursing in a garbled and most unladylike fashion, the disheveled moll struggled to his hairy knees and scrabbled across the deck in an effort to recover his belongings. Now that he had lost his coiffured bob and headband, his beard looked ridiculously wild and out of place. What's more, the front of his chin and dress seemed inexplicably covered in blood.

Did he cut himself?

People giggled.

The transvestite paid no heed. He stood up, straightened his hem, fiddled about in his purse for a moment and . . .

Bang!

The sudden retort was deafening and totally unexpected.

Everyone froze, including the shooter, who stared incredulously as his target turned to face him without the slightest sign of injury.

"Fuck me!" Yamato hissed. "Is that Guiteau dressed as a hooker?"

Yamato looked closer and concluded that, yes, underneath the layers of ridiculous face paint, powder and flouncy clothing, their fugitive from injustice had got the drop on them and tried to shoot someone in the back.

So who's his target?

The atmosphere around the out of place Blue Suit twinkled, making it appear as if he were standing inside an invisible snow globe full of transcendent glitter. The bullet hovered before him, spinning round and around until he decided to pluck it from the air.

A thrill surged along Yamato's spine.

I knew there was something off about our latest arrival. Due to his imprisonment at the hands of the Sibitti, Yamato had never seen the Angel Grislington. But he had heard about him, and had read every report there was on the cherub in minute detail. *And if that's not our man, then Altos must have someone visiting they didn't tell us about. Either way . . .*

Champ signaled to him, and his gesture seemed to convey the feeling, *what the hell? Who do we take first?*

Circumstance decided for them.

Bang! Bang!

Guiteau continued firing, and the winter wonderland sparkled brighter.

The corner of Grislington's mouth lifted in an ugly sneer. He flicked each of the slugs away from him, and for the first time, seemed to regard his attacker with some degree of comprehension. His eyes flared and began to glow.

Galvanized into action, Yamato drew his sword and leaped forward. Guiteau was nearer to him than the angel, his arm still outstretched, so Yamato acted instinctively and chopped down with all his considerable strength.

Guiteau grunted in pain and the weapon fired again. Only this time it did so from where it came to rest on the decking, still firmly grasped within a severed hand, the nerves twitching to the commands of an unseen puppet master. People screamed and tumbled to the ground as bullets tore through unprotected shins and ankles. In moments, the gun's magazine was empty.

Stamping closer, Yamato then elbowed Guiteau on the bridge of his nose, knocking him into Champ's path. Champ didn't hesitate, and slammed his bowie knife deep into Guiteau's neck.

In defiance of the severity of the wound, the assassin drove his head backward, butting Champ in the face. Surprised by the force and direction of the move, Champ released his grip and went sprawling.

Now free of restraint, Guiteau wiped fresh gore from his chin and scuttled away a few steps. With bloody fingers, he fumbled for something hidden within the folds of his waist sash. Forced to use his weak hand, it clearly took him much longer than he would have liked, for he tore at the fabric like a demented beast and snarled with every painful exertion.

A hidden weapon?

Yamato gamboled swiftly toward him and slashed upward.

Whatever Guiteau was so desperate to reach joined the gun on the floor, clutched within his opposite, amputated fist. Yamato had no time to celebrate, as he wanted to ensure he'd neutralized the threat. Spinning on the spot, he lashed out, intending to add Guiteau's head to the growing number of trophies lining the deck.

He missed.

Not because he was slow, far from it. But the angel was faster.

Yamato's arm went numb as his mystical blade, the *Sword of the Gathering Clouds of Heaven*, absorbed the potential from two sizzling bands of lustrous energy. The beams cut off, but Grislington's pupils continued to shine like the moon in a midnight sky. In that gaze, the Hound glimpsed the power of eternity unmasked.

Then he heard a gargled scream from behind him. He turned just in time to watch Guiteau disappear over the edge of the observation deck. Arms and legs flailing, the unfortunate wretch was wreathed in silver flames that had already seared away his clothing and blackened his flesh.

One down . . .

In moments, Champ was by Yamato's side, Abaddon 6000 pump action shotgun held at the ready. Denizens scattered, creating a halo of empty space between the Hounds and their prey . . . if *prey* was the correct term in this situation.

"Any fewkin' suggestions? I know Guiteau was our target but there's no way we can ignore public enemy number one." Champ eyed the angel dubiously and racked a cartridge into the chamber. "Can you imagine the bounty if we manage to take him?"

If *being the operative word . . .*

"Fear not, minions," Grislington interceded, "I ran into your master not thirty minutes ago across in the slum you call Olde London Town, and found him to be equally unimpressive. I had hoped my journey to these far shores might furnish more in the way of intellectual stimulation and a degree of respite from those who seek to use me to further their own petty ambitions. Alas, it would seem my newfound freedom is beset by hurdles and meager mentalities."

Well used to working with each other, Champ and Yamato fanned out, hoping to divide the angel's attention. To no avail.

"As is the case here. Do you seriously think to succeed where your master failed?" To emphasize his point, Grislington reached inside his coat.

The Hounds reacted instantly. Champ fired, and Yamato let fly with a clutch of poisoned throwing stars. Neither hit anything but thin air.

Yamato cast his senses out into the ether. But it was too late. Whatever methods Grislington had used to travel were very effective. He was long gone, and no hint of his presence remained. Replacing his sword within its sheath, Yamato started toward the low railing over which Guiteau had fallen.

"So what do we do now?" Champ moaned.

"Now? I think we'd better—"

"That was a fucking angel," a voice from the crowd declared. Its tone betrayed the awe its owner so clearly felt. "An actual goddam true to life angel."

"Don't be stupid," someone else mocked, "the only angel we have in this godforsaken place is Altos . . . or the fallen. And *this* one was nothing like any of them."

"Yeah, he looked like he could actually handle himself."

"Careful," another hissed, "you don't know who might be listening."

Heads ducked and people glared from side to side, wary of imaginary foes, completely forgetting the deadly predators standing only yards away.

"Well, I think the first thing on the agenda should be the immediate sanitization of this area," Yamato sighed. "Can you imagine how pissed Daemon would be if news got out?"

He stood to one side and gestured. "Shall we?"

Champ's face set into a wicked grin and he cocked the shotgun for a second time.

"I knew this day would turn out right."

They set to with gusto and less than a minute later, the observation deck was awash with the screams of the dying and echoing essences of those already on their way back to the Undertaker's lair.

As their last victim expired in a shower of dust, Yamato spied a couple of limbs that had failed to dissipate. He beckoned to Champ, and they walked over to inspect the mystery members.

The first appendage was a right forearm and hand clutching an ivory handled Cult .45 pistol.

That's Guiteau's weapon. So why hasn't—?

"Hey, I like the look of that." Champ was quick to leap on the gun and hold it up for inspection. He seemed particularly enamored by its bulk. "Nice weight to it. Adds a bit of sophistication to my already charmin' mystique." He sniffed, tucked the weapon away inside his coat, and after a moment's deliberation, did the same with the severed arm.

"Consider them confiscated."

Yamato bent to examine the second article.

Well, would you look at that?

"It looks like Chopin and Tesla have started dishing out their toys to all and sundry."He peeled back the fingers of Guiteau's left hand so that Champ could see.

"A travel orb!"

"It certainly is, my friend. And if it's in working condition, Daemon might be inclined to forgive us for missing the clues and letting our prey slip through the net."

"Slip through the net?" Champ coughed and hacked a vile sticky mixture onto the deck. "Shoot, brother. We're dealing with a fuckin' angel here. Even the boss has trouble with him. And as for Guiteau, we didn't fail. Grislington just did our job for us and ghosted the fucker. He'll be on the way back to the slab as we speak, so all—"

Yamato caught on to his partner's line of thought.

"So all we have to do is get over to the Mortuary and ensure our foul-breathed fiend revives said fugitive with all haste."

Champ slapped Yamato on the back, and chortled, "Where we'll make him sing like a bird as we cut him up all over again."

"Good thinking." Yamato flipped the portal generator and its attached limb to his friend. "You take care of these, and I'll let Daemon know what's occurred. If what Grislington said was true, they must have had a bit of a run in only a short while ago. I'm sure Daemon will be only too eager to find out why Chopin and Tesla are now targeting our favorite harp-strumming refugee."

And if it were up to me, I might be inclined to help them.

Chapter 10: Virtual Reality

Ducking into a side road, Nimrod led the way toward a service lane sandwiched between two street lamps. Each damaged light leaned upon the other, creating the impression that they formed an entrance to another world.

What lay beyond only seemed to confirm that fact, and as Gemini stepped across the threshold, she couldn't believe the transformation. In the space of a mere score of steps, the glitz and glamour of Rue de l'Hôtel de E'ville with its bars and bistros and elegant shops had faded away to reveal the broken, crumbling underbelly of the true Perish; a place that was as dark and foreboding as the damned souls who inhabited it.

Nimrod paused at the next junction they came to, and bent to Gemini's ear.

"Keep your guard up. While there are few who can match us, this place may surprise you, for the vagrants that frequent these hovels are predatory and will be swift to exploit any perceived advantage."

"It sounds charming."

"Oh, it is." The faintest of smiles played across Nimrod's lips. "You'll see."

He turned and strode confidently into the gloom. Gemini followed close behind, and found herself transposed into
a sprawling suburbia of cardboard boxes. A veritable ghost
town, where broken pipes and leaky roofs dripped discordant
rhythms that vied to entice her toward mysterious stairwells
and basement delivery chutes threaded like arteries through
the subdermal layer of the commercial empire about them.

Serenaded by a bronchial harmony of coughing, wheez-
ing and psychotic grumbling that rolled endlessly from the
depths of pneumonia-ridden lungs, Gemini turned on the
spot, transfixed by what she saw and heard.

"It's like a virtual city hidden in plain sight within the
shadows. I've never . . . phew! Pity there's nothing virtual
about the smell."

Nimrod's voice echoed out of the dark. "I told you it
would surprise you."

The deeper they trudged into the piss-stained distillery,
the stronger the blend of ammonia and stale body odor became. Soon, the heady bouquet of rancid putrefaction connected at an unerring level with the stench of fermenting
trash, transposing the atmosphere into a genesis of mutated
exigency. So bad was the all-pervading stench that Gemini
feared she would never be clean again.

The air hummed a literal counterpoint to the drone of
thousands upon thousands of insects. But that wasn't surprising, as closer inspection revealed the presence of dozens of
corpses littered here and there. Bloated and forgotten, picked
clean of valuables long ago and then discarded, they festered
in their own decay.

Gemini had no idea why the bodies hadn't dissipated and
returned to the Slab. But then she remembered:

Ah, the Reap– Daemon mentioned there were pockets like this scattered throughout the underverse. And nowhere more so than here in Perish.

She stooped to examine the putrid legacy of the remains closest to her.

What a way to go, caught in the moment between new death and reassignment, suffering on and on, until you either rot away or something eats you.

That thought served as a reminder.

Gemini edged back the sleeve of a threadbare overcoat and jiggled the skeletal fingers dangling from the cuff like a desiccated fan. Gnawed extremities gave evidence of hell-rats at play.

Aha! So that's why Nimrod brought me here. She scanned the immediate vicinity for rodent unlife. *But where are they?*

Extending her burgeoning senses out beyond the rubbish-strewn steps and stuttering candle lamps, Gemini delved deeper into the veiled interiors of abandoned basements and other substructures.

There!

Squeals of alarm met her gentle telepathic query, and shoelace tails slithered off into the darkness like miniature serpents.

I suppose I should have expected such a reaction. In a place like this, down-and-outs who haven't seen a proper meal in this side of forever will look upon even the vermin as tasty treats. She snorted to herself softly. *Just like the rest of us, then.*

"Nimrod," she whispered, "stop for a moment and stay as still as you can."

He did as requested.

Gemini noted with interest how, despite his size, Nimrod blended into his surroundings, erasing any suggestion of his existence.

She was impressed.

And he doesn't need a chameleon mesh to do it. Now that, I have to learn.

Clearing her mind for the task at hand, Gemini shuffled forward and made herself comfortable within a nest of broken masonry. Once ready, she removed several items of used clothing from her knapsack and placed them on the ground beside her. She took her time, arranging the garments into two neat piles, side by side, as if offering them for sale or inspection to a potential customer.

One for Tesla, one for Chopin.

Satisfied, she whistled softly, held out her hand toward her partner and clicked her fingers. Two small parcels sailed out from the shadows. Gemini snatched them from the air and ripped the packets open, revealing a total of six juicy cuts of beef tenderloin, worth a small fortune on the white market.

Gemini concentrated, and then projected an invitation out into the darkness whilst making a show of placing the steaks onto some of the larger bricks, well away from any source of danger. Happy with her arrangement, she squatted down to wait.

"How long now?" Nimrod kept the tone of his query low.

"As long as it takes. Direct conversation is still new to me, so I'm doing all I can to radiate feelings of friendship, safety and food. Our little friends are skittish, but I think they'll respond once they realize we mean them no harm. When they're close enough for me to judge their tongue more precisely, I'll try to open a dialogue. But it won't be easy." Gemini gestured toward the urban jungle about her.

"Look how asphyxiating and oppressive this place is. And we've only traversed the back alleys of one street. For this to work, we'll need the support of virtually every single colony in the city, so not only do I need to learn the nuances of each sub-dialect, but we've got to offer them a big enough inducement to ensure they reach an accord."

"Oh, don't worry about that," Nimrod's mental veneer was confident, "I can guarantee that anyone helping us bring Chopin and Tesla to heel will never have to pick for scraps again."

"That should do it. Food is always . . . hang on!" The slightest sound issuing from a shattered drainpipe caught her attention. "It looks like someone has come to check us out."

Gemini stilled her thoughts and strove to radiate nothing but good vibes.

"Psst, psst, *psst.*"

The pitter-patter of tiny feet through water signaled the approach of an envoy.

She held her breath and something edged forward into the light.

A miniscule nose appeared first. Then silver whiskers perched on the end of a long snout, shivering and twitching in a constant search for hidden danger. Pink triangular ears came next, sprouting wildly from a tufted brown head. Finally, a diminutive body emerged, Buddha tummy and all, with delicately crafted miniature claws held prayerfully before it.

"Well, hello you," Gemini crooned, "nice to meet you. My name is Charlotte, but you can call me . . ."

And in some abstruse, mystical fashion, Gemini's gifts transposed her words into a form the little creature before her could understand.

The hell-rat relaxed, shuffled closer, raised itself up onto its hind legs and sniffed.

As deliberately as she could, Gemini hefted Chopin and Tesla's clothes before the ambassador and explained what would be required. Then she indicated the food and highlighted the benefits cooperation would bring.

The rodent *squeed*, kinked its head to one side, and then scuttled forward to examine the prize.

Sharp—and surprisingly large—yellow fangs nipped down to grasp the bloody steak by the fat. Then, amid a great deal of huffing and puffing, *Ratty* dragged the sample peace offering away into the inky blackness.

"What now?" The tone of Nimrod's voice betrayed his amazement at what he had just witnessed.

"Now we wait again. They have to decide if they can trust us enough to put themselves at risk by spreading the word into other territories."

"Put themselves at risk?"

"Of course. Even in the world above, just being a rat doesn't automatically protect you from other rats. Some colonies are mutually antagonistic and will attack without provocation in a search for food or in protection of their turf. You can guess how that aggression is bound to be exacerbated here in hell."

"Hmm. I'd forgotten about that," Nimrod admitted. "Perhaps you'd better ask our furry friends what *they* think might help smooth the process and speed things along? I'm sure Daemon could use his Perishian contacts to provide all manner of additional incentives."

"I'll bear that in mind."

The Hounds fell into relaxed silence, and the minutes dragged by, as if lead weights tethered each second. Eventually, something registered at the edge of Gemini's perceptions.

She stiffened and squinted off into the gloom.

Nimrod sensed the immediate change in his partner's mood. "Company?"

"You could say that," Gemini mumbled. "Damn. I think we're gonna need more steaks."

"What makes you say that?"

She jutted her chin toward the shadows. "They're coming."

"The rats? How many?"

"All of them."

The darkness filled with thousands upon thousands of twinkling eyes.

*

Deep beneath the streets of Olde London Town, the brick-lined galleries of the main sewers resounded with the echoes of pursuit. Water splished and filth sploshed in time to erratic footfalls. Every now and then, bursts of frenzied activity resonated with interludes of hacking sobs as the terrified victim tried to catch both his breath and his bearings.

The endless chain of low wattage emergency beacons dotted along the apex of the tunnels stretched off into the distance. But their wan light did little to dispel the midnight embrace leaching into every nook and cranny, and if anything, only served to define the darkness into tighter clusters.

Isabella Castile slowed her pace and judged her prey's progress.

It had been like this for more than an hour, ever since her quarry had discovered his second wind, in fact, and a determination to fight against the seeming inevitability of his situation.

Why Isabella had chosen this particular denizen, she didn't know. Maybe the color of his hair, the cut of his pinstripe suit, the way he turned his nose up at those around him. None of it mattered now, for once she began her hunt, she continued until she added her victim's name to a growing list of damned souls who found themselves, at her behest, in dread repose upon the Undertaker's slab.

His haphazard course through the maze was a clear indicator of the Blue Suit's panic, and the notion that he would leave his fate to happenchance only spurred Isabella to greater efforts. That, and the sour aftertaste lacing his pheromone-ridden trail.

Isabella reached the latest in a long line of junctions. Pausing just long enough to taste the ether, she quickly determined his new route and set off with a fresh spring in her step and a deepening ache in her loins.

Not long now, my sweet. Not long.

A cruel smile stole its way across her lips.

Plunk!

The betraying splash tolled like a death knell in the dark.

Halting her advance, Isabella hugged the shadows along the far wall, and sang: "Can you hear what I hear?"

Her tuneful query elicited nothing but silence.

Creeping forward, she peered around the lip of aside shaft, her fingers testing the air like spider legs on a web. "And can you see what I see?"

A knife appeared in her hand where nothing had existed before. Then it was gone, traversing the fifty-foot gap in the blink of an eye.

A grunt coughed out of the gloom, then a stifled curse. Moments later, the filthy waters slopping about Isabella's feet turned crimson.

She stepped out into the scant illumination offered by a meager cone of light from the ceiling and was rewarded by a sharp intake of breath.

"No, please. I'll give you anything you want," was all the Blue Suit managed to gasp before calamity fell upon him.

*

Mesmerized, Tesla watched as the supine figure of Isabella Castile arched up from the bed before him at an impossible angle.

And another one bites the dust.

She remained in that backbreaking position for a full minute as wave after wave of ecstasy flooded the ether in the most evocative enticements imaginable.

Nonplussed by the intensity of those feelings, Tesla distracted himself to avoid being swept along in its wake. Only with the greatest resolve could he immerse himself within the tumbling statistics portrayed by Isabella's vital signs monitor.

Her excitement gradually abated and she relaxed back down onto the sheets.

Tesla saw something within the readout that gave him cause for concern.

Leaning forward, he adjusted one of the controls adorning the ornate headband encircling Isabella's head. Made of polycarbonate alloy and embellished by a number of ultrafine needles, the RSD—Reality Schism Device—was a snugly fitting contraption that also covered her eyes. Nevertheless, Tesla was able to note the moment the telltale bloom of rapidly flashing lights leaking through from around the edge of her ocular attachment reduced in intensity. Satisfied that no further disparity would be visible within the computer-generated paradigm, he sat back and relaxed.

"How's she doing?" a voice from behind him enquired.

Tesla turned to find Frédéric Chopin, his partner in crime, waiting; beverage in hand.

"Surprisingly well. I just need to incorporate several more tweaks into the overall calibration of the RSD and then the simulation should generate a fully integrated automotive sensory bond."

"Ingenious," Chopin mused, "that modern technology can so easily recreate what it took His Satanic Asswipe an age to construct." He nodded toward the sated woman on the bed. "And even more amazing that you are able to use your fabrication to satisfy her unholy desires."

"It's quite simple really," Tesla responded modestly. "I merely devised an assortment of scenarios in which Isabella can indulge herself. Remember, her cravings magnify here in hell. She lusts for the kill. So, by incorporating divergent locations and varying degrees of difficulty into the program, we cater to that longing in a way that should keep her fully occupied between assignments without any additional threat to us or anyone else."

"And you call this a . . . what?"

"A Reality Schism Device or RSD for short: it generates a virtual playground of endless scope for our subject's hunt, without the need to snatch actual victims off the street."

"Ingenious, as I say—" The figure on the bed abruptly began to thrash about and fight against her restraints. "What's happening?"

"The nature and setting of Isabella's last pursuit must have whetted her appetite more than I anticipated." Tesla's hands skimmed the controls like a maestro. He pointed to one of the screens where the phosphorous lines were spiking rapidly up and down. "Do you see how her fight or flight responses and respiration have increased?"

"So what will you do?"

"Do? Why, give her what she wants. It'll keep her in fine fighting fettle and free of the zombified lag we've seen in others induced by the Damocles blades over long periods." He nodded toward their charge. "Isabella needs to stay sharp. This machine will ensure she does so without the added danger of emotional overload."

Chopin fell silent, so Tesla set about entering the codes for another simulation into the master computer. On this occasion, he thought it best to keep their assassin engaged for a much longer period, and adjusted the program to compensate.

Several minutes later, Tesla pressed a final button and watched as Isabella relaxed into the environment of her latest make-believe world.

That should keep her occupied for a few days at least.

He turned to look at the empty bed on the far side of the room.

And once Guiteau gets back, I'll sort something out that will help them blend their talents into a more effective team. He glanced at the clock on the far wall. *I wonder what's keeping him.*

Chapter 11: Give the Man a Hand

Destabilized Sheolspace continuum or no, good news was good news at any time of the figurative day or night, and the message I'd received from Champ and Yamato had me riding the rapids of the cosmic highways for the third time in less than twenty-four hours.

A run-in with Grislington himself, no less. And from the sound of it, not long after he'd chickened out of a confrontation with me back in Juxtapose.

I chuckled over the obvious karma at work.

Talk about being in the right place at the right time. One badass angel badgered beyond belief, and one bona fide fugitive from injustice well and truly fucked over in the space of five minutes. Not a bad day's work, even if I do say so myself.

The trouble was, the more I thought about it the more I realized the circumstances didn't add up, and my initial pleasure slowly turned to consternation.

For one thing, it didn't sit well that the clue I recovered from Guiteau's cell led us directly to the man himself. It raised the inevitable question: Why?

Killer or not, Guiteau was no match for my Hounds, and Yamato's telepathic report testified to the truth of that matter.

Before our cherubic friend decided to intervene, my guys had been literally chopping Guiteau into little pieces.

And as irritating as I found Chopin and Tesla, they weren't stupid. I had never known them to waste their resources with such blatant disregard. So springing Guiteau from a maximum security asylum stank to High Hades: Guiteau had no chance of avoiding nearly immediate recapture.

I don't believe for one moment that Chopin and Tesla would sacrifice their minion so easily. Unless, of course, Guiteau has orders to make a play on the angel. But that doesn't make sense. How would Chopin or Tesla know to send him there? The only reason our celestial nut job left Juxtapose in the first place was because I threatened to tear him limb from limb. If we hadn't crossed paths, Grislington would still be in Olde London Town right now, swanning around in his own little spaced out world, wasting time and pretending to be important.

The implications of ordering such a hit were mind-boggling.

Crazy or not, Grislington's a powerful adversary and way too strong for the likes of a mere assassin . . . and probably my Hounds too, truth be told.

I chewed my nonexistent bottom lip as I mulled things over.

So what am I missing? Is all this linked to the seraphinite murders in some way? Are Chopin and Tesla trying to send a message? If so, to whom? Me? Satan? Grislington? Someone else? Dammit, this is . . . this is . . .

The conundrum was beginning to irritate me. Every time I thought of a logical line of reasoning, it did nothing but leave a dozen more unanswered questions in its wake.

Not good enough. I need to—

An unexpected deviation to my projected course interrupted my rambling.

What the hell?

Nearing the threshold of the Azazel hypergate, I had entered an area beset by gravitational eddies and vortices that could snare the unwary and snatch them away into badness knows what. Postulating had distracted me so much I had almost become the latest casualty in a long line of victims. It was an understatement to say that my current surroundings slammed into focus with alarming clarity.

Switch on, idiot!

I reined my awareness back to where I needed it most and concentrated on the esodesic threshold separating me from my desired destination.

Further questions will have to wait. Guiteau's not going anywhere until the Undertaker decides to revive him. I smiled. *And when he does, the boys and me will go Spanish Inquisition on his ass until he spills the beans . . . along with the rest of his internal organs.*

Positive thinking did the trick. The esoteric plane flared, and I found myself on the Azazel Plaza under a menacing sky that threatened a downpour at any moment.

It never rains . . .

"Boss. You're here already?"

I turned to find Champ and Yamato standing not five yards from me.

"I aim to please. Good news prompts me to travel fast." I motioned for them to join me as I strode off along the sidewalk. "Have you been waiting long?"

"No. We've only just arrived ourselves." In reply to my look of surprise, Yamato explained, "It took us longer than anticipated to ensure the scene was properly sanitized. Do you realize how many CCTV positions there are on that one observation deck alone? Champ and I thought you'd appreciate it if we ensured the Babel News Network didn't catch wind of the event, so after we'd taken care of the witnesses, we took our time destroying every camera, every server, and everyone on duty in the security office."

I checked my stride and stared at him.

He smirked. "The management didn't like it but . . . hey ho. Tough shit and job done."

Good lads . . . Hang on?

Something Yamato had just mentioned tweaked a nerve.

"You say you've just arrived? All the way from Filth Avenue, that's pretty nifty footwork. How did you . . . ?"

Yamato hefted a silver-gray orb in one fist. "Oh yes, that. Well, seeing as we were in a rush, we thought we'd try *this* out. Perks of the job and all that."

He glanced toward Champ. Their eyes flared.

"What a rush," each murmured in unison.

I knew what they meant. The first time I remembered using a multi-phasic portal generator I had been overwhelmed by the head-over-heels sensation it invoked. 'Invigorating' didn't go anywhere near to describing it.

"And you're all right? You didn't discern any weird side effects?"

They looked at each other more intently and shook their heads.

"Other than a pressing urge to pee?" Champ declared. "Not a chuffin' thing." He started hopping from foot to foot. "I'm not jokin'. Can we get going, boss, I'm gonna burst if we don't get inside soon?"

Typical Champ.

Bowing theatrically, I gestured toward the end of the street.

"By all means, feel free. And take your old man's bladder with you."

Champ didn't need any further prompting and set off like a hamstrung pony, setting a brisk pace that Yamato and I were hard-pressed to keep up with.

Less than a minute later, we turned a final corner and surveyed our destination. A place that every denizen of hell has experienced at least once in their miserable existence and wished they hadn't.

The Mortuary.

From a distance, that great edifice seemed enveloped within a pernicious shroud of impending doom. A fitting accompaniment to the legend inscribed upon a one hundred-foot long pediment above the main entrance: *Abandon Hope, All Ye Who Enter Here.*

Though only several stories high, the Mortuary filled an entire city block and seemed to loom over everything else like a frozen tidal wave of barely restrained malice. But that was probably due to the fact that its ancient walls radiated an air of dread so profound, passersby refused to walk on that side of the street.

My position reminded me of a moat around a castle. Except here, the Mortuary had a ring of paving slabs protecting its ramparts rather than water.

As if it needs protecting. This is one bastion that will never suffer the indignity of being stormed . . . except by Champ.

As we hit the curb, Champ revealed his growing desperation by breaking into a run.

I guess he really does need to go? A pity. I can't remember ever seeing a restroom inside. This should get interesting.

Brakes screeched, tires squealed, and horns blared. It mattered not. Champ barely slowed as he forded the stream of bumper to bumper traffic like a newborn fawn.

I almost felt sorry for him. Almost.

Grinning from ear to ear, Yamato and I followed close behind and sniggered as Champ reached the other side and vaulted the steps four at a time, only to come to a shuddering halt before the main entrance.

Ah, that'll be . . .

We closed the gap and, sure enough, I recalled another reason why people tended to avoid this place like the plague. The smell. Even at this distance I could discern the insidious odor of putrefying flesh and rank decay emanating from inside: *the fetor of death and a clear indicator of the Under-taker's lack of oral hygiene.*

It got worse the moment I pushed through the revolving doors and entered the foyer proper. Somehow, the unsavory tang of cheesy feet and toe jam interweaved with the fabric of the air, producing a stench that crawled down your throat and tried to throttle you from the inside.

Doing my best to ignore the eye-watering effluvium, I turned on the spot and looked about for signs of unlife.

Nothing.

Our footfalls echoed along empty corridors, where ranked offices marched away from us in every direction, their shuttered windows giving no hint as to the nature of the business conducted within. I found it amazing to think that in all the times I had visited here, I had never seen any of them in use.

"Ooh, yes."

Until now.

One of the doors to my left was ajar, and blissful expressions of relief issued from within, along with something that sounded like running water pattering onto linoleum.

That's when I realized Champ was missing.

"Hades help me. He wouldn't?"

"He would," Yamato countered. "This is Champ we're talking about. He may be the underworld's best tracker, but he's the worst possible example I can think of when it comes to unsociable etiquette."

Yamato then gave me a full sensory replay of some of the many disasters he had witnessed over their years together, and concluded, "Remember, this is the guy who put 'what the faux' into 'pas.'"

"Tell me about it," I muttered, scanning the halls for signs of our inevitable sour-faced escort, "we're here to get the Undertaker's help, not literally piss him off."

And as if by magic, the Undertaker's chief bellboy was there, appearing from the shadows like a conjugation of downcast thoughts and doleful rejection.

As emaciated as ever, Mr. Happy possessed a complexion so sallow that his skin looked molded from dough and squeezed into the ill-fitting lab coat that hung from his frame like a drape. I honestly thought I was looking at a *Brides of Dracula* reject, for when he moved, he seemed to glide across the floor instead of walk.

Has he got a skateboard hidden under there?

I didn't get the chance to find out, for Champ chose that moment to make his entrance.

"By Satan, that's better." Slamming the door loudly behind him, he made no effort to conceal what he had been doing, and made haste to dry his hands on Mr. Happy's pristine smock. "C'mon, let's get this party started."

Mr. Happy wasn't impressed.

"Now that your esteemed colleague has finished fouling the premises," he grumbled, "you may follow me. My master is waiting."

And with that, he was off, sighing along the corridor like a specter in search of somewhere to haunt.

His pace wasn't taxing, and my Hounds and I kept pace easily. Nonetheless, in no time at all we had passed the long line of interview rooms, storage cupboards and empty cubicles that led toward the wrought-iron staircase giving access to the underground chambers.

I was itching to see how Mr. Happy would navigate that obstacle without moving his feet, but once again circumstances conspired against me.

The Undertaker had obviously been renovating; he'd replaced the knee-trembling span with a brand-new, state of the art, helter-skelter-style moving escalator. Replete with multispeed baggage rail, it sported a number of speakers along its length, through which a weird combination of muzak and jazz played in a constant loop. A masterful stroke of genius, for thirteen floors later, I found I couldn't stop humming the infuriating tune he had selected and was ready to hang myself.

And I wasn't alone.

I had noticed Yamato and Champ tapping their toes along to the rhythm a number of times on the way down. On each occasion they would catch themselves, *tsk* or grimace, and stop, only to find themselves repeating the process a few seconds later.

A clear case of psychological warfare of the highest order.

Bastard!

And the mind games continued once we reached the bottom.

The Undertaker was indeed waiting for us. Instead of his usual garb, however, he was strutting round and around like a peacock, attired in tweed check-patterned shooting jacket and trews, Highland wool over-socks, and Scottish brogues.

Oh, you have got to be yanking my chain?

With a well oiled double-barreled shotgun resting casually over one shoulder, and his plaid cap perched at a jaunty angle, he had either come to see us off his land or was in the middle of a photo shoot for one of hell's most prestigious hunting periodicals, *Field & Scream*. I seriously expected to see a pack of hunting dogs come baying out of one of the side wards at any second.

My own Hounds were too stunned to say anything and just stood there, mouths agape, an incredulous look in their eyes. I spotted the way their hands kept twitching toward their weapons, and got the distinct impression they would rather be expressing their distaste by altering the cut of the Undertaker's suit.

Yeah . . . Most likely from the neck up.

I didn't know what brand of shit Astarte, Queen of the Dead, was shoveling the Undertaker's way lately regarding his fashion sense. Whatever it was, this idiot was swallowing it down, dung flies and all.

"How's the grouse infestation?" I teased.

"The what?"

"The grouse infestation. Forgive me, but with the way you're dressed, I thought you must be plagued by rabid wildfowl of some sort?"

It took a moment for my jibe to sink in.

"Oh, this?" The Undertaker struck a pose. "No, no, no, I'm just getting in the mood for a spot of discipline is all."

As he spoke, the Undertaker stepped forward and brought his gun to bear.

Boom! Boom!

Mr. Happy flew back through the air and hit the wall, leaving a large red smear across the tiles as he slid down into a heap on the floor.

The Undertaker calmly handed his weapon to a waiting stooge and wiped his palms on a silk handkerchief.

"While I am a patient man who allows his staff a great deal of leeway," he explained, "I do not appreciate it when they fall asleep on the job."

He gestured toward his unfortunate lackey, who was struggling to breathe around the inconvenient holes in his chest. "Buttkiss is supposed to greet all visitors as they arrive in a timely fashion . . ."

Buttkiss? His name's Buttkiss? Bloody hell, no wonder he always looks irritated.

"And although we don't get all that many, he knows the consequence of allowing them to wander. Especially if said visitors gain access to private areas, only to use them as their own personal toilet."

I glanced at Champ. Empathic to a fault, he was failing miserably to hide his mirth behind a poorly placed fist, and was turning a rather disturbing shade of red in an effort not to wet himself all over again.

The Undertaker appeared not to notice, and continued, "Though harsh, my punishment will be merciful. His time on the slab will teach Buttkiss the error of his ways and allow him a period of personal reflection before he returns to work."

Unbelievably, Buttkiss stirred.

Struggling into a sitting position, his eyelids fluttered open, and through a froth of scarlet and green fluids, he gasped, "Thank you, master, you are most kind."

Then he expired, fading from view in a mist of rotten eggs and wet fart.

I turned to regard our host in a new light. Regardless of the fact I hated his guts, I couldn't compromise discipline in the ranks and I rather liked the way he had handled the matter.

Fuck! Get a grip, Daemon. Next thing you know, you'll be sending him a Hatebook fiends request.

We shared a moment.

I knew he felt it too, for the Undertaker appeared as self-conscious as if he had walked in on an orthodontist's convention.

"Anyway," he snapped, "all pleasantries aside, you're obviously not here on a social visit. What do you want?"

"Your help, actually, with a recent deader."I expanded my awareness and transferred a précis of current events directly into his mind. "One Charles Julius Guiteau. Absconder from Cadavers Lunatic Asylum, Slay'em, Black Massachusetts, and as of an hour ago, freshly thrown from the top of the Empire Stake Building." The Undertaker's eyes bulged. "As you can appreciate from the details you are now privy to, we need to know exactly what he was doing there and why."

"My, my," the Undertaker simpered, "the great and mighty Reaper coming to me for advice. What is the underworld coming to?"

And the moment is ruined.

Several underlings scampering about nearby paused from their ministrations to listen. I couldn't let this slight to my authority, however minor, go unanswered.

Stepping forward, I loomed over him, ignited my eyes and clenched my fists. Poison-tipped studded spikes sprang out from each knuckle.

"Are you going to assist us," I whispered, "or do I need to make a statement?"

My simple approach did the trick. Bad Breath sobered instantly.

"Of . . . of course. No need to get feisty, I'll do anything to help our Dark Father's officers of injustice." He turned and swaggered off in the direction of his office as if nothing untoward had taken place. "Please accompany me; we'll see if this chap's essence has coalesced sufficiently to register."

We followed, and soon immersed ourselves in the ebb and flow that was the Mortuary.

As always, the bowels of this place were a hive of pathological activity. Minions were everywhere, scurrying like ants from one room to another, carrying all manner of visceral remains and obscene embellishments that reminded me of the invasive nature of their work. Drills whined, saws buzzed and those throats that could, screamed, creating a contrasting dissonance that somehow managed to blend together into a wash of white noise. A surreal experience, especially when you factored in the idle background chatter of ordinary folk going about their everyday business.

Halfway toward Slab A, we veered away from the main corridor and into a side passage. When the Undertaker led us toward a highly polished door with a sign on the wall next to it that read *Collections*, I had an idea where we might be heading.

Inside, more than a dozen geeks were busy, doing whatever it was nerdy stooges do on computers containing endless ranks of scrolling names and enigmatic symbols.

The Undertaker strolled across to a chubby little minion sitting apart from the others. Blessed with a ridiculously large pair of bottle bottom spectacles, he appeared far more studious than his companions and I assumed he must be some form of supervisor.

"Oswald," the Undertaker intoned as he leaned across the workstation, "please bring up the latest schedules."

While he did as directed, I didn't miss how Oswald gagged slightly and leaned away from his master.

Interesting, working here obviously doesn't make you immune to olfactory assault.

A large panel sprang to life on the wall above the entrance behind me, containing a similar inventory to those on the smaller screens.

"What are we looking at here?" I enquired.

"These are the fresher and reanimation lists," the Undertaker replied without taking his eyes from the file before him. "Basically, my staff prioritizes the candidates into each day's order of business. I like to keep things logical, so I ensure to leapfrog the newly dead with those awaiting reassign– Sod it! I can't see him."

He grasped Oswald by the shoulder. "Please enter a specific tasking for Charles Julius Guiteau."

Short stubby fingers danced like tarantula legs across the keyboard.

Moments later, the result appeared in phosphorous green glory:

Charles Julius Guiteau.
DOB: Sept 8 1841 – Freeport, Illinois
DOD: Jun 30 1882 – Washington, D.C.
DOR: Jul 2 1882 – New Hell. #289554MS:ADT11872
See attached file for further details.

The Undertaker studied the readout and pondered its contents.

"Ah yes, Guiteau. A most intriguing case. I remember him because he wouldn't shut up. An abject failure in life who only ever managed to get one thing right, he seemed plagued by a weird Munchhausen-Walter Mitty complex. I quickly tired of the nonsense he kept spouting and replaced his larynx with razor-blades. And for good measure, I ramped up his ability to kill by cursing him with an overwhelming compulsion to murder anyone he formed an attachment to, or those he felt might be in a position to help him. If memory serves me, I later added a little modification or two to his DNHA sequence at the behest of Doctor Livingstone out at Cadavers Asylum. Evidently, they wanted to adopt a more aggressive form of behavioral therapy, and I was happy to obli–"

Oh, for badness sake, he'll go on all day if I let him.

"And where is he now?" I prompted.

"Let's find out, shall we?" The Undertaker seemed to remember where he was and why we were there. He turned back to his flunky. "Oswald, highlight the current whereabouts of Guiteau's spirit, would you? There's a good lad."

Once again, the sound of machine-gun typing echoed around the office.

The readout flickered: *Searching . . .*

A few minutes later, we had our result: *No results found for Charles Julius Guiteau. Please enter new search parameter or try again.*

A sense of impending *oh for fuck's sake* began to niggle in the back of my mind.

"Should I be worried?"

"Not really . . ." The Undertaker looked thoughtful. "You say Guiteau was thrown off the Empire Stake Building what, an hour to an hour and a half ago?"

I glanced at my Hounds who nodded in reply. "Yes, that's right."

"That explains it then. Guiteau's essence probably hasn't filtered back sufficiently to fully coalesce. It happens once a denizen has been here a while, as their tincture tends to thicken."

"So we have to wait?"

"No. I'll just have to carry out a manual recovery. I don't do it very often because of the energy required. But seeing as you've stressed this is an emergency, I feel impelled to make an exception and demonstrate one of the more refined aspects of my many talents."

At last, a little willing cooperation.

I stood to one side. "Then by all means, *except* away."

The Undertaker grinned and stalked toward the open stairwell at the rear of the office.

Several minutes and a score of switchbacks later, we arrived outside a set of blast doors warded by a bristling force field. At over fifty tons, each great slab of metal displayed scars and pits from centuries of use. The word *Hub* was stenciled across the central join in bold red letters.

Neither Champ nor Yamato had been here before. They were in for a treat.

The energy field cut off and the metal leaves grated ponderously back into wall recesses on either side. A gaping chasm more than two hundred yards across stood revealed. Despite its size, the chamber filled by swirling multicolored brume looked as if a gas-giant planet lurked within.

Addressing my Hounds, the Undertaker announced, "Welcome to the heart of my empire . . ."

I knew what that turbid ball represented. Nevertheless, that didn't prevent the Undertaker from reveling in the moment.

Spreading his arms wide, he enthused, "This is the composite of all souls awaiting restoration. It includes the essences of those recently arrived in latter-day hell, along with the already damned. Think of it as a devilish synthesis of the foulest kind, a black hole of maleficent intent that attracts the sum of an individual's life—who they were, along with what they did, warts and all—and draws it together here for my scrutiny."

"So what are all those dark splotches?" Yamato asked. "See? Those ones there, exploding up through the energy bands. There are hundreds of them . . . maybe thousands."

"That, Yamato Takeru, is pure unadulterated sin. Dastardly deeds, despicable desires and dark secrets, stirred to fruition and laid bare for my inspection. These are the particular aspects upon which I base my judgments for suffering . . . under the guiding tenets of our gloriously Vindictive Father, of course, whose guidance—"

"And how will you use this to help us?" I interjected. "You mentioned something about a manual override?"

"Manual *retrieval*, actually," the Undertaker countered, clearly vexed by the interruption. "Come, I'll be glad to demonstrate my arts to you."

The last time I came here, we descended a ladder on the right side of the anomaly, which led back under the structure and into a concealed cave; from there, we summoned the Grumbles. On this occasion, the Undertaker led us around to the left until we arrived at a small platform extending toward the evocation itself.

With an air of superiority, he sneered, "If you don't mind, please remain on the gantry. The process creates a backwash that many find distasteful and hard to manage."

Distasteful? This is hell, you arrogant prick. What are we going to find repellant?

The Undertaker didn't bother explaining himself further. Instead, he made a great display of rolling up his sleeves and edging forward until he was within touching distance of

the sphere. Then, he extended his arms until his hands submerged within its boiling currents.

At first, nothing happened.

Then the Undertaker stiffened. His spine arched over and
his head fell back. The muscles along his arms tensed and
bulged. Almost immediately, I sensed a tangible buildup of
unseen energy. Pupils black as pitch yawned wide. I saw the
Undertaker encompassed within a nebula of Teutonic particles. In response, the tumultuous bands orbiting the maelstrom slowed and then froze in place, allowing myriad cy-
clones of sin to rage free.

The midnight corona surrounding the Undertaker's form
sparked amethyst and blue. In a heartbeat, all of the miniature singularities came together to form one giant eye; a bottomless well that bruised more than a quarter of the sphere's
volume in dreadful potency.

Moans oozed out from the void, bringing with them lurid
flashes and twisted thoughts, nightmare fears of discovery
and compounded feelings of shame.

See? What's he going on about, this is perfectly norm—

Then the first wave of sugar and spice hit me.

Hale and hearty, it was resonant with the joys of spring
and the rush of love's first kiss; of tender compassion for
those less fortunate and the wellbeing experienced within the
arms of one you cherish. Close on its heels came expressions
of tenderness, intimacy and loyalty; from the safety felt within a caring home environment to the stability gained from
family itself; of trustworthy friends and hard work rewarded.

The torrent continued gushing forth in a deluge of sickly
sweet sentiment that was as cloying as it was repulsive. Surprised, I stepped back. Such emotions were foreign, alien to
my nature; they made me feel dirty.

Fortunately, the flood darkened the longer it continued.

Years of fidelity tainted by betrayal; lives full of promise soured by wasted potential; the bitter resentment of the insignificant; isolation amidst a crowd of uncaring self-centered people; peace and contentment became hatred and misery. Anything and everything good squeezed and strangled until the last breath of decency died.

It took me a moment to realize I was witnessing a medley of transgression as experienced by a multitude of souls in their spiraling decay into immorality.

Now that's *more like it.*

Without warning, the concentrated accumulation of sin bloomed outward like the unfolding fronds of a huge liquidescent flower. Then it burst, shedding petal-like droplets into the shimmering ocean around it. As they sank into the depths, the entire mass began revolving again, every whichway at once.

The Undertaker's head snapped forward. He took a moment to regain his balance, pulled his arms free, and stepped back.

I couldn't contain myself any longer. "Well?"

"No, it isn't." He looked perplexed. "I'm sorry, Reaper, but there's absolutely no trace of Guiteau's presence within the hub."

"How is that possible, because unless he's learned to fly, there's no way . . . ?"

A new realization overwhelmed me, bringing to mind my conversation with Doctor Livingstone at Cadavers:

"What happens when he runs out of fingers?"

"That's just it, Reaper. He doesn't. The Undertaker cursed Guiteau with superior regenerative faculties. They grow back in a matter of hours. And the fun thing about it is, when they do, the nerve endings will have been tweaked so

his sense of touch becomes even more sensitive to physical stimuli than before."

The Undertaker noted my expression. "What have you just thought of?"

"Tell me, how extensive were the modifications you incorporated into Guiteau's DNHA?"

The Undertaker scratched his chin. "Initially, just his hands. But after his third suicide attempt, the adaptations were extended." He caught his breath. "You don't think . . . ?"

"Yes, I do. I suspect he not only survived the fall, but managed to crawl off some place where he'd be able to regenerate sufficiently to make a clean getaway." Turning to my Hounds, I asked, "Did you check the environs at street level?"

"We did," Yamato replied, "but not until after we'd sanitized the scene and picked up the remains. Naturally, we assumed a fall from that height would spread Guiteau's ass all over the pavement like it does everyone else's. You know the score. That's why the sidewalk surrounding the Empire Stake Building consists mostly of large grilles leading directly into the sewers. It saves some poor flunky from having to clean up the jumpers' blood all the time. I can only assume—"

Something Yamato just said tweaked a nerve.

"Wait a minute. Did you say there were remains?"

"That's right, up on the observation deck. If you remember the details of my report, I managed to chop both Guiteau's hands off. Only after Grislington had fled and we'd ghosted everyone did we realize that the gun and portal generator were still there on the floor, clenched within each of Guiteau's fists."

"And where are they now?"

Yamato glanced toward Champ, and for once, his partner had the decency to look embarrassed. Removing the missing limbs from the folds of his robe, he tossed them over.

"Dang it, boss. I was saving these. It's not like Guiteau's gonna miss them."

Ignoring his complaint, I examined each appendage and was shocked to find the flesh as pink and fresh as if unlife still circulated through the veins. I passed one to the Undertaker.

"Did you realize your machinations might have this effect?"

His professional curiosity aroused, the Undertaker appeared fascinated by certain aspects of the severed hand. He continued manipulating the fingers and palm as he spoke.

"Not at all. Doctor Livingstone wanted Guiteau to be able to recover quickly so they could employ a sustained torture regimen. I never dreamed his system would mutate in such a manner."

"Can you undo it? Or at least think of a way to use these body parts to track his remaining essence?"

"I don't know. It's not something I've ever had to do before, but I'll give it my best shot."

"Good, please do that." I turned back to my guys. "So, which one of you has Guiteau's weapon?"

This time, Champ didn't bother trying to explain. Shamefaced, he produced a silver Cult .45 from one of his pockets and held it out to me, handle first. I noticed the grip was made of ivory.

How quaint. Guiteau obviously likes to remind himself of his one and only success.

As I hefted the gun in my hand, I noticed a faint clinking sound coming from inside.

Hello, has something fallen loose?

I shook the pistol lightly; discerning that whatever was causing the noise appeared to issue from the magazine. Ejecting the clip, I discovered that Guiteau favored a specialized, custom-made twelve round polymer arrangement known for its smooth feed action.

So really, nothing should have worked free. Unless . . . ?

Depressing the retention pimple, I slid the floor plate to one side and found a thin wafer of metal pressed against the lining of the magazine itself. I picked the item free and everyone crowded round. One glance confirmed my suspicions.

"Well, would you credit that, it looks like we've found the next piece of our jigsaw."

Inscribed into the fragile metal with exquisite care I saw words. Expanding my astral sight, I opened my mind so everyone could see:

1 – 1 – 2 – 3 – 8 – 13.
As you can see,
This sequence is sorely lacking.
But can you find the key?
The answer lies in darkness,
Where rings lie within rings,
Guarding a secret
Without a circle in site.
You are Chosen, Reaper,
But few are worth their salt,
So be guided by the stars.
Delapsus Resurgam.

I recognized the style immediately.

Wow, Tesla doesn't mess about. This is as cryptic as fuck!

"It seems we have to find the key that will unlock the meaning of the clue. Any suggestions?"

"I'd have thought it was obvious," the Undertaker chuckled. "Can't you see? The answer has to be five."

My Hounds and I turned to stare at him in amazement.

"How in Hades' name did you work that out?"

"It's easy. Those numbers form part of the Fibonacci
mathematical sequence." In reply to the furrowed brows arrayed against him, he explained, "The Fibonacci sequence
starts at one, but every subsequent number is the sum of the
two preceding it. One plus one equals two; one and two is
three; two and three equals five; three add five is eight, and
so on and so forth."

I was astounded.

"Since when have you been a math genius?"

"I'm not. It's just that Astarte has badgered me to broad-
en my uncultured horizons over the past several months, and
I've started reading a lot more poetry. The Fib sequence just
so happens to be a form of specialized prose I've recently applied myself to." He tapped the side of his head. "It's very
good for the mind."

"And for us, it seems . . ." Addressing everyone again, I
continued, "So, bearing in mind the key is five, how does that
relate to the rest of the passage?"

I enlarged the representation again and, as was my cus-
tom, started to reason out loud.

"The answer—or what we're after—lies in darkness.
Obviously, in a guarded or secret place. And although it's
a location where no circles are in sight, we'll nevertheless
find rings within rings. Does that relate to something like the
Olympic emblem they have topside? If so, we're out of luck,
because no such buildings exist in hell. Then there's the reference to salt. It's a preservative. Also called sodium chlo-
ride. It makes things taste nice."

I browsed through the verse again.

"And it's linked to a star in some way . . ."

"Daemon?"

Yamato spoke so quietly that I didn't respond at first.

"Wait a minute. 'Worth your salt' is a nautical term relating to sailors who have proven their value. They're certainly guided by the stars, so does this mean we'll be forced to rely on the pirates to help—"

"Daemon." This time, Yamato shook me by the shoulder. "I suspect the clue might be a word picture relating to something else entirely."

"What do you mean?"

"The Fib sequence says five is the key, *but* the answer lies in darkness. So I worked backward from the star reference. Stars shine in the vault of the heavens, hiding mysteries people have never been able to fathom. It got me thinking . . . don't those who supposedly practice black magic topside do so in secret? In the dark, under a night sky where they won't be disturbed? Witches focus their will with the aid of a five-sided star, a pentacle, and they make use of a circle of salt to protect them during their summoning. Few ever manage to obtain tangible results, but those who do are said to rise up and . . ."

He let the suggestion linger.

Yamato, I could fucking kiss you.

Just thinking of the word *pentacle* brought to mind one of two of the most heavily fortified citadels in New Hell. The Pentagram, a complex housing the highest divisions of our Dark Father's infernal intelligence infrastructure: The Stake Department, the Ministry of Injustice, and the headquarters of his super secret police, the Devil's Own.

I visualized the layout of that stronghold and the wording of the clue made me smile, for the site was indeed without circles. Nevertheless, five separate polygon-shaped buildings in concentric rings formed one vast pentagram and a lasting monument to Satan's sovereignty.

And like its military counterpart across the water, the Hexagon, it houses some of the deepest, darkest vaults in existence.

"Gentlemen, it seems we have a winner."

Everyone started congratulating themselves.

While they did that, however, my attention remained fixed upon two of the passages within the concluding section of the poem:

You are Chosen, Reaper . . .
Delapsus Resurgam.

Chosen. It's capitalized. I've heard that expression before. Oh, no . . .

The room about me faded and, as was happening more often lately, I found myself transported back more than six months to the incident that had so drastically changed my unlife. The Angel Grislington had been droning on and on, doing his best to misdirect me by the sheer volume of his words. Words that invoked a startling vision I was loath to relive again:

The weight of the cosmos arched away in all directions. Resolved to respond to the greatest slander of all time, He Who Causes to Become framed a thought, and the heavens condensed into a single point.

A quorum gathered. Shrouded in nebulas and dark matter, they met to discuss a strategy. Debate raged until The Word issued a decree and passed judgment. From on high, He Who Causes to Become watched. Approval radiated throughout the gathered assembly and a prodigious circular table made of purest jasper appeared. Upon it, a rainbow of prismatic brilliance glittered within an unquenchable fire. Each color represented an aspect of mastery encompassed within the jeweled hilt of a sword of majestic power and purpose.

One by one, the host came forward and He selected the Chosen. They each took their stand, drawn to the character of the weapon most suited to their nature. The celestial vault flared as each champion arose, flaming blade held on high.

A new hope was born to meet this challenge. They sallied forth, and dark clashed with light. Storms raged for an age of days throughout the firmament and quaked within the fundament. Justice, terror by determination, answered outrage. A great dragon hurled downward to the abyss, and a third of the stars went with him. The heavens stood cleansed, and chaos was prevented.

But victory came at a price, for some were lost.

Certain phrases rang out loud and clear:

The Chosen; heavenly champions selected to contend against Satan and the fallen angels; wielders of the Vidium Swords of power; some were lost.

"Delapsus Resurgam," I mumbled, "when I fall I shall rise."

Bugger! Now *it makes sense.*

"Don't celebrate just yet," I snarled. "If they're after what I think they're after, we're all in the shit."

Chapter 12: Love is in the Air

When they so desired, the Sibitti were glorious to behold.

Born of the union between gods and men, they could clothe themselves in a semblance so alluring that they beguiled the eyes of lesser beings.

Attired thus in magnificent splendor, the living arsenal in human form convened upon the observation deck of the Empire Stake Building were busy plotting vengeance and cruel destruction.

"And you say this human lackey made a direct attempt upon the angel, here in front of witnesses?" The First's incredulity was evident. "Alone and unaided by artifice or device?"

"Apart from his pitiful disguise, it would appear so," the Fourth replied. "Although it is more likely the assassin's actions were but an opening gambit in a much larger, and perhaps more devious stratagem."

"How so?"

"Insanity aside, the cherub's proclivity for destruction speaks for itself. Black Keep is no more. He now possesses his heaven-wrought blade. What's more, I have no doubt that Chopin and Tesla—strategists that they are—would be well aware how ill-advised such an attempt would be." He paused to meet the eyes of each of his brethren. "I believe their intent was to ignite greater conflict by drawing the Reaper's Hounds into the fray. Though to what end, I have not yet fathomed."

The air crackled with barely suppressed passion as all seven enforcers contemplated the prospect of battle joined. Nevertheless, one was more cautious than the others.

"I would have thought that was obvious," the Second ventured.

As he stepped forward, the most beautiful of Erra's personified weapons projected an image of Yamato Takeru and Champ Ferguson into the ether between them. "We all witnessed, firsthand, the unbreakable spirit these creatures possess. Facing calamity, mutilation and pain heaped upon pain, they did not waver and made our enterprise appear trifling. That they are competent is without question. Regardless, I doubt their exuberance would last long against the angel's might unleashed. No, they would be forced to call upon their pack leader for aid, and *that*, blood of my blood, is the apocalypse I suspect Chopin and Tesla work toward." The Second looked toward the Fourth and inclined his beauteous head. "Though, like my brother, I fail to see the sense in such foolishness."

"A sound line of reasoning," the First acknowledged, "and something for us to contemplate as we expand our efforts to audit this circle fully. Which brings me neatly to another bane of contention; the Reaper himself, a creature that would wreak havoc if left unchecked."

"Left unchecked?" the Second countered. "It sounds as if you are overly anxious to test his mettle, a course both rash and fraught with danger. I was there in Dark Cairo, don't forget, along with the Sixth and Seventh when we bested him. And although we despised his frailty at the time, in all truth he faced us undaunted in his hour of weakness. Though different in nature, the Reaper's service is as pure and uncompromising as our own. Once engaged, those who fall prey to his fury find no escape or relief, for Grim is as relentless as he is merciless. He shows no remorse for those who err. No pity. He cannot be bought and is as unwavering in his devotion to his master's ideology as we are to our own. Are those not principles we should respect?"

And there, the Second reveals his secret heart.

The First wasn't surprised. Of all Erra's champions, the Second was the entity most blighted by empathy. The First decided to test the water: "I get the distinct impression you would rather recruit the Reaper to our cause than throw him down and mount his head on a pike?"

"And why not?" The Second bared no shame in his admission. "We have curried favor from the strong and powerful before; Kur of Ki-gal and Irkalla of Arali to name but two. Such a potent force for judgment would be a powerful ally and enhance our labors considerably."

"We need no allies to fulfill our mandate. Retribution and havoc without mercy is the mark by which we measure ourselves. The Sibitti are a force of nature, unyielding and indomitable, sent from on high to flay the unworthy and expose hypocrisy. No, Second, we should be wary of inviting the unknown into our circle, especially when sanctioned by the tincture of a misbegotten kingdom eaten away from within by ills of its own making. Have you not felt it? The paradox of this Reaper who bears a capacity so familiar, so evocative that we are . . ." The First paused and changed tack: "Fifth, you have been following Lucifer's pet. Have you discovered aught that might assist us?"

The Fifth stepped forward.

"During the limited time I have observed our enemy, two things immediately became apparent. One, the Reaper is stronger than before. Without question, whatever augmentation his Infernal Charlatan bestowed upon his puppet continues to unfold at an alarming rate. What's more, in his latest quarrel with Grislington, the more enraged Grim became, the greater his mastery of the situation. And it was no mere posturing either; a fact I can testify to, for no sooner had the angel fled than Grim pierced the cloak obscuring me to make a direct challenge."

The Fifth paused to share his memories of the incident.

As he tasted the extent of Grim's power, the First was forced to concede that here—at last—was a true force in the making; an authority worthy of the Sibitti's full attention. That fact unnerved him. And from what he could discern, it alarmed his fellow enforcers too.

Never have I witnessed such a horrific amalgam of barely restrained violence and proficiency. And his prowess continues to burgeon apace! What *is he? Such a contradiction would thwart the ambit by which we exist. He . . . he cannot be allowed to continue.*

Perturbed, the First tried to get things back on track.

"Fifth? You said two things were immediately apparent. What was the other?"

The Fifth waited in silence until he had everyone's full attention, then: "Our talents allow us to distinguish the hearts and minds of sinners, to discern the truth from what they have seen and felt and experienced. Because we usually employ such aptitude as weapons, I fear we sometimes miss the subtle nuances that adroitness would otherwise reveal. For example . . ." He beckoned his kin closer, and the keen, shimmering edge of excitement compromised the smooth veneer of his thoughts. "As vigorous as Grim was in defense of his realm, his response paled into insignificance when compared to the moment he perceived the female Inquisitor might be exposed to danger." The Fifth opened his mind once more to emphasize the truth of his statement. "Do you see? The tension between them was palpable, and involved a complex tapestry of both agápe and erotic overtones."

"Still?" The First was shocked. "But they can no longer embrace. She will expire at the slightest touch, whether or not his mortality aura is activated."

"True. Nevertheless, residual feelings remain, and if anything have been exacerbated by their enforced separation."

The Seven fell silent as each ruminated on the proffered morsel.

Eventually, the First posed a question.

"Brothers, do you feel there might be a way to exploit this news?"

"There might be," the Second replied swiftly, "but only if we are prepared to look elsewhere for assistance."

"Elsewhere, after what I just said? Explain your reasoning."

"You know as well as I do that there are those rare ones in hell who are contrite, repentant of the sins committed in life and compounded here beyond measure."

"Contrite?" the First almost laughed. "Such saintly ones are few and far between. And you're in the wrong realm if you expect to—"

"Oh, but we're not."

The Second's statement cut the First dead.

Having claimed everyone's attention, the Second continued, "It is known that I am the most empathic of us all. A quality some of you look on as a weakness, which is a pity. For as is so often the case, while you are content to visit vengeance upon righteous and unrighteous alike, *I* make more of an effort to actually listen to the thoughts, fears and hopeless expressions of those upon whom I pass judgment. During our years here, I have heard a name uttered by many in their greatest hour of need. A name that evokes hope in those seeking absolution."

"Hope in absolution? How would that be possible?"

"From what I have determined, this person is indeed a saint; a precious soul sucked into hell by artifice and duplicity. Now one of Satan's most prized possessions, she still advocates love as the means by which all ills can be conquered."

"Just who is this prize?"

"She is known as Saint Teresa of Ávila."

"And you say she's here in hell?"

"From what I have determined, yes. Deceived by the Father of Lies into thinking her visions were of diabolical origin, she has been trapped here ever since by seeds of self-doubt."

"Then we must act and seek out this mystic who sees the unseen and knows the unknown. Perhaps *she* can devise a method by which proscribed intimacy can effectuate the Reaper's downfall, along with the rest of this damnable circle."

The First's proposition proved instantly agreeable. United and focused toward a single purpose, the Seven quickly reached a consensus.

Regardless, the First still wished to press a hidden agenda to the fore.

"Second, have your insights granted you knowledge of this saint's whereabouts?"

"Alas, no. All I have managed to glean from the thoughts of those slain in evaluation so far is that she resides somewhere within the fractal bedlam that is Juxtapose."

"Hmm." Although his mind was already set on its course, the First made a play of pondering the issue deeply. "Then establishing the whereabouts of this mystic is now a priority. Fourth? Fifth? Abandon your current observations and join with the rest of us. Tread cautiously. Neither the Reaper nor his puppies must catch wind of our intentions."

"And how do you propose we keep it from them?" the Seventh demanded. "Shall we tiptoe around like frightened children and peep out from the shadows?"

Ever zealous, the Seventh unwittingly provided the First with the opportunity he had been waiting for.

"Why, I'd have thought that was obvious. For too long we've danced in the Reaper's shadow. I would suggest the best thing we can do is act as the damned expect us to act. To do otherwise would be suspicious. We are Sibitti, sent to rend, tear and destroy. To create havoc on an epic scale that demands attention. Such a course will afford us ample opportunity to determine the whereabouts of this *Saint Teresa* through the souls we analyze, as it allows us to hide our true purpose in plain sight."

The Seventh's ardor threatened to ignite the atmosphere. "And if our malevolence *demands* the attention of the Reaper himself?"

"Such a confrontation is inevitable." The First's statement rumbled from his throat and the building shook. "Better to settle the issue once and for all while all seven of us are gathered as one. Grim may be a new force to reckon with, therefore it would be a course of wisdom not to let him beco–"

"I'm sorry, gentlemen, but you can't be up here," a female voice intruded. "We're still cleaning up after today's—Oh my!"

The First turned to find a lone officer belonging to the Empire Stake Building's security detail standing at the entrance to the observation deck's lobby.

"I . . . I didn't realize anyone was still up here after this afternoon's ruckus." She took in their glowing countenances and heroic stature and batted her eyelids, clearly enamored by their presence. "Please, I'll escort you all downstairs to the nearest bar or restaurant."

The woman gestured, stood to one side, and held the door open.

"Why, thank you, dear lady," the First replied, walking swiftly toward her, "but that won't be necessary."

A shining sword appeared in his hand. It flashed, and clove the unfortunate guard from head to crotch. Before the two halves of her body had a chance to peel apart, the First drove his fist through her ribcage and tore her yet-beating heart from her chest. Muscle squelched and blood squirted as he bit down then swallowed the mush of his prize.

Let judgment commence.

Moments later, the other enforcers fell on her, devouring eyes, tongue, ears and liver in quick succession.

Unworthy. Unrighteous. Ungodly. Chattel fit for destruction . . . Audit complete.

With a pass of his hands, the First restored his robes to their immaculate condition. He waited until his kin had done the same, then bellowed, "To work, brothers. We have pandemonium to unleash."

*

To anyone looking on, the scene within the isolated cavern might best be described as ridiculous—or surreal at best—for a tall, rather distinguished-looking fellow dressed in an expensive well tailored suit was sitting on a rock near a seething pool of magma.

A neat pile comprising a handmade overcoat and shoes, cotton socks and silk tie lay on the floor next to him, creating an odd accompaniment to the glittering sword across them. Gentleman's trousers, rolled up to the knees, allowed him to scrunch his toes in the fine white sand of a tiny beach encompassing the lava.

A blazing band of golden light streamed down through a void at the exact center of the chamber. Emerging at a point just shy of the cave's apex, it thundered into the fiery cauldron below, generating a malodorous mist of crackling, energized steam.

However, it seemed the fates had conspired to keep the grotto reserved as a place of welcome respite, for a constant flow of clean cold air blew out from the rift, adding just the right counterpoint to keep the Turkish bath environment cool enough to remain remarkably invigorating.

Not that it mattered, for the sole occupant was of heavenly origin and immune to such insignificance as creature comforts.

Nevertheless, he was deeply troubled.

Decisions, decisions.

Lost in thought, the Angel Grislington stared into the shimmering hearth of the fire and absentmindedly stooped to pick up a pebble from the floor.

He turned it over and over and rubbed it between his fingers for a while, before tossing it toward the coruscating ribbon of plasma.

Vzzt!

The stone disappeared in a flash of green light.

"I suppose I should have expected the fallout to create a winter pall of discontent," he mumbled to himself, "after all, my escape did destroy their little prison, and Satan isn't the type to take a kick in the teeth lying down."

Grislington reminisced for a moment on memories of another time and place, and of the character of a fellow cherub who was never satisfied with his lot.

"Hubris was Lucifer's undoing. And ever since He Who Causes to Become chastised him regarding his behavior in the Garden of Eden, he harbored the most irrepressible resentment. The seeds of rebellion germinated that day. And look what it led to. A fall from grace and a third of our number lost to madness . . . and worse."

He giggled and his eyes flared with sudden intensity.

A feeling I've come to know with the intimacy of a lover.

With a shake of his head, Grislington focused his thoughts back on the here and now.

"And the cost? The Reaper and his Hounds are constantly on my tail. Chopin and Tesla are in a sulk because I won't surrender what they want. And goodness only knows what their insufferable, mentally lobotomized monkeys will get up to next. Oh yes, and I've also got the Sibitti thinking they're being extremely clever by spying on my movements from a distance."

He lobbed a larger rock into the lurid beam.

Zzzzt!

"I just want to relax and enjoy myself. To unwind and catch up with the time I've lost. And, of course, I'm just itching to see what Satan's done with his little corner of the underverse since his expulsion."

A poignant realization caused Grislington to acknowledge hidden blessings.

"Still, at least Grim and his blunt instruments have kept a lid on things. I can only imagine how bad it might get if all the sycophants and bravados infesting this hellhole caught wind of the fact that a wingless angel walks among them. *Taxing* wouldn't even begin to describe it. Mind you, how would they react if they found out about *him*? It would . . . they would—"

A troubling thought crossed his mind: *If it got too bad, it might mean I'd have to leave. But could I actually go back?*

Grislington's eyes glazed over as he stared off into the distance of forever.

I don't see how. Incomplete as I am, I might try for an eternity of tomorrows and never get anywhere further than—than—?

He leaned forward and kinked his head to once side.

Otherworldly hosannas pulsed out from the void, offering sweet solace to all who would listen.

How quaintly familiar.

On a whim, Grislington stood and walked toward the withering shaft of light. Due to the inherent sovereignty of his nature, the torrid conditions within the environs of the pool didn't intrude on his wellbeing in the slightest, and as he neared the beam, his essence meshed to the cleansing resonance of God's Grace and lifted the celestial backdrop into pristine clarity.

Adulatory in scope, the choir's appeal became much more personal, promising condolence and release, fellowship and love, life renewed and service restored; if he would only take that final step, activate his sword and step on through to . . .

Home.

"They don't know about my wings. But if I could, would I really want to go home?"

He listened more intently and suppressed a shudder.

"I don't think so. Not yet, anyway. All the hassles aside, I love it here now and am having far too much fun. Speaking of which . . ."

*

Tenebrous currents intervened, and once again Frédéric Chopin found himself battling the overwhelming compulsion to take that fatal last breath that would put an end to the insufferable existence that was his own personal hell.

As usual, the elusive sprite remained just out of reach. Whirling lazily within a froth of spiraling turbulence, it seemed determined to tease him and test his resolve.

Oh no you don't, I've not come this far to falter now.

Chopin knew instinctively what he must do. Calming his heart, he cleared his mind and stopped struggling. Then, in a supreme demonstration of self-control, he ignored the crushing press of the encompassing abyss and concentrated instead on the sword he knew rested within his actual hands back in the safety of his sumptuous drawing room.

He envisioned himself gripping the jewel on the weapon's pommel. Almost immediately, a skittering sensation infused his ethereal awareness with a burning chill that ate its way through his epidermis and down into his core.

Good, it's working.

Now linked to the totem on both sides of the esoteric bridge, Chopin focused his will into a needle of intent.

I command you. Stand forth and manifest.

A shockwave blossomed outward from his position, followed by an eruption of silver-gray effervescence that tingled across his skin as it propagated its way toward the surface far, far above.

Then the bubbles cleared and his prize stood revealed: a flaxen weave, thick and luxuriant, shining like the sun and crowned by a skull possessing an impressive set of curled horns. It sparkled coldly under his scrutiny, hinting at hidden possibilities.

The Golden Fleece. I always thought it the stuff of myth and legend. Just wait until—

His victory was short-lived: Chopin's strength drained from his body as if a tap opened at his feet. Overcome by bone-deep exhaustion, he kicked out feebly, only to find he couldn't prevent the void from sucking him deeper into the endless black below.

It must be a consequence of employing the power of the gem. Hell and damnation, I'll have to let go.

He did. And no sooner had Chopin surrendered his hold than the thalassic bands constricting his movements dissipated. He shot upward like a cork. As he rose, bright spots flashed behind his eyes, revealing scintillating details of a hidden location.

So that's *where they've stashed it away. I'll soon—*

Pain, as sudden as it was intense, coursed through Chopin's limbs and on into his extremities. Distracted, he was unprepared for the thundering bore that rolled into him and swept him away. The world devolved into a sickening, tumbling rush. Before he realized what was happening, Chopin's consciousness slammed back into his body. Air exploded from his lungs. Though grounded, the giddy dance continued, and he fell to the floor, thrashing and jerking like a rabbit caught in a snare.

Crash!

A metallic clattering sounded right next to his ear.

"Frédéric?"

Someone called out to him from a great distance.

He tried to discern where the voice had come from, but the quality of its tones fluttered about his head several times before lifting into the heavens like a billowing flock of starlings. As the cloud rose higher, it condensed, morphed, and took on a distinct form. Stunned, Chopin watched transfixed as a huge pair of wings appeared. Motionless, they hung in the air above him, reeking of antiquity and power.

At first, Chopin thought them as white as snow. But the more he looked, the more he realized the feathers possessed an unearthly iridescence that shimmered like mother-of-pearl through all the colors of the rainbow, and more.

"Frédéric?"

Reality returned with a vengeance.

A fulgurous bolt seared the top of Chopin's head in blazing agony. He just had time to flip onto his hands and knees before he started retching. Over and over again he heaved, discharging the contents of his stomach so violently that he feared his intestines might rupture.

At last, the spasms subsided.

Gasping for breath, Chopin blinked his eyes open to find a wastepaper basket placed on the floor before him.

Nikola Tesla loomed nearby, a look of concern inscribed across his features. He rushed to assist his friend to his feet.

"That looked a tad difficult to endure," he mumbled.

Chopin groaned.

Merciful God! I feel completely drained.

With Tesla's help, Chopin stumbled across to a nearby couch, flopped onto the nearest cushion, and tried to still the tympanic hammers creating havoc within his heart.

He waved away the customary glass of chilled wine that awaited him.

"Thank you, but not just yet. I fear I'd merely spill the contents over my shirt instead of down my throat." He gestured to a small drum table next to him. "Be a kind fellow and pop it there. I'll drink it in a minute or two."

Tesla did as asked and took a seat opposite.

"You look as if you've been hit by a truck."

"Coincidentally, that's exactly the way I feel. Please, give me a moment."

Chopin took a few minutes to compose himself and tried to make sense of the jumbled images still cavorting through his mind.

Ever eager, Tesla couldn't contain himself for long.

"So?"

"Well, the good news is that the *Sword of Uncovered Secrets* works like a charm. The bad news is that its modus operandi must involve a whole host of cryptic factors I hadn't anticipated, for it takes a hell of a lot out of you. Seriously, Nikola, I'm dead on my feet and could sleep for a week."

"But it obeyed your command?"

"And then some. Not only did the blade reveal our elusive artifact to be none other than the Golden Fleece, lost by Jason in the vicinity of ancient Athens, but I now know its purpose and current place of concealment."

"All that from one quick hit?"

"Yes. I suspect that's why I feel like death warmed up. Depending on the task at hand, the sword must draw on the adherent's life energy until all secrets reveal their truths and questions have answers. Unforeseen obstacles and all."

"Are you saying it can anticipate the hurdles you're going to face and adapt to provide a solution?"

"It would appear so."

"You'd better take small steps then, until you've fathomed its limits. The last thing we want is for you set it a task that would drain you to the point of expiration."

"True. But I'll still need to press ahead regardless. The Fleece is now an essential factor to the eventual success of our plans."

"Essential. In what way?"

"Remember, our afflictions prevent us from carrying anything through to completion without consequence. Without the intervention of proxies, your devices become deathtraps, while I succumb to bone-breaking impediment. Even with the newfangled recording device you provided so I can compile small sections of music at a time, look how long it's taken me to complete my last concerto. Months. A luxury I simply won't have when it comes to using the Scroll of Divergent Union. You know the specifics of the Scroll's activation. I'll need to get the incantation right first time." Chopin nodded toward the *Sword of Uncovered Secrets* still lying on the floor where it had come to rest. "Because of *that*, now I will. The restorative effects of the Fleece will allow me to pierce the veil between realms while you breach the pearly gates using the shard of the Key of Sighs. I tell you, Nikola, now all the pieces are coming together; we can't fail. I'll be reunited with my precious Amantine, and you'll gain access to the power source you've craved for so long to— to—what?"

For a reason Chopin couldn't fathom, Tesla was frowning deeply and shaking his head.

"Is something wrong?"

Tesla edged forward in his seat. "Far be it from me to stand in the way of true love, but now that we stand on the cusp of achieving our dreams, I realize there might be a flaw in our plan, and it's a bit of a party-pooper."

"A flaw?"

"Perhaps I've missed something, Frédéric, so you tell me. Once the envelopment drops, how exactly are we going to reach the pearly gates? We're in hell, don't forget."

Chopin was momentarily flummoxed.

"Why, I'd naturally assumed we were going to use an orb. Or our rings. Perhaps a combination of the two with one of the new booster packs?"

"As did I. But the longer I've thought about it, the more I realize it might be too risky. You saw how a pocket existing outside of normal Sheolspace protected the Black Keep on the Isle of Cogs. And that was just an isolated prison. Do you imagine the boundary into paradise itself will be warded by anything less? I have a terrible feeling that if we attempt to bridge the gap using artificial means, we'll have the heavenly host on us like a ton of bricks and baying for blood. No, I fear we might need to search for something more, something natural and specific to the celestial environment itself if we hope to succeed."

Crestfallen, Chopin reached for his drink and gulped it down in one.

An unexpected thought caused him to catch his breath. He choked and jerked forward. Through a spray of sputum and wine, he spluttered, "The wings!"

"Wings?"

Awestruck, Chopin gazed at the sword with newfound respect. When he looked back to his friend, he beckoned him closer and muttered, "Let me tell you about a little surprise I received at the end of my last vision quest, and what I think it means."

Chapter 13: Delapsus Resurgam

Surrounded by a squad of high reavers, Champ, Yamato and I rode the freight elevator in silence down into the bowels of the Pentagram.

I had forgotten how vast this place was but that was probably due to the sheer scale of one of hell's greatest bastions, which tended to dwarf the senses of those who only visited every once in a while.

Arranged over five floors and with an identical number of sublevels, His Infernal Majesty constructed the Pentagram from a quintet of concentric pentagons linked together by a succession of strategically placed ringed corridors. Together, they formed an edifice possessing 6, 666, 666 square feet of floor space; almost half again as big as its military counterpart across the Ptomatic River; the Hexagon.

Within the Pentagram itself, only half of the total area served the needs of the thousands of intelligence advisors, interdepartmental liaisons, demons, Blue Suits and Devil's Children who flocked here to work on a daily basis. The rest contains a number of dedicated safety shelters for VIDs to occupy in times of crisis, and of course, the fortified bunkers housing prohibited artifacts and some of the most destructive weapons ever devised by damned souls.

The high reavers encircling us made the cage seem cramped and claustrophobic. Not surprising, as they were twice the size of their *normal* cousins. Possessing gleaming yellow eyes and fangs, horned spurs the size of daggers on each of their six armored legs, and coiled tails with vicious-looking stingers at the tip, they epitomize devilish corruption. An unholy fusion, where the worst of human and arachnid traits blended into an amalgam of barely controlled savagery.

Just the thing to deter unwanted visitors.

Or they should have been, especially when you considered what they had to support them.

Due to the nature of the work undertaken here, the Pentagram boasted a highly automated security system. Including segregated modular checkpoints, cross spectral scanners, infrared and motion detectors, and backed up by old-fashioned CCTV and the aforementioned reaver patrols, every square inch of the more sensitive areas are under constant observation.

On the surface, just what you would expect from an infernal institution of this significance.

It did, however, have its drawbacks at times like this when I was aware of information they weren't privy to.

I received no reports of suspicious incidents or triggered alarms. Therefore, I wasted nearly half an hour trying to convince the duty supervisor from the PFPA (Pentagram Feral Protection Agency)to do something about the break-in I was sure had taken place right under their collective noses.

They took my accusation as an insult.

The watch commander sneered, "Why the fuck should we listen to you? This is our little kingdom, and we're always on the ball. Don't you think we'd know if there was a problem? None of the systems have been activated, so stop wasting my time."

I stopped wasting time all right.

My scythe chewed through the room like a blender on steroids, reaping her sorry ass there and then, along with every other PFPA officer present, except for one. I let him run for help with my admonition ringing loudly in his ears: "Bring me someone with the balls and authority to get things done . . . or you're next."

He did.

Samael, rousted from his private suite, arrived frightfully pissed. He didn't often use his chambers within the outer ring, and when in residence ne brooked few disturbances. Spitting fire and brimstone, he stormed into the PFPA office, only to come up short as I ignored his protests and casually highlighted my current mission. I showed him the clue, and at the same time emphasized what I thought it meant. When I then went on to remind him that I answered to Satan, and Satan alone, and that I was being delayed by the unnecessary hurdles experienced at the hands of his incompetent staff, he turned the air blue and then red, by executing each and every single one of the security detail still on duty with his bare hands.

An awesome sight and a timely reminder of what I would have to contend with when I eventually faced off with Grislington.

However, my little scene achieved its purpose. With an escort in tow, we were now on our way to the precise scene of the "maybe" crime.

Nonetheless, it was taking forever. I was sure the lift only had two speeds: *Slow* and *You Might As Well Give Up and Die Of Old Age.*

It had taken us more than ten minutes to descend to the basement, but at last it looked as if we were about to arrive.

The hydraulic whine cut off, and unbelievably, our speed reduced even further. Almost stationary, we crawled the final few feet until the car came to a stop, bouncing like a yoyo several times before coming to rest with a groan. Then the cage doors slid back to reveal a circular hub area from which a number of hallways radiated away like spokes on a wheel. The sign on the wall read: *Sublevel 5*.

Amid a frenzy of tapping talons that sounded like two gangs of opposing secretaries engaged in a type-off, the grand alpha shepherded us around the bend toward a dedicated passage marked: *Section 13*. A transparent floor-to-ceiling hydraflex-cronimium composite barrier barred the way, protected by a double-barreled .50 Brimstone-Gehenna cannon with auto-track and lock feature.

Looking along the corridor, I could see half a dozen further emplacements situated next to a corresponding number of access points.

"So what have we got here?" I asked the alpha.

"Each checkpoint tessts different asspects of your nature. The firsst being voicce recognition. Nexxt is a retina scan. The third, aural; and so on until you reach the bunker guarding silo six at the far end."

"So you have feet on the ground too?"

"Only the mosst senssitive treasures are warded thus with a PFPA agent and fellow reaver. Neither is allowed access to the spensse itsself, and each musst watch the other as much as the item they are charged to protect."

"You don't trust them?"

"This is hell, Reaper. What elsse would you exxpect? The contents of each vault must remain ssecret. Both guards have specific orders to kill the other sshould they stray from accepted protocol."

"And do they ever get to find out what they are guarding,

for example, by CCTV coverage of what's inside each repository?"

The alpha laughed. The sound reminded me of someone choking to death.

"No. The silos are half filled with hellfuricaccid, into which an open bell-bottomed chamber has been partially submerged. While the team iss able to monitor the interior of the main cell in order to enssure the accid bath remains undissturbed, what transspires within the smaller ventricle remains beyond their ken."

A sound strategy.

"And do you keep digital records of all comings and goings?"

"Of coursse. The library iss extenssive and is held for thirteen years in the grand archive. But we hold local copiess here for up to one month."

Excellent.

"Then by all means . . ."

I gestured and let the grand alpha take the lead. He ushered us through the battery of security checks and we arrived at the sentry bunker without incident.

A squat block of reinforced concrete, the post measured a mere ten by fifteen feet. Apart from the entrance, only one other exit was apparent; down at the far end next to a large triple-glazed window. From where I was standing, that door appeared to be an airlock style hatchway giving access into the main vault itself.

Closer still, a pair of workstations dominated the remaining space. Positioned facing each other in the exact center of the room, each was equipped with two terminals. The first was a normal computer; the other displayed a total of eight different images, presumably from CCTV positions within the silo.

The grand alpha made the necessary introductions.

"Walter, Kirith. This is His Infernal Majessty's Reaper. His ignoble companions are the Hell Hounds Champ Fergusson and Yamato Takeru. You are to exxtend them every disscourtessy."

Both officers nodded and went to stand by their respective stations.

"How long have you been on duty?"I asked.

"We started at sixteen hundred hours," Walter, the human, replied, "and are due to stay until midnight."

"So you've been here, what . . . ?" I glanced at my timekeeper. "Just over three hours?"

"Yes, that's correct."

"Have you noticed anything untoward, anything at all? The slightest detail might have relevance in the case I'm investigating."

Both guards looked toward each other for a moment and shook their heads. Walter added, "No, nothing. It's been as monotonously quiet as always."

That raised an important point.

"So how do you maintain a constant state of alertness? I mean, look at this place. It must get boring just sitting around the whole time?"

"It is rather tedious," Walter admitted, "but we have to physically check the external corridor every half hour. And in between, we ensure to carry out an eyeball scan of the acid bath through the window. Then, of course, there's the video game Samael laid on."

"A video game?"

"Sure," he beckoned me over to his desk, "come and see."

As I walked across, I discerned one of the pictures from within the CCTV unit flicker, and then flash onto the main screen of his terminal. Walter reacted like a man possessed. Slamming his hand down on a red plunger situated next to his keyboard, he made haste to activate a joystick attached to the arm of his chair. I noted with interest how the enlarged image began to pan around the interior of the main chamber.

Eyes riveted to his screen, Walter explained, "This interruption occurs at irregular intervals throughout our shift. When it does, we have to acknowledge it as quickly as possible by depressing the button as you saw. I'm now completing a full scan of the silo, and . . ."

His hand punched the knob again. "Now my reaction time gets logged on the central computer. At the end of the month, all the results from each of the bunkers are correlated, and those possessing the top ten fastest aggregate speeds will be rewarded with an extra unpaid day off."

"What happens if you miss one?"

"Your score gets wiped back to zero. Not good, as you never want to end up in the bottom three."

He made a cutting gesture across his throat.

Ah, the dreaded reassignment: a clever way to keep everyone motivated and eager.

Aloud, I continued, "So, neither of you encountered anything suspicious nor out of the ordinary today?"

"No. As I mentioned, it's been as quiet as the grave."

"And what about your predecessors?"

"They didn't mention anything." Walter tapped an open ledger at the end of the double desks. "As you can see. If anything of note happens, we have to record it in here as well as log it electronically."

"Who did you relieve?"

"Gath of the reavers, and one of our auxiliaries . . ." he leaned forward to check the name, "Daphne Hemlock. She replaced Joe Bonadonna, who was last month's competition winner. He chose to take this morning as his bonus day."

Something about Walter's aura was off. I decided to let it ride for the moment and turned to the grand alpha.

"Is what Walter described normal practice?"

"Yes, Reaper. Samael is keen to enssure all thosse who operate within the highesst ecchelons of the Devil's Children receive bassic training in the responssibilities handled by other strategic possts. It enables us to multitassk in the event of an emergency. As Hemlock works for the intelligencce section of the narcotics divission of the Diabolical Enforcement Agenccy, she is well qualified to assisst with staff shortages here."

Hmm, an innovative strategy. Bold, too.

I paused to work out the time factor involved and turned to Walter's teammate.

"Kirith, would you bring up the CCTV archive covering twelve noon today until the duty change. In particular . . ." I strolled to the end of the room and took a quick peek at the layout inside the silo. Spotting what I wanted high up on the domed apex, I pointed and continued, "I'd like to see the record for that top camera. It looks directly down onto the bell chamber and will afford the best view."

"Ccertainly, Reaper. Pleasse wait one moment."

I was surprised to discover the versatility of Kirith's talons. By the time I walked back, the desired clip was ready to play. The readout across the top of the VDU stated: *Daily Archive 5/13-6.Camera 1:ADT12006. Time Reference: 12:00—16:00. Start point—12:00:00:00.*

"What setting would you prefer? We have human sstandard with replay speed of times sixxty-four. But I can increasse that to one thoussand for enhancced denizzens."

"Excellent. Give me a moment to prepare, and then hit me with everything you've got. Max it out."

Opening my senses, I stepped back a pace and adjusted my perspective. Once I had cut away all outside distractions, I blended both ordinary and astral sight together and allowed them to become a malleable whole.

I raised my hand . . . then let it drop. "Go!"

The onscreen image flickered, and the readout suddenly jumped forward as if boosted by a temporal ramjet. My consciousness followed, tuned and ready to react.

Mundane time ticked by, and the calmness of the dappled picture before me gave no indication of its relationship to the chaotic rush of numbers as they cascaded upward in an incoherent stream.

It didn't take long for the normal flow of seconds to reach a minute. Then two. When the three minute marker had come and gone, I was beginning to suspect I might have erred.

Perhaps we miscalculated the time of—?

"Stop!"

Something had caught my eye. There and gone in an instant, it nevertheless registered on a subliminal level.

Kirith was exceedingly quick; the timer froze on: *15:45:22:79.*

"Now go backward at times one hundred."

I stepped forward and peered intently at the screen. My peripheral vision showed me the others doing the same around Walter's computer.

Less than a minute later, my senses flared a warning again.

"There."

Forewarned, Kirith responded much quicker this time around, and the readout halted at: *15:30:18:79.*

"Good lad. Now scroll forward again at regular speed. Let's see—"

A bright flash issued from directly underneath the bell chamber. Even under normal conditions the intrusion was exceedingly swift. Kirith moved to freeze the counter again, but a gesture from me stopped him. "No, let it play out. I want to—do you see that?"

Ripples proliferated across the surface of the bath. Worryingly, they issued from the direction of the airlock.

"Jumpin' Jehoshaphat," Champ cursed from the other side of the table. "Did someone go into the acid?"

"Someone or something," Yamato added ominously.

Grasping Kirith by the front shoulder platelet, I hissed, "Bring up those cameras pointing toward the hatchway."

The screen blinked and divided in half, revealing two distinct views of the airlock itself; one from up close, the other from the opposite side of the repository.

Glancing repeatedly from side to side, I studied both aspects as play resumed.

Nothing?

My finger drummed on the table. "Try once more."

Still nothing?

"Kirith, do it again, but this time set the replay to one tenth speed. Keep the frames as smooth as possible."

The incident unfurled in ultrafine slow-motion. As it did so I discerned the tiniest jump in digital clarity: a mere shiver, but enough to give me a clue.

Gotcha!

I leaned across the desk and edged Kirith out of the way. "Let me play with the controls for a moment."

"What have you spotted?" Walter murmured from the opposite side. "I can't see jack on my terminal."

"I'll show you in just a second. Hang on. "As gently as my palladinium-encased finger would allow, I stroked the pad and teased the timer forward until the incongruity clarified. "*There*, do you perceive where the records have been doctored?"

My triumphant declaration elicited a cloud of puzzled expressions.

Beckoning for patience, I adjusted the readout to show the angle from the far side of the vault only, played it through once, and then paused the playback. "Do you notice how the pool inside is completely calm? There's nothing that can disturb it. No wind, no fans, and no foreign objects swimming around. All security measures are static and therefore, unable to influence the acidic medium. However . . ." I pressed *replay* and the mirrored sheen of the bath abruptly distorted into multiple little ripples. "Now do you get it? Those waves are already in full flow. They didn't just appear on the edge of the screen and work their way across. And if you look closely, you can see where they're actually bouncing back off the near wall. Someone with a lot of know-how tried to corrupt the cameras covering the door. They didn't want us finding out a crime had taken place until it was too late. We were fortunate they were in such a rush."

"What makes you say that?" Walter asked.

"Look at the readout."

Everybody did. It said: *15:30:52:71.*

"That time corresponds closely to the mysterious flash from inside the bell chamber. I'm betting our agents weren't on the same team. One, alerted in somehow to an incident within the prohibited area, went to check and . . . *bam*! The so-called partner revealed their true colors and disposed of the other in the only way that might give the guilty party a chance to get away."

"By shovin' them headfirst into the vat?" Champ sounded surprised. "Why not just cut their throat and be done with it?"

"Because places like the Pentagram and Hexagon have essence detectors. It forms part of their heightened defense package. Murder might be our number one pastime here in hell, but we allow no unsanctioned killing that imperils state security. Any unwarranted disruption sets off an alarm and an automatic lockdown." I looked toward the grand alpha. "Correct?"

"Yes, Reaper. Your premisse is entirely accurate."

"And I'm betting those sealed silos are the only places in the Pentagram where someone's tincture might linger without triggering any kind of response. Right?"

"Again, you are mosst perceptive."

"Wait a moment," Walter interceded. "You also said whoever did this was in a rush. How would you know that?"

"It's simple," I tapped the screen in front of me, "the clock indicates this incident occurred just before your changeover. Fortunate for us, as our fugitive from injustice didn't have time to edit things as smoothly as I'm sure they would have liked. Think about it: when you and Kirith came on duty, did any of the automatic logs show an opening of the airlock? Did an alarm trigger? Did anyone notice anything out of the ordinary?"

"Why, no."

For some reason, Walter's face had turned ashen and he was finding it difficult to swallow.

"There you go. Our killer was skilled. Very skilled. But the glitch in the replay shows they simply didn't have time to cover *all* their tracks. Speaking of which . . . What time did you arrive for duty today?"

Walter appeared suddenly awkward and his complexion blanched even further. Once again, black tendrils of guilt coiled around the extremity of his aura. "I . . . er . . . I got here at three fifty-two, several minutes ahead of Kirith."

I loomed over him and lowered my voice. "And?"

"Ah, shit." He looked desperately toward the grand alpha. "I'm sorry, boss, but Gath wasn't here when I arrived."

The alpha skittered forward, claws clacking, eyes smoldering, tail stiff and erect. A sure sign he was angry. I held up my finger to forestall his outburst.

"What do you mean, he wasn't here?" I growled.

Walter was now sweating profusely.

"I— I mean he'd already left . . . or so I thought. It happens now and again. We get called up to the supervisor's office at the end of our shift, so we leave before we're supposed to."

On this occasion, the timbre of his spirit revealed he was telling the truth.

Did you know about this? I sent to the high alpha, mentally.

No, I didn't. While I'm aware of the practice, it creates a possible breach in security, so it's frowned upon. It was interesting to note how the sibilant hiss of the reaver's speech was absent from his thoughts. He concluded, *Nevertheless, when it does occur, each agent is supposed to log the incident so we can monitor who might be abusing the courtesy.*

Noted.

I swept the vent of my robe to one side, exposing my scythe. Walter's eyes bulged.

"Why didn't you report it, Walter?"

Walter licked his lips and glanced repeatedly around the room. His respiration increased dramatically.

"I— I didn't want to. She said . . ." Then he ran his fingers through his hair and threw his arms wide. "Look, I fucked up. You know it. I know it. I was going to report it, honestly. I even mentioned to Daphne I'd have to record it in the book, DEA officer or not. It *is* protocol after all . . . but . . ."

"But?"

"Reaper. She's a very good-looking woman." He leaned forward and motioned me closer, as if attempting to keep what he was about to say confidential. "She . . . she said a few minutes either way wouldn't really matter, especially as she was willing to . . . to . . ."

"Spit it out, man."

"She offered to meet me after work tonight and have sex with me." He bowed his head in shame, and mumbled, "And I haven't had sex in such a long time."

I couldn't quite believe what I had just heard. But everybody else did.

While the reavers maintained their composure, my Hounds started sniggering, and graphic suggestions as to what would now probably happen to the naïve romantic before them bounded back and forth.

Signaling for silence, I removed my weapon from its holster and placed it on the table in front of Walter. He eyed it dubiously and leaned away.

The simple fact of the matter was that this poor schmuck had screwed himself over by falling for one of the oldest tricks in the book.

"How in Hades' name did you think she'd be able to live up to her promise without the both of you facing the consequences? You know what happens to denizens of hell wh–"

"I now, I know," he interjected, "but Reaper, Daphne works in the narcotics division. They go undercover all the time and get themselves into all sorts of situations. She said her department was the current custodian of"—he peered around the room again—"a certain item of clothing that allows a couple to . . . you know, complete the act."

Champ and Yamato howled with glee. This time, their

sidesplitting gales of laughter joined the buttock-clenching shriek of nails on a chalkboard, a sure indicator that the reavers laughed along with them.

Foul telepathic caricatures littered the ether, portraying the most despicable and brutal forms of congress. And in every one, Walter was being rogered senseless by an endless parade of participants, all of whom ejaculated hungry scorpions and spiders in their semen and wore bright red spandex underpants encrusted with the accumulated residue of centuries of sexual deviancy.

Flushed with embarrassment, Walter's neck and cheeks turned bright pink.

"Well, what do you expect, you idiot?" I bawled, slamming my fist onto the desk. "They're only emphasizing what you've brought on yourself by being stupid."

He stared up, a pleading look in his eyes.

"It was a simple mistake, isn't there anything you can do to make it go away?"

"What, like parade your fuckup all over Twatter, Boo Tube and Hatebook, and leave it at that? I don't think handing your fate over to the cutting trends of unsocial media is gonna work, do you? Yes, it was a mistake, and you must be simple to have fallen for it"—I paused—"but as it so happens, there *is* something I can do to make it all go away."

"What?" The bright dawn of hope flashed across his features.

"This."

I gestured, and he flew over the desk and into my outstretched hand. My death touch manifested, and a moment later, he went limp as the unlife left his body.

Maybe the Undertaker will be more lenient . . . I shrugged, *but somehow, I doubt it.*

Without waiting for his remains to dissipate, I turned to

Kirith.

"Cancel any alarm that sounds and make up another copy of the breach on a separate DVD. Start it one minute before the incident and play it through until after the unauthorized elimination of Gath. Then add a slow-motion version at the end and superimpose it into the main feature so it's obvious what the viewer needs to be looking at. Print three discs: one each for His Infernal Majesty, Samael, and myself.

"Champ, Yamato. Go to the main security office and sequester all records of every camera leading from this repository up to the DEA offices. Not for one moment do I think she actually went there, but we might gain something from watching her actual route." Mentally, I added, *I suspect this Daphne Hemlock to be one of the leaks we learned about a while ago. This is our first real break, so notify Bella and Donna and start running crosschecks of the Hell Data Net. I want to know* who *she is; everything, down to what time she usually takes a dump.*

They nodded without changing expressions.

Finally, I addressed the high alpha.

"As the reavers are beyond reproach, I'd like you to notify your squads to initiate a full lockdown of the Pentagram. Get dedicated packs to cover the exits. Nobody goes in or out until I say so. Once I say so, the rest can join Champ and Yamato in a methodical search. Don't waste your time with physical checks. She's one of the Devil's Children, so she'll be far too canny for that. Use her latest psident and aural patterns from file instead. No matter what guise she wears, she won't fool your heightened senses. Oh, and if anyone does spot her, make sure she doesn't try to use any form of ripcord. I want her mind intact and ready for the Inquisitors."

"Undersstood." He paused, and evil intent manifested in the air about him. "I take it my brood brothers may use forcce to enssure her compliancce?"

"Of course. Beat her to a bloody pulp if you have to, just ensure her brain and memories are ripe for retrieval."

"Exxcellent. It will be so."

As the high alpha tap-danced from the bunker, I removed my cowl and weapon holster and laid them in a neat pile across my scythe.

"You're going inside, then," Yamato stated.

"Yup. It's about time I discovered once and for all what we're actually dealing with, so do me a favor. I have a feeling I'll need my wits about me, so don't disturb me unless it's urgent, okay?"

"Got it."

Dismissing all other considerations from my mind, I approached the airlock and positioned myself in front of the sensor. A coherent ray of amber luminescence stabbed out, quickly widening to envelop my entire body from head to foot in a wash of honey-colored exuberance.

For some reason, a growing feeling of peril wormed its way down my spine.

I wonder . . . ?

"Daemon Grim recognized," a metallic voice intoned, "sixty-sixth degree grandmaster of the First Order of Shâitan. Hell's Reaper. Chief bounty hunter and master of those appointed as Hell Hounds."

The shaft condensed to form a nucleus of radiance before my eyes.

"Reaper, state your security code."

"Daemon Grim. Infernal serial number: Six, six, six, alpha. Zero, zero, thirteen."

"Qualify with opening sequence."

Encompassing the glowing sprite within one hand, I reverted to ancient Hellanese:

"*Seáis Daûmen Grÿrmm, Satanase Thanatos (*I am Daemon Grim, Satan's Reaper). *Déane chmoúgh dareshetom mi dreó sgadhanise* (Recognize my authority and open to me now)."

The beam cut off and the first door slid open. Striplights blinked on, and a small anterior passage measuring some five by seven feet stood revealed. No sooner had I stepped inside than the hatch slid shut behind me and my sixth sense alerted me to imminent danger.

Two hi-tech photon accelerators dropped down from hidden recesses in the roof before me. Dual pinpricks of ruby light manifested within their targeting arrays. I never knew what came next, for a heartbeat later I reacted on instinct and decimated both posts with twin bolts of arcane lightning.

I knew it.

My sense of relief was premature. A faint hissing sound intruded. I sniffed the air and discerned the telltale scent of caramel. A quick scan along the far wall confirmed more than half a dozen interior vents now open to the insidious brume within the silo, and a lethal mephitis congealing upon the floor.

Problems? Yamato's telepathic query grated with concern.

Nothing I can't handle. It would appear Miss Hemlock's ingenuity knows no bounds and she had the foresight to add a few booby-traps to the defensive measures in an attempt to take out whoever came this way next. The cubicle is currently filling with hellfuric vapor. Once the pressure has equalized, I'll blow the exit and get this over with.

Just as well you removed your cowl then? Yamato's mind-tone smacked of humor.

Yes, I've grown rather fond of that one. Which reminded me: *And Yamato? Stay sharp. This bitch clearly means business. If you find her, I'd appreciate your making it clear that so do we.*

Don't worry. I intend—oops, gotta go. Champ will start breaking things if I leave him alone too long.

I watched him as he rejoined his partner, who was attempting to remove a memory disc from one of the CCTV units using his head and fists. Cursing, I swallowed down a twinge of exasperation and returned to the task at hand.

A fine sheen of caustic mist now coated my form from top to bottom. So much so that in some places, tiny bubbles had beaded together like vicious little teardrops in an effort to eat their way through to my nonexistent flesh. Fortunately, palladinium was one of the most resilient alloys in existence, and the sizzling invaders made no impression on my armor's integrity.

Right, this has gone on long enough.

Striding forward, I put my boot to the door.

Boom!

The reinforced plating crumpled, and a distinct concave indentation marred the once smooth purity of its outline.

I stepped back and kicked again, much harder this time.

Booom!

The entire hatch deformed and creased outward. Pressure seals ruptured and weight-bearing struts squealed in protest.

One more should do it.

Booom!

Crack!

With a resounding snap, the inner airlock flew free of its hinges, taking chunks of metal and masonry with it and bringing down a shower of debris.

It felt as if I had stepped into a sulfurous sauna, for the air was as hot and moist as the heart of a sea serpent's lair. Very few possessed the fortitude to endure such a mordant environment for long. Happily, I was one of them.

Mesmerized, I edged forward and watched as the acid consumed all trace of the sturdy barrier in less than six seconds. Show over, I then took stock of my surroundings.

The repository was more than fifty feet wide and twice that high, and built from Dpoxy-saturated, brimstone-baked concrete. A combination that not only proofed the lining against the corrosive atmosphere of the vat, but ensured the entire structure would retain its tensile strength without compromising fatigue resistance.

A slender finger of the same material rose up from the vault's deck and disappeared into the open end of an upturned dome positioned at the exact center of the open space.

I projected my farsight inside the confines of my target.

From what I could discern, the tip of that shaft ended in a flat even platform just above the *acid line*. I couldn't be sure, however, as something prevented me from bringing the image into clearer focus.

Hmm, it must be a telepathic fuzzer of some sort to thwart long-range snoopers.

Straining against the warping effects of the psychic defense, I tried again and this time managed to clarify certain aspects I would need to know. The shelf was a mere ten feet in diameter, and seemed connected to the edge of the internal casing via a series of six slender support rods. A slim plinth made of an unknown material rose up like a microphone stand in the middle of this arrangement to form one of the most elegant locking brackets I had ever seen. Unfortunately, the jaws of those restraints stood empty. And from the shape and size of the encompassing groove, it looked as if my suspicions would prove correct.

Deferring to caution, I erected a powerful shield and phased down through the pool and up onto the ledge. No sooner had I materialized than I discovered why I'd had trouble penetrating the shielding. The interior of the bell had a coat of sheolanite resin, an experimental psychoactive polymer capable of absorbing most forms of extrasensory stimuli and reflecting it back toward its originator. Satan had recently added multiple layers of this substance to the walls and floors of his favorite palaces in an effort to reduce inadvertent eavesdropping into his affairs.

The ache behind my eyes testified to its effectiveness. Of all the denizens of the underverse, very few could match my finesse when it came to metaphysical dexterity. If it gave *me* problems, our Dark Father's secrets would remain where he wanted them, safely tucked away out of the reach of fickle ears and prying eyes.

Nonetheless, sheolanite wasn't the only hurdle I faced. The atmosphere within the confines of the chamber sparkled with residual celestial energy of such dominion that before I knew it, my knees folded and I reached out toward the pedestal to support myself. I made contact with its strange glasslike structure, and my sensibilities flared. In moments, my perceptions drifted upon currents long forgotten, along with those previously unknown to me:

Contradictory images and feelings flooded the ether. In them, I was both Alpha spark and Bãlefire, the precocious light of perpetuity unleashed, pitted against the omega of timeless night. The sensation was most disconcerting, for my very essence contended against itself in an endless war of attrition; a battle where neither creation nor destruction could win for fear of destroying the delicate balance that by necessity ensured the immortal coil could exist within me.

Memories, artfully concealed, tugged at the edge of conception.

Something significant stormed against its restraints at

the core of my psyche.

Your identity is shattered. You must become a chimera of my devising.

Beware! There is a hole where your heart once beat to a fanfare of legions.

The sands of time shifted. In answer to a summons from on high, I ascended the planes to stand before a translucent table, pulsing with emerald green radiance. Circular in shape, it held an array of glittering swords arranged to form a giant iris, transcendent in scope. The pommel of each weapon bore a jewel of majestic clarity. Such acute blades and so imbued with power that the slightest movement sent prismatic reflections careering along razor-sharp arêtes and off through the length and breadth of the universe.

Far below, shrouded by nebulas and antimatter, a dark army brooded. Fed by malice, bolstered by numbers and pride; unwavering in their determination for rebellion and indifferent to the suffering their actions would bring, its generals issued a challenge.

Selecting the weapon most suited to their nature, bastions of truth stood forth to contend with harbingers of slander, and soon, the void echoed with conflict as each side sortied, one against the other.

Tempests and tumults raged for apparent eons, until the accuser and his champion were cast down, and their angels with them. Lashing out, they sought to wreak one last travesty upon the Just, but He Who Causes to Become then moved to counter.

Like an inconsonant Möebius loop, the firmament writhed in horror as chaos scourged the cosmos in irreconcilable poles of stunning magnitude; energies so unfathomable that they consumed the natural balance around them, only to spawn something else in their stead. The Divide, a mystical barrier which ever separated one reality from the other.

And it did. But the consequence of victory was deep abiding sorrow, for some bright stars were lost to the limbo of neverwhere and neverwhen, trapped between a moment of then and now where the serpent could tempt them still. And tempt them he did, in a mocking welcome that dared all to partake of unnatural cravings.

A few cowered. Some called for aid. Then the agent of the Almighty's justice, his true angel of fire and flame, stood forth undaunted. The fallen horde surrounded him, thinking him easy prey until his obsidian gold sword reaped vitriolic judgment by the thousands.

Still, the Titan was alone, weary and unaided, and his enemies were many. Waiting for that moment, Lucifer's champion of war stood forth. Crimson lust clashed with discipline and ebony. Sanity perished and was consumed, defiled, and dark Lucifer, in the guise of all that is bright and beautiful, waited transcendent, to fashion his most atrocious of miscreations.

The scales dropped from my eyes to utter blindness.

Delapsus Resurgam, when I fall I shall rise, a travesty, whole while yet incomplete.

Without warning, reality flexed back in on itself and I once again found myself within the bell chamber.

"Unholy shit!" My voice resonated to the close confines of the cavity. "What the fuck was that?"

A tingling sensation tickled its way along the extent of my nonexistent epidermis and I reached down to trace a finger along the back of my opposite hand.

My every sense is supercharged and overcompensating for the armor, but . . . ?

I inhaled, and the mastery saturating the air rushed to fill my lungs.

I'm attuned to the nature of the artifact that once was in here.

A clear and distinct impression popped into my mind.

The Sword of Uncovered Secrets—*Sarnáel.*

How did . . . ?

Another echo still lingered. Something now somewhat faded, but grandiose nonetheless. Without fear, I reached out to embrace its signature.

The Sword of Seraphim Speed—*Adonìjah.*

I can distinguish each Vidium essence and know its true wielder as if . . . ?

My consciousness pounced upon alien recollections I shouldn't possess. But no sooner had I latched onto them than the genesis of those memories faded from my supernal grasp. Their departure imbued me with a deep sense of loss. In some inexplicable way, I sensed real tears forming within the crux of my residual fleshly template.

Oh, this cannot be happening.

"Get a grip, Daemon," I snarled to myself, "and get out of here. This place is buried away like a crypt for a reason and, shields or not, it's anathema to your true spirit."

Suitably chastised, I forced myself to concentrate on the plinth again. A sliver of treated parchment protruded from the edge of the collars. Snatching it up, I unrolled it, blinked my eyes clear, and read:

> Bring me the head of the savior,
> An Old Lady still gasping for breath,
> Who wanders a garden of insanity
> Where Sarah, in lament, now rests.
>
> Bring me the blanket of life,
> A fleece to envelop my charter.

Gold wrapped, this mortal coil
Sparks nothing but death.

Bring me the keys of release
And a yard in which to turn for your answer,
For your thimble will lie redundant
In the eye that no camel will ever Thread.

"Tesla again," I mumbled aloud, "and he's either being kind or slipping. This one isn't even difficult, although I thought the Golden Fleece was just a fable from Greek mythology?" I folded the clue and edged it inside my gauntlet. "Still, I can use my Inquisitors for this. I have enough of them to surround—"

Daemon?

The telepathic hail was faint but familiar, but worryingly, laced with the bitter aftertaste of dread.

"Strawberry?"

I eyed the restrictive dome encompassing me and realized I needed to move fast. Concern added impetus to my determination, and no sooner did I think it than I had materialized back inside the security bunker in front of a startled reaver. Ignoring Kirith, I opened my mind and punched my awareness through the Sheolspace continuum.

"I'm here, Strawberry, what's happening?"

Oh, Daemon, thank badness. I've been trying for a few minutes . . .

A sense of calamity intruded.

"What in damnation is happ–?"

Juxtapose is under open attack.

"Attack? Who would be that stupid?"

The Sibitti.

A cold fury froze me to the spot. My black heart

crystallized and stopped beating.

"How many?" I growled.

About me, the foundations of the Pentagram began to shake.

All of them.

"Where?"

Just across the river from the Den of Iniquity.

Rage and insult moved me to action.

They dare to target us?

I gestured and my cowl enveloped me once more.

Clang!

My staff of office slammed into my outstretched hand, extended and ready for battle. In one fluid motion, I raised it high and hammered the spiked heel into the floor.

Utter ruination congealed about me as the Bãlefire answered my call. In moments, a crown of scarlet flames danced upon my head and a storm of midnight hue swathed me in a seething cloud-mass that scoured the room with yellow and purple bolts of lightning.

"Call the Hounds," I thundered. "Tell them to use the orbs and meet me at the Black Tower. Rouse the Inquisitors. Have them activate the keep's defenses and stand to. Then notify His Infernal Majesty. We have a challenge to answer that must be met." *At last, I get to test my mettle.* "Whether we live or die, they'll never cross Satan again."

I cared not that the command post about me shattered and crumbled, crushed to dust within a gyre of increasing potential. As the unutterable potency of the underverse bent to my will, all I could think of was the bloody revenge I was about to inflict on those who did not deserve to exist.

Every denizen in hell will talk about this day for all eternity.

Fixing my destination in mind, I formed a portal and

slammed myself toward destiny.

Chapter 14: The Maleficent Seven

Swathed in cloud and rain, the Sibitti masked their approach amid an expanding pall of gloom. It mattered not that the bells of Little Ben had only just struck 4 a.m. This was Olde London Town of the Juxtapose level of hell, and it was always busy. A throbbing conurbation where the flotsam and jetsam of the damned tangled together twenty-four hours a day, seven days a week, in a shipwreck of crime, vice and hate.

Erra, ancient god of plague and mayhem, watched from on high as his enforcers settled to the ground just south of Black Tower Bridge and surveyed the surrounding brume of new dead, old dead, and the dregs of every vile cesspit humanity had ever fomented.

I hope their confidence is well founded. Long have they chafed to attack this circle directly. Still, their proposal is sound, and if it works will satisfy their lust for contention as it restores their confidence. It will be gratifying to audit this mire and rid it of some of the detritus it has so clearly accumulated.

Attired in muted outer raiment, his sons of heaven and earth went largely unseen, for their cowls flapped and fluttered in the strengthening breeze like insubstantial scraps of

247

thought sent to dishearten the unwary on a dark and stormy night. Those who caught sight of the wraiths out of the corner of one eye shivered unknowing, and merely tightened their grip upon unbuttoned coats and unruly umbrellas before increasing their pace, keen to be home and away from the worsening weather.

All that changed, however, once the Seven threw back their hoods and spread out to form a circle.

Traffic ground to a halt and pedestrians stopped to stare as a standoff ensued. Appearances were deceiving, for no one had yet realized the danger represented by this ring of strangers that began to shimmer as horns blared and curses flew. Denizens had heard of the evaluation, of course. Everyone throughout the many layered underworld had sought news on the devastation unleashed elsewhere, and especially across in New Hell. But as yet, none believed they would ever be threatened here.

Discerning the mood of the rabble, Erra chuckled to himself.

That's about to change.

The First of the Seven turned his eyes to the heavens as if looking for guidance.

Despite their serene countenance, Erra sensed his weapons waxing hot, impatient to be about a slaughter long deferred.

"You may proceed," he whispered into the wind.

The coterie of death moved as one, expanding their formation again until they faced all points of the compass. A gesture quivered through their ranks and gleaming swords appeared, brandished high in the glare of headlights and streetlamps.

Only then did the screams of the surrounding crowd cause a chrysanthemum burst of scrambled panic away from danger. In moments, an expanding wave of terror filtered out into the surrounding streets and across the bridge.

Vehicles crashed, and unfortunates trampled one another underfoot. The Sibitti lingered, as if content to allow hysteria do their work for them, and in that lull, gave no overt sign of the peril about to befall one of Satan's most precious strongholds.

Somewhere, an air raid siren wailed. Several others quickly picked up its call. Then a dozen more joined in, until a proliferating resonance warbled out across a skyline that bled into obscurity and shadow.

"Come then, Satan, and face us," the First called into the night, "bring your harbingers and show us your quality . . . if you dare?"

The Seven waited.

Only a resounding silence answered their challenge.

Stamping forward, the First of the Seven reversed his blade and stabbed its tip into the ground. Splinters radiated away from him across the tarmac like fingers of asphalt lightning. Lengthening, they spawned a series of fissures that rent the earth in one place after another, spilling conveyances and smaller buildings alike into widening chasms. The primary archway leading onto the bridge shuddered as bricks—stressed by unexpected shearing—exploded, showering fleeing denizens in a volley of lethal shrapnel. Small craft moored along nearby havens smashed together in freak swells, and damned souls cried their last as each hungry abyss silenced their protests in a final crushing embrace.

In that brief opening gambit, more than a thousand of the unworthy perished without recourse. Burst pipes spewed water and effluent onto sidewalks already slick with rain. Snapped cables lashed out blindly, spitting sparks and flames onto those too slow or injured to care. Nodding in apparent satisfaction, the First resumed his place.

The Second now strode forward to circle his brothers. Surveying the carnage about them, he cast his refulgent gaze upon those fools in the distance who thought they were safe. His eyes crackled with energy and encompassed fleeing wretches immediately in a skein of electrified intent. Spinning like marionettes, damned souls, helpless to resist the charged commands of their puppet-master, danced and jerked, coiled and writhed, until eventually they blackened and fell, gums bared in a rictus of death.

Erra noticed the moment his second cut the strings, for scores of spent bodies flopped limply to the ground; their final expirations marked only by wisps of oily gray smoke curling idly from lips crisped to ash.

Clutching his sword to his chest, the Third of the Seven stepped back into the center of the ring. He took a deep breath and exhaled a freezing haar high into the sky. The rain instantly transformed; each drop becoming an icy splinter of death, cruel and sharp. Shards heavy enough to puncture steel and pierce flesh hammered down onto the arrested flow of traffic. Muted cries echoed out from those still trapped in vehicles impaled again and again by a verglas fusillade offering no quarter. The Third breathed once more, and those wails ceased as shocked casualties were coated in a rime that frosted their blood lilac, then blue, and finally, unsullied white.

In conclusion, the Third waved his dazzling sword in an arc through the air. Even the river succumbed to his might as a glaze of ice clenched its way from one riverbank to the other. Without waiting for the transformation to run its course, the Third turned on his heel and nodded to the next enforcer in line.

The Fourth didn't even bother to lower his blade. Instead, he merely pointed with one finger toward those hiding in doorways or cowering within the ruined shells of nearby buildings. Where his hand passed, boils broke forth, covering faces and exposed skin in a sea of blisters that swelled and popped as if the flesh on which they festered then melted. People fell to their knees, gagging and retching, helpless to prevent congealing fluids drowning them from the inside out. Eventually they weakened, only to expire in pools of their own filth.

His work done, the Fourth smiled, lowered his weapon to the ground, and ran that same finger of destruction across the pommel of his weapon with loving care.

So great was the press of those clamoring to cross the bridge that panicked folk made little progress. Tight packed, they pushed and they shoved and they jostled—falling more often than not—only to be trampled into bloody pulp by those too terrified to care for any but themselves.

Spotting their dilemma, the Fifth of Seven broke into a run. As he moved, his cloak fell away, revealing a churning, tumbling matrix of flickering death. Honed and needle sharp, he tore into the milling throng like a razor-edged tornado, lopping limbs and shredding sinews left, right, and center. Having cut a swath through the main body of the crush, he whirled unpredictably from side to side, spilling guts and opening throats, and putting those who still possessed legs to rout.

As abruptly as it began, the whirling dervish stopped and a glowing Titan stood forth; sword shining, knee deep in severed heads, torn torsos and the spilth of intestines.

"It is fitting," he declared, though to whom, Erra could not discern.

Now the Sixth moved forward to face the River Tombs directly. Taking position, the enforcer thrust his blade toward the heavens. The falling torrents turned into a deluge of biblical proportions, its leaden weight flattening anything that moved and knocking breath from the lungs of victims desperate to cling to whatever measure of unlife they had left.

When it came, respite was as sudden as it was unexpected, for a squall blew in from the west that swept all signs of the storm away and out toward the sea. Even from his position high in the cloud mass, Erra could hear the cries of release from those who thought their nightmare ended.

Their relief was short-lived.

Down below, the ground began to tremble and a distant growl lifted itself above the background din of a city under siege. A dark mass appeared on the horizon, roaring closer and higher with every passing second. In less than a minute it had clarified into a foaming frothing wave-cap of malevolence. Amazingly, the towering cliff yet restricted itself to the confines of the frosted Tombs. But there was a reason for that: the Sixth reached out with one hand as if inviting an embrace from a long-lost friend. Then he clenched his fist and the crest broke like an avalanche, thundering down out of the night sky to smash the ice apart and scour the banks clean of any sign of life. Jetties, docks, wharfs and quays; waterside developments, walkways and ornamental gardens—anything and everything that once identified the river's course as part of a throbbing metropolis disappeared amid turgid currents that scourged one of Olde London Town's greatest landmarks raw.

And still it came.

The weight of a mountain struck Black Tower Bridge square on. Ancient stones thrummed and metal girders squealed. And as the ninety-foot high wall of glacial water sped by, the thousand-ton leaves of the center span went with it, tumbling over and over in an aquatic blender that gradually pulverized tempered steel into scrap.

Only then did the breaker begin to subside.

Taking his time, the Seventh marked those that yet remained alive and shrugged his mantle free. Heroic in form, he looked magnificent as he hefted his sword in blazing arcs that fried the air and blistered concrete. Feral glee scarred his countenance, and an abrupt concentration of incendiary focus caused all those within his sight to howl in pain. Some dived for cover behind walls and ramparts. Others threw themselves into exposed sewers or the river itself. Regardless, no matter where they stood or cowered, stragglers recoiled in panic as embers kindled deep inside their bodies.

That heat grew exponentially, sparking an expanding eruption that rushed through organs and airways alike until it burst from every orifice and exploded from every extremity.

Denizens ignited, careering hither and thither like phosphorous flares until they could stand no more. Flesh seared and cracked. Ululating screams choked off. Carbonized bones crumbled and fell.

Suddenly, all was still.

The circle came to completion and the Seven gathered together again; magnificent, maleficent, and whole.

Erra descended to assess the result of the night's foray.

A great arc almost a mile wide lay in ruins along the south bank of the Tombs. Fires raged and smoke ascended on high. Buildings weakened by elemental attack continued to topple, adding their substance to the wreckage already lining the streets in a testimony to agony and desolation. All that remained of the bridge were two shattered towers and bare stumps where ornate archways once stood proudly. And of the thousands filling the streets with a constant flow of hell's unliving essence, none remained.

"Well done, my Seven," Erra boomed, "a fitting demonstration of our intent. Perhaps now Satan will take heed and accede to the audit he knows—"

A swirling vortex appeared in the sky above them. Condensing, the cloud thickened, generating fulgurous bolts that charged the ether with violet and citrine potency.

"It would seem someone comes to answer our challenge . . ."

The maelstrom descended toward the earth and the entire region rocked as death on two legs thundered into the ground on the other side of the river.

". . . though I fear it is not Satan."

A moment of doubt clutched at Erra's bowels.

And now, we shall see . . .

*

Far below the dark and dirty streets of Perish, Nimrod and Gemini awaited the outcome of a most extraordinary meeting. Their plea for aid (and the benefits thereof) in the hunt for Chopin and Tesla's lair had made a huge impression on the hell-rat colony they had originally approached; so much so that word of the proposal had spread like wildfire throughout the length and breadth of the city, quickly reaching the ears of the *raft council.*

A hunter of men, denizens, and other entities for millennia, Nimrod had never realized sewer vermin possessed such sophistication, let alone the need for government, but Gemini soon put him right. Working as interpreter, she had revealed that the many communities interspersed throughout the lowways and byways arranged into rodent fiefdoms that corresponded to all twenty horrondissements above, along with an additional zone ringing the outskirts of the capital itself. Those fiefdoms formed seven larger shires, each of which existed under the oversight of a reeve, one of seven *rat-meisters* that answered to the king.

Nimrod was shocked to discover such a creature existed until Gemini emphasized that was the only way any degree of order could be maintained amongst so many antagonistic factions crammed into the limited space provided by the subterranean arteries beneath the city. The labyrinthine passages might amount to thousands of miles in length, but there were more than thirteen million rats, and without oversight, anarchy would ensue. Therefore, anything that affected the overall safety of the raft nation as a whole took priority and received the utmost respect.

The offer delivered by Gemini the previous evening had been taken seriously, and the Hounds escorted here, to one of the largest sewer terminals in all of Perish, where they could await the verdict of all seven reeves now gathered in moot.

Situated beneath the Opera Carnage, Place Venôme junction, at the border of the First, Second, Eighth and Ninth Horrondissements, the hub was more than a hundred feet in diameter and formed a huge conical bowl fed by no less than four main and thirteen tributary pipelines. Edged by vaulted arches and crisscrossed with stone colonnades, it looked more like the interior of a gothic cathedral than a city-sized toilet pan.

Ignoring the faint resonance filtering down from the world above, Nimrod used his augmented sight to gaze about him in wonder, for a sea of glittering eyes suffused the darkness with a twinkling luminescence that made it appear as if the heavens had been transposed onto the domed roof of the terminus.

It was obviously an auspicious occasion. More than fifteen thousand hell-rats from hundreds of different colonies were crowded onto the shelves, railings and overhangs surrounding the main sluiceway, and yet, not one of them seemed intent on misbehaving. In fact, so quiet were they that all Nimrod's keen hunter's senses could discern was the occasional nuzzling sound of fur being groomed free of bothersome fleas, or the squeak of youngsters being chastised for daring to show impatience.

Over to one side, Gemini abruptly ended her latest conversation and scooted back across to their place of honor on the gantry spanning the primary bore.

"Heads up," she whispered, gesturing back over her shoulder. "Something's coming."

"About time," Nimrod grumbled. "It's been—what? Four, five hours now? I'm beginning to lose track of time."

"You can't blame them for being cautious. This is the biggest thing to happen to them since the creation of the fiefdoms, so they're not going to rush into a decision." She glanced behind. "But it looks like they're about ready to make an announcement."

Nimrod glanced across to where Gemini had indicated and noticed a gentle glow stirring in the deepest recesses of one of the smaller influents. As that light source drew nearer and became more defined, he began to appreciate why the governing body of the rodent population was called the raft council, for a floating mass appeared from out of the darkness and evolved into a candlelit isle of drifting refuse. Consisting of twigs, smashed wooden crates and what appeared to be an old tractor tire covered in a weather-beaten tarp, it was indicative of the subterranean culture, where unwanted garbage could always be turned into someone else's treasure . . . Or, in this case, something far grander.

A thick layer of cushions in contrasting shapes, sizes and colors was scattered across the top of the trash island. Some were hand stitched and looked to be made of satin or velvet. Others were bog-standard foam-filled polyester. One was a 1970s discotheque reject; its lurid yellow cover smothered in rents, stains and cigarette burns. Regardless of how much the patchwork arrangement clashed, it was apparent to Nimrod that the creatures before him carried authority, for not only were they much larger and better groomed than their myriad subjects, but an escort of bobbing heads surrounded them, swimming alongside in a protective cordon.

The reeves had been accorded places of respect around the outer edge of the mound, while the king himself took center stage, enthroned upon (of all things) a child's car seat; though how such an item had wound up in hell, Nimrod couldn't fathom.

The procession came to a stately halt beneath the Hounds' position and the king stirred from his resting place. Fat of body, long of whisker and gray of snout, it was obvious this unusual denizen of hell was past his prime, for his fangs had yellowed with age and his eyes possessed a milk-white cast that hinted at future blindness. Nevertheless, he held himself proudly, and without ceremony got straight down to business.

A stream of clipped chittering rang out, and Nimrod watched, amused, as Gemini uttered a halting reply and raised her hand to stall the little monarch midsentence.

"What's wrong?" Nimrod whispered.

"For one, I've just advised his majesty that you don't speak their dialect, so I'll have to interpret as we go along. The other thing is that he's talking in a form of modern rodent-French. I told you, I haven't been here in a while, so it's taking all my concentration to get my head around what he's saying."

Hell-rats speak French?

Notwithstanding the magnitude of the setting, Nimrod had to smother laughter. Covering himself with a make-believe coughing fit, he spluttered, "Please continue, but link with me so I can discern what you're saying. We don't wish to offend, after all."

Gemini relayed what was happening to their host, and then opened her mind. Nimrod immediately felt himself meshed to his new partner's level of understanding. The sensation was rather odd, for he now saw the world about them as if experiencing it through Gemini's senses.

The king cleared his throat as if to compose himself, and then began. "*A près des pour parlers avec mes nobles, votredemandé a* étéaccepté (After consultation with my barons, your request has been accepted). *Chaque fief aidera à la question de la chasse les humains que vous cherchez* (Every fiefdom will assist in the matter of hunting the humans you seek). *Leurodeur sontété absorbés par mes fonctionnaires* (Their essences have been absorbed by my rat-meisters) *qui na la transmettre à lieutenants responsables au sein de chaque shire* (who will pass it on to responsible lieutenants within each shire). *Ne crains pas, nous allons attra perces renégats a court mesure* (Fear not, we will catch these renegades in short measure)."

"That's good to hear," Nimrod replied solemnly, "and as promised, the crime lord presiding over the south side of the river—and his associates—will ensure you and yours are kept well supplied with fresh meat."

Gemini translated Nimrod's assurances, whereupon the king sought a little clarification.

"*Qu'entendez-vous par frais? Nous sommes bien conscients que les humains dispapaissent au décèsporte en enfer*

(What do you mean by *fresh*? We are well aware that humans in hell disappear at death's door)."

"Ah, fear not. They will be fresh in the sense that each . . . *delivery* . . . will be bound, gagged, and still unliving. But, of course, we expect your kin to ensure such ones never escape to tell the tale."

No sooner had Gemini conveyed his reply than an excited *chirrup* told Nimrod all he needed to know.

Aha! It would seem no translation is required on this occasion?

The king jumped nimbly down from his throne and scurried across to the gantry. Tail swishing, he stared Nimrod in the face, bit his paw, then held it out to the giant in front of him.

Dumbfounded, Nimrod crouched down and extended his right hand. His host leaned forward and carefully nipped the tip of his little finger with one sharp fang. Then, with the utmost gravity, the king pressed his claw to the blood that welled from the small incision.

A resounding squeak trilled around the chamber, repeated by those rats looking on from side tunnels. In moments, a fanfare was echoing along the sewer system, announcing the result of the meeting to the underworld's underworld.

Party to the meaning of the noise about her, Gemini grinned from ear to ear.

Nimrod beckoned her closer.

"Once everyone has calmed down, we'll head straight to the Awful Tower and get Don Pérignone to send the first consignment. It'll be best to catch them in a good—"

Nimrod? Gemini?

The strident telepathic voice—laced as it was with anger and urgency—cut the celebratory chatter dead.

"Strawberry?" Nimrod leaped to his feet. "What in Satan's name is going on?"

Get your asses back to the Den, now. Olde London Town is under attack.

The mental picture relayed at the same time made Nimrod's blood run cold.

"The Sibitti?" he gasped. "In Juxtapose . . . Strawberry, we're stuck in Perish. Even if Vane were here, the *Lone Ra*–"

Forget that, it's taken care of. Pascal Fléau will meet you on the ground in the next few minutes with the orb you recovered at the Brass-Steel. Dodgy or not, Daemon said to use it and join us here in making our defense.

"Understood." Nimrod glanced at Gemini and jerked his chin toward a set of metal ladders at the end of the scaffold. She made haste to extend a hurried apology to their hosts and then set off at a run. "We're on our way."

Hot on Gemini's heels, Nimrod couldn't help but ponder the situation they were rushing toward.

One way or another, what takes place in the next half hour will seal the fate of everything we've worked hard to achieve. A conversation he'd had with His Infernal Majesty the last time Daemon had been injured sprang to mind. *And the worst danger comes from the unlikeliest sources.*

Chapter 15: Reaper

As everyone was aware, the conflicting gravitational eddies riddling the Sheolspace continuum made inter-circle travel hazardous at the best of times. Lately, even the use of sanctioned gateways had become more perilous, thanks to the Sibitti, who seemed determined to maroon denizens wherever they could in order to make their confounded audit run smoother. Nevertheless, I possessed something that rendered their schemes invalid, something I looked upon as the ultimate living cosmic buoy: the Bālefire.

A vibrant, animated milieu of stunning potential, it saturated the molecular nature of infernity in such a way that its heartbeat actually anchored my anathematized soul to hell.

And of all the places in the underworld, nowhere was it more resonant than at the Black Tower in Juxtapose, a location that acted as a lodestone to my dark essence as it was a haven to my ungodly lusts. So, upheaval or not, it was a simple matter for me to tune into the accursed pulse I knew so well, and will myself here.

The Sibitti made a mistake in choosing to attack so close to the seat of my power—a fact they will shortly discover to their cost.

Manifesting high in the clouds above the Den of Iniquity, I discerned how swiftly Strawberry had responded to the
threat of danger. The keep's mundane and esoteric defenses
were armed, and the battlements sizzled from the raw energies now coursing through the fabric of their ancient stones.

The Inquisitors had deployed tactically: Leonard "*Crush-
er*" Skeffington and Myra "*Black Velvet*" Star manned the
northern walls between Devious Tower and Ravens Tower;
the *Red Baron*, Ferenc Nádasdy and his wife, Elizabeth Báthory, our very own *Blood Countess*, patrolled the ramparts
of the western sector. Until the Hounds arrived, Strawberry
had assumed a position at the southeastern corner of the castle, right on the crook of Devil's Point.

As a thunderbolt personified, I blazed toward the ground
and allowed my gaze to sweep across the carnage on the
south side of the Tombs. From my vantage point, it looked as
if a giant hand had reached down from the sky to raze a cres-
cent-shaped swath of land stretching more than half a mile
from the river.

City Hall was a broken shell: Neckwringer, The Shard,
and Rotters Field were nothing but a festering liquefied
graveyard of semi-dissolved, putrid corpses; Weepers Lane,
Unfair Cloister, and The Draught had been transformed into
a burnt-out ruin all the way back to Druid Street. Even the
Tombs embankment bore the scars of an abrasion that had
excised all distinguishing features from her banks.

I had to admit, what I saw appealed to me and it picked at
a scab of grudging respect hidden deep inside. Death was my
living, carnage my delight. And this . . . ?

This *is the embodiment of what hell should be. Unfair.
Unjust. Unbearable suffering, corruption and misery.* Then a
spark of fury blasted that sentiment away. *But only if it's sanctioned by His Satanic Majesty first.* My resolve hardened and

the sigils adorning my armor steamed anew. *And especially not when Erra's personal butt-monkeys do the inflicting.*

Seven such butt-monkeys stood in a loose circle on the approach to the far side of the remains of Black Tower Bridge. And if I wasn't mistaken, Erra himself was with them.

I smashed into the ground outside the fortress like a meteor, generating a shockwave that radiated away like a supersonic dinosaur-obliterating firewall. No sooner had I landed than a flash high up on the eastern bailey indicated that Champ and Yamato must have used their portal generator to follow in my wake.

Good, two to go.

Addressing Strawberry, I amplified my voice. "The others?"

"Nimrod and Gemini should be with us any second. I had the GDSI agent, Pascal, take the orb to their location at the raft council meeting."

Raft council?

In reply to my subliminal query, she answered, "We don't have time. I'll tell you about it later . . . if we—"

"We will. Don't worry. And what about my Dark Father?"

"Summoning his angels as we speak. Fortunately, he received a heads-up from Samael. It seems your manner of departure caused quite a stir over at the Pentagram, so backup is on the way."

A secondary burst of light right next to Strawberry's position signified the appearance of Nimrod and Gemini.

Good, my general is here.

"Nimrod. Take command and ensure the inner grounds are free of all noncombatant personnel. I want the moat's sluice gates opened so the Bãlefire has an opportunity to flood the outer ward by the time Satan arrives. If you manage to do nothing else before the inevitable shit hits the fan, make sure the walls are prepared."

"I understand," he replied. "And you?"

Cocooned as I was in a web of purple and gold energy, I allowed just a hint of the overwhelming passion coursing through my veins to peek through.

"I've got too much power too close to the surface doing nothing." I turned to face the Sibitti. "And I need to express it."

A hint of anxiety leaked through Nim's aura.

"Don't worry. These fuckers were quite content to play the big *I Am* when they caught me with my pants down in Dark Cairo. I'm itching to find out how keen they are to flex their pecs now I'm all fired up and ready to play."

For emphasis, I allowed my blazing crown to burn incandescent for just a moment before quenching the flames.

Nonetheless, Nimrod remained uneasy. "But Daemon, there are seven of them this time. And Erra's right behind them."

"I appreciate your concern. I really do. But people tend to forget one important fact. He's an ancient Babylonian plague god. His ass-lickers are sons of heaven and earth. *They* don't belong here; I do. Their quintessence is alien, contradictory to the natural functioning of the entire underworld. Mine resonates in harmony with its very tincture. You carry a spark of that same authority within you." I cocked a thumb toward my waiting adversaries. "It's about time they got a taste of their own medicine, and this is just the occasion to deliver it. They've overstepped the mark; I'm going to cut their legs out from under them."

Turning, I channeled my intent along my staff and held it high. Then I stalked down the interceding berm toward the bridge. The Sibitti closely scrutinized my approach, and I noticed how they all began edging nearer together, as if closing ranks and barring the way to their master.

Good. The mere fact they're worried tells me my hunch is right.

Once I reached the approach road, I thought it wise to use the lull before the storm to study my enemy. It was the first time I had ever seen them manifest in human form. Nevertheless, I recognized three auras immediately, and one of them in particular.

So you're the assholes who tried to take advantage?

I labeled them in my mind.

Mister Muscles gets all hot under the collar. Pressure Cooker doesn't like to get boiled. What's more, he *chickened out of a one-on-one under Skull Isle. And Pretty Boy likes to sneak up on you in storms. And as for the others? We'll see soon enough.*

Blazing with devilish theurgy, cowl flapping in the breeze, I waited for my enemy to make the first move. Now that they were all together, I wondered how they would actually play it.

Probably bullshit and bravado, especially now daddy's here to hold their hands and tuck in their shirttails. The last time out, they had tried to provoke me. That wouldn't work on this occasion. *So, I might as well set the tone and take the game to them. After all, actions speak louder than words.*

The asphalt ended abruptly in sheared-off cables and shattered concrete stumps hanging from the end of deformed and twisted steel rods. I strode confidently forward until I could go no farther without getting my feet wet.

Now we were only two hundred and fifty yards apart.

As slowly and deliberately as possible, I slammed the heel of my sickle into the road and turned it to stone.

Watching, waiting, I stared at them, a pocket battleship of charged potential and midnight menace.

My provocative actions worked like a charm.

One of Erra's enforcers raised his voice:

"Will you not respond, Reaper?" he cried. "Have you no answer to the folly heaped upon your city?"

This close to them, I received a distinct sense of individuality coming from the First.

I decided to ham it up a little, as irritated folk tended to act irrationally.

Here's hoping.

"What? Would you like me to say *thank you*? Bring you flowers or chocolates?"

The First's expression turned to one of puzzlement. Then his frown deepened.

Pressing my advantage, I continued, "This is hell, you idiot. Contrary to what you might have seen in other circles so far, it's supposed to be a place of gross injustice and eternal suffering." I made a point of surveying the surrounding devastation. "Not a bad show . . . for beginners. But if you're so intent on doing my job for me, you'll have to learn to do things properly. I hope you do. I haven't had a break in like . . . forever!"

"You would make light of so much carnage?"

"On the contrary, I never make light of inflicting carnage. It's my sole purpose for being. Denizens get things far too easy, in my opinion. All you've done is clear away some of the chaff." I swept my arm across the expanse of the city. "You want to create havoc? Please, be my guests. I'll even join you if you like, just to ensure things are done right."

Mr. Muscles couldn't contain himself any longer. As before, the moment he opened his mouth, I received an impression of identity from the Seventh.

"He is merely posturing and trying to delay the inevitable."

"No, he speaks truth," the Second—aka *Pretty Boy*—intoned. "Are you blind to the clarity of his sincerity? For all his faults, this creature does not lie. He lives for death."

"Pah!" Seven was in a bad mood. "Sincerity? He seeks to assuage our anger in—"

"I know *you*, don't I?" So quietly did I speak that I cut the Titan's mounting diatribe dead. "Unlucky number seven. *You* were one of the cowards who caught me with my pants down at the Spouting Pyramids. I have to admit, I've thought about that day quite a lot since then. I'm sure you remember, too, how run down I was. How drained and weak I felt. You were lucky there, weren't you? Strange that, for all your supposed power, three of you couldn't finish me off, eh? And do you recall how I didn't beg for mercy, even though you tried to rub my face in how superior you were?" I chuckled to myself. "Tell me . . . if I didn't ask for quarter then, what makes you think I'd be interested in doing that here, especially now I'm fully empowered and can do things like . . . *this*?"

Faster than thought, I phased and put my entire weight and speed behind the mother of all uppercuts.

A satisfying *crack* graced my ears, and the Seventh went spiraling backward through the air to crash to the floor at three of his brothers' feet. He rolled over and over, almost knocking them down.

Third, Fourth and Fifth . . .

I had obviously made the right impression. Defying his best efforts, Mr. Muscles couldn't get his namesake to work, nor could he get to his feet unaided.

My personal maelstrom condensed about me as I strode into the center of their ring. Spinning on my heel, I faced them all in turn.

"You go to all this trouble to draw my attention and think I'll be too afraid to respond?" I threw back my head and laughed. Augmented as I was, the sound fractured nearby concrete posts. "You've not done your homework."

They were good, I'd give them that. Nobody panicked or overreacted. Seventh apart, their swords came up and they dropped into combat-ready crouches, holding themselves on the balls of their feet. I could taste the anger and malevolence radiating from them in waves. They wanted so badly to take me; but they were also uncertain.

The Fourth glanced behind him at Erra, as if looking for guidance.

Following the direction of his gaze, I nodded and addressed the god of plague and mayhem directly. "You seem perplexed, Your Majesty. But what did you expect? Did you honestly think I would run away and hide? Just because I'm worked off my feet tracking down scum doesn't mean I've gone soft on you and yours. I have a job to do and your idiot antics are getting in the way of that. If we had crossed paths sooner, this would have been settled already." I jabbed my finger at the Fifth and Sixth standing side by side. "Ask them. Both of your *personified weapons* have bumped into me in passing. One recently, the other some months ago back on Skull Isle when I reclaimed my Hounds—who, by the way, are up on my castle's battlements just waiting to even the score. Both your lackeys were wise enough to back down then. I suggest you do the same now."

I stalked across the gap and positioned myself within touching distance of the Fourth.

Ignoring him completely, I regarded only Erra. "You have no idea what you're dealing with. Up until now, all you've faced are petty demon lords, vassal god-kings and minor nobility aspiring to positions beyond their pay grades.

No wonder you've vanquished them all. They had no spine, no real power; and those that did, you fawned to. Did you not realize we know all about Kur of Ki-gal and Irkalla of Arali?"

I noticed that the First of Seven in particular bristled at my accusations.

Stalking the inner circle, I looked each enforcer in the eye.

"You have never faced anyone like me as I am now: someone who makes you look like wannabes. Personified weapons? Personified amateurs, more like. I've reaped more souls than all of you combined. Do you want a lesson in how to kill?" I threw my arms wide. "Well, here I am. What are you waiting for? Come and get me."

As before, the First seemed to take my taunts to heart. I could taste the hatred burning inside him like sweet nectar working its way toward ultimate release.

Egged on by his ardor, several gleaming sword tips leveled toward me.

"I would advise caution, brothers." Once again, the Second spoke out. "There is no falsehood in him. Like us, he is an instrument of design and although different in many ways, he is as bound to his task as we are to ours. He is . . ." The Second's countenance glowered as his mental caress probed the deepest recesses of my soul. "Pure? Odd that a denizen of hell should be so cursed."

"Pure?" The First spluttered, still incensed by my presence and the challenge raised by my accusations.

Imbibing his spirit, I discerned that this monstrosity, more than all the others, was accustomed to commanding a degree of subservience from those around him. It made him presumptuous. Condescending.

The First ignored his comrade's advice and virtually spat on me as he hissed, "You don't expect to survive us, do you?"

Concentrating, I opened my crux to the entirety that was the Bãlefire. Warped creative energy that defined the depth and the length and the breadth of all the circles of hell rushed to answer my summons. In a heartbeat, the Phage about me bloomed, quenching nearby fires, shattering the foundations of all remaining structures and eradicating those undead remains that had as yet failed to dissipate due to the Sibitti's interference.

"What did you say?" I whispered.

"I said that no insect like you can possibly expect to survive this encounter." His arrogance sealed his fate. "We are sons of heaven and earth. You are nothing but—"

In the blink of an eye, I closed on the First and lifted him by his throat high into the air. His sword slashed down and sparks flew as I redirected the force of his blow along the length of my staff. With a twist of my wrist, I hooked my blade around his hilt-guard and tore the weapon from his grasp.

His brothers rushed to aid him. Before they had taken two steps, I encased us both within a sphere of incandescent mastery.

Yanking the First closer to my face, I growled, "You might very well be a son of heaven. But you are also a product of the earth, a mortal element I can exploit . . . *thus*."

Manifesting my death touch, I commenced draining his essence from him, while outside the shield, the Sibitti worked their mighty arts . . . to no avail.

"Don't you idiots get it? I don't care what you try to do to me, for I am neither dead nor alive. Here in this realm, I walk the boundary between such mundane labels. I am a true juxtapose made flesh, unleashed on the masses to foment fear and harvest the unworthy." Something clicked and then cracked open deep inside me. "You can't undo what I am unless the latter-day levels of hell cease to exist."

My craving became feral, almost rabid in its intensity. I increased the drain of the First's life force and noticed for the first time how large his soul-well actually was. The First was fortunate; had he not been what he was, he would have expired already.

But the majesty of his tincture provided a strange side effect.

Gravity seemed to squeeze in around us and the gales that had buffeted the city during the attack increased. Cimmerian in nature, they darkened, thickened, and started to corkscrew inward from all points of the compass to form a tornado. Then they ignited in a blaze of violet and golden majesty that poured the all-sustaining pith of the underverse down into the core of my being.

The same sense of dislocation I remembered from when I destroyed the Black Keep at the Isle of Cogs now enveloped me.

I am the Bãlefire. Brimstone incarnate, made flesh.

I am also part of the Heavenly Light, celestial beauty eclipsed.

Perpetual discordance personified. At war with myself—within myself— Because of myself, I am the very anathema of my own existence.

I relived the nuance of every feeling:

Limitless potential waited within the nucleus of the smallest atom.

Memories, hidden within a vortex of confusion, tugged at the edge of comprehension.

Something significant clawed for air within the very core of my soul.

A red-hot spike of flame anchored my semi-corporeal shell to reality. As I descended toward my body, a world of contradictions gyrated wildly about me. Good and evil; ecstasy and agony; right and wrong; glorification and debasement. The cracks widened and chaos threatened, raging against restraints long in the making but now tenuous at best.

Something huge, something ruinous, slavered for release.

For a moment, I was in two places at once.

What?

What?

Who am I?

Where am I?

This is not my armor. The last thing I recall, I was ascending to face . . . ?

The last thing I remember, I was falling into the . . . ?

Then Sheolspace inverted, and solidarity of mind and purpose returned once more—along with a need to express my rage.

"I know who I am," I snarled through gritted teeth, "the Reaper, through and thro–"

Around me, the Sibitti backed away, clearly appalled.

I must have released my grip during my psychedelic side-trip, for two enforcers held the First between them and were dragging him away toward Erra.

Unholy shit, how did I not finish the job?

At a signal from the god of plague and mayhem, they vanished—all except one.

The Second hand remained behind and stared at me, a mixture of fascination and abhorrence inscribed across his finely wrought features. His gaze crawled with an energy that seemed to delve into the furthest reaches of my soul as it roused me to hunger.

"You are more than you appear to be . . . Gods help us all."

I've heard that somewhere before?

The Second folded from sight to the accompaniment of a rumbling sky and terra that was very much on the infirma side of things.

As the last of his features disappeared, a pair of intense glowing eyes invoked memories of a time and place I would rather have forgotten.

You are more than you appear to be.

Feeling hyped to an unerring degree, I stirred from my waking dream and leaned on my sickle for support. A crushing weight threatened to burst my head at any moment. I tried blinking rapidly and massaging the back of my neck. But it was no use. I needed to act, and act fast. Reversing my grip, I pressed the jewel of my scythe firmly into the ruined soil and, without thought or direction, channeled the vast potential of simmering might back into the realm from which I had siphoned it.

The response was immediate. Floodwaters began to recede. Stagnant pools dried out. Shriveled and diseased foliage distended to bloom gray-green once more.

As the pressure eased, the dizziness abated. I sped the process by turning my attention to the surrounding ruins, roadways and shattered span. A sparkling mist materialized upon the ground at my feet and undulated away like an inverse mushroom cloud. Where it passed, sparkling motes illuminated the brume with fulgurous effusions that sizzled and popped and filled the air with the delicious aroma of rotten eggs and ozone.

High and proud, buildings stood restored. Highways gleamed as if freshly laid with sulfur and pitch. Even the bridge looked magnificent; its new gothic allure portrayed by exaggerated spires, crenels and spider web cables.

Then thunder pealed across the firmament as Satan and his angels appeared. Resplendent in feather-winged serpent guise, they descended swiftly toward me in a spiraling loop, swords shining, tails charged, manes full and overflowing with murderous intent and deviltry.

Landing only yards away, they took in my feat of re-creation and muttered amongst themselves. I sensed that something about my accomplishment had unsettled them. A few exuded auras of barely restrained malice. Fortunately, the Father of all Lies wasn't amongst the dissenters—or if he was, he hid it well.

Satan studied me closely.

"Yes . . . you do seem rather bloated in all the wrong places. I think your self-rejuvenating codex may have something to do with that, even though we'd given it a tweak to ensure you . . ."

He went silent for a moment and came to an abrupt decision. "Come closer, Daemon. It's about time we returned you to a more natural form."

In response to my bemused telepathic query, he added, "Your augmentation produced some rather unexpected side effects today, side effects that will no doubt elicit a more concerted and aggressive response from our would-be auditor of hell. I have a feeling I'm going to need my armor back sooner rather than later."

His Infernal Majesty had obviously been communicating with his choir, for they maneuvered into a similar formation to that employed by the Sibitti. As they did so, Satan raised his arm and flared his talons wide.

A hurricane formed right above us. Strangely devoid of encircling winds, it churned and moiled about itself in a concentrated, isolated nucleus that stained the heavens in ruddy amber and rose-gold hues from one horizon to the other. Then, like a crucible filled with sorcerous coals, the eye contracted, spewing a hammer strike of thaumaturgic rage onto the anvil of fallen angels gathered below.

The cascade intensified, warping the atmosphere in silver and blue-black streaks that coiled out to strike the ground, vegetation, water and buildings alike; anything, in fact, that would assist such excessive potential to earth itself.

In response to an unseen signal, the quorum raised their weapons, tips pointing toward my position next to Satan. I felt the air tingle, and then an efflux powerful enough to level cities exploded outward, engulfing me in the unadulterated quiddity of the Bãlefire, but an aspect I had never tasted or witnessed before.

This is the polar opposite of what I'm used to. And it seems to . . ?

Before I realized what was happening, my consciousness refracted in a million different directions at once, only a few of which I was able to comprehend:

Here, I surfed along celestial waves of limitless scope. There, I floated free, at peace and lost to the orgasmic rush of perpetual agony. In another reality, I bathed in diabolical energies that blended to my soul and bent to my will, perverting the very nature and order of life.

And even though these sights, sounds and sensations consumed me, a tiny kernel of awareness was cognizant of the fact that Satan was taking his time to manipulate the sigils engraved into my helmet, cuirass and pauldrons. Seconds dragged into minutes as he methodically worked his way down my body and onto my vambraces and each cuisse.

A bolt of ice-cold vitality shocked me to the core. Scorching its way through my nervous system, it gripped me by the spine and jolted me into the air, arms and legs splayed upon a torture rack of elation.

The tail end of the colossal discharge smote the crown of my head, and without understanding how, I just knew I was changed.

Flames licked a coating of frost from the surface of my skin, for skin it was; actual flesh made whole again; and more. As I looked on, the phosphorescent radiance faded and the only evidence that the armor had ever existed were the tattoos now covering my body. Each mark occupied the exact same place and was the perfect representation of a former glyph. With a thought, I accessed their potential. My reward consisted of an instant hit of raw power.

Oh yes, that *will do nicely.*

The fact that I was buck naked didn't register until my Dark Father waved a taloned claw in my direction, and snapped, "Perhaps you'd care to use some of your excess energy and attire yourself as befits a hero of hell?"

Hero? Is this a test? Not friggerty likely.

In my mind's eye, I conjured a picture of the only garb I had ever felt comfortable wearing. A blinding flash, followed by a blast of cinders and a vacuum concussion—and my trademark cowled trench coat, boots and gloves materialized where they belonged.

Fuck yeah! The king of Goths is back.

A masterful eyebrow arched upward in surprise. "I'm the Reaper," I explained, "what else am I going to wear?"

Satan shrugged and gestured. A miniature implosion within the palm of his hand followed, together with a waft of rotten eggs. "Here, I do believe you'll need these as your complexus settles down," he said, holding out a pair of Ray

Burns. "I've attempted to return you to a semblance of normalcy, but you're like a chrysalis. Badness knows how you'll end up. It'd probably be wise not to take any chances. I'd put them on right away if I were you."

Semblance? Chrysalis? I let the obvious questions ride.

Doing as instructed, I donned my sunglasses and murmured, "What now?"

Satan's eyes smoldered like slavering fangs.

"And now, my Reaper, I'd really like it if you'd put your new enhancements to use and make haste to rid my kingdom of certain thorns in the flesh that are becoming rather . . . bothersome."

I gestured, and my scythe slammed into my outstretched hand.

"I'll get right on that."

Chapter 16: The Old Lady

In spite of the setback caused by the failed Sibitti incursion, my team and I were able to get back down to business with relative ease; a task assisted by the recovery of the vortex generators. Because of them, Champ and Yamato quickly returned to the Pentagram to follow up on several fresh leads, while Nimrod and Gemini had departed not twenty minutes previously with the intention of consolidating our new accord with the raft council (now that I knew what that was) back in Perish.

That left me free to pursue my own agenda. And in this regard, I had been lucky . . . twice.

For one thing, Satan's act of restoring me to human form nearly backfired for I had tucked the latest clue within the gauntlet of my armor in an effort to keep it safe. Needless to say, the note vaporized during my transformation. However, fortune favored the bold and my close to eidetic memory saved the day.

As I stood outside my current objective in the cool predawn air, I was able to review the poem in its entirety, mentally:

Bring me the head of the savior,

An Old Lady still gasping for breath,
Who wanders a garden of insanity
Where Sarah, in lament, now rests.

Bring me the blanket of life,
A fleece to envelop my charter.
Gold wrapped, this mortal coil
Sparks nothing but death.

Bring me the keys of release
And a yard in which to turn for your answer,
For your thimble will lie redundant
In the eye that no camel will ever Thread.

I had to chuckle, for in their haste to test me the Sibitti
had unwittingly helped me in a second way, by launching
their attack in the very city the rhyme had indicated I would
find my next clue: Olde London Town.

Things were most definitely starting to look up.

An action, coincidentally, in which I was engaged at this
precise moment, as the entrance portico to the Bunker of
England here in Bloodneedle Street was as imposingly high
as it was arabesque and wide.

Not to be obsessive, but it's best to check. As I peered
about my environs, I recited those parts of the verse that had
so easily led me here:

"An Old Lady who wanders a garden of insanity;
where Sarah, in lament, now rests"—*and what was it, oh
yes*—"gold wrapped; keys of release, and a yard in which
to turn for your answer; in the eye that no camel will ever
Thread."

Established in 1694 under royal charter, the Bank of England, as this great entity is still known topside, is the second oldest central bank in the world, and the model upon which other similar institutes have been based. Situated in Threadneedle Street, she earned the metonym *The Old Lady of Threadneedle Street* or simply, *The Old Lady*: a name from the legend of one Sarah Whitehead, said to still haunt the gardens of that great edifice in the land of the living.

Sarah once had a brother—Philip Whitehead—a disgruntled former employee of the bank who was found guilty of forgery in 1811 and executed for his crime. So shocked was Sarah to discover the circumstances of her sibling's demise that she became unhinged, and every day for the next twenty-five years went to his office in the hall of cashiers, asking to see him.

When she died, Sarah was buried in the old churchyard that later became the bank's garden, and her ghost was said to wander the streets even now, where she would accost strangers at night, asking, "Have you seen my brother?"

It was obvious her shade yearned for a reunion that would never come, for while her soul was stuck in limbo, Philip had descended into hell where Satan, ever eager to stick the knife in, had devised the ultimate punishment.

In life, Philip abused his trusted position and coveted money above all else. Therefore, after his arrival and induction, he had been appointed *Chancellor of Coin* at the Bunker, and placed in charge of the repository housing some of hell's greatest treasures, proscribed artifacts—and in the most delicious twist—its gold bullion reserves, estimated at a value in excess of Đ544,500,000,000.00.

The daily temptation for him to pilfer would be unbearable. As were the consequences, for every time he touched things forbidden, part of him would turn to gold. It was a foregone conclusion that one day he would be an unliving monument to Midas himself, mounted on the Bunker's steps as an everlasting testimony to Satan's perverse genius.

I sighed. *There's nothing like an unhappy ending to make a true story worthwhile and heartwarming.*

Although in all honesty, I found nothing heartwarming about the ease with which I had solved Tesla's latest clue. Up until now, they had been blatantly obscure. But this last one was far too simple. Even the slightly cryptic reference to the yard-long special keys used to unlock the vaults hadn't been lost on me.

Which means they're up to something.

I chewed my bottom lip for a moment, and then put my doubts aside.

It's no use wasting my time trying to second-guess them. I'll just let events unfurl around me as I did before, and when they get too close, bam*! I'll take their heads.*

Satisfied, I moved toward the main entrance, only to discern at least a dozen different kinds of scanning and tracking systems locking-on to me.

Just what I'd expect from one of the most heavily fortified bastions in hell.

Either the sensors included some of the latest psidentic upgrades, or somebody inside recognized my restored profile and clothing, for a bank teller emerged from the atrium and trotted down the steps to meet me.

But this was no teller anyone from topside would be familiar with, for the underworld filled such positions with seven-foot tall Minotaurs. Granted the ability to *read* anyone stepping onto the bank's precincts, they would declare—or *tell*—of their arrival to all and sundry . . . even if it was only 5:00 a.m. And, of course, if that visitor happened to be on the *Wanted* or *Undesirables* lists, the Minotaur was more than capable of stomping and goring them to a bloody pulp before calling on the relevant agents of injustice to scrape up the remains.

Dressed about its muscular torso in butler's tails, starched black shirt and bold red bowtie, the teller portrayed a smart and elegant welcome to the establishment, regardless of the fact it trailed fizzling pools of pitch in its wake.

"Announcing Daemon Grim, Satan's Reaper and chief bounty hunter," it intoned, "leader of those called Hell Hounds and Inquisitors."

Several passersby stopped to stare. One or two even dared to snatch a picture on their mobile phones. I let them.

Good. That's all it will take. The rumor mill will spread the news of my return to human form in less than an hour.

A tinge of Bãlefire seasoned the air. Turning back to my escort, I noticed his crimson eyes glowering like hot coals.

Aha! So that's where he gets the authority to read auras.

"Bad morning, Mister Grim." The Minotaur spoke with a surprisingly soft voice and held out his hand in welcome without the slightest sign of fear. "My name is Geoffrey, and if you'd kindly follow me, I'll take you to see the chancellor. Fortunately, he's here twenty-four hours a day, as our Dark Father has seen fit to deny Mister Whitehead the privilege of sleep or time off."

"Oh, really?"

Nice one, Boss. And a crafty way of making eternal torment drag on longer than it already does.

Geoffrey led me inside, through the foyer and on into the boundmasons' parade, a welcoming area possessing a strange checkerboard floor design that flowed off through a series of identical rooms and wide archways toward the six main banking halls.

This was the first occasion I had ever visited the Bunker, but even a cursory glance revealed that interior, designed to fool the eye and confuse the senses. Every separate area made a perfect square of equal dimensions. Light shone from a single central lantern suspended from the ceiling and supported by a main spire and pediments in each corner. Decorated porticos with baroque embellishments held trelliswork of glass and mirrors descending to the floor and creating a dazzling riot of light and dark that made it difficult to work out where one chamber ended and the next began. I adjusted my perceptions to compensate and detected a variance in the camber of the floors. Each possessed a different angle that would cause those with poor eyesight to wander aimlessly round and around in circles.

A man of genteel appearance waited for us at a small display cabinet situated against the nearest wall.

Philip Whitehead, I presume.

Even at a distance, I could see the telltale flicker of gold along one side of his throat and the entire length of two of the fingers of his left hand; a sure indicator the chancellor had given into temptation on more than one occasion in the past.

Geoffrey bowed silently and trotted off, leaving me alone with my host.

"Reaper," Whitehead grunted by way of greeting, "glad to see someone in authority can be bothered to display a modicum of competency."

Without further explanation, he turned on his heel and stalked away. It was obvious he wanted me to follow, so I did. Nevertheless, it was plain to see the chancellor was also a man with a whole world of woe crowding in on him.

"Problems?"

"You could say that," he snapped back over his shoulder. "A place like this will always be full of temptation to those of us who work here, Reaper. A fact I myself can testify to." He waved his disfigured hand toward me. "Regardless, since the new security systems were installed several years ago, not one gold bar, not a single diablo or even a speck of dust has gone unaccounted for: a superlative record for hell, let me tell you. So, imagine my immense delight only one hour ago when I discovered an Omega Class artifact had gone missing."

"An Omega Class artifact? One hour ago?"

"Yes, kept within an isolated and specially sealed vault, and barred to all but those few who possess undecipherable keys. Due to the nature of the defenses around them, we leave those items well alone and allow them to mothball. We only break a seal once every five years to check the contents, and then we lock them right back up again."

"And I take it you carried out an audit tonight?"

"Indeed. And with such a sensitive article involved, I'd have expected a more enthusiastic response."

"Enthusiastic, in what way?"

"I notified MI13 of the breach at four o'clock. Four o' bloody clock. When they didn't bother showing, I thought I'd better contact your department." He suddenly halted and turned to look me in the eye. "I only made the call what, four or five minutes ago. Damned impressive."

He started forward again, and I hadn't the heart to burst his bubble and tell him about the clue that had preemptively led me here.

"Well, you can relax; SIS weren't being derelict in their duties. They were a little busy dealing with the threat presented by an attack from all seven Sibitti."

"The Sibitti, eh?" he murmured. "That's nasty."

He wasn't really listening. In fact, I got the distinct impression nothing outside his own personal little kingdom would matter to the late, great, Philip Whitehead. I decided to test my theory.

"Yes, all seven of them assaulted the Den of Iniquity. Erra, too. Worse, they brandished inflatable cucumbers and fought from pantomime horseback. Fortunately, I claimed a time-out, and then beat them back with a lethal combination of good looks and razor-sharp wit."

"Oh, there's nice."

Gotcha! You've marked your cards, matey. Before this is over, I'll have thought of a fitting way to remind you never to disrespect me again.

By now, we had reached a circular area more than eighty yards across. The sign above the archway said *Rotunda*. After the perfect uniformity everywhere else, it looked oddly out of place. A series of workstations and long counters formed its outer circumference, leaving the open expanse clear and free of obstructions.

As in other chambers, the floor slanted away at an angle. But here, everything sloped gently downward to form a shallow silver bowl five feet in diameter in the exact center of the room. Without bothering to explain what we were doing, Whitehead led me toward that feature.

The closer we got to the disc, the stronger the tingling sensation that had begun to crawl across my newly restored skin.

That's a lot of energy for such a small space.

Whitehead noted my interest.

"This is the code key," he said with evident pride, "the only entrance into the wyrm chamber that guards the way to the vaults and repository far below us."

We stepped onto the platform and found ourselves enveloped within a shimmering orange light filled by glowing liquescent blobs of divine and arcane puissance. Several of my tattoos flared whenever any of them strayed too close. Scanning the globules, I recognized the distinctive signature of God's Grace and the Bālefire. If such mastery came together in this environment, it would be akin to introducing matter to antimatter. Catastrophic.

"Please get on with it," I murmured, keen to retain the flesh I had so recently reacquired.

Whitehead didn't appear to be concerned in the slightest, and said, "Have you seen my brother?"

I wondered who he was speaking to, until I realized the personal phrase he had just uttered was an acoustic cipher. *Ouch, that has got to hurt.*

The haze about us dimmed and everything went black.

Without knowing why, I suddenly felt restrained in some way. However, it was difficult to ascertain the reason for such a notion because the darkness was absolute and seemed to stretch off toward infinity.

I raised my fingers.

"*Leightansîn bi aotrom* (Let there be light)."

Nothing happened.

What the . . . ?

"This is the new security measure I was talking about earlier," Whitehead mumbled. He seemed distracted, and I heard a scraping sound, as if the sole of his foot was scuffing the floor.

Click!

The dais beneath our feet illuminated with a soft red fluorescence, and I was able to confirm that we were literally in the middle of nowhere. Two damned souls, marooned atop a floating disc of light in the middle of a vast and empty ocean of nonexistence.

"Where . . . ?"

"It's a specially fabricated rupture beyond the Sheol-space continuum," he explained, "a place in between, that exists outside of the normal laws of physics, metaphysics and whatever other *ysics* you care to mention. Your abilities won't work here."

"No shit?" My stomach churned at the thought of any-thing that could so easily counteract my power. "How in Sa-tan's name was it created?"

"I haven't the faintest idea, old chap. All I do know is that it took His Infernal Majesty and his entire coterie of fallen an-gels some considerable time and effort to anchor the schism here. To reach any part of the main vault or the repository it-self, you must now pass through this eye of nothingness. If you don't possess the right key, you'll be marooned here un-til the platform fades and you end up falling into . . . badness knows what."

The last stanza of my clue sprang to mind and a shiver ran down my spine:

Bring me the keys of release
And a yard in which to turn for your answer,
For your thimble will lie redundant
In the eye that no camel will ever Thread.

Was Tesla talking about this *place? I thought the clue was a play on words referring to Threadneedle Street?*

I spun on the spot, but no matter how hard I tried, I simply couldn't penetrate the weight of eternity that had us clutched by the balls in its merciless grip.

"So now what?"

"Now I do this." Whitehead walked to the edge of the po-dium, cupped his hands to his lips, and yelled, "George? This is Philip, the chancellor of coin. I'm here with the Reaper,

Daemon Grim, and we need to gain access to vault one three one seven."

Like a sponge, the perpetual midnight surrounding us soaked up his every word, making it seem as if nobody had ever spoken.

The radiance beneath our feet turned amber.

In view of the slight change in circumstances, I expected someone to materialize in front of us, or for the platform to take us somewhere else, but after a few minutes of waiting around with nothing happening, I realized I was sorely mistaken.

Then I heard a strange resonance.

Whup—whup. Whup—whup.

Faint at first, something was nevertheless sailing the gulf toward us.

Whup—whup. Whup—whup.

The sound indicated something huge and ponderous.

Whup—whup. Whup—whup.

As it drew nearer, I noticed a golden-green glow throbbing in time to the cadence of each swishing echo. Every pulse hinted at a long sinewy outline, resplendent in many scaled hues against the inky backdrop. In spite of its obvious size, I was struck by an imbued sense of ultimate poise and grace.

Whup—whup. Whup—whup.

Then I remembered that Whitehead had called this place "wyrm chamber" and I understood what I was looking at.

"Well, screw me blind. It's a goddam dragon!"

The leviathan swooped in to hover before us in a hurricane blast of heat and sulfur. So close did it come that I thought its wings might buffet us from our fragile perch. I was sure I could smell my hair singeing.

Staring at this legend made flesh, I tugged at Whitehead's arm, and hissed, "I thought George was supposed to be the name of the knight?"

"I'm not deaf, you know," the beast replied with the weary fortitude of one who has told the same story a thousand times before, "and I'm not *that* dragon. That was Lilith. As the chancellor said, I'm George."

"My bad," I apologized, "this is only the second time I've ever seen one of your kind, and the first chance I've had to actually converse."

Eyes like white-hot suns regarded me for a moment, then the great horned head arched backward and I had a clear and unobstructed view of the moment George's pyro-sacs ignited deep in his chest.

What the fuck? "Chancellor . . . ?"

Abilities or not, I still had my scythe and the dragon was within leaping distance. As I reached inside my cowl, Whitehead's hand restrained me. "Wait!"

Flame washed across us moments later, but amazingly, it didn't burn or even scorch my clothing.

"You are worthy," George snickered, sounding eerily like a mutant donkey braying, "and may proceed."

With that, the great lizard began to cough and retch until he regurgitated a metallic lever-type key more than three feet long onto the floor. It clanged loudly as it struck the smooth metal of the disc, and lay there, sizzling in bile and other caustic juices.

"For badness sake, George," Whitehead complained, "we are in a bit of a rush, you know. The Reaper's here to investigate the lapse in security. I'd appreciate it if you'd stop dawdling."

George grunted disdainfully, but lowered his head until his long and supple neck had uncoiled to its full length above us. He took a breath, then exhaled through his nostrils, showering us in ice crystals. In seconds, everything cooled enough to touch.

Whitehead moved forward, and I realized that an over-sized keyhole had appeared in the center of the dais. Kneeling, Whitehead closed his eyes and touched the key's shoulder above the shank.

"I am responsible for my sister's death."

A chime trilled through the air, whereupon the key slid along the floor and into the vacant opening. Then the oval-shaped bow began to turn of its own volition.

Clunk, clunk, clunk, snap!

The surface of the platform turned green and melted away, and I fell through into a fluidic medium. I expected to get wet, but no sooner had I plunged into the waiting vat than my senses reeled and I found myself somewhere else entirely.

What in the blazes?

From what I could see, we were now inside a bare stone cell, completely unadorned except for a grille in the center of the room and a couple of burning torches set into braziers against opposite walls. The atmosphere was warm and dry, and the slabs making up the compartment appeared free of mold and damp.

The metal grate demanded my attention, for it flickered within a heat mirage and emitted the betraying buzz of re-pressed power.

Whitehead walked toward it, stopped, and invited me forward: "If you'd be so kind as to do your thing, Reaper?"

Confused, I merely stared at him, so he continued, "Well, don't look at me. Only denizens who possess both damned and celestial dexterity can open the wards in here."

Denizens who possess . . . ? On a whim, I tried to project my farsight down through the granite blocks. *Hey, my abilities work aga– Wow!*

An incredible sight met my astral eyes.

Below us, two gigantic chambers nearly a mile in circumference were positioned one on top of the other. A short, ten-foot wide tunnel separated each. Water from the lower half fed in a constant loop into the upper level via a series of directional high-pressure pipes, creating a churning maelstrom above and a blistering cataract below.

Conditions within the narrow stricture must have been extreme, for I couldn't begin to calculate the volume of liquid passing through.

I zoomed in and spotted a spider's web network of filaments stretched across the midway point of the bore.

So what purpose does that serve?

"It's like a colossal egg timer," I muttered, "except it uses water instead of sand."

"That's right, and artifact one three one seven—the Golden Fleece—was positioned on the mesh you will have no doubt discerned through all that turbulence, yes?"

"The Golden Fleece?"

I recalled another portion of my latest clue:

Bring me the blanket of life,
A fleece to envelop my charter.
Gold wrapped, this mortal coil
Sparks nothing but death.

Oh, very clever. I thought Tesla was referring to the hellectrified meshing they use to cover the bullion pyramids. Once sealed under Satan's royal charter, no one except the highest ranking officials may go near, or they get fried. I laughed out loud. *But now I see Tesla's really done his homework.*

Taking my outburst as a sign of surprise, Whitehead carried on. "Yes, despite your high standing, there are relics down here you wouldn't have dreamed of. Totems of myth and legend that would cause mayhem if the populace was ever to discover they existed; and other things too, talismans straight out of your nightmares that would curdle the blood in your veins." He fingered a ripcord around his neck. "A heavy burden to bear, let me tell you."

"I don't get nightmares, Mister Whitehead, both they and my inner demons are frightened of me. Besides"—a sneaking suspicion began to gnaw at my liver—"I'm more concerned as to how your intruders managed to breach the fracture. You say it's pervasive in nature? Tell me, does it negate all forms of manipulation, mundane as well as occult?"

"Of course. Our Dark Lord even saw fit to install a celestial fuzzer to prevent heavenly intrusion."

"And how long has this level of security been in situ?"

"Phew . . ." Whitehead scratched his head. "For the Omega Class items? Just under three years."

So how did Tesla and Chopin circumvent the rift? The orbs might be versatile, but they can't operate outside of the normal Sheolspace or spacetime continuums. The Isle of Cogs proved their limitations. I suffered a moment's doubt. *And there is no way they could adapt them to work where neither divine nor devilish means hold sway; or is there?*

I felt sure the answer to this conundrum would present itself if I could still my thoughts enough to—

"Ahem?"

I turned to find Whitehead gesticulating repeatedly toward the hatch.

"If you please, Reaper. I'm just as keen as you about discovering how they overcame our defenses. And although the conditions inside are somewhat volatile, there might yet be sulforensic evidence available by which investigators can identify the scum responsible for bringing shame on this great institution."

His aura tingled red and black along the edges.

To say nothing of the fact your own ass is on the line. An earlier determination came to mind. *Now,* that's *an idea. If my deliberations have to wait, I just might bring your punishment forward.*

Aloud, I replied, "I'm right on it."

Walking swiftly across to the grate, I saw that it was indeed warded by two seals; one a heavenly sigil, the other inscribed in ancient Hellanese. Adjusting my position, I stood above them, legs wide, and placed one boot onto each character.

Dual esoteric signatures coursed up through the soles of my feet, along my spine and into my brain. Blending with them, I discerned what I needed to do to disable each one safely.

I see. It's an orphic binary code linked to the medium below. Simple yet effective, for very few would be able to add the heavenly element to the simultaneous telepathic axiom.

Shutting my eyes, I did my best to adopt a more tranquil aspect. Once achieved, I formed the prerequisite words in my mind and broadcast both celestial and occult variants at the same moment I spoke that same phrase aloud.

Te-up vas'nuph—Fliutdúseg. "Wet water."

Both glyphs illuminated like magnesium flares.

Crack!

The trellis began to swing up and over, forcing me to step aside. A deafening roar swelled from below. Whitehead backed away grimacing, his hands pressed firmly to his ears. I adjusted my sensitivity to compensate and looked down into the squall.

A luminous cauldron awaited, a pelagic borehole of death filled with aquamarine and turquoise currents, twisting and surging along at cyclonic speeds.

Hmm, a blender doesn't have to have metallic edges to chop you to pieces. Ah well, best get this over with.

Divesting myself of my cowl and weapon, I made a small pile on the flagstones next to the grille and placed my sickle at the very top.

I wonder if he'll go for it.

"Look after these, will you?" I said, without a second glance, "I won't be long."

And with that, I stepped up to the lip and jumped straight into the abyss.

Within a heartbeat, I was spinning head over heels and tumbling round and around so violently that it reminded me of the sport three enforcers had inflicted on me the year before during the ambush at the Spouting Pyramids of Geyser.

Damnation, the things I do to keep the Boss happy.

I was thankful I had suspended my respiration. The water was icy cold, and had I tried to simply hold my breath, the temperature and pressure would already have me gasping for a lungful of air.

The overload increased as suction pulled me down.

Submitting myself to inordinate gyroscopic forces, I projected my awareness through spume and froth. And this time, the speed at which I approached my target actually surprised me. Instinctively adapting to the flow, I allowed my molecules to blend with those of the torrent around me, then waited until I was on the final approach to the quivering web of cables. As I passed, I willed myself to coalesce slightly.

Even in my semi-somatic state, the press of water was stupendous, and it was only with the greatest degree of difficulty that I found I could move.

But it was enough.

My hand brushed against something resinous, something smooth and flat. Holding on tight, I fought against the relentless compression and rounded on my prize.

A resinous wafer had been wedged between the strands of the net. About half the size of a computer tablet, it was transparent and appeared to contain a crisp piece of watermarked paper that carried a stenciled message.

Fresh directions, no doubt.

Encompassing the clue within my tenuous threshold, I immediately phased away from the effervescent madness and materialized next to a startled chancellor of coin, who was desperately trying to extract my scythe from his body.

True to form, Whitehead hadn't been able to resist the temptation to meddle, and judging from the angle of impalement, had been inspecting the jewels along the main shaft of the sickle when he had given in to the impulse to press one of them. The medusanite tip had extended, piercing his belly and exiting via his ass, pinning him to the floor.

Now that gives a whole different meaning to the expression "tearing him a new one."

Whitehead was having difficulty breathing. A mixed pool of blood, urine and other foul juices tarnished the stones at his feet, and a fine sheen of sweat trickled down the sides of his neck to stain his starched white collar gray.

Strutting around him like a rooster, I clucked, "Did I forget to mention? Nobody can touch my weapon without triggering certain . . . safeguards." I paused in case he had something pertinent to say in reply, but all he could manage was a protruding bottom lip that quivered uncontrollably, and a shocked, wide-eyed expression. I continued, "That must really pinch. If you'd like me to end your misery, tell me: is the only way back to the wyrm chamber by the same way we came in?"

"Ye . . . yes, that's right," he gasped.

"Then if you want to live, you'd better act quickly, because I've got places to be and I'm certainly not leaving my scythe where it is."

I gestured, and my staff shot from its position with a morbid sucking sound. Unfortunately for Whitehead, it also ripped most of his entrails free. Voiding his bowels, he fell to his knees, whimpering.

In such a confined space, the stench was overpowering.

"What the devil have you been eating, man? Now hurry. If you want the pain to stop, take us home."

Catching his breath, Whitehead managed to lift his head, and groan, "The Old Lady of Threadneedle Street."

The air flickered and the darkness of the rupture returned, although the podium still glowed green from our previous encounter. George had remained close by, hovering like a gargantuan bat above his prey. I suspected that time moved very differently in this physics-warping pocket of non-reality, so didn't bother asking the obvious question.

"George, I'm glad you're still here. Listen closely . . ."

Reverting to ancient Hellanese, I declared, "*An moàithresh Satanase Thanatos, se lùthnech Sûktét—a' tráihlmeasg cumaech'd* (In my capacity as Satan's reaper, I invoke Shok-teth—the bond of compliance). *Do mogéill cumhach'd* (Submit to my authority)."

Impervious to the existence of the void about us, the dominion invoked by the utterance of one of Satan's most sacred tenets induced George's inbred compliance.

"State your demands, Reaper. I am compelled by ancient writ to obey."

"Seal all vaults and repositories until further notice. Allow no one in or out, and process no further deposits or withdrawals until someone from the Inquisitors' office notifies you, in person, that business may resume. Is that clearly understood?"

"It is, and shall be done."

I heard a faint sob behind me. Glancing back, I could see Whitehead looked as if he was about to breathe his last.

"George, are you able to activate the code key to send me back?"

"Under certain circumstances, yes, I am."

"And Shok-teth covers such a situation, yes?"

"Indeed it does."

"Excellent."

I held up one finger to ask his forbearance and strolled casually over to where the chancellor of coin had collapsed in the final stages of stupefaction. Placing my boot against his shoulder, I growled, "Sarah would still be ashamed of you," and pushed him over the edge.

Bad riddance.

"Then if you please, George, I have a riddle to decipher and more scumbags to kill."

Chapter 17: Joining the Dots

The Angel Grislington stood alone upon the torch deck adorning the highest point of the Statue of Lost Liberty and braced himself against the gales, for thunder and lightning blared in across the Frantic Ocean, bringing with it a storm front that corralled the rain into a seething mass intent on flaying the resolve of every denizen it encountered.

Though immune to the piercing chill and frenzied riot of icy shards that pounded his skin in a needle wash, he nevertheless found the tempo of the deluge soothing.

He looked down from his vantage point and out across New Hell Harbor, then on toward the Madhatten skyline, and thought back on the titillating events he had so recently witnessed in Juxtapose.

"A conjunction of possibilities looms on the horizon. How in heaven's name Grim hasn't connected the dots yet, I'll never know. Is he so blind, so preoccupied with trivial pursuits, or so content with being a lapdog that he fails to realize what he is?"

Grislington reexamined the specifics of the confrontation that had excited him.

"How extravagant were the flames that burned within him, and how poignant, for the answer to the riddle that is his identity was right there in front of him. Without guile, he acted on instinct and his true nature almost broke free; and against Erra and his Seven, no less!"

The angel shook his head at the audacity of Grim's strategy.

"Artfully played." Then a profound notion struck him: "Although not as cunning as the Arch Deceiver, I think. How prudent that Satan would arrive late. Perhaps he imagined solving two problems in one masterstroke? After all, what better way to remove a growing threat to your sovereignty than in an orgy of mutual destruction against those who would expose your shortcomings by their audit? Careful, Lucifer, lest you totter too close to the edge and fall prey to the fallout of your own finagle."

Spine-tingling laughter pealed through the air, revealing how close this celestial being faltered to an abyss of his own.

"And what brinksmanship. Notwithstanding the evident shock displayed by his fallen cronies, Satan continued to play the dutiful father. '*Look how I have empowered you, my son. Elevated you. Made you a prize above all others. Only you can protect my realm from those who would see all we have achieved together thrown down.*'" Grislington appeared incredulous. "And thinking he is nothing more than a child seeking the approval of his betters, Grim lapped it up. No wonder he wastes himself on wanton excess."

A mad gleam entered the angel's eyes.

"The Reaper is a chrysalis all right, one standing on the edge of a metamorphosis that will rock the very foundations of hell. All he needs is the right kind of stimulation, the right nurture to mature and transform . . . And I think I know how to provide it."

That gleam focused sharper as Grislington scanned the threadwork of flickering sodium arteries woven from thousands of glowing streetlamps on the other side of the harbor. Their light was sickly, lurid and vile; the perfect accompaniment to a city overflowing with denizens who infused the ether with emanations of lust, greed and depravation.

"And where better to start than here? This rabble needs stirring up. There must be hue and cry. Outrage and fear in one place after another." A moment's inspiration brought joy to his still beautiful face. "I know, perhaps I'll have more fun playing one side off against the other. What better artifice to provide the motivation for growth?"

His smile slowly turned into a lopsided leer that revealed the depth of the deranged landscape lurking within.

Grislington's head dropped forward as if contemplating a moment of prayer. His fingers caressed the jewel of his weapon. A ripple passed through his substance, and moments later, a Titan in dusty raiment wielding a shining sword stalked the highest palisade of one of hell's most infamous landmarks.

If it looks like an auditor and it talks like an auditor, it had better damned well act like one. But which of the seven to play, and how to proceed?

His astral gaze bored down through the statue and into the Bãlefire chamber beneath the island.

Of course, this monument is dedicated to Satan's glory and reminds all those arriving in New Hell by sea that here is a place under his pernicious protection.

The evil smirk returned.

Grislington stepped forward into empty space and allowed the force of gravity to hurtle him headlong toward the foundation pedestal, more than two hundred feet below. He struck with the force of a mountain, and as the island witnessed the power of heaven unleashed for the first time in an age, it cracked wide, the waters rushed in, and all hell broke loose.

*

The repetitive thudding sound didn't falter once as it echoed through the walls of the Deputy Director's private suite—*Diabolical Enforcement Agency – Drugs Division.* A sure sign to Yamato Takeru and everyone else gathered in the conference room that Champ Ferguson had caught his second wind and was now well into his stride.

Situated on the top floor of the southeastern wing of the Pentagram, the Director's offices afforded commanding views of the Ptomatic River and the ornamental swamp bordering two of the parking lots. Not that its privileged aspect would mean a great deal to those on the receiving end of the steady torrent of pain and misery raining down on them at this moment.

Yamato smiled. While Champ was one of the most uncouth individuals he had ever met, and someone who possessed the restraint of an enraged bull hyped up on redflag-laced amphetamines, he was nevertheless an effective examiner, a proficiency first honed during his years as a Confederate guerilla during the American Civil War.

And, of course, on occasions like this when time is of the essence, it provides certain dividends.

Sudden silence made everyone look up from what they were doing. A reaver skittered out of the ancillary room the Hounds had commandeered for interrogation and ran off into one of the adjacent offices.

No doubt another snippet of information on which I must act immediately.

As the door swung shut, the pressure hinge slowed its

progress and Yamato was able to get a good look inside.

Champ knelt on the floor opposite the only suspect left alive, one bound with duct tape, hand and foot, into an office chair. A single glance confirmed the fellow had suffered a most intensive form of questioning, for his features were marred by a sea of bruises and broken teeth. At least one ear had been ripped off, and ruby stains spread from multiple lacerations about his cheeks, neck and chest, and down across what remained of his once white shirt.

Only one left, eh? Unholy shit, he's not hanging around today.

From what Yamato could see, Champ's blood-spattered face was becalmed, even serene as he carefully removed his victim's intestines via a small incision in the subject's stomach. Working slowly, and hand over hand, he neatly coiled the growing ring of entrails into a mound on the floor between them. As he labored, he hummed a quiet tune and rocked gently to and fro on his heels.

He caught sight of Yamato watching and gave a cheery wave.

"Just wrappin' things up. Gimme a minute or two, and I'll be done."

He winked, and the door closed with a hiss and a click.

Several of the secretaries who had gathered in the conference room to assist the Hounds in retrieving data from the system appeared shocked by what they had just witnessed. They stared at Yamato as if he had sprouted horns.

Yes, ladies, he thought to himself, *guilty by association.*

Smiling sweetly, he ignored any further silent protestations and continued his examination of Daphne Hemlock's file.

So, my Hounds transferred our lady of the hour here from the Palais de L'Injustice *across in Perish, along with*

Jeremiah Quinine—who, as luck would have it, Champ is torturing as I read the latest sitrep, which tells me that both she and Quinine indulged in a strange ménage-a-quatre *with two fellow workers, Ivy Hedera and Lily Foxglove. Their relationship became public knowledge; they faced discipline, and then policy guidelines, strictly enforced, caused their reposting at their own expense to avoid any possibility of compromised intermediaries.*

"Hmm, I have a feeling it was already too late by then."

Yamato flicked channels to view the disciplinary records of each suspect.

"As I expected. Perfect. Until this incident, they were exemplary denizens, as you would expect of Devil's Children."

But why not split them up completely, just to be sure?

Yamato enlarged a third screen showing each agent's work profile.

"Aha! Quinine and Hemlock had an affinity with each other's minds, essential for undercover work And yes, the same goes for Hedera and Foxglove. Although in their case, they were posted to Vilencia together."

Something about the situation still struck Yamato as odd.

Strange that so many agents from one department should suddenly start having problems with professional misconduct?

As a precaution, Yamato began a separate search, looking for further common denominators.

At that moment, the door to the interrogation office crashed open and Champ strode back into the conference room, whistling a merry tune and licking the blood of the detainees from the palms of his hands.

Yamato struggled to keep himself from laughing, for one of the typists was staring at his colleague in open-mouthed revulsion. Champ caught sight of the ill-conceived expression and, true to form, extended an inappropriate finger, maintaining eye contact with her as he slowly sucked the offending digit clean from top to bottom . . . top to bottom . . . top to bottom . . .

Okay, Yamato sent telepathically, *cut the crap and let's talk.*

Champ continued leering at the woman for a moment longer, then bared the identical finger of his other hand. "Pretty missy," he called, wiggling his eyebrows at the same time, "I don't suppose you'd like to clean this one for me?"

For good measure, Champ waggled his tongue.

Oh, for Satan's sake.

Repulsed, the secretary quickly looked away, and Champ started to walk across to Yamato's desk. Unfortunately, he kept his hand extended and proffered it to everyone in turn until they all found something else to occupy their attention.

These souls are helping us, Yamato scolded. *I know it's difficult, but do show a little restraint around them.*

"Ah, I was just havin' a little fun, is all," Champ muttered out loud. He came to sit on the corner of the desk. "And what I lack in manners, I make up for in results."

Suddenly alert, Yamato leaned forward.

"Do tell."

"Not that it comes as too much of a surprise, but Quinine and Hemlock are definitely on Chopin's payroll. Hedera and Foxglove, too. From what Quinine could fathom, it all started about a year ago when they met a high falutin' doctor at one of the places they used to hang out at in Perish."

Cream and his damned concoctions, no doubt.

"The doc went there with a couple of friends. One was a wiry little runt who kept rubbin' his hands together; and the other, Quinine described as kinda intense, with eyes that could melt lead. Anyhoo, although they didn't end up spendin' too much time together initially, it looks as if the skinny guy would send the Children a thext, and they'd all feel an overwhelmin' compulsion to meet up and do stuff."

Subliminal conditioning? Aloud, Yamato added, "Stuff?"

"Quinine couldn't explain it clearly. There was some kind of mental block preventin' him from sayin' or rememberin' certain things. That's why I took so long with his interrogation. I had to overcome the obstruction and go deeper. Even so, I was only partially successful as I ended up killin' him, but at least I got a few addresses before he eventually checked out."

"Did you not think to keep him undead for long enough so that Strawberry and her team could interrogate him properly?"

"Jumpin' Jehoshaphat, brother," Champ complained, "I couldn't really give a fuck. It's not my job to go diggin' into the whys and the wherefores. I just catch 'em and smoke 'em and leave all that fiddly stuff to someone else."

Ping!

The results of Yamato's latest query were ready. As Champ continued to pontificate, Yamato chose to ignore him and flicked through the various entries instead.

". . . not what we do. Anyway, it doesn't matter . . . I've snuffed 'em. Bad Breath has his magic ball of tricks . . . still there, stashed away under the Mortuary. When they're reassigned, he'll be able to get what we've missed and—"

"You say you managed to get a few addresses?" Yamato cut in. "Would you mind telling me where?"

Champ thought for a moment.

"Several we already knew about in Perish, Dark Cairo and here in New Hell. But he seemed mighty reluctant to give up Vilencia, and one by the Colonosseum across in Rime."

"The Colonosseum borehole?"

"Yup, that's what I thought. All sorts of icy shit leaks through from the frozen wastes of Niflheim. They have fogs that create dead pockets, mists that suck you into temporal mazes and haars that will freeze your balls where you stand. I tell you, outside of Juxtapose, which is too close to our lair, it's the perfect place to hide."

"I'm inclined to agree, old friend," Yamato tapped the screen, "because the list of alternate accommodations I have here doesn't mention Rime at all. You've done well."

Champ's face brightened at the compliment.

"So we have a little skiin' trip in front of us?"

Yamato studied the computer screen and pondered their options.

"Yes, I believe we do, but don't pack your winter woolies just yet. Remember, Hedera and Foxglove are much closer. What say we try to kill three birds with one stone and swing by the other addresses first? It'll take a few days, but you never know . . . ?"

"I'm game for anythin' that involves killin'."

"Round trip it is, then. And once we've removed any possible threat from Hemlock's cohorts locally, we can take our time tracking the lady herself. I don't care how deep she goes into the frozen wastes; we'll ensure there are more than just chestnuts roasting on an open fire when we catch her."

"Brother, I suddenly feel in a carin' sharin' mood," Champ crowed. He held out his hand, bloodied little finger extended. "Would you care to clean my pinkie?"

Yamato began to salivate.

"Do you know, I think I will?"

*

No matter how Chopin tried, he couldn't seem to ease the constant pressure still building between his temples. It felt as if a tiny gremlin highway maintenance crew had somehow managed to burrow in through his spine, with the sole intent of employing a whole host of jackhammers against the inside of his skull.

He moaned aloud and curled into a tighter ball on his bed.

"Assprin?" Tesla offered. "Or what about a Badvil?"

Chopin waved his associate away. "Thank you, but no. You know how I feel about being force-fed any form of medication."

"Well, you've got to take something. I need you back on your feet as soon as possible and that won't happen if I keep pouring chilled wine down your neck."

The mere mention of his usual remedy gave Chopin an idea.

"Perhaps an icepack might work?"

"I'll go get one in a moment." Tesla sat alongside his longtime co-conspirator and placed the back of his hand against a clammy forehead. "I told you the side effects of using the orb in such a manner would be dramatic. The odd hour here and there gives us an advantage. But to distort the reality fields to such an extreme creates a temporal fugue that can unhinge weaker minds. We were fortunate to emerge with our sanity intact."

"It had to be done, my friend. How else could we elude the schism? Thank badness such contrivances are as costly to Satan as this one was to us. If he'd had the time and circumstance to create more, we'd be marooned here in this uncreative shithole with no way of fulfilling our ambitions." Chopin craned forward and made an effort to focus on Tesla's expression. "Anyway, *you* don't seem much the worse for wear."

Tesla removed a box of painkillers from his top jacket pocket and waved them in Chopin's face.

"That's because I've been popping half-a-dozen of these every hour or so. Bathmat tongue aside, they *do* work. I wish you'd try them."

Chopin's head flopped back down onto the pillow and he groaned again, fearful the eggshell fragility of his cranium might shatter and spill its stir-fried contents across the sheets. "No, no, no. I don't think I could stomach the taste, or the constipation."

Tesla sighed. "Then you'd better hope your method of recovery doesn't cost us too dearly. The culmination of years of planning is at hand, and I cannot operate the sword alone. Unless . . . ?"

Though blighted with pain-induced tunnel vision, Chopin couldn't miss how Tesla's face lit up as he hit on an idea. "You seem to have been blessed with a moment's inspiration?"

"What about the Fleece? If the mere thought of touching it on your vision quest generated temporary respite, just imagine what its invigorating presence would do now."

"I cannot, Nikola. Remember, the periapt is as mysterious as it is rare. Try as I might, I have discovered no definitive guidelines regarding its use. Can I draw on its authority but once, as was the case with the Cup of Tartarus, or a thousand times? No, for fear of undoing all we have striven to achieve, I dare not invoke its might now. Our patience has weathered the passage of decades; it can endure a few more days until I am strong enough to attempt the *Sword of Uncovered Secrets* unaided. Once we have the key to entering the Colonnade unharmed we can move swiftly, for there will be nothing to stop us. Not Satan. Not the paradox that is Grim. Not even that accursed angel who seems hell-bent on causing mischief and needless confrontation."

Tesla chuckled and started toward the door.

"Then I'd best get your icepack. The sooner we reduce the swelling between your ears, the sooner we can end this."

Watching him go, Chopin felt a moment's concern.

"Nikola, what of our thorns?"

"Already taken care of, Frédéric. Our gardeners have been dispatched, and I imagine that any time now, they'll begin pruning."

*

Following my daring escapade where I had plucked the latest clue from the devil's cauldron of all traps, it had claimed pride of place on my dining room table. And there it remained, for I was no closer to understanding its contents now than I had been two days previously, when I had returned home in triumph.

For the benefit of my latest visitors who had volunteered to try to help me crack the code, I projected an enlarged version of the complete verse into the air.

It read:

Pinioned within a silvered sheen
I have no substance,
For it is a medium portraying a mere perception of death
Whilst liberated from the excess of time.
Congruence and confluence are but flightless messengers
Encapsulated in an eternity of personal reflections,
A colonnade of captured moments, always changing,
Where liberty stares back, forever lost.

"I see what you mean about obscure," Ferenc Nádasdy, one of my best Inquisitors, acknowledged. "I've always prided myself on possessing an analytical mind, but this? Gods, can Tesla not write in a manner that other intellects might at least have a chance of understanding?"

"You don't understand *me* half the time, sweetie," Elizabeth Báthory, his wife and co-interrogator chirped as she waltzed past us, naked as the day she was born, dancing to unheard tunes. "So when you think about it, you're in the perfect position to make sense of the nonsensical, yes?"

Ferenc and I made eye contact. Because of the depraved excesses she had enjoyed in life, Elizabeth—aka the *Blood Countess*—was usually off in Batshit Crazy Land at the best of times. But every now and then, the childlike logic of her altered sense of perspective could really kick you in the nuts. And this was definitely one of those moments.

We did our best to ignore her, and I picked up on Ferenc's last inference. "Yes, Tesla's an out and out genius and everybody knows it. There's no need for him to be so incomprehensible. And yet he is, which makes me wonder if he still wants to make a point somehow."

"Make a point? Ha! What's the point in making a point if no one actually understands it? All you do is end up looking like a blithering idiot."

"Precisely." I threw my hands in the air and stomped across to my sound system. "This still doesn't help us get any closer to what's really going on."

So far, this conundrum had eluded the sharpest intellectuals on both my teams. Whenever anything like this had bothered me before, I would usually put the immediate problem to the back of my mind and let it simmer there whilst busying myself with other tasks—completing reports, assisting in the dungeons, training with my staff, even listening to music—as all such chores had helped in the past. And yet, here I was, forty-six and a half hours later, no closer to understanding what I was looking for, or where. My in- and out-trays were empty, my Inquisitors put through their paces, and I even whiled away some time in idle reflection while listening to my complete collections of Bauhaus, Evanescence, and Clan of Xymox.

And still no inspiration.

"That's it then, this problem calls for either Nightwish or Disturbed." I juggled two CDs between my hands. "Nightwish it is—"

I popped the disc into the player, turned up the volume, and let the melodic sound of Floor Jansen's voice fill the air. Elizabeth immediately changed step to match the tempo of some actual music, while Ferenc tapped his toes and leaned across the table to take a better look at the wafer-ensconced message itself.

He picked it up and turned to face me.

"And you say Chopin and Tesla managed to negotiate a void schism and then break into an Omega Class vault, just so they could taunt you with *this*?"

"Yup, making off with none other than the Golden Fleece in the process."

"Incredible."

"Bloody frustrating more like. If the Isle of Cogs debacle achieved one good thing, it proved once and for all that the orbs do have their limitations. They might be able to wreak havoc anywhere within the spacetime and Sheolspace continuums, but they can't operate beyond it, bec–"

"And don't forget the rest, rest, rest," Elizabeth twittered as she flounced by.

I tried to carry on as if she weren't there.

"Because as we know, the Bunker fracture lies outside the normal laws of physics and metaphysics, so it's impossible to breach or circumvent by any known mundane or arcane contrivance. An unnerving experience, let me tell you."

"Easy peasy lemon squeezy." On this occasion, Elizabeth curtseyed before performing an unerringly perfect *attitude derrière* ballet move.

Both Ferenc and I stopped to stare.

"What do you mean, my love?" he crooned.

The frenzied cast to Elizabeth's eyes melted away and she adopted a more conversational posture and tone.

"I mean, *tempus fugit,* darling, or perhaps *tempus est fluidum* would be more accurate in this case."

"What?" *Time is . . .* I wracked my brains, dragging up a spot of Latin to ensure the obvious was, in fact, correct: *Ah: time is fluid.*

Elizabeth turned a rare lucid look my way and added, "You forgot the contents of your own report, Daemon. Understandable, I suppose, with all that's been going on." She tapped the side of her head with a finely manicured finger. "You must have scrambled your wits. Welcome to the club." Then she giggled. "The orbs don't only take you anywhere you want, they take you . . ."

"Anywhen!" I breathed, thunderstruck to have overlooked an obvious factor of their function.

At that moment, the "Yours Is An Empty Hope" track started playing on the CD.

Hmm, even Nightwish karma seems to be taking a dig at my expense.

Then I sobered, for Elizabeth's timely reminder struck another chord.

"So that strange malady I suffered on my visit to Cadavers Lunatic Asylum must have occurred because I inadvertently triggered the temporal component. That's how I gained so much time on Chopin and Tesla, more than . . ." My face fell. "But I don't know how I did it or if I'll be able to do it again?"

"Only because nobody thought to show you how it's done, silly," Elizabeth stated so matter of-factly that my jaw dropped. Dancing up to me, she stood on tiptoes, pushed my chin up with one finger, kissed my nose, and concluded, "But you'll soon learn." Then she let out a loud gasp and fell to the floor.

Ferenc's shoulders dropped as he gazed at his wife's form, spread in dramatic repose across the Persian rug. He sniffed and muttered, "Stop being childish, Lizzie. You know you're one of the few who can touch Daemon without consequence."

One hazel eye blinked open. "You mean I'm still alive?"

"No, my love, you've not been alive for a very long time," he bent to help her to her feet, "but what we have here and now will suffice."

They embraced for a moment and enjoyed a brief kiss; then Elizabeth was off again, dancing with the fairies to a melody clearly at odds with the music currently issuing from the speakers.

I smiled. The quirks of their relationship were unique and reminded me that now I was back in human form, I had a lot of catching up to do. Once this was all over, I would have to find some way to get all sorts of personal and down and dirty with Strawberry.

Overactive death touch or no.

Sadly, such reunions would have to wait, as Elizabeth's insights had presented me with the seeds of another idea I needed to pursue.

Tapping on the back of a chair, I drew Ferenc's attention

and looked down at the tablet in his grasp. Then I glanced at his wife and nodded.

"What do you think?"

Understanding my intent, he replied, "It's certainly worth a shot. Hang on . . ."

Ferenc reached out as Elizabeth capered past and caught her in mid frolic. Holding the clue before her face, he adroitly steered her toward the table. Like a moth to a flame, Elizabeth took a seat and immediately became engrossed in the subject passage, her head kinked to one side.

Softly, he whispered in her ear. "We'd really appreciate your help with this puzzle."

I held my breath as her gaze skimmed the contents of the poem.

She read it again, and this time her lips moved and she started to whisper certain phrases out loud. Suddenly, her eyes flared and a look of immense sorrow clouded her features.

With tears streaming down her cheeks, she cried, "Poor angel, to be thus emasculated and teased with the means of his escape."

Angel?

An electric shock coursed along my spine. "What do you mean by 'escape'?"

But it was no use; Elizabeth had buried her head in her arms and now sobbed uncontrollably. I backed away and gestured for Ferenc to step in and console his wife.

"Comfort her, get her lucid, and for fuck's sake, get a more detailed explanation of what she meant, ASAP. Understood?"

"I'll do what I can."

Leaving them alone, I strode out of the dining room and off toward my study. I had to work hard to suppress the static sparks of excitement skipping along the surface of my skin, for although the subject matter of the clue still remained a mystery, one important aspect about this latest escapade was now glaringly clear.

For Chopin and Tesla to leave me a cryptogram like that means they're ready to involve all the key players together in one place. Well, fools rush in . . . So I think I'll take my time and try to determine why *it is they want the angel and me to confront each other. And at the same time, I'll get Bella and Donna to find out what they can about the time travel aspect of the portal generators. Who knows; if I play this right, perhaps it'll be me springing an endgame of my own choosing?*

"And blood will flow."

Chapter 18: A Cat Among the Pigeons

From the outside, there was nothing to distinguish this particular apartment block from all the others crowded together here in Plaza del Górgona, in the ancient gated municipality of Vilencia, Juxtapose.

Like every other structure in the city, it had been constructed in a baroque castellan style from solid stone replete with internal and external gargoyles and buttresses, arched double-leafed casement windows leading onto balconied pediments, and an assortment of exterior climbing weeds. The effect did much to add an air of steadfastness and significance to this, one of the oldest districts in Hisspania.

The inside of the premises, however, proved another matter entirely.

Doors to four ground floor residences stood ajar. Blood pooled in thickening gobs on rugs, against varnished skirting boards, or trickled in trellised patterns between floor tiles as large as paving slabs. In several places, whitewashed walls bore stains in a brazen Picasso-esque explosion of gore and entrails.

Of the residents themselves or their bodies there was no trace, for they had already begun the process by which their

essences would return to the one place in the entire underworld that everybody feared: the Mortuary.

Those responsible for the carnage still stalked the halls,
keen to ensure none were in a position to signal a warning to
their target and thorough in their determination to erase all
witnesses from existence.

Charles Guiteau edged up the stairs leading to the first
floor, silenced gun in hand. "Are you sure this is the right address?" he whispered around a mouthful of blood.

Isabella Castile closed her eyes, raised her chin and
sniffed the air.

"Oh, she's here all right. Her scent is . . . *distinctive*.
Moist, succulent, and if I'm not mistaken, contains the heady
tint of controlled panic."

"Why? Do you think she knows we're here?"

"No. I suspect that particular aroma is due entirely to a
sense of impending doom. The Reaper and his Hounds are on
her tail, and as clever as she thinks she is, Miss Hemlock un-
derestimates their tenacity. She's in a rush to be away."

"She's gonna get a shock when we turn up then," Guiteau
snarled, his face creased in a mixture of pain and delight, "as
we'll give her a sendoff she's not expecting."

"Keep the noise down. She's a DEA agent and if she
hears any unusual sounds or even suspects—"

"Watch out!"

Guiteau suddenly ducked back into the stairwell and pantomimed for Isabella to look up high, along the near wall of
the next landing.

Scooting close to the railings, Isabella edged around the
corner until she spotted what Guiteau had seen.

I noticed a tiny covert button camera positioned on the
ceiling at the far end of the adjoining passageway. Close to

an exterior window, it would afford its operator a clear and unobstructed view of the entire corridor on this level.

Isabella's eyes flared.

Shit! If we'd brought the orb with us instead of stashing it, this wouldn't have been a problem.

"What do we do now?" Guiteau croaked. "Blow our way in?"

"Shut up, I'm think–" At that moment, the door opposite their target opened and a dusky beauty stepped out.

"*Hola, hermosa niña* (Hello, beautiful girl)," she breathed.

Attired in a dark blue dress suit, crisp white blouse and highly polished black shoes, it was immediately apparent to Isabella that she was looking at a local Blue Suit.

Isabella glanced down at her own navy skirt.

Perfect.

Jumping forward, she pushed Guiteau back against the wall, held a finger to her lips, and handed him her gun.

The click of heels on tiles signified their next victim was approaching swiftly.

As the Blue Suit rounded the corner, Isabella smiled and embraced her like a long lost friend. "*Encantado de concerte* (Nice to meet you)."

Although confused, the young woman relaxed and automatically responded in kind, only to stiffen a moment later as the stiletto blade pierced her heart.

Isabella glanced at the name badge.

Lucia.

Deftly removing Lucia's jacket, Isabella stared into the dying girl's eyes and supported her in her arms as she gently lowered her onto the steps.

That's it, my lovely, give me your memories. Go on, give me—

Their light fading, Lucia's pupils suddenly dilated. She went limp, and it was Isabella's turn to savor the sweet rigidity of impalement shared as an orgasmic wave surged across her.

Up close and personal is always best. Isabella could hear Guiteau's breath rattling in his chest. She glanced up and confirmed he was clearly aroused. *Though not with everybody.*

Standing, Isabella swung her arms into the appropriated jacket and reclaimed her gun.

"Have you got the plastic explosive?"

"Huh? Yes, yes, I have. Why?"

"Okay, prime it and keep it in your hand. We're going to walk toward Lucia's apartment as if we belong here. It's only ten yards away, so we'll be on target in seconds. I'll pretend I'm not well, so drape your arm around me and keep your head low, like you're giving me sweet-talk and support. As we arrive, I'll fall back against the wall on the far side of the door. That way, you'll be able to use my body as cover and affix the putty to the bitch's lock. If she's looking through the camera, Hemlock might get suspicious but won't really know what's going on until it's too late."

"And the back blast?"

"I'll mumble something about needing fresh air. Just lead me toward the window. Even on a three second fuse that should put us outside the concussive arc."

"Sounds like a plan."

Guiteau removed a small block of wax from his coat pocket and inserted a small metallic rod into one end. He fiddled with the cap for a moment, swallowed repeatedly to clear his airway, then looked up. "Okay, ready to go."

In tandem, they moved through the hallway, Isabella moaning and groaning and leaning heavily upon her chaperone, Guiteau offered appropriate reassurances whilst ensuring he supported his charge, allowing no opportunity for her to fall.

Professionals both, they didn't rush but made their slow and painful way toward their goal.

Isabella tripped and fell back. "Satan help me, I'm going to be sick—"

"Quick, this way," Guiteau offered, rushing to assist, and dragging his companion toward the safety of the nearby casement.

Boom!

The percussive wave blew dust and myriad bits of shrapnel into the corridor. Isabella felt the floor heave beneath her feet. Guiteau was already running, gun up and held at the ready. Arriving, he put his shoulder to what remained of the door and disappeared inside.

Hot on his heels, Isabella adopted a more cautious approach and paused for just a moment at the entrance to scan the layout.

A single hall stretched out before her, culminating in an open area that looked like a kitchen. Closer still, paired doorways on either side of the passage blocked the way to further mystery.

Up ahead, Guiteau approached the first room. He gripped a brass handle and started to twist. Abruptly he tensed and went rigid with shock, teeth bared. Isabella heard a distinct sizzling sound, before the smell of scorched flesh and singed hair became overpowering.

A figure darted out of nowhere, running right to left from the back of the building toward the street side. Isabella saw a bright flash and ducked.

Clack. Clack.

Blood misted the walls and Guiteau careened away from the trap with two neat bullet holes in his neck and cheek.

Quick as lightning, Isabella returned fire and sprinted inside. Projecting her senses forward, she caught the distinctive neon-red glow of intense passion.

Someone is in fear and trying to escape.

Moving with uncanny speed and agility, Isabella leaped ahead and bowled into the kitchen just in time to catch a silhouette, dark against the midday light of paradise, outlined against the window.

Oh, no you don't.

The figure braced itself on either side of the sash frame and then jumped.

Isabella reacted and a scream split the air.

The assassin smiled with satisfaction, for while the bulk of her target's body dropped from view, an arm remained behind, skewered to the interior wall by the knife firmly embedded through the back of a delicately proportioned hand.

A scrabbling sound issued from outside and a face reappeared above the sill.

"That's quite far enough, my lovely," Isabella crooned. "Chopin and Tesla asked me to relay their thanks for all the hard work you've done on their behalf. Sadly, it's time to bring your invaluable assistance to an end."

She edged closer and pressed the barrel of her gun against Hemlock's forehead.

"But there's so much more I could still do," Hemlock gasped, "if you'd tell—"

"Our employers don't agree," Isabella snapped. "And don't concern yourself with incriminating thoughts and memories. I'm using rip-bullets. You won't remember"—*Phut!*—"a thing."

Hemlock's head rocked back, tearing her hand free of its mooring . . . almost. A long streak of blood trailed away from a single remaining finger, which had been wedged against the guard of the stiletto. Retrieving her dagger, Isabella allowed the digit to fall to the floor and contented herself by licking her weapon clean.

"Mmm." The tang of a coppery reward made her stomach flutter.

Such a shame I didn't have time to play. Never mind, with this one down, I still have two more I can satisfy my urges wi–

"Seven shades of unholy shit!"

Guiteau's cursing grated like jagged talons across the silken landscape of her nerves. Disturbed, Isabella reluctantly returned to the land of the unliving. Tapping the flat of her blade against her lips, she watched as Guiteau staggered into the kitchen, massaging the side of his neck and face where bullets hit him. His wounds, she noted with interest, were already knitting over.

"It gets worse every goddam time," Guiteau complained. A slight tremor and rumble of thunder shuddered along the length of the street outside. "I tell you, Charlotte, if Chopin and Tesla don't let me have some form of payback against the Undertaker, I just might have to go off-book. He's making my unlife an insufferable misery."

"Suck it up, you baby. This is hell; what do you expect? Anyway, I don't know what in Hades you're complaining about; most denizens would bite off their arm for the ability to heal quickly, even if you do gargle every time you speak. The way you're carrying—"

Something impinged at the edge of her awareness. Something dangerous.

Guiteau noticed her look of concern. "What is it? What's wrong?"

Ignoring his query, Isabella sprang to the window and peeped outside, only to duck away almost immediately.

"Fuck! Hell Hounds."

"Here?" Guiteau spluttered, spraying blood across the floor.

"No, swanning around in the darkest depths of purgatory." She rounded on her partner and started dragging him along the hallway. "Of course *here*, you fool."

"How in Azazel's name did they manage to get this close without you sensing them?"

"Easy, they have a portal generator. Probably the one they recovered from you after your last encounter with them."

Guiteau glanced at his hands and sneered.

"But what if Hedera and Foxglove return?"

"You think that's likely with Hell Hounds sniffing around?" Isabella chided. "No, they'll have fled to the next rendezvous, where they await Hemlock's arrival. Fortunately, we know where that's likely to be."

"So we're simply going to run away?"

Isabella checked her stride to look Guiteau in the eye.

"Unless you'd like the ninja menace out there to finish the job he started on you at the Empire Stake Building, yes. Now cut the macho bullshit and let's get going. We have a job to do."

*

Weapons drawn and senses sharp, Champ and Yamato edged silently forward through the debris.

Champ dropped to one knee at the ruined entrance to the apartment to examine various fragments and scuffmarks within the rubble. Maintaining cover, Yamato stood over his friend and continued to scrutinize their surroundings.

"What do you see, Champ?"

"Well, if I'm readin' the spoor right, whoever trashed this place left in a hurry, and from the look of it, only a few minutes ago." He leaned back and pointed toward a rear fire escape at the end of the landing. "Thataway."

"So, we just missed them . . . pity."

"'Fraid so." Champ's face creased in grudging appreciation. "They're good too. In spite of their rush, they took the time to clear up. Apart from the obvious destruction, there's hardly anythin' to betray that the assassins were here."

"It looks like we were right to swing by this address first, then?"

Yamato noticed the dark stain spread across the back wall and drew his partner's attention to it.

"Yeah, I saw that," Champ acknowledged, "but whose blood is it: Hedera's, Foxglove's, or Hemlock's?"

"There's only one way to find out for sure." Yamato altered his perspective and allowed his astral sight to float through the interior of the apartment. "I'm not picking up any unlife signs, but you can never be too sure. I tell you what, let's do a quick sweep and see what we can find. You cover the rear, and I'll clear the rooms overlooking the main street."

In three, two, one—go!

They peeled away from each other and crashed through their respective doors.

Yamato found himself in a well appointed bedroom, fashionably furnished in Spanish oak fitments. Nevertheless, the place was a mess. Various items of clothing hung from half-open drawers and closets or trailed in disarray along the floor. An overturned suitcase lay on its side, its contents strewn across the quilt.

Whoever was here got disturbed. Then he examined more closely the items chosen for travel. *And they were intending to go somewhere a damned sight chillier than the balmy shores of Juxtapose: We were right.*

Encouraged, Yamato proceeded next door and discovered a spacious lounge filled with large couches, a widescreen TV, coffee tables and a separate work desk equipped with an expensive-looking computer. The light at the base of the tower unit glowed blue, signifying a machine left running until reaching standby mode.

Grasping the mouse, he swished it from side to side and was rewarded by the whine of the system rebooting.

"I got diddlysquat my side," Champ muttered as he entered the room, "till I entered the kitchen, that is. There are at least two types of blood residue across the floor, wall, and windowsill in there. Exterior stonework as well. What about you?"

"Odd indicators here and there that someone was planning to leave in a hurry. Though the evidence tends to suggest they didn't make it."

"You think someone got ghosted?"

"You tell me. Were there any trails leading away from this place out in the street under the kitchen window?"

"Nope, not a single one."

"There you go then. All the signs indicate one of our targets was here, they got disturbed, and were dispatched with prejudice."

Champ spied the computer. "So, what have you got there?"

"I'm just about to find out."

Yamato hunkered down in front of the screen as the last page to be used illuminated. It revealed an open unaddressed email that nevertheless looked complete. It read:

We'll be waiting for you at Perry & Bing's cabin. XXX

Above it were two photo attachments showing topside entertainers from the latter half of the twentieth century.

Yamato chuckled. "Well, well, well. It looks as if the information you extracted from Quinine about Niflheim was spot on."

"In what way?"

"Look at the wording of the message. It says '*We'll* be waiting' That has to be from either Hedera or Foxglove. I'm betting Hemlock tipped them off as soon as she'd murdered the reaver back at the Pentagram and they got out of here fast, leaving a little pointer as to where they wanted to meet up."

"How do you know they're definitely talkin' about Niflheim though?"

Yamato tapped the screen. "That's Bing Crosby and Perry Como. Black Velvet likes to listen to them while she's interrogating prisoners back at the Den: something about creating the right mood." He shrugged. "Anyway, I've been forced to listen to their music enough to know they both had hit songs that were extremely festive in nature. Put it all together and what we have here is a cryptic clue from Hedera and Foxglove that lets Hemlock know exactly where to go."

"Ha! They're in for a long wait then."

"True, at least until we find out where in Niflheim they've gone."

Champ suddenly frowned.

"Hey, was the computer off when you got here?"

"No, it was on but had gone idle, why?"

"I'm just thinkin'—odd for me, I know—but if it wasn't illuminated and our assassins only left just before we arrived, does that mean they won't know about the message?"

Nice spot.

"That's a strong possibility."

"So we'll get there ahead of them?"

Grasping his partner by the shoulder, Yamato tried his best not to spoil a rare inspirational moment. "I'd certainly like to think so, my friend, but when has hell *ever* been that easy on us?"

*

The Angel Grislington was in a distinctly sour mood. Sheathed within a sphere of invisibility, he had concealed himself in the long grass high on a hilltop overlooking one of the busiest theme parks in New Hell, brooding over his lot.

And with good reason.

In the guise of various Sibitti enforcers, he had spent the last few days conducting a series of lightning raids in one realm after another, committing atrocities, each more audacious than the last. To no avail, it seemed, for no matter what he did, his acts failed to assuage the growing dissatisfaction gnawing away at his soul.

Yesterday, his toils had culminated in the quenching of the Fire Falls of Infernium, situated within Lower Hades; a feat triggering subterranean earthquakes that had not only destroyed hundreds of square miles of the Kilner Wilderland, but had also generated the release of noxious fumes into the atmosphere that had poisoned thousands.

This morning, he had started his day by boiling dry the Scourge Fens of Plagus. That act had caused the ever-present clouds lingering above the swamp to combust and, because they were caustic in nature, the ensuing conflagration had resulted in scores of denizens being flambéed alive.

And yet, not once had his actions elicited the response he had hoped for.

"It seems that unless I confine my efforts to New Hell itself, or its nearby principalities, neither Satan nor his minions care a fig. How does Erra stand it? Where is the sport in destroying those who are incapable of offering meaningful resistance? And what satisfaction can he possibly gain from vanquishing those who are already downtrodden and beaten? No, I tire of this charade and hanker for something different."

Grislington stretched his shoulders. The tightness across his back still lingered, regardless of the fact that millennia had passed since his diminution.

"If only I were free to express my essence in the way I was created to do." His gaze came back into focus and skimmed the stain smeared across the vast and distant horizon. "But now I am like this world; a pale reflection of my former self and a fitting addition to endless decay and drudgery."

That notion struck him as funny.

"But at least I've not been corrupted as much as my most worthy antagonist, shortsighted fool that he is. I really must take the time to educate him as to his true nature before the end. Talk about putting the cat among the pigeons. It's bound to make our inevitable confrontation so much more interesting."

Grislington sighed and looked back down into the valley where a growing crowd of denizens were lined in anticipation. The sign looming above them caught his eye.

Misery Land—Welcome to the Epcut Center.

The wording of the banner gave him an idea. He smiled and a familiar fire stirred within him.

Epcut . . . Why not? A final fling before things come to a head and I move on to pastures new. And of all the Sibitti, I haven't truly explored the range of his particular form as yet. Who knows, perhaps this time my endeavors might draw a response from the Reaper?

Grislington flexed and his semblance expanded to become an ablation upon the earth, a vortex of whirring blades that chopped, hacked, minced and diced every rock and root, stalk and shoot within his sphere of influence.

Thus attired, he issued a shrieking challenge that cut the air apart and descended like a banshee upon the unsuspecting crowds below.

Chapter 19: Down and Dirty

It had been a long and grueling day—all twelve hours of it—and despite their resilient nature, both Nimrod and Gemini were bone weary tired.

As she divested herself of her kit, Gemini glanced across at her partner and could see Nimrod was already beginning to work the kinks out of his back and neck. She couldn't blame him. He was a head taller than their leader, Daemon Grim, and bulkier too. Yet many of the tunnels they had traversed in the subterranean highways and byways beneath the grimy streets of Perish had been so low that even Gemini was forced to stoop. That meant Nimrod had been bent almost double for most of the time.

How the hell he managed to cover so many miles without complaining, I'll never know.

Gemini had to admit, that was one of the characteristics she liked about him. Nimrod was quiet, resourceful, and only expressed himself if something needed to be said. Comfortable silences were the norm, and truth be told, Gemini preferred that as their working relationship suited her own preference for peace and solitude.

She noticed Nimrod had commenced the stretch routine he liked to engage in at the end of their workday, so she made haste to strip down and grab the first shower.

Tonight, they were guests of Dorothée Babineaux, one of François de UnBorn's mutual business associates, and thereby, someone on the Reaper's unofficial payroll. Babineaux had provided them with a tiny little apartment in the St Merde district of the Fifth Horrondissement; a hidey-hole normally used as a safe house for itinerant hit-men and mercenaries in the employ of Don Pérignone. While basic, and smelling much like the neighborhood in which it was situated, the studio was relatively clean and dry and most importantly, was tucked away from prying eyes.

Entering the bathroom, Gemini lingered by the full-length mirror to give herself a quick once-over.

She had always been athletic, but since her recent enhancement Gemini had noticed certain differences. It was as if her elevation into the Ancient Disorder of Hell Hounds had caused her body to bloom into its full potential—and beyond. She was leaner now, and far from making her look gaunt, it only served to accentuate her figure. The process had also generated an additional vibrancy within her essence, something that emphasized the luster of her hair and skin. She positively glowed with unhealth and vitality. Even the ruined side of her face had been transformed, and the ravaged parchment effect now added a blunt starkness to her countenance that made her look shockingly beautiful. Something she hadn't felt in a long, long time.

And now, someone had taken notice of her.

Champ Ferguson. She snorted and turned on the water. *An out and out rogue if ever there was one and not my usual type at all.* Adjusting the spray to an arctic pulse, Gemini stepped in. *Mind you, it's not like I have a type anymore.*

Jets of cold water pummeled her flesh like icy needles, kneading her aches and pains and blasting the cobwebs away. Letting her self-discipline slide, Gemini submitted to a moment of rare relaxation and found her thoughts drifting.

I don't suppose I should complain. It's not like I get an endless queue of suitors, especially here where the consequences of any close relationship are likely to involve getting eaten alive by a swarm of mutant spiders and scorpions.

Out of the blue, Gemini was struck by a sudden realization.

Hey, we've been so busy from the moment I joined, I forgot about the other privileges extended to the Hell Hounds and Inquisitors. I can touch Daemon now, skin to skin, without being zapped. Does that mean my augmentation has affected me in other ways? Can I have sex again?

She did her best to dismiss such a line of reasoning, but found it more difficult than she realized, especially when an uninvited fancy began worming its way into her subconscious.

Idiot! Like you'd ever be that lucky.

The image intensified.

Mind you, I think I'd say to hell *with the consequences and bring on the arachnids if our illustrious leader ever found himself in need of a bit of company.*

Whatthefuck?

Feeling suddenly like a child caught with her fingers in the cookie jar, Gemini dialed the temperature as low as it would go and braced herself against the arousal-numbing chill.

Yet still the fantasy lingered.

Oh, for Satan's sake. I'm like a schoolgirl with a sudden crush.

A loud knocking at the bathroom door saved the day.

"I hope you're not using up all the hot water in there?" Nimrod yelled, his voice laced with humor.

"Ha ha, very funny. You'll be glad to know I've saved most of it for you. I'll be finished in a few minutes; whatever you do, please don't burn your tiny—"

An odd, fleeting impression brushed against her mind. *Is someone calling me?*

"Gemini?"

She could tell by his tone that Nimrod realized something was amiss.

"Hang on," she called back.

Slamming the faucet off, Gemini stepped out of the shower, closed her eyes and stood there, listening with as many of her new found faculties as she could employ.

Hello? Is anybody there?

For a moment, all she could discern was the water dripping onto the tiles at her feet. Then the telepathic hail came again, more determinedly this time.

Gemini dropped to her knees.

Don't be shy. You know we have the blessing of the ratmeisters and the king, so it's quite safe to come out.

The door opened and she sensed Nimrod entering the bathroom. His aura burned with curiosity and concern. Gemini raised a hand to forestall his questions, and repeated her psychic invitation.

A scrabbling sound issued from the drain in the center of the floor, along with the faintest of squeaks. Extending her talons, Gemini leaned forward, forced her nails beneath the cover and prized it loose.

A twinkling pair of eyes glared up out of the darkness. Gemini pursed her lips and sat back. "Tsst, tsst. C'mon. You know we won't hurt you. You're obviously an emissary from the raft council, so you are under our protection."

An elongated head peeped up over the rim, wet fur glistening and bristled nose twitching. A prolonged sequence of chittering and chattering followed, which somehow made complete sense to her the longer the rat kept talking.

"What's he saying?" Nimrod enquired.

"Well, for starters, *he* is a she, and her name is Brown-Tail. She's a special envoy from the king, sent to notify us that the rat-meisters are proud to announce they've found our fugitives."

"Already?" Nimrod spluttered. "But that's fantastic. Where?"

"That's what she was just telling me. They don't have suitable words to describe the addresses we use, so they sent Brown-Tail because of her affinity for telepathy. She's going to share her memories and actually show us where Chopin and Tesla are."

"She's been there?"

"It looks that way. Wanna join in the fun?"

"Are you kidding?"

Scooting forward, Nimrod grabbed a couple of towels from the rack. One he draped across Gemini's shoulders, the other he folded and placed across her lap. Apparently satisfied, he settled in beside her and fell silent.

Thankful of the gesture, Gemini turned back to their visitor.

"So, how do you want to do this?"

Brown-Tail didn't reply. Instead, she scampered up onto Gemini's knees and raised herself up on her hind legs. Fixing Gemini with what could only be described as a look of sheer concentration, the little rat went abruptly still.

Gemini felt a buzzing sensation behind her nose. Brown-Tail's gaze bored into her, and the orbs of the rodent's eyes seemed to grow larger and larger and larger.

She's opening to me . . . where the hell are we?

One moment Gemini felt the cold hard press of the tiles beneath her and the prickle of goose-pimples along flesh yet exposed, and the next, she was careening at breakneck speed along a dark and humid expanse full of contradictory sounds and smells.

So sudden was the change that it took Gemini a moment to realize she was witnessing events from the perspective of a rat, where everything would appear much larger than she was used to. The scene possessed an astral component that was rather disconcerting, for while her sight retained a nucleus of pristine clarity, her peripheral vision remained clouded within a spectral corona of diffuse light.

It must be the way Brown-Tail recollects things?

Gemini made a conscious effort to let go, and soon she was bobbing along like a phantom will-o'-the-wisp amid an undulating carpet of furry bodies, all intent on one thing: *Find the humans—Find the humans—Find the humans . . .*

As fellow clan members branched away, the seething mass gradually thinned and Brown-Tail was left to her own devices.

Time jumped forward and events took on a different and more personal dimension:

She finds herself alone and approaching a junction near the outskirts of the city. As she passes a side duct, something tugs at a shared memory and her olfactory receptors sting in recognition. She stops and scuttles back, alarmed and shocked to have actually detected an aroma so recently shared amongst the shires by the rat-meisters.

There!

Blended in among the mephitic backwash, a tart and distinctive fragrance makes her nostrils quiver.

Squeee!

She pauses to send news of her discovery to other patrols nearby and sets off to investigate. A host of feelings assaults her from all angles: hope, fear, delight, and terror.

A smaller conduit beckons. Running water trickles down into the arterial channel, bringing with it an anamorphic blend of scummy dross, refuse and unwanted body parts that humans tend to think cease to exist once they are flushed away.

A beetle, in the wrong place at the wrong time, crawls out from underneath a mound of decomposing feces and becomes an unexpected snack and welcome distraction from the hunt. Strength replenished, she's off again and the walls close in about her as the incline here increases and space decreases.

Minutes later, she finds herself on a communal gallery beneath the foundations of a row of houses. Before her, a church organ array of pipe work stretches off in a multitude of directions, each one serving its own unique purpose. She stops to listen and sample the bouquets presented by each one.

Voices filter down from above; muted, hollow, resonant; engaged in relaxed conversation and heated argument alike. And with them, a familiar, insidious percolation.

Here, this is the den of our prey.

A heady affirmation of victory makes her fur and whiskers bristle with suppressed excitement. She feels relief when the pitter-patter of tiny feet approaching becomes evident. Others have responded to her call. Challenges and queries ring back and forth.

Some venture to the surface. Bins are examined, doorsteps sniffed, and open windows peered through. Others stay below to confirm the scent is indeed accurate.

Success. A sense of jubilation and reward spreads throughout a growing swarm.

Caution now as she follows instructions to the letter. She approaches an open drain. The denizens above are large and dangerous, unfriendly toward her kind; their environment alien and hostile. However, traffic is quiet and the footfalls of passing humans few and far between.

She ventures upward, into a world bright and vast compared with hers, below. Dark railings loom over her; wide stone steps meet her stare with theirs. A door the color of blood bars the way. Here she sees strange patterns across its shiny exterior.

I must memorize their size and shape: 13.

At the end of the street, a fellow pack member sends a similar image of a sign that identifies the given name of this surface artery: *Rue du Val de Harme.*

She looks about.

I must get higher and show exactly where this place is in the city.

A nearby streetlight reaches toward the heavens, its ornate workings providing handy footholds and free passage to wires above that stretch away toward other abodes.

Round and round, up and up.

In the distance, the trellised outline of Satan's Finger dominates the horizon and threatens the clouds. Searchlights near its pinnacle comb the streets below, as if scouring the shadows for those seeking to escape. In front of that monument, the twinkling splendor of the marsh burns with a fierce and natural counterpoint to all-pervading insanity. Closer still, the flaming tower stands like a lonely sentinel over the bone gardens where humans once buried their dead. Now devoid of permanent residents, it is home to those who have fallen foul of the crime lord ruling the south side of the river, for they lie in misery—bound and gagged—awaiting their fate and providing fresh delights to those who can dig and burrow their way in.

Crack!

Zing! comes a harsh report and rush of wind as something flies past her.

"Fucking vermin."

A human below, leaning out of a window with a gun? Fleeee . . .

And the connection severs:

Blinking her eyes open, Gemini felt as if she were waking from a dream and discovered she had stopped breathing. She kick-started her respiration again with a shudder, and Brown-Tail skipped down off her lap.

Gemini turned to Nimrod. "I hope you saw all that?"

"I certainly did, and from what I can ascertain, Brown-Tail's recollections fit perfectly with the clue provided by Al Catraz earlier in the week, remember?"

"He has the balls to want what he cannot have, and lives beyond the opus ring in sight of Dante's hangout . . . "

Nimrod continued, "That's thirteen, Rue du Val de Harme, in the Genitaux district of Perish. Did you see the line of sight approach Brown-Tail provided? The Awful Tower, Chomp-de-Marsh, Montpyre Tower and finally, Montpyre Cemetery. All of them point like a needle to the narrow district sandwiched between Morgue le Kremlin and Port de Gentilly on the outskirts of the city."

"That's just beyond the Thirteenth and Fourteenth Horrondissements then, or as the clue says, the opus ring. Get it?"

"Correct, and a place where a former maestro no doubt seeks to create a new defining work. Oh, very good."

Gemini was stunned. "So we've got them?"

"Almost. Now we plan our assault. If you'd been with us last year, you'd know Chopin and Tesla are extremely thorough annoying little bastards, and we can't let our apparent success make us sloppy. For all we know, if we try to storm in there using the orbs, we might run smack-bang into a trap. Tesla invented the damned things, don't forget, so we don't know if he's ringed his home with any countermeasures to their operation, or indeed, if he can booby-trap the one we have into exploding in our faces."

"So what do you propose?"

Nimrod held out his hand to help Gemini rise from the floor.

"Well, you're a stealth expert. What say I get onto Daemon and see if he wants to join us in a surprise assault of your design?"

"Me? But I've only just joined the Hounds."

"It doesn't matter. I might lead the pack, but Daemon likes everyone to use their initiative. If you impress him now, it might open all sorts of doors later."

Gemini liked the sound of that, until a sudden flush of her cheeks brought back a recent fantasy she had worked hard to suppress.

If only it could be the one to his bedroom. "I—er, I'll start thinking about that right—"

Squeak!

Gemini looked down. Brown-Tail still waited patiently on the floor.

Shit, I forgot.

"I'm sorry." Gemini bit her finger and extended her hand toward the rat king's emissary. "I do apologize. Here, take this as a reward and tell the meisters we'll be contacting them shortly with details of a plan we'd like you all to take part in.

I think you'll enjoy what's coming. Considering the speed of your work, the Reaper's bound to show his approval in ways you've never imagined."

Brown-Tail drank her fill and then skittered away down the drain without a further word or twitch of her whiskers. Gemini watched her go for a moment and turned to find Nimrod studying her with a rare glint of humor in his eyes.

Suddenly conscious of her nakedness, Gemini bristled with indignation: "Getting a good look, are you?"

Nimrod waved and chuckled: "No, not at all. I was merely thinking you rushed in here first in a bid to get all nice and clean, and now you've got to put your dirty clothes back on."

"What?"

"We've got to plan things as quickly as possible, Gemini. That means we'll be back down in the sewers in an hour, two tops. You know as well as I do, the last thing you want giving you away in an environment like that is the distinctive aroma of fresh kit."

He's right!"Oh, for Satan's sake." She eyed the sullied mound of her uniform out in the main room. Even at this distance, she could see it nearly crawling of its own accord.

Nimrod's mirth grew into gales of laughter.

She grimaced. "If you'd like a repeat performance of the ass-kicking I gave you during my trials, please continue. I can't think of a better way of getting all sweaty again."

The hysterics abruptly stopped, and Nimrod backed out from the bathroom.

"Very unladylike. Perhaps that's why we all love you so much." Then he winked.

Gemini threw a towel straight at his face.

Nimrod was quicker, and the door slammed shut.

Men!

Chapter 20: Layers Within Layers

I found it difficult not to hover.

Elizabeth had proven so insightful earlier in the day that I thought she would crack the clue wide open in a matter of minutes. Instead, the code seemed to hold her captive and enthrall her by its complexity. She had been completely still for more than thirteen hours, and it was driving me nuts. *If this carries on, I'll wear a hole in the floor from all the pacing up and down.*

A mental hail pulled me up short.

Samael?

Reaper, have you been keeping an eye on current events?

His mind-tone was laced with sarcasm, which immediately put me on edge.

I can't say I have, sorry. I'm a little busy tracking down an ever-growing band of fugitives from injustice and unearthing high-level moles who seem intent on undermining His Infernal Majesty's sovereignty. Can you be a little more specific?

I'm referring to the random attacks by Erra's personified weapons.

Oh, those? Yes, I'm aware they've taken to skulking about, mostly in the outer regions. So long as they stay there I'm not really bothered.

So, you feel New Hell isn't worth the effort?

His jibe caught me off guard.

New Hell again? When?

Not thirty minutes ago. From the look of it, this strike was carried out by the Fifth. Word is, he left quite a mess behind. They've closed the Epcut Center while they await sulforensic examiners.

Epcut Center? At Misery Land? What does the Boss have to say?

He's keen for you to look into the matter personally. He'd like you to remind those assholes of what will happen if they insist on being . . . provocative.

I couldn't resist a bit of payback.

Aren't you a bit insulted he didn't ask you *to look into it?*

Well, you're the boy with the golden—if somewhat heavily tattooed—balls. I'm thinking he probably gave you the task to see if you could actually finish the job this time and do what you were created to do. Like exterminate them?

Touché. Tell him I'll get right on it. I wouldn't want his chief messenger boy to get all sulky.

His mind-tone refused to rise to the bait.

Poor attempt, Reaper. We've always been messengers of one sort or another, fallen or not. That's what angel means, after all.

He severed the connection.

A couple of things Samael had just said tweaked a nerve.

"What the fuck was he driveling on about? *Do what I was created to do?* And where have I heard that term 'messenger' recently?"

Before I had a chance to think deeply on the matter, another telepathic call interrupted my train of thought: *What the bloody hell does he want now?*

"Yes?" I snapped, mentally and verbally.

Daemon?

Nimrod? Sorry, I thought you were some high-pocketed smug bastard for a moment. How can I—? Then I discerned his mood. *You have good news?*

You could say that. The raft council has only gone and done it, they've actually found Chopin and Tesla's lair. Gemini's putting together a little strategy to pay them a surprise visit. I thought you'd like to join us.

Karma was taking a dump on me from a great height.

I'd love to, but I can't. I've just this minute been tasked with a more urgent matter.

More urgent than Chopin and Tesla?

I'm afraid so. It's the Sibitti again, throwing teddy out of their collective pram with another tantrum. Unfortunately, their latest one was over in New Hell.

Ah, I see. Nimrod was quiet for a moment. *Would you prefer for Champ and Yamato to join us, or are you okay for Gemini and me to go ahead with this on our own?*

You'll have to fly solo on this one, Nimrod. Champ and Yamato are hot on the heels of our snakes in the grass and will shortly be freezing their butts off in Niflheim. The responsibility will do Gemini good and enforce the fact she's operating at an entirely different level now. Enjoy yourselves. When this is all over, every single major thorn in our flesh should be out of the way except for Grislington himself, so we'll make him a special pack outing.

Excellent. Good hunting, then.

I could taste his anticipation even from this distance.

You too. Then I thought it best to make a distinction before things got underway. *Just remember, we need Chopin and Tesla in an unhealthy enough state for Strawberry and her team to extract information. Don't let Gemini go too psycho.*

Understood. But is it all right to take their limbs? They don't need arms and legs to answer questions.

He had a valid point.

Then by all means, take those away. Just leave enough pain-sensitive nerve fibers in situ for the Inquisitors to play with, and go vent some steam.

The ether fell silent.

"As will I."

*

Looking down from the advantage afforded by his throne mound, Erra was thankful for the eternal and resilient nature of his personified weapons. The confrontation with the Devil's Bastard had shaken them badly, especially the First, who took several days to recover. But recover he had and, currently, all seven of them chafed to release their frustrations in direct conflict, as they were designed to do.

And now that they are determined to use their wits as much as their obvious power, events should unfold apace.

Erra put that hope to the back of his mind as his primary enforcer stepped forward to address him.

"It is as we suspected," declared the First. "For whatever reason, the angel now tires of his sport and seeks out that by which he hopes to regain his liberty. A pity, for as we shadowed his movements and consumed those scant survivors left in his wake, we were able to conclude that his actions did much to sustain our reputation."

"And you are sure of this?"

"Yes, he terrified the casualties. And when we consider the fact that so few were left alive in Juxtapose to bear witness to Satan's proclamation of victory, or to see the transformation of his Reaper, Grislington's disruptions only contradict those claims and make his seem like boastful propaganda."

Erra seized his opening.

"Speaking of Grim, have you determined what tactics to employ should you encounter him again?"

"We have, and a timely revision it was too, for we have grown lax and content to bask in the limelight of our superiority." The First glanced to those of his brothers who were present. "While our natural style of battle will suffice for the masses, it is our opinion that only a combined and sustained assault by all of us together will suffice, especially if we also utilize the divergent qualities of our elemental natures in tandem."

The First paused to display an ethereal representation of their strategy in the atmosphere between them.

"You see? The Second and Sixth will employ their variant capacities and create opposing hurdles. So will the Third and Seventh, and likewise, the Fourth and Fifth."

"And what of you, my prime examiner?"

"I will supplement each pair as they rotate in an effort to keep the Beast off balance."

To Erra's eyes, the First appeared to be holding something back. Intuition spurred him to press the matter immediately: "You have something else to say, perhaps?"

"I do, for it is our firm belief that the Reaper will be further weakened by the time any such confrontation manifests."

"On what do you base this assumption?"

"On the basis that we have made progress regarding a recently proposed policy." The First advanced a few steps to the base of the mound, and continued: "Sire, as intimated, we made sure to follow the angel's movements as it spread mayhem, and in each case were able to audit those scant survivors left at each scene. At last we have secured the breakthrough we have been waiting for. You will note that both the Second and Sixth are absent? That is because they responded to the outcry following Grislington's latest attack at the theme park in New Hell and appraised those close to death. They discovered a small group of zealots who follow a denizen known as *The Saint*, or *Saint Teresa*. As they lay waning, each called out to her for help and the strength needed to forgive the atrocity heaped upon them. I am told they reeked of love."

"And what transpired?"

"Second and Sixth consumed their hearts and were able to determine that she is ensconced within the isolation wing of Wormblood Scrubs on the outskirts of Olde London Town. We seek your blessing to proceed with our attempt to gain both her trust and her insight as to how we can spread this benign quality in its entirety among the damned of hell."

"And you think she will listen to your petition?"

"If what the Second has to say is accurate, I am sure of it."

Erra found it difficult to hide his elation.

"Then by all means, proceed, and do so with all haste."

*

As Chopin traversed the dark and gloomy passage, a tenebrous gray mist undulated about his feet, clearly visible despite the fact his only light came from an unknown source somewhere overhead.

The hall itself was devoid of all features. There were no doors, fixtures or fittings, and so far as he could see, even the seams where the walls bled into the ceiling were bland and indistinct. It seemed to Chopin as if the brume was designed to absorb any and all signs of life.

He stopped to look about him.

A black void trailed in his wake, appearing identical in substance to the one leading the way not ten yards beyond his current position. Each matched his pace with a precision that left him in no doubt that he was being cocooned within a web of tangible nonexistence.

I don't think I could imagine anything more soul-destroying than being marooned in a place like this.

Steeling his resolve, Chopin set off again and remembered a vital aspect to this altered form of existential existence.

Don't try, do!

No sooner had Chopin applied that principle than his progress was interrupted by the sudden manifestation of a cold steel barrier before him. He pulled up short and turned to look back the way he had come, only to find the passageway had closed in on him from that direction as well. Spinning on the spot, he discovered he was now in a space barely larger than a shower cubicle. The walls in front and behind were balanced on either side by two opposing floor-to-ceiling mirrors. At least, he thought they were mirrors, even though they failed to recognize his presence as if his existence were not significant enough to be acknowledged. However, the silvered sheen of their surfaces was far from empty.

A pair of giant wings, as tall and wide as Chopin's body, graced the reflective medium on both sides. At first glance, he thought them like everything else in this sterile environment—blanched of all color and haloed in an anemic blush of diffuse light. But the longer he stared, the more Chopin realized they shimmered and sparkled with a vibrancy so powerful that his mundane eyes were insufficient to comprehend their nascent majesty.

That the texture of their matrix should be balanced thus within a moment of time is remarkable. How on earth such a thing was contrived, I cannot begin to fathom. The cogency involved must be . . .

Chopin broke the spell and made haste to remove the seraphinite from within his pocket. Fist clenched, he thrust his hand toward the shimmering plane of the barrier, only to stub his knuckles.

"What? But I—" *Don't try, do!*

Remembering his link across the esoteric bridge, Chopin focused on the *Sword of Uncovered Secrets* and concentrated.

I command you. Stand forth and manifest. Reveal the key to unlock this enigma.

The hairs on the back of his hands prickled as an electric current trilled through the ether. He blinked, and a figure stood behind him where no one had been an instant before. Tall and slender, it appeared at once fragile and imposing; permanent, yet as fleeting as a candle's flame in the wind.

It's Gris— No, wait. It's what Grislington would have looked like if he'd never been held captive in hell.

Fixated upon his goal, the figure of the angel glided forward and peered into quicksilver refractions. Then he went still. A rush of wind sprang up out of nowhere and swept past Chopin's face, bringing with it a fleeting kiss of gossamer softness, along with a sense of *knowing*. Grislington blazed bright, and his entire being illuminated, giving the impression his skin was dusted with diamonds. As the glare faded, Chopin discovered that the images within the mirrors had been miraculously transposed back to where they truly belonged. Grislington flexed his chest and back muscles, and his newly-restored wings extended away from him, creating a halo of transcendent energy that defied the strictures of the restraining walls and pierced the veil between worlds.

A tangible shockwave swatted Chopin away. Thrown head over heels, he floundered for a moment before a bile-inducing drop claimed him. Plummeting, he fell through fire and ice and slammed back into his body.

His eyes snapped open.

As always, Tesla was waiting, chilled remedy at the ready to counter the crushing migraines that use of the *Sword of Uncovered Secrets* induced.

"And?"

"Well, there were one or two surprises," Chopin confessed. Shuffling into a sitting position, he seized the proffered drink and held it to his forehead. "For one, seraphinite won't be enough—"

"It won't?"

"No. The vision made it plain that the presence of an actual angel will be required to open the way. Evidently, there is something specific about Grislington's life force that creates the harmonic required to cancel the temporal web." He shrugged. "We've no choice but to bait him into getting there before us."

"And what of the other dangers?"

Chopin thought for a moment upon what his brief contact with the divine periapt had revealed.

"Under no account are we to look into the mirrors squarely. To do so will activate the gravity trap. Additionally, if you allow more than one at a time to capture your image, you'll literally be torn apart."

Tesla looked genuinely shocked.

"Then how are we going to traverse the gallery?"

"By making sure our insurance policy is also in attendance. If we play this right, our antagonists will be too busy trying to outmaneuver each other to pay any real attention to us. Of course, it'll be vital to stay as close to their shielding energies as possible to neutralize the influence of the gravity wells, but that can't be avoided." Chopin downed his drink in one. "Then we jump in, snatch our prize, and get the hell out of there using our rings."

"Indeed. Just as well we're prepared for just about anything, then?"

Chopin grimaced.

"Ah yes, and about that . . ."

Chapter 21: Time to Make a Statement

With its gray stones, black wrought-iron fencing topped by spikes, white granite steps and crimson-colored door sandwiched neatly between a double-fronted aspect, the specified residence on the other side of the thoroughfare looked like every other house paraded along Rue du Val de Harme. Ordinary. Except that Gemini knew that the events unfolding within number 13 were anything but ordinary.

Peeping through the sheers of the premises opposite, Gemini scrutinized the exterior features of their target one last time, then allowed her eyes to glaze over. In moments, her perceptions had sunk down through the asphalt and into the network of pipes and sub-tunnels running below the entire neighborhood. An army of rodents from nearly a dozen combined fiefdoms had gathered there, under the leadership of three rat-meisters, to provide whatever support the Hell Hounds might need in the coming raid.

Two further packs had assembled at either end of the street, and an entire mischief currently owned the alley running along the back of number 13, where Nimrod waited patiently for the signal to pounce.

Traffic flowed scarcely at this time of evening and would remain light for a further hour at least.

"Good," Gemini mumbled to herself, "everyone is nearly ready."

As a precaution, Gemini attempted to scan the interior of their objective, to again find her probe rebuffed by a subtle yet resilient shield.

I daren't push it for fear of triggering something. She sighed. "Okay, physical breach it is. We'll just have to trust that the intelligence our little friends provided is accurate, and rely on them to scamper from room to room as we enter."

Cautious and heavily shielded, Nimrod's thoughts intruded.

Is everything set?

"Yes," Gemini replied aloud, "although I still can't get an accurate picture of what's waiting for us inside. Fortunately, we know the layout of these properties, and Brown-Tail's packs will be quick to provide important updates as they spread throughout each floor."

Don't be too downhearted. Chopin and Tesla aren't idiots, so this was never going to be easy. They're bound to have taken precautions following the raid on their former apartment across in Place Venôme, so the faster we get in there, the less time they'll have to respond with anything nasty. Are you sure you don't want me over there with you on the main assault?

"No, I'll be fine. I'm certain I can overcome any barriers without drawing attention to the fact we're here until it's too late. Not to put too fine a point on it, you are a strapping lad and about as subtle as a Fourth of July celebration on steroids. And while I'm sure you'd help get the job done, Chopin and Tesla's toys will see you coming from the middle of next week and they'll pull one of their disappearing acts. I'm hoping to catch them with their pants down." She paused to project a dual image of Chopin and Tesla, facing each other on opposing lavatories in a pose reminiscent of Rodin's *The Thinker*. "Wouldn't it be marvelous if we could make that happen?"

A rarified smile filtered back.

If you managed to pull that off, I think Daemon would try his damndest to get you anything you wanted.

"Anything? I'll compile a list then, and make sure our boys are served up hogtied on a platter with their own balls in the place of an apple. But we'll discuss the specifics in a little while." Gemini decided the banter had gone on long enough. Opening her mind wide, she addressed everyone standing by, both above and below ground. "Listen close, everybody. The show will be kicking off in a few minutes. Get ready for my signal."

Gemini turned to consider the occupant of the house she had commandeered; a respectable-looking lady whom the misdeeds identified as Angelique Noir. Mademoiselle Noir had been bound and left face down on the parlor floor. Clearly terrified, she started to squeal around her gag and did her best to wriggle away as Gemini marched across the room brandishing one of her combat knives.

"I really am sorry," Gemini murmured, "but you were in the right place at the wrong time. In the past, you'd have been left well alone, as I've never involved bystanders in my hits. But now I'm a Hell Hound and accountable at an entirely different level." She shrugged, pushed her victim over onto one side, then squatted down beside her. "I simply can't afford any loose ends that might jeopardize the outcome. But don't worry. I'll personally ensure the Undertaker gives you a favorable reassignment."

Gemini drew her blade across the young woman's throat before deftly spearing her brain through the left eye.

Mademoiselle Noir grunted, stiffened, and then exploded in a shower of dust and vapor.

Padding through to the kitchen without so much as a backward glance, Gemini removed her trademark cowl, activated the chameleon mesh interwoven into her flaytex bodysuit, and faded from sight. Everything went still.

She had always been able to move about furtively, but since her elevation, Gemini's capability for stealth had increased a thousandfold. When added to her Bãlefire-magnified strength, speed and agility, this made her a formidable opponent, as her new teammates had discovered recently during her final trials.

And now, I get to use these skills for real . . . at last.

Breaking cover via the rear exit, Gemini sped down the service lane, cut left onto the main sidewalk, and left again until she stood directly opposite number 13.

She looked up at the main entrance. Like every other property on this street, number 13 boasted a hardwood six-panel door adorned with a laminated four-leafed window fan. Property misdeeds showed each one fitted with standard five lever deadlocks and supported by a further two rack-bolts positioned six inches from the top and bottom of the frame. A sturdy set of precautions under all but the most pressing circumstances—such as the presence of a Hell Hound, of course, no matter how diminutive her outward form might be. As none of the exterior windows were easy to reach, the door would provide the most practical option for rapid entry.

Mounting the steps like a whisper, Gemini pressed her ear to the cool oak surface and listened. Notwithstanding the acuity of her senses, she received no impression of movement inside. In fact, it seemed as if the very concept of noise had been drained from the abode entirely. Confident in her ability to remain undetected, Gemini braced herself against the casing and boosted herself up to look in through the glass.

A carpeted stairway, flush against the wall, occupied the space on the right. The landing at the top branched both ways. On the ground floor, doors led off to what plans had shown were a drawing room and study on opposite sides of the hallway that led to the dining room and parlor. Out of her sight, Gemini knew that the rear of the property contained a wide kitchen and access to the basement.

Gemini received an indistinct impression the house might be empty.

Brown-Tail, she called, *can your people hear anything down there through the pipe work?*

After a moment's pause, an impression came back signifying a combination of unnatural silence and incertitude.

Okay, let's take this a step further.

Lowering herself back down to the floor, Gemini placed her hand against the uppermost panel where the deadbolt should be. Making sure of her position, she began pushing harder and harder until she discerned the slightest movement around the top of the frame.

Aha! It only moves in a millimeter or two, but that speaks volumes.

Using her foot, she repeated the process at the bottom until she was rewarded by the tiniest of creaks.

They're not set. So either our targets aren't at home or they've been careless. Gemini didn't need to speculate. *And I'm betting on the former, which means we could lie in wait until they return, or . . . ah, dammit! I can't take the risk. We'll go in with all guns blazing.*

She glanced up and down the deserted street.

Brown-Tail? Ask the rat-meisters to start bringing your people to the surface. No one is around at the moment so you can all line up in front of the house. Be quick.

Gemini tested the integrity of the door as she waited and managed to ascertain the exact situation of the main lock's workings. As she probed each section, she also discerned a miniscule current running through the fabric of the wood. She recognized the frequency of that energy and tested the wall on either side.

It's a dampening field. Her discovery quashed any remaining doubts they were at the right address.

Only Chopin and Tesla would go to such lengths.

A scrabbling sound echoed out from the drain behind her. Gemini turned in time to see a tufted brown and gray head pop up above the curb. She blinked and two more appeared. Then ten more. Then thirty. Soon, the sidewalk and spaces beneath parked cars teemed with bristling little warriors, all ready to play their part.

Right, time to get things moving before some idiot comes along and spoils things by shrieking. Expanding her awareness once more, she zeroed in on Nimrod and made contact. *The brown stuff is about to hit the fan. Listen for my countdown and go on my mark.*

Roger that.

Gemini retreated into the middle of the street. While she lacked both height and weight, her positive application of the augmented capabilities she did possess more than made up for it—a fact she was about to demonstrate.

Nimrod? Begin your assault in . . . three, two, one. Now!

Had she been visible, Gemini would have become a blur of indistinct motion the moment she set off. Hitting the curb, she hopped across the sidewalk, skipped straight up to the middle step, twisted to one side and with a final bound, bunched her knees to her chest. Just before making contact with the door, Gemini kicked out with both feet as hard as she could. The shock of impact jarred her from heel to jaw.

A satisfying *crack* and *ping* signaled the moment the lock snapped and fittings went flying. They were followed almost immediately by the scratching of hundreds of tiny claws on concrete, then on wood, as the waiting pack swarmed inside and up the stairs.

Gemini felt a brief flush bloom across her skin as the dampening field collapsed. Maintaining her momentum, she surfed along the hallway for a moment on the remains of the door, and then gamboled backward toward the front of the house. No sooner had she landed than she jinked left into the drawing room.

A crash from the rear of the property signaled Nimrod's arrival.

Free to employ her abilities fully, Gemini deactivated her chameleon sheath and sent out a refined psychic pulse in an effort to detect other unlife forms.

Not a goddam thing? Either they're really not here or they've masked their signatures. I'd better warn the others.

Resorting to both verbal and mental speech, Gemini declared, "Okay, everyone, listen up. We're in, but the game isn't over. Our primary targets are Chopin and Tesla. Take them alive if you can, and remember. This is their home turf, so they may be hidden and they might resort to the use of arcane relics.

"Brown-Tail? If your people encounter strange energies or the humans themselves, report directly to Nimrod or me and we will assist you. Once we have them, we can concentrate on the recovery of proscribed artifacts.

"Nimrod? When you've completed your sweep of the cellar, I'll meet you in the entrance lobby and we'll commence a search of the upstairs together."

A number of affirmations rang or squeaked back.

As she was speaking, Gemini skirted the perimeter of the drawing room. She began a second circuit, and this time chose to weave in and out of the furniture. A tingling sensation in her toes gave her cause for concern.

What was that?

Backtracking, she pushed the coffee table away, kicked a sumptuous Persian rug to one side and uncovered a cunningly concealed floor safe beneath a transparent mantle. The lever had been cranked down, indicating it was open.

Bait, perhaps?

Kneeling beside her find, Gemini carefully prized off the cover. Next, she removed a length of twine from one of the pouches on her belt and looped it around the handle. Having done that, she trailed the cord up over the adjacent table and beyond, so that it hung down behind the largest of the couches. Taking cover behind her foam-filled shield, Gemini tensed and yanked hard.

The lid shot up with a loud *clunk*!

Then everything went quiet.

Determining it was safe to proceed, she crept forward and peered inside the box. The abstruse vibrations were a lot stronger now the top was open, and Gemini was forced to sniff away a runny nose and wipe her eyes.

Unholy shit, what did they keep in there? It's almost as if . . . ?

Then the import of what she had just uncovered slapped her in the face.

They've gone. And I bet this place has been stripped clean of anything useful.

She recalled several reports of previous encounters where the Hell Hounds had attempted to close the gap on the elusive pair.

The team has always wondered how these scumbags manage to stay one step ahead. I'm betting it's something to do with the temporal application of their rift generators. Daemon only warned us about it this morning. But if so, we—

Her line of thought was disturbed by a frantic chittering from the doorway.

"Brown-Tail? Why aren't you—?" She stopped to listen as the raft council's liaison expressed her concerns. "What do you mean, they're not moving?"

This time, Brown-Tail let loose with a stream of agitated squeaks and trills. While Gemini had difficulty keeping up with the translation, she had no problem whatsoever understanding the picture the little rat projected directly into her mind. In it, Nimrod approached a large open chest, apparently fixated upon its contents.

But if he is, his stance is distorted in some way.

Then Gemini realized her partner was in the midst of taking a step.

Is this on freeze frame?

She zoomed in closer, and was amazed to see Nimrod's leading foot descending toward the floor, albeit at an impossibly slow rate.

A time ambush! "Brown-Tail, warn the rest of your people," Gemini hissed as she launched herself at breakneck speed toward the basement.

As she ran, Gemini considered her options.

Make an assessment first and then report it afterward.

She arrived at the kitchen within three seconds, amid a flood of panicking rodents.

Lingering at the top of the rear stairs, Gemini scanned her route ahead and could taste the esoteric resonance emanating from below. All she could discern through that haze was the presence of one damned soul, surrounded by multiple little hotspots that she knew belonged to the retinue of rats in Nimrod's company. To all intents and purposes, those unlife signs appeared normal. They just weren't moving.

So how large is the trap? She shook her head in frustration. *Only one way to find out, I suppose.*

As a precaution, Gemini drew her knives. Infused with the purest essence of Bãlefire, she knew her blades would warn of any mystic mischief her own senses might overlook. Nonetheless, that knowledge didn't make her feel any better. Holding her weapons before her, she waited for the last of the rats that could do so to flee the cellar before edging down into the unknown.

She soon reached the bottom and was surprised to find an immaculately kept work area. All manner of benches and shelves laden with clean well-oiled tools lined the walls, and several other tables had been placed at regular intervals about the open space in-between. Nimrod was down at the far end toward the rear of the property with his entourage of frozen helpers, and from this angle, she could see he was only two or three steps away from the open trunk.

Waving the daggers to and fro in the air before her, Gemini gradually worked her way forward until the tip of one blade flared the deep ruddy color of metal being heated in a forge. She released it immediately, and wasn't at all surprised when it hung suspended in the air for a moment or two, until a flash of Bãlefire caused it to droop toward the floor. The overall effect made Gemini think of invisible wax melting.

So it's viscous in nature and susceptible to manipulation. That means . . .

She spied a crowbar on a nearby work surface. Snatching it up, she used the hooked end to knock her weapon free of the restrictive field. The knife fell to the floor and gouged a chip from the concrete.

That gave Gemini an idea.

As quickly as she could, she sheathed her weapons, scooted back to the same table and started searching through several boxes until she found one containing an assortment of nails, screws and carpet tacks. Grabbing a handful, she edged left from the score mark and encircled Nimrod's position, flicking screws and nails as she went. Soon, Gemini had marked the extent of the tau-field in glowing little beacons.

Hmm, it's only about ten feet in diameter. But how the hell am I going to get him out of there?

Gemini scrutinized his position. It had changed slightly, as his leading foot was now resting on the floor. His expression also spoke volumes, for she could see the beginnings of a frown crawling across his face.

Aah, he must have cottoned on to the fact something's wrong within his timeframe. Then she followed the line of his gaze. *Either that or he's only just seen what's inside the box.*

Interest roused, Gemini shuffled as close to her partner as she dared and sprang into the air. Surprised by her own strength, she was forced to stop her head from banging against the ceiling. Nevertheless, in that brief instant she was able to gain an unobstructed view of the chest's contents.

A series of bright blue LEDs flashed across the angular surface of a pyramid-shaped device. Whatever power emanated from that contrivance caused the air to shimmer, and once again Gemini's vision teared. As she began to descend, she just caught sight of a series of filaments leading from that gadget into a larger than usual portal generator.

I was right. They have used a tempo–

A tiny *ping* alerted her to a carpet tack falling to the floor in front of her.

Hello?

Gemini tugged on a nail close to where the tack had been. It resisted her efforts for a few moments and then, with the greatest reluctance, started to tease free. As she worked on it, another screw dropped to the floor on the other side of the sphere. She marked its position and came to a sudden realization.

The threshold is collapsing in on itself!

Fighting against the inclination to rush things, Gemini stood back and watched as most of the tacks she had thrown into the viscid film fell free over the next few minutes.

Yes, it's definitely shrinking, and from the look of it, at a rate of about an inch every sixty seconds. She did the math. *Shit! At this rate, it'll take nearly two hours to dissipate.*

Gemini turned on the spot and looked up and down the length and breadth of the cellar. Her gaze fell onto the discarded crowbar, and the beginnings of a plan took form in her mind.

I wonder?

Retrieving the jemmy, she hefted it a few times, then threw it as hard as she could toward a spot just in front of Nimrod's location. Because of its additional weight and speed, the heavy tool pierced the temporal field to a greater extent than the smaller objects had. All the same, once the trap activated, the crowbar slowed and came to a stop mere inches from Nimrod's head.

So, something bigger and faster should, in theory, be able to penetrate much farther. She glanced at her daggers. *And if the Bālefire does its work, such an effect might be magnified enough to knock Nimrod—and me—free . . . or at least clos-er to the edge.*

Gemini made her decision.

Time to update the Den.

Biting down her apprehension, Gemini cleared her mind of the million and one things crowding in on her and sent the hail; the first time she had attempted such a thing unaided since her augmentation.

"Daemon?"

There was no reply.

"Daemon?" she called again, much louder this time. "Can you hear me?"

The ether remained silent.

"Fuck it, I knew—"

Gemini?

"Strawberry?"

Yes, it's me. Sorry for any misunderstanding, but if the boys are away, I usually keep a metaphysical ear open for anyone trying to make contact with HQ. Is there anything I can help you with?

Overcoming her surprise, Gemini related a no holds barred précis of the events within the target property, including their failure to anticipate the trap.

So, Nimrod's okay? Strawberry's mental voice was laced with concern. *He's just stuck in some weird time-warp until it dissipates?*

"That's right. But I'm loath to leave him there until it does. You ought to see the way this place has been cleared out. It reeks of arcane and celestial power. I've got a terrible feeling Chopin and Tesla are planning something big. We all need to be on our toes, and as quickly as possible."

So what do you propose?

"I want to snap him out of it. Literally."

Gemini displayed the nuts and bolts of her idea, and waited to see what Strawberry might advise.

Do you think it will work?

"The way I see it, we've got no choice but to try. The others are all busy, so if I do nothing, we'll be stuck here for a few hours anyway. If I make the attempt and fail, it's not like anything will get worse. But if it works, you might have a couple of extra Hell Hounds on tap that Chopin and Tesla weren't expecting."

Bad luck, then.

"Here's hoping. I'll contact you as soon as we're free of the house. You might want to dispatch someone to secure the place as well in the meantime. Oh, and it would be a good idea to let the others know we're out of commission until this little problem is solved."

Will do.

Strawberry cut the link and Gemini was left alone to implement her plan.

After pushing the intervening tables out of the way, Gemini judged she had enough of a run-up to hit maximum speed. Removing her knives once more, she reversed grip so the pommels were uppermost and strolled to the far end of the basement. Once there, she lowered herself to the floor and adopted a stance similar to that of a sprinter at the beginning of a race, except that in Gemini's case, she would be using the wall as a kickoff point instead of starting blocks.

She took several deep breaths and made an effort to control her heart rate.

Here goes nothing.

Focusing solely on her objective, Gemini rocked backward and forward. Once, twice, three times . . . pause.

After a deep inhalation, she erupted toward the trap like a thunderbolt.

Chapter 22: Things Uncommon

At my insistence, the Epcut Center remained shut. The facility's manager didn't like it, of course, but then again, I wasn't really concerned whether he met his monthly quotas or not. Neither was I moved by sentiment or respect for the dead. My job was to get to the bottom of any act that threatened the instability of His Infernal Majesty's sovereignty; and on that account, this incident qualified with bells on.

Bearing in mind what I needed to do, I was particularly thankful for the way in which Satan had woven together the various levels of latter-day hell, for it wasn't only the realms that gradually bled one into another; over time, the crux of every denizen did too. None of us was entirely corporeal. As such, each circle was able to absorb the esoteric imprints of particularly heinous events. The stronger the emotions generated, the greater the impression. So, as I wandered about the taped-off scene of the latest Sibitti atrocity, I was able to literally drink in the ambience of what had taken place.

Terror dominated, along with lesser amounts of impotence, resignation and outrage; an exotic mélange I found both intoxicating and arousing.

Gods, but this is more like it. Why my dark father has me chasing after idiots when I could simply be emptying the streets of dross, I don't know. I ached to inflict such losses on a grand scale. *Still, we were born to serve . . . or were created for that purpose if Samael's little slip was anything to go by.*

I lingered at the scene of a particularly gruesome slaying. The atmosphere still sang at its memory so I took the time to separate each brutality from the next, savoring the distinct horror of every last moment the victims had to share.

It was magnificent.

And to my surprise, there was something distinctly *off* about it. Intrigued, I tasted another sample and sure enough, an overwhelming sense of ennui soured an otherwise appealing bouquet.

The Sibitti relish their charge, as do I. They live for conflict and have never displayed such a wanton disregard toward their reason for existence. And while they've been loath to face me since my augmentation, once they are *unleashed, they are relentless and committed to their task.*

I found this revelation confusing. All joking aside, the Seven were tribal in their purpose. Unflagging and hungry for death. Except for the growing arrogance of the First, they had no need for charades or airs and graces. They acted the way they did out of necessity. As weapons, forged for one thing and one thing only . . . which is why the aftertaste of boredom I had detected seemed completely at odds with their usual temperament.

Extending the range of my probe, I walked in a larger circle and endeavored to capture an overall impression of the entire occurrence.

Aha, it was the Fifth. And he came from the hillside to the east, the only one that's been left undeveloped. I skimmed through the incident on fast-forward. *Having descended upon those denizens waiting in line, he started slaughtering them and . . . ? Hang on, he's just butchering them. Not once is he stopping to consume their organs or carry out any form of appraisal.*

A tingle coursed along my spine.

Was this not an audit? So far as I can see, he doesn't seem to be making any attempt to judge them. Even his expression looks grim. It's as if he's forcing himself to act.

A sneaking suspicion sprouted in the back of my mind.

Look at that! Now the attack is over, he's leaving the wounded alive and is simply strolling away.

Changing focus, I concentrated on those echoes expressed by the badly wounded. In spite of their miraculous reprieve, trepidation and fear of prolonged agony drenched the ether in an evocatively refreshing mist of misery and despair. Some called out to God, others a whole host of saints, thinking such deities might save them. Sipping from such a panic-laced ambiance made my heart thump like a jackrabbit on heat.

This is what hell could be like . . . Would be like, if I had my way.

Time leaped again, on this occasion to the moment two more entities arrived. I recognized the pair immediately. The Second and Sixth.

With calm but focused savagery, they dispatched those wretches still clinging to unlife. Economical to a fault, they were quick to take advantage of whatever was at hand. Brains, hearts, livers, eyes and tongues. Devouring anything and everything from which a judgment could be made.

I wonder?

On a whim, I tuned in to the resonance of their gluttony. Enlarging the experience, I then compared it with a full sensory overlay of what the Fifth had done. It was quickly apparent the two attacks were completely at odds.

While the Second and Sixth's actions were natural and enacted without fear of consequence, the Fifth's seemed contrived.

It's like he's fulfilling a role.

A mere spectator to past atrocities, I homed in on the Fifth again and watched as his wraith ambled away from the carnage he had so expertly wrought, and back up the prominence from whence he came.

My earlier sneaking suspicion now hammered away inside my skull.

Fulfilling a role . . .

No! It can't be?

Punching through the ether, I phased up onto the rise and opened my senses wide.

The area was open and exposed to the winds whistling down from the frozen wastes of the far north. Each gust bit like a knife and whipped my cloak into distorted whorls to match the frenzied dancing of the long grasses about me. I had always found the desolation of such places relaxing. Closing my eyes to the hypnotic dance of the reeds, I reached out with my consciousness and began prizing the threads of the Sheolspace continuum apart. Fortunately, a powerful afterimage still remained.

"Well, screw me blind," I spluttered, "it *was* Grislington all along. So how many—?"

"I see you are as attentive as you are mighty."

Without warning, I felt the tattoos across my body burn hot. Those I could see flared red, and before I knew it, I was sheathed in a layer of palladinium beneath my cowl.

How did he manage—?

The Second of the Seven stepped away and raised his hands in a nonthreatening gesture. "The rumors are true, then? You have been returned to your former state," his gaze flicked across the armor, "though once again, Satan has seen fit to grace you with unprecedented favor."

Instant aggression helped me fight down a double dose of astonishment. Faster than the eye could follow, my scythe flew from its sheath and into my hand, extended and ready to dispense deadly gratification.

"Your casual approach doesn't cut any slack with me. And you're being incredibly naïve if you don't think I'll kill you as soon as look at you." I spun on the spot, just to be sure."Especially as you've been foolish enough to come here on your own."

The Second betrayed no sign of alarm, other than to take another backward step.

"I assure you, Reaper, I offer no threat or duplicity. On the contrary, I am merely an observer drawn to the angel's accomplishments and am as puzzled as you are as to the reasons he would go to such lengths to foment outrage."

The enforcer's aura was extremely powerful, and glittered with the faultless clarity of pure unadulterated honesty.

Fuck me, my day keeps getting better and better. Then a simple truth struck home. *And, of course, he has no reason to lie.*

No sooner had I acknowledged this fact than the sigils adorning my breastplate throbbed with a baleful green light, and the armor seemed to melt into my skin.

"An impressive addition to your already considerable arsenal," the Second murmured, "as if you weren't already formidable enough."

"Flattery doesn't work either," I snapped, "unless there's an expensive meal and chocolates involved." Then I remembered something about this particular entity from our last encounter back at Black Tower Bridge. Making a rare attempt to hold my temper, I asked, "So, how about granting me the benefits of your enhanced insight? If you're so concerned, why do *you* think Grislington went to all this trouble? I bet this isn't the only one of his attacks that's been blamed on your illegal auditing."

The paradox lowered his arms and adopted a relaxed posture.

"Who knows the mind of one of the oldest creatures under creation, Reaper, especially one driven insane over countless eons by loneliness and despair? Such bitterness and loss would be hard to endure." He turned away to stare at the shroud glazing the distant horizon in thick gloom. "This is the reason I ponder, long and hard, why the cherub chose to remain in hell after regaining his liberty. Even without his wings, Grislington has the means to travel nearly anywhere. So why stay? Is it to seek revenge, recover his sensibilities or, like you, does he seek to establish the true nature of his altered identity?"

Like me? "What the blazes are you dithering on about?"

The Second stiffened and I felt an inrush of potential.

"My apologies, Daemon Grim. Much might have been achieved had I been allowed to test my theory. Summonsed, I am constrained to obey."

And with that, he folded out of sight.

Why does no one in this godforsaken hellhole ever speak in plain English?

A whole plethora of questions and thoughts crowded in on me. But one in particular niggled more than most.

Of course, I'm so used to seeing Satan's many guises that I tend to forget he's a fallen angel himself. Angels have wings. It's a natural extension of their being. But Grislington doesn't have any now. Thunderstruck, I made a connection. *So, what can his wings do that the* Sword of Celestial Arches *can't? And would hope of their retrieval be enough to keep him here while his mind is so fragmented?*

Then another firework fanfare exploded across the landscape of bright ideas.

Hey, I wonder if this has anything to do with what Elizabeth was twittering on about back at the Den?

"Poor angel, to be thus emasculated and teased with the means of his escape."

I thought that related to the sword? The Boss did plant the damned thing right in front of him in his cell after all, and then teased him with it by putting it just out of reach. I never stopped to think about what he might have done with Grislington's wings.

Turning to face directly into the frigid embrace of the wind, I threw my arms wide and allowed it to soothe away my agitation. Then I came to a decision.

"Stuff this. The Sibitti weren't really involved and will have to wait until another time. If Grislington is after his wings, Satan only knows what he might get up to."

Although . . . wouldn't it be better just to let him go, and good riddance?

And just like that, my priorities changed.

*

Having squeezed through the Colonosseum Borehole several hours earlier, Champ and Yamato immediately ran into a snow-covered brick wall, for while the clue they had recovered from Daphne Hemlock's computer in Vilencia was descriptive, Niflheim turned out to be more of a primordial wilderness of relentless blizzards and drifts than expected. As such, the reference to *Perry and Bing's cabin* had initially produced an endless list of possibilities. So many, in fact, that the Hounds had been forced to waste an hour while the experts in such matters—Bella and Donna Nightshade—interrogated their systems for indicators that would help narrow the margin.

Although vexing, it was an hour well spent, for the girls had come up trumps.

Thousands of chalets there might be in such a sparsely populated realm, but only three had drawn their interest. *Let it Snow*, *Magic Moments* and *Sleighride*. All were isolated, and each and every one was situated along the frozen shores of Hvergelmir Lake, which lay far beyond the ice crystal forests of Raknagar, the northernmost city of Niflheim.

Champ and Yamato pounced on the proffered morsels and put their multi-phasic generator to good use, traversing vast distances in moments and making up for lost time.

It was obvious the first two properties were dead-enders. Despite being in a good state of repair, they exuded a bone-deep chill that only occurred following months of abandonment or disuse. A deathly deciding factor in such an inhospitable place, where attrition didn't need any excuse to exact a heavy price.

However, their final candidate, *Sleighride*, looked much more promising.

Constructed from black juniper, the lodge's steeply angled roof was thick with snow; a sure sign it was well insulated. Alpine-style doors and windows, tightly shuttered, graced both northern and southern aspects, while a wraparound veranda draped in a full complement of yard-long icicles completed the picture-postcard scene. An open hut stood to one side, fully stocked with freshly cut logs. Opposite, a modern hi-tech garage looked oddly out of place in such a winter wonderland setting.

Smoke curled in lazy spirals from the top of a stone chimney, only to be dispersed by the thick foliage of surrounding pine trees. While there were no obvious signs anyone had made their way to or from the cabin in a long time, there were clear indicators of recent trips to the wood store, where amateurish attempts had been made to mask a trail of footprints.

Well used to the ways of the wilds, the Hell Hounds had spent another hour silently circling the cabin and its environs. Watching, listening and waiting. A fruitful endeavor, for they discovered several tripwires and nearly a dozen pressure-activated antipersonnel mines protecting the approaches, and a particularly nasty laser grid and a tooth-jarring dampening field covering the property itself.

To Yamato's thinking, their targets were definitely inside, and despite their best endeavors may as well have hung a sign out front: *Open For Being Killed Business.*

An insubstantial phantom, he drifted out from the ever-present haar saturating the tree line in a sheen of mystery. "Well," he enquired, "is it Hedera and Foxglove, or not?"

Motionless amongst the verglas ferns bordering the fringes of the forest, Champ looked like a frost-covered mannequin, stiff and white, barely moving except for the occasional flare of his nostrils, which Yamato noticed were now quivering rapidly.

"Oh, it's them all right."

"What makes you so sure?"

"Can't you smell 'em?" Champ sounded incredulous. "Incompetents that they are, they at least made an effort to cover their tracks movin' about outside. However, it seems the dozy Jezebels forgot that odors are more noticeable in places like this where there's no pollution. Once they got indoors, they doused themselves in perfume . . ." He sniffed.

"Plagus eau de toilet by Jean-Paul Guillotine if I'm not mistaken, same as back at the apartment. I tell you, buddy, if we were any closer, I'd have a sneezin' fit."

Yamato inclined his head in acknowledgment of his partner's assessment. All of them possessed superlative skills to one degree or another, and among the Hell Hounds, Champ stood supreme as a tracker.

I'd missed that one. Thank goodness he's more attentive than he looks.

"And what of our elusive assassins? I must confess, I haven't sensed sight or sound of anybody else since we've been here."

"I think it's safe to say we've got the jump on 'em." Champ sounded confident. "They left in a hurry and were obviously keen to get here ahead of us. That means they didn't have time to get any proper thermal gear. You know as well as I do, it's colder out here than a witch's tit in a brass bra. That's why I suggested we simply hang around for a while. There's no way they'd be able to endure these conditions for as long as us and still be fightin' fit."

Sound reasoning, and eloquently expressed.

As Yamato absorbed the implications of Champ's logic, he decided it was time to make their move. "Bearing in mind the security measures they've deployed about their little abode, how would you go about getting inside?"

Champ shook his head, blinked away a glazing of ice from his lashes and cast an expert eye over their target.

"Well, the orb is out, that's for sure. The dampenin' field around this place is tuned so high my dick's threatenin' to burst out my britches spittin' spiders and scorpions . . ."

"Thank you, brother. I can't begin to describe the delightful image you've just conjured in my mind. So what would you recommend that doesn't require such a graphic description?"

"Seriously? I'd recommend a *hard* entry." Champ grinned and patted his loins. Then he jerked his chin toward the south side of the property where the trees and foliage had grown closer to the cabin itself. "Through that window there."

"And if it's barred?"

Champ stood, causing a layer of hoar frost to break free from his clothes. As it showered about his feet in a miniature snowstorm, he reached inside the folds of his cloak and withdrew his ever-present Abaddon 6000 pump-action shotgun.

"Ah, that's nothin' Big Bertha can't handle."

"Does that mean you're volunteering to breach?"

"I guess so." Champ gestured toward the lodge. "Shall we go and spoil their day?"

Yamato's eyes glazed over as he attempted to push his astral gaze through the dampening field for the umpteenth time that day. Once again, he only managed to capture a fleeting impression of what was inside before overwhelming pressure threatened to burst his head apart.

"All I'm getting is a feeling of two frightened girls who are desperate to find a way out of the mess they've dug themselves into. I'm almost inclined to offer them protection."

"What the fuck?"

"Why not? After all, their former employers have turned against them, and we share a common enemy now. They know they don't stand a chance alone, so they might jump at the opportunity to tell us what they know in exchange for safe passage out of here."

Champ's eyes narrowed.

"And *once* we're outta here?"

"Why, they'd no longer need our protection and we'd be forced to extract further information—as required—by fair means or foul." Now it was Yamato's turn to smile. "Though, knowing our track record, it'd most likely be foul."

"You know, I kinda like the sound of that. It's just cruel enough to be classy. Let's go and put the window in and see what they say."

Suddenly businesslike, the two bounty hunters melted into their environment and crept forward. So professional were they that even their passing didn't leave an impression in the snow, and after a few minutes, they were in the perfect position to avoid the laser grid and begin their final approach.

Going fully tactical, the Hounds reverted to telepathy.

How far out does the shield extend? Champ asked.

About two to three feet from the walls.

And you're positive it's only a psychic fuzzer?

Yes. Its resonance is unusual, but my examinations have revealed it seems to effectively mute all forms of extrasensory manipulation within its threshold. Why?

Oh, you'll see.

Champ led the way until they were so close to the property that they could hear voices coming from inside, along with the occasional *clink* of glass on glass.

Are they havin' themselves a party? Champ chortled. *Hell, I love gate crashin' parties.*

Celebrate all you want after we get inside, Yamato retorted. He released a farseeing pulse into the surrounding forest to ensure they were still alone. *The sooner we get this mess sorted, the sooner we can all relax.*

Jeez, keep yer hat on. It was just a suggestion.

Without further argument, Champ lowered himself into the nearest drift and rolled forward toward the chalet, flattening the snow as he went and leaving a compacted furrow for Yamato to follow. He stopped just short of the outer veranda. *Wouldn't want to spoil the surprise now, would we?*

Wriggling back, Champ adjusted his position, checked his weapon and tensed. *All set?*

Yes.

Then here we go. Up and over the railing in three, two, one . . . Now!

Champ sprang forward at a run. This time his feet crunched with every step.

Yamato drew his sword and lingered to check on the progress of his probe. It was nearly a mile out and fading but it had done its job, for he now knew they were entirely alone.

Boom!

A gap the size of a manhole cover appeared in the shutters, blowing the windows inward. Yamato set off, and by the time he had closed on the porch, was hot on his partner's heels as Champ crashed inside. Hitting the floor a moment later, Yamato rolled and collided with an upholstered easy chair, sending it tumbling across the room. Capitalizing on the distraction, Yamato scanned the interior. In that instant, he saw Champ had already engaged someone over by the fireplace to his right. Yamato gamboled left, away from his partner and toward the only other occupant, who had just emerged from the kitchen area.

Wide-eyed with shock, she was frozen to the spot. Glass fragments and a wet patch on the floor marked where she had dropped her drink.

The female noticed Yamato staring at the stain and glanced down, only to find the tip of a mystically empowered sword poking into her throat. Fear radiated from her in waves. She gulped and stepped back.

"Look at me." Yamato tapped her on the bottom of her chin twice with the flat of his blade. "So which one are you?"

"Wha . . . what?"

"Which one are you? Ivy Hedera or Lily Foxglove?"

"I . . . I'm Lily. Ivy's over there." She frowned. "Does he really need to be that rough?"

Something heavy hit the ground behind Yamato, and the sounds of struggle suddenly stopped.

"Crazy fuckin' bitch," Champ muttered.

Yamato tried to scan what his colleague was doing, only to be rewarded by what felt like a spike being driven into his temple.

Yeow! Have they—?"Is the dampening field active *inside* the property as well?"

"Yes, it is," Lily replied. "Daphne suggested it would be a good idea to install them at our hideaways so our stray thoughts wouldn't give us away. That's who we're waiting for, actually. We . . . we ran into a bit of bother and she suggested we—"

"You'll have a bloody long wait then, girlie," Champ interjected from across the room. His laugh sounded harsh in the aftermath of the attack. "Let's just say she's had her breathing privileges revoked."

Lily's brows flared, and one hand flew to her mouth.

Oh, for pity's sake. Yamato circled to one side and cast a filthy look toward his partner. Aloud, he continued, "No, we didn't kill her. Someone beat us to it. Someone, I might add, who is on their way here as we speak."

The young woman before him seemed to deflate. He decided to press the advantage.

"The way I see it, you can either wait for whoever Chopin and Tesla have sent to butcher you, or you can talk to us and get a bit of payback. Who knows, what you have to say might even be valuable enough to keep you alive, or at the very least, qualify you for a less . . . *invasive* form of reassignment."

"What? The Reaper and his Hell Hounds showing mercy? Since when has that ever happened?"

Yamato stepped closer.

"Wrong answer. You should be asking, 'when has the Reaper ever lied?' You know his reputation. If you qualify for his special dispensation, then even Satan won't touch you. It has nothing to do with mercy, and everything to do with expediency. He favors those denizens wise enough to assist him in his many duties. And don't forget, we have ways of extracting information from you whether you're undead or not. Either way, we'll get what we want. Make it easier for us, and you might benefit in the long run."

As a final incentive, Yamato leaned in and whispered, "After all, eternity is a very, *very* long time."

Lily stumbled, and then collapsed into a nearby kitchen chair. Yamato watched impassively as all the fight seemed to drain out of her.

I do believe we have a winner.

"Ah, fuck it. Why not? I told them we should have come clean at the very beginning when we first thought we'd been influenced by that damned smarmy bastard of a doctor. I never liked him, you know."

Cream? "Oh, really?"

She straightened. "What do you want to—?"

Crack!

Crack!

A neat hole appeared in the center of Lily's forehead and she was propelled backward to the floor. Yamato caught the distinctive scent of a rip-bullet and rolled away, drawing a handful of ninja stars from his belt pouch as he did so. He came to his feet and movement out of the corner of one eye alerted him to further danger. Twisting instinctively, he ducked, let fly and gamboled again.

Thunk! Thunk! Thunk!

The shurikens embedded themselves in the wall where a woman had been standing only a fraction of a second before.

Gods, but she's fast.

Boom!

Big Bertha roared, blowing a gaping hole in the couch behind which the unknown female had taken cover. But she wasn't the target. Her partner was.

A second head peeked out from behind ruined cushions.

Guiteau? So that must mean the second shot was for—?

Yamato glanced toward Champ's position. Sure enough, Hedera's body had already dissipated. He nodded toward his partner, and Champ began to unload his weapon into the furniture, starting at the end where Guiteau was hiding.

Sidling toward the opposite end, Yamato relaxed and held himself ready. Among the Hell Hounds, he was known for his elemental affinity. Employing those abilities now, he created a glaze of ice across the floor where he knew their enemy would emerge.

When they came, both assassins were surprisingly swift. They went down almost immediately in a tangle of arms and legs. Yamato was upon them in an instant, his sword cutting left and right in his first pass.

Two severed gun frames and top slides fell to the floor, barrels and silencers all.

If they were surprised by his dexterity, Guiteau and his companion didn't show it. They stood warily and edged closer together, back to back. Yamato found himself facing the woman once again.

Despite her predicament, she held herself regally and appeared calm and aware of her surroundings.

"I don't believe I've had the pleasure?" Yamato crooned as he positioned himself for his next thrust. He inclined his head slightly. "Yamato Takeru, once known as Prince Ōsu of Japan."

"Isabella," she returned the gesture, "once Queen of Castile. It is rare to find a true gentleman in such a place." She gazed disdainfully at Champ as he moved to Yamato's side. "Especially when one consorts with such riffraff. Still, we have each other. And as befits a meeting of royal blood, I bring a gift."

As smooth as silk, Isabella removed a small pyramid-shaped device from behind her back. Covered along one side in twinkling blue lights, it looked so small and inconspicuous that at first glance, Yamato thought he was looking at an electronic alarm clock.

Isabella smiled and, with fluid grace, gently tossed the gadget toward him.

"Careful," she warned, "it's delicate and might break easily."

A flare of alarm coursed along Yamato's nerves. He started to shy away and shout a warning, only to watch helplessly as Champ ignored him to reach out and pluck the offering from midair.

Yamato heard a high-pitched hum and felt a skittering like invisible insects across his skin. His own voice seemed to slow and deepen as it ground to a halt.

Then everything warped. The air tinged pink, and both intruders disappeared from sight.

Chapter 23: The Maulin' Rouge

The Angel Grislington fought melancholy. A gnawing dissatisfaction with everything he had achieved since his release festered inside him. If he didn't do something about it soon, that irritation would demand an uncharacteristic, cataclysmic release.

In an effort to appease his frustrations, he had come here, to one of the most infamous nightspots in all the many circles of latter-day hell: the Maulin' Rouge.

Founded in 1889 in the world above, the Moulin Rouge was best known as the birthplace of the modern-day form of the can-can, a dance routine originally introduced by courtesans to seduce the rich and influential into parting with cash or favors.

But as the world later came to appreciate, the Moulin Rouge was more—much more—than a mere sleazy venue. Its founders, Charles Zidler and Joseph Oller, had meant to capitalize on the opportunities blossoming in an increasingly vast and impersonal nineteenth-century Paris. They located their new venture in the Montmartre district of the Eighteenth Arrondissement, an area that had managed to retain a bucolic village atmosphere despite its extravagant setting. Because of this, the Moulin Rouge quickly became known as a place where people from all walks of life—workers, residents, artistes, businessmen, the middle classes, elegant ladies and foreigners passing through—could mix and enjoy the freedom of unbridled pleasure without fear of prejudice or judgment.

Needless to say, when the original nightclub mysteriously burnt down in 1915, the underworld was keen to put such profligacy to better use. Before the month was out, residents of Boulevard de Cliché, in the Eighteenth Horrondissement of Perish, witnessed a spectacular rebirth, for the neon-red windmill and gaudy revolving signs of the earthly establishment were transposed into the Maulin' Rouge, a cesspit of brutal and decadent excess. A venue where stocking-clad fillies would engage in kick fights to the death, and a whole host of cabaret hopefuls judged them on their martial prowess before the worst were hung, drawn, quartered and guillotined at their patrons' displeasure.

Yet, as popular as these acts were, they were but an aperitif to the main course: *An Evening with the Minotaur*, a nightly extravaganzaat which those denizens who had fallen foul of the local injustice system were thrown to their fate.

To cater to this event, an adjustable labyrinth had been built beneath the glass floor of the main restaurant so that diners and other clientele could witness the tribulations of those served up for their entertainment.

The premise was simple. Offenders were released at different points around the edge of the maze with the goal of reaching a cage at its center. If they made it, they would be pardoned for their crimes and their records expunged. But the Minotaur never made it easy, for it was wily and relentless and possessed preternatural senses and strength that allowed it to home in on its victims with uncanny precision.

Nevertheless, a few were lucky enough to evade the creature from time to time. And that's where the audience came in, for it was their job to try to persuade the more naïve miscreants to follow their *helpful* directions from above . . . usually straight back into the arms of the beast.

A great deal of mirth and merriment ensued when such a tragedy happened, for the Minotaur didn't like looking foolish and would work itself into a frenzy, epitomizing the name of the establishment by goring, battering and rending such unfortunates limb from limb before gnawing on their bones and stomping the mauled remains into a bloody pulp.

As had, in fact, just happened right beneath Grislington's table.

Unfortunately, neither the spectacle of the event nor the rich tapestry of the establishment's history could relieve the angel's sour mood. His sumptuous meal lay on the plate going cold, the Armand de Brigand sat fizzing forlornly in its glass, and the summary execution so clinically performed right under his nose went unacknowledged.

Grislington lingered instead on cherished recollections of an endlessly burnished landscape, an existence where modulating moods and pulsating thoughts added vibrant solidarity to the celestial medium. In such a place, intent was as substantial as reality. Purpose was tangible. Applied will was a potent catalyst to the creative blueprint spanning the length and breadth of the universe. He tried with all his might to stay submerged in the soothing balm such memories brought, but all too soon his consciousness spiraled inward, and his perspicacity became captive once more to the profanity of the here and now.

Rapturous applause caused glass railings and numerous other fitments positioned about the show floor to vibrate, refracting the light from chandeliers and table candles alike into a million different possibilities.

That little detail only reminded Grislington how pale a reflection hell was, and left him feeling gloomier than ever.

I don't belong here, that's what it is. No matter how I try to fool myself and make excuses for the loss endured during my confinement, the quintessence of this place is a scourge upon my soul. I yearn for higher things, austere though they are in comparison.

Only half awake, he suffered the boisterous celebrations in silence.

What an empty, meaningless existence. Trapped betwixt life and true death, they seek to fill their twilight world with revelry and delight, failing to realize what a fruitless charade it is. He sneered. *Eternal torment, my ass. Eternal licentiousness, more like. No wonder the Sibitti were dispatched. Even Daemon Grim would do a better job if left to his own devices. At least* he *wants the underworld cleansed of worthless chattel.*

Grislington again became lost in the bewildering fugue of his imagination.

As do my long lost brothers of the heavenly host. My goodness, but that would be an event to see. Purification of the sternest stripe to put the Sibitti to shame.

So consumed was he by his meandering that Grislington didn't notice that room went silent, or that he had started to verbalize his internal debate.

"I need to be away from this feculent mire and its fouled sensibilities. But where? My sword can do much, but it could never breach the Divide, for it was not forged with such majesty in mind. Earth and its mortal plane, then? But how shallow and paltry that would be after the exuberance I have experienced here."

"You fail to heed me, angel? Am I so far beneath you that you would—?"

"No, I desire to return where I was created." A pang of sorrow pierced him to the core. "But to get there, I need that which was taken from me. How will I—?"

"Wings you want, is it? Then why do you fail to acknowledge my existence?"

Snapping free of his daydream, Grislington found everybody staring at him in wide-eyed amazement. Some kept glancing toward the floor. Following the line of their gazes, he discovered the Minotaur pointing at him.

"Ah, I have your attention at last," it boomed. A toss of its great head sprayed blood from its horns and jaws across the maze wall. The brute made a show of addressing the other patrons, who crowded forward to get a better look. "So, realizing it is but a shadow of its former self, our heavenly minion seeks solace in the recovery of that which can make it whole again."

Murmurs sprang up in one place after another.

"An angel? Here?"

"That's not possible, is it?"

"Is this part of the act? Are they going to fight?"

"I've seen Altos, and that looks nothing like him. He must be an impostor."

Grislington didn't like the way things were progressing. He glanced toward the exits.

"Have you nothing to say, messenger?" the Minotaur taunted. "Do you need to run away and hide, or do you have permission from Big Daddy to take action?"

Thus the Minotaur crossed an invisible line.

One moment, Grislington's primary concern was preserving what remained of his shattered anonymity with as much dignity as he could muster. Then something in the fiend's tone demanded response. He surged to his feet, knocking tables and chairs out of the way so he could gain a better view of his accuser.

Sensing confrontation, wiser damned souls and those of a more cowardly disposition fled. Most stayed put, content to wait and see how things developed before making up their minds. Realizing they might be in for a once in an un-lifetime treat, a reckless few continued edging closer, endeavoring to secure a prime spot.

"What do you know of my wings, vermin?" Grislington snarled. "And how can you know of such things when you are naught but an abomination?"

"Regarding the how, that's for you to find out. As to the what? More than you, it seems. Perhaps I should make the effort to collect them myself? They'd make a fine addition to my home, don't you think?" The Minotaur gesticulated with one hand and absentmindedly began scratching at its rump with the other. Then it tensed, adopted a look of fierce concentration, and farted. "Do you know, I think I will? I'll keep your pretty pinions in my cage as a lesson in futility to others."It grinned. "A fitting parallel, don't you agree?"

And with that, it turned and trotted off into the labyrinth.

Grislington went white with rage, and in that moment his glamour fell away, revealing him fully for what he was. Now people did fall back. Some in fear, others in horror, while yet more shied away out of a sense of shame and humility, for here was a being whose very gaze hinted at the purity to be found in madness and utter ruination.

The angel's brows furrowed and twin laser beams thundered from his eyes, melting the toughened glass at his feet as if it were nothing but a thin film of wax, and sending a crazy paving network of cracks splintering away across the floor.

As light as a feather, Grislington dropped down into the dirt. Ignoring the stench of rotting flesh and years of decay, he set off after his quarry.

Echoing laughter teased him as it resonated along the system of interconnecting corridors. The patter of shuffling feet from above as diners overcame their shock and pitched forward only added to his disorientation. Checking his stride, Grislington dismissed such interference and allowed his senses to reach out through the warren of twists and turns until he located his tormentor.

I have you now.

He set off, straight as an arrow and oblivious to the presence of intervening concrete and metal impediments that sought to hinder his progress. In mere seconds, he had closed on his target. Demolishing a final obstruction, Grislington slammed his delicate fist into the side of the monster's head.

It went down as if poleaxed. Nonetheless, Grislington was dealing with a Minotaur, and they were forged of sturdy stock. Rolling to its feet, the beast lowered its bulk and reacted instinctively. It charged.

Lifted into the air, Grislington was propelled backward and smashed into a wall. Bricks crumbled and shards went flying. The brute kept pumping its legs, as if attempting to grind him to powder.

Absorbing the force of the attack, Grislington calmly raised his elbow high and stabbed it down onto the base of the Minotaur's neck. Knees as thick and sinewy as tree trunks sagged. He struck again, and this time the fiend dropped to the floor, stunned.

In one fluid motion, Grislington grasped his adversary by the horns, twisted, and drove the heel of his palm into its face. A sickening *snap* rang out. The monster fell, prostrate upon the ground. Moving to sit astride his foe, Grislington then thrust his fingers deep into its chest.

Gore spattered across the stones, though not one drop thought to sully the pristine radiance of the angel's feet or robes.

Leaning down, Grislington sneered, "You are vanquished, unworthy insect. Now tell me, quickly before you expire: what do you know of my wings?"

Too weak to answer, the beast glared up defiantly.

Swiftly, Grislington seized the Minotaur by its snout and ripped its nostrils open. It squealed and a gurgling sound purled up from its throat.

Oh dear, it seems to be drowning in its own blood. "I asked you a question. Tell me now, and I might alleviate the suffering of your passage."

Once again, the smoldering coals of the creature's gaze bored into him. But this time, the atmosphere shimmered and Grislington found himself transposed to another place. There, he looked down from on high upon a luxuriant barbaric bastion. Although its stones were dark and its aspect brooding, he recognized enough of its basic features to remember where he had seen such a stronghold before in its natural form.

I know that place! It was featured in some of the literature the jailers used to leave in my cell. On earth, they call it the Palace of Versailles. So is this . . . ?

The ether quivered again. This time, Grislington espied a long vaulted hall full of mirrors and candles. He couldn't quite make out what lay hidden in shadow at the far end of the chamber, but the inference was clear.

A thrill of hope electrified his entire body.

At last. And once I am whole again, this realm will be open to . . . ?

The Minotaur began to struggle beneath him. Releasing the nuance of the vision, Grislington allowed his mind to clear and regarded his victim with an air of detachment.

"Thank you. You seem to have served your purpose rather well. I suppose the best thing you can do now is . . . die."

Faster than a striking viper, Grislington's fist snaked out and shattered the top of the monster's skull. It stiffened, twitched once, and went limp. As it faded from view, Grislington threw back his head and let out a cry of triumph.

Now everyone will fear m–

His gaze came to rest on a familiar face in the crowd.

Tesla?

Surprised, Grislington focused on the scientist, only to watch helplessly as he disappeared from sight.

"My, my. It looks as if my previous stalkers have been busy preparing a little finale of their own?" He clenched his fist and the air blazed in argent majesty. "It'd be a pity to deny them one last curtain call. After all, when it falls, an entirely different show will commence."

*

Wrapped in multiple layers to combat the chill of the dank night air, Chopin nevertheless shivered uncontrollably. He didn't know if that was due to his increasingly fragile constitution or the jitters eating away at his nerves the longer he was forced to wait.

Tesla should have been back by now, with Grislington in hot pursuit. I wonder what could be keeping him.

Chopin poured a mug of steaming hot coffee from a stainless steel Thermos and settled back against the bole of the nearest tree. Savoring the warmth radiating through his hands, he did his best to calm his fears and remain alert.

I'm being paranoid. We're well prepared and our rings will give us an edge against anything the angel might try. I just don't like hanging around this close to the enemy.

Tendrils of thick cloying mist wound their way out from the forest, only to undulate down into the valley toward their target a mere half mile away; the Palace of Verse and Sighs. A symbol of absolute monarchy and a tribute to Satan's vanity, the exterior of the citadel was a lavish affair; a mixture of French baroque and the fetishly gothic. Ornamental gardens of outrageous taste punctuated neatly manicured lawns with oases both refined and grotesque. Complex external balustrades and railings adorned chic, well crafted walls. And spike-garnished towers sat in crowning glory atop pillars of volcanic sheen. An overload of architectural extravagance, the palace nevertheless retained a sense of symmetrical orderliness that only hinted at its true purpose.

And tonight, we'll crack this place wide open in one of our most daring escapades to date, and I'll be a step closer to the one I love.

To pass the time, Chopin began a final check of the equipment and artifacts they would be using.

"Okay, what have we got? A Dagger of Damocles, just in case we need to negate anything nasty. The Mermaid's Pinto to pierce unforeseen shields. One of the Fishwives' nets for a shroud of invisibility. A spare orb to counter any temporal obstacles. Two microgravity pyramids to put some space between us and the inevitable hot pursuit. And finally, the *Sword of Uncovered Secrets*. Yes, it looks like we're all—"

The air before him puckered slightly, and Tesla appeared. Despite the gloom, Chopin could see his friend grinning from ear to ear.

"I take it all went well at the Maulin' Rouge?"

"It certainly did," Tesla gushed. He pounced on the near-by flask and helped himself to coffee before explaining further. "I didn't even have to trigger the ripcord capsule in the Minotaur's brain. Grislington took care of the beast for me."

"Grislington? You mean he . . . ?"

"Yes, and with surprising gusto. It's the first time I've ever seen him lose his temper and it was quite an eye-opener. The restaurant was in uproar. I thought he was going to trash the place until I made sure he could spot me among the crowd."

"And that did the trick?"

"I've no doubt."

"So he'll be on the way here?"

"Soon. I mitigated us a ten minute window, so we've got time to pack our stuff and get into position before we light the blue touch paper." Tesla snorted in ill-concealed mirth. "And there will be fireworks, believe me. Don't be fooled by what Grislington looks like; Grim will have his hands full tonight."

Chopin's mind raced, ten to the dozen.

"Speaking of Grim, what about him and our other loose ends?"

"Being tied off nicely as we speak." Tesla paused to squeeze Chopin firmly by the shoulder. "And we have the *Sword of Uncovered Secrets* to thank for that. I tell you, that thing is an absolute devils' end. Who would have thought an Inquisitor would be open to such manipulations?"

Chopin shrugged. "I was surprised myself. Unhinged as she is, there's nothing tangible for the coercive sequence to bond with. It's only in those rare moments when she slips between madness and lucidity that the compulsive element can take hold and work its magic." He sniffed. "Pity it's only temporary."

"It will suffice. Our board is set once more and other pieces are in play. Now we've got to ensure everyone is in the right place at the right time to benefit from the results."

Tesla's assurances reminded Chopin of their immediate priorities.

"So what now?"

"Now? I suggest we use the remaining time wisely and make our first jump into the Sentinels' Square. It's one of the outermost gardens, and because of the resonance given off by the Wyrd tree, most of the reaver and demon patrols avoid it like the plague. However, we're going to use the tree's leaves to boost our own strength and test the extent of His Royal Ass-wipe's new sheolanite shielding."

"Won't that attract attention?"

"If it does, we'll be long gone by the time anyone responds, and they'll be left thinking it was something to do with the tree's psychoactive properties. Either way, our maneuver will have served its purpose. My early scans revealed a predominance of the new resin lining the walls of the entire Colonnade. If that's the case, Satan's eagerness to protect his privacy will work in our favor, because we'll be able to wait right on the doorstep and no one will be any the wiser."

"Grim might though. And if he doesn't work it out, the angel certainly will, especially after that little escapade at the Maulin' Rouge. Neither of them is stupid."

"True. But that's why we have to make sure they're sufficiently distracted by each other to not worry about us until it's too late." Tesla downed the last of his drink before checking his watch. "Time's a' ticking. Are you ready?"

"I've been ready for decades. Let's get this show on the road."

Chapter 24: Putting Two and Two Together

"Bollocks!"

I had just ended a long-distance call with Bella and Donna Nightshade across in New Hell, and couldn't help venting out loud. Notwithstanding their usual tenacity, the girls had been hard-pressed to pin down how the temporal component of the portal generators actually worked. In all fairness, that wasn't surprising given the limited amount of time they'd had to investigate the matter. And I couldn't complain. If I insisted on rushing them, it could lead to all sorts of risky anomalies, time shears and chronological incongruities. Chaos theories aside, the last thing we wanted were alternate-dimension Chopins and Teslas running around . . . Or more Sibitti, come to that.

Swallowing my disappointment, I decided to pursue another area of investigation where I was sure to have better luck. I took a seat at my desk and cast my astral senses down into the dungeons. Despite the late hour, I knew someone would still be at work.

"Ferenc?"

His reply came through after only a moment's delay. *Yes, Daemon?*

"Is Elizabeth with you, and is she orbiting anywhere near

this part of the solar system? I'd really like to get her insight on something."

Give her a few minutes, will you? We've just completed a twelve hour stint and she's showering. Ferenc projected the gory image of blood-soaked saws and blades lying across a pile of entrails on the floor. A nearby assortment of spikes and butcher's hooks still had hunks of lacerated flesh hanging from them. *As you can see, she got rather carried away.*

Cool. That's my girl. "As soon as possible then. I'm in my study."

Understood.

While I waited, I decided it would be a good idea to run my eye over our latest clue again. I felt confident, for I was now armed with a perspective afforded by three recent conversations with Samael, the Second of the Seven, and Elizabeth respectively. Mere snippets on their own, each had acted like an important piece to a jigsaw puzzle, granting me a clearer view of the bigger picture.

Placing it before me, I read:

Pinioned within a silvered sheen

I have no substance,

For it is a medium portraying a mere perception of death

Whilst liberated from the excess of time.

Congruence and confluence are but flightless messengers

Encapsulated in an eternity of personal reflections,

A colonnade of captured moments, always changing,

Where liberty stares back, forever lost.

"Okay, bearing in mind I now appreciate that '*messenger*' means angel, and that a flightless Grislington has obviously been weakened or diminished in some way by his loss, I now need to understand *how* Satan sought to flaunt his victory in Grislington's face."

I examined the poem once more, taking my time to search for certain keys that would unlock its meaning.

"It isn't as obvious as sticking a sword in the ground out of reach, that's for sure. No, with something as intimate as an angel's wings, he'd make the rub much more personal."

Hmm. Personal . . .

I skimmed the last half of the verse for a third time and considered what I knew about my dark father.

"Like Satan, Grislington was a cherub, one of the higher echelons of the heavenly host. So, it was one hell of an achievement to be able to capture such a creature. The thing is, Satan couldn't exactly advertise his victory to all and sundry like he normally does. In fact, he did just the opposite and sequestered Grislington in an ultra-secret facility on the Isle of Cogs, a place detached from the normal Sheolspace continuum. But if Grislington was already in maximum security, why take his wings and put them somewhere else entirely?"

Then it hit me.

"Because they have to be more than mere trophies. They must be able to do something that would cause havoc in the wrong hands." I wracked my brains. "Where would he put such an accolade?"

Think personal . . . What would exasperate Grislington the most?

The penny dropped.

"Of course. If Satan was denied the opportunity to crow about his conquest, he'd make damned sure his ill-gotten gains were paraded somewhere he could gloat over them any time he wanted, and invite other select parties to do the same at his pleasure. So it would be somewhere exclusive. But where? He has any number of such residences throughout the underverse and can . . . Hang on . . . "

Simple logic took over.

"On display or not, a totem that important would still be subject to the strictest precautions."

I reread the last few lines:

A colonnade of captured moments, always changing,
Where liberty stares back, forever lost.

"A colonnade of captured moments . . . staring back. Captured moments. Colonnade."

Those phrases struck a chord, and I jumped as an ice-cold shock coursed down my spine and along the surface of my skin.

"His Infernal Majesty's chief residence here in Juxtapose: the Palace of Verse and Sighs! Not only is it constantly patrolled and bristling with all sorts of arcane and mundane security protocols, but an entire section of the sanctuary is dedicated to his past victories. What's more, it incorporates the Royal Theatre, where Shakespeare and Marlow are forced to reenact the most glorious of Satan's battles every Halloween. Where better to put such a prize, especially as the entire west wing is devoted to the Colonnade of Eternal Reflections, a hall full of mirror cages where only the most precious of his mementos are kept?"

Bloody hell, I think I've only gone and cracked it!

At that moment, Elizabeth burst into the room, naked as a jaybird and still dripping wet from her shower. For some reason, she appeared unusually serious.

"Elizabeth, is everything all right?"

Marching straight up to me, she placed her fists firmly on the desk, leaned across, and hissed, "Whatever you do this night, make sure you don't get caught in the moment."

Doing my best to ignore the hypnotic beads of water trickling down her breasts toward her nipples, I mumbled, "Caught in what moment?"

"Just take care not to be enamored by your own loss."

What the fuck planet is she on today?

"Elizabeth, I'm sorry but you're not making sense. Why would I need to guard against my own loss?"

She made no reply, except to lean further across the tabletop until we were almost nose to nose. The intensity of her gaze was electric, and as I stared into her eyes, I felt the world begin to spin:

A Wyrd tree stands, tall and proud, at the center of an ash-covered stone garden. Its ruby-colored leaves defy the surrounding desolation and glow with a rose-gold phosphorescence that infuses the entire area with warmth and hope.

Under its benevolent radiance, barren soil darkens and new shoots spring forth, promising rebirth where only death had so recently ensued.

Feelings of confusion and isolation dominate.

"Where . . . where am I?"

"Fear not," a deep and commanding voice intones, "all will be well again, eventually."

"Again?"

"Trust me. You will be refashioned and forged anew into something better."

"Better?"

"You'll see."

Hands turn me to squarely face the light of the tree. Its leaves chime and dance to the caress of an unfelt breeze. The sound of a distant choir recedes, while closer, a chanting chorus rises in unison.

A desire for slumber bows my neck and my palms come to rest upon the pommel of a great sword.

"What is—?"

"No more questions. Sleep now. Though it takes an eternity, you will be mine."

Unattainable oblivion descends and time marches on. Detached, I am yet aware that seasons come and seasons go, their natures corrupted by a cancer gripping this actuality in a way that bends it to another purpose. Vitiated, that tarnished essence becomes as natural and invigorating as life itself . . . And I am changed.

A full moon shimmers in a cloudless, magenta-ochre sky. Resonant with purpose, its argent purity focuses the night like a lens, and fills the now lush square with an expectant hush. It has snowed, and a virgin glaze powders the garden in a crystal white cocoon as cold and brittle as the heart that no longer beats within my obsidian chest.

From the edge of that oasis, I maintain a silent vigil, waiting patiently, knowing that the day will come when I will be unleashed upon an unknown enemy. But for now, I wait . . .

The soft *crunch* of feet upon icy flakes intrudes as a lonely figure walks the unblemished parchment of the path. Hooded in scarlet, her footfall is light and leaves an indented score along its length.

Without a word, she approaches and stands before me. Pale fingers draw back the cowl, and burnished, strawberry-blonde hair that blazes like fire in the moonlight cascades down around her shoulders. She is beautiful, and glows with an ethereal warmth that signifies she is at one with her surroundings.

I feel as if I should know her from somewhere, for this woman bears a familiarity that is as appealing as it is instinctual. She climbs the pedestal on which I stand and stretches up toward my ear.

Cupping her hands, she whispers, "The Divide has been established and the curtain is in place. It's time to wake up—awake—wake up—"

"Daemon, can you hear me? Daemon?"

My perspective turned inside out and I found myself back within my study. Somehow, Elizabeth had squirmed her way across the table and was almost sitting in my lap.

"Thank badness," she gasped, "I thought I'd lost you there for a moment . . . Or should I say *found* you? From the look on your face, I thought you might have slipped through into my reality for a while." She giggled and tapped my bottom lip with one of her fingers. "What a topsy-turvy pair we'd make, eh? Though I think Ferenc might have something to say about that. Naughty, naughty, Reaper."

"I er, I don't know what you . . ."

Elizabeth smiled sweetly, then a switch flipped inside her head and the glint of steel returned to her gaze.

"Just remember what I said, Daemon. You are wading into dangerous waters. When you find out where the angel wants to go, don't let its actions divide your loyalties and encapsulate you in an eternity of sorrow and regret. Know where you belong, and believe in what you are."

With that, Elizabeth arched backward, curled off the other side of my desk, and cartwheeled gracefully from the room.

I have got to get me some of whatever it is she might be taking. How the blazes . . . ?

A flash of inspiration had me sitting bolt upright: *'Where the angel wants to go . . . '*

I put all the clues together and the picture finally became

clear.

"Unholy shit! For all its power, there's one place the *Sword of Celestial Arches* can't encroach upon. Heaven. To do that, it would need to be able to drop the veil and traverse the prohibited area. And the only thing I know of that has the power to cross the Divide is . . ."

Oh fuck!

Only at that moment did I begin to comprehend the depths of the angel's insanity:

If he drops the veil and leaves it down, there'll be pandemonium.

Chapter 25: Out of the Blue

The bell sounded and Tara prepared herself for her first guest of the day. A laborious task, it nonetheless helped ease the tedium of the past twenty-three hours spent locked in a ten-foot by eight-foot isolation cell.

While most of the remaining prisoners at Wormblood Scrubs maximum security prison never got to interact with other denizens, His Satanic Majesty had insisted she serve a special form of penance by being forced to spend her precious free time listening to the gripes and pathetic excuses of those who felt they had been unfairly condemned to an eternity of suffering. A thankless task and a particularly inventive twist of the knife in her case, for she was under compulsion never to reveal her true identity.

One of the four jailers escorted a disheveled female inside the visitors' area. Tara could tell by the way the other woman's eyes flinched around every facet of the room that she was a fresher; newly arrived in hell and ripe for exploitation.

She's no doubt still in a state of self denial and firm in the belief that any moment soon she'll wake up, and all this will be nothing more than a bad dream.

Her caller shuffled forward and took a seat on the other side of the table. After a nervous glance to ensure the guards weren't standing close enough to hear their conversation, the woman leaned across and in a conspiratorial tone whispered, "Are you Teresa, Saint Teresa of Ávila?"

"In spite of what you might have heard, I'm no saint. And when you think about it, what would such a person be doing in a place like this? The name's Tara. And yours?"

"Mandy." She looked crestfallen."I'm sorry. I was told—I mean, they said . . ."

Yes, a definite fresher. Still finding her feet and desperate to clutch at any hope to keep her dream of a reprieve alive.

"I take it you're seeking absolution?"

"Absolution? Goodness me, no. I'm under no illusions about what I did. He was an abusive drunken shit who liked to take his shortcomings out on me any time he'd had one too many. In the end, he deserved what he got. But . . ."

"But?"

Mandy's expression said it all.

"Let me guess," Tara continued, "you can't understand why, after putting up with such behavior for years, you finally snapped. And that one act bound you to an eternity of"—she gestured about them—"this?"

"Well, yes. If there is a loving Almighty,"—the room shuddered and distant thunder rolled—"why would he allow it? I loved my husband. Even when the beatings became more regular, I thought it must be something I'd done, or failed to do properly. I tried my best to change, to be a loyal wife, but it got worse and . . . and . . ."

Ah, the stereotypical never-ending story. "And in the end, you couldn't take it anymore and killed him?"

Mandy's eyes stared into an echo of the past and she nodded her head."I honestly thought I was going to die that night. He kept hitting me and hitting me. When I came round, he'd fallen asleep and—"she sighed—"God knows I tried. I really did."

Another tremor shook the ground, closer this time, and the roar of a lightning strike boomed nearby. Tara felt pain in her ears and noticed how the guards were becoming fidgety. Somewhere, a siren began to wail.

Mandy swiveled in her chair."Is this normal?"

Without warning, the far corner of the room blew inward, overturning furniture, throwing Tara and her guest to the floor and showering everyone in a billowing rain of bricks and dust. The two warders nearest the exit were mown down like wheat, and as the remaining pair rushed to assist, they combusted in a sharp concussion of flames and ash.

By the time the first sooty flakes of their incinerated vestiges hit the floor, everything was deathly still. Then a wind sprang up out of nowhere. Acting like a vacuum, it sucked the choking cloud away in seconds.

Blinking back tears, Tara peeked around the side of an overturned table and was astounded to find a heroically-proportioned Adonis standing close to the breach in the outer wall. Next to him, an equally impressive individual demanded attention; for he was one of the most exquisite creatures she had ever seen. Resplendent in rich mantles and carrying glittering swords, she immediately knew who these entities were.

"To what do I owe the distinction of being singled out by two of the Sibitti?"

The handsomer of the two stepped forward.

"Do I have the pleasure of addressing Teresa Sánchez de Cepeda y Ahumada?"

In the presence of such might, Tara attempted to answer truthfully, but gagged over her words. She tried again, only to feel her throat constrict so badly, she almost choked.

The demigod's gaze seemed to bore down into her soul. One finely chiseled brow arched upward. He gesticulated and the pressure within her chest faded.

Tara gasped. "I am free of coercion!"

"A trifling matter for one such as I." He strode closer and bowed formally. "I am the Second of Seven. My companion for this special venture is the Seventh. By your reaction, I take it you are indeed the Saint Teresa of whom I've heard so much?"

"I am, though I must confess, I don't see why you would go to all this trouble to make my acquaintance unless you seek to audit me?"

"I bloody well knew it!" Everyone turned to look at the only other survivor of the attack, Teresa's visitor, Mandy. "I wondered why you were so blasé about my question when word on the street knows it's you that's in here. I can't wait to . . . to . . . What's happening?"

The Second did nothing more than raise a finger. Mandy's skin started to shine. The glow intensified, brighter and brighter, and she caught her breath. Inexorably, an explosion of angry sparks and an evaporating pink mist brought an untimely end to her interruption.

Teresa watched, appalled, as the enforcer inhaled the fetid greasy eddies left behind by the poor woman's passing.

"Hmm, she was contrite, and honest about the circumstances of her damnation. A rare treasure in a place such as this." The Second graced Teresa with his full attention again. "And no, dear lady, we are not here to measure you. Just the opposite, in fact, for we come seeking your assistance."

Despite the danger, Teresa found herself laughing.

"Erra must be sorely troubled indeed if he is forced to turn to an unworthy for aid. What could I possibly have that would interest the god of plague and mayhem, and that his personified weapons do not already possess?"

The Second knelt at her side and offered Teresa his hand. Only once she had accepted and climbed unsteadily to her feet did he deign to reply. "Why, you are able to access a power that neither I nor my brothers are fit to wield. Love."

"Love?" Teresa was astounded. "Please explain."

"In truth, our methods within this particular realm have proved insufficient. The human spirit—accursed or not—is indomitable when dedicated to a source it finds inspiring. Other hurdles aside, brute strength and terror have failed to exact the results we expected."

"By 'hurdles,' I take it you refer to certain champions in Satan's employ?"

"Indeed. And one in particular."

"Then forgive me for asking, but what do you expect a fragile flower to accomplish where mighty oaks have failed?"

"Do not tarry overlong," the Seventh interjected, "their security forces are beginning to respond and will detect our presence if we linger."

The Second became more insistent.

"We have heard it said that while still alive, you advocated love as the perfect medium through which to bring about change. Having been sentenced unjustly, do you feel this is still the case?"

"Of course. Satan may have scored a minor victory in the greater scheme of things by fooling me into condemning myself, but he failed to appreciate the seeds I would sow upon my arrival here. My secret heart has never faltered. I learned to accept what is unjust in order to serve the needs of the many. Why do you think he locked such a prize away in a place like this? In weakness, my influence grows, and I have yet to employ the greater abilities at my disposal."

"And what would you seek to instill in the undeserving chattel of this realm?"

"It's quite simple. We cannot change the past, but what we do in the present reveals much about the person we've become. No matter how great the sin, love is the most powerful force in the universe for good, and for repentance and fine works. Our Infernal Majesty fears revolution."

The Second stood tall and smiled. Unbelievably, the gesture made him appear even more beauteous than before.

"Just what we needed to hear. Tell me, how would you like the opportunity to express your message without fear of contradiction throughout all the circles of hell?"

"Are you mad? Satan's response and that of his Reaper would be swift and deadly. I would not invite such tragedy willingly, especially as the Undertaker would no doubt be tasked to emphasize the error of my choice."

"Good point." The Second appeared to consider the matter for a moment. "Then what if the Sibitti chose to protect you while you approached the matter from a more circumspect angle?"

"Explain yourself, sir."

"You are a mystic, Teresa, a modern-day sage who by your own admission has the authority to influence hearts and minds, and even the inclinations of others. Few in hell possess such a gift. What if you were free to foment a medium by which love might burgeon more openly?"

"They're on the way."

The Seventh's warning went unheeded and the Second continued. "For example, you once propagated the belief that love alone gives worth to all things, yes?"

"That is correct. And I still stand by that notion."

"And yet, is not the basic human right of intimacy, of companionship, denied those sentenced to this affection-starved world? How can love ever hope to flourish in such a sterile environment?"

Teresa shrugged. "Love comes in many guises, not all of them intimate."

"True. And yet, what a subtle way for the Father of All Lies to prevent a person from remembering their simple humanity? When one fails to embrace another for fear of the consequences, do they not slowly wither away and die inside?"

And once dead inside, they are no longer truly human. "I see your point."

The Second pressed his advantage.

"If Satan is allowed to keep the masses isolated from such a fundamental expression of their nature, there is no hope. Wouldn't you like to be an inspiration to millions, an inspiration that demonstrates the reality that a fresh start is achievable?"

Regardless of the urgency of the situation, Teresa pondered the question seriously.

Would I? Although the consequences would be grievous until change was forced.

She came to a decision.

"One of the worst transgressions is procrastination. I would be deserving of my judgment had I the power to do something yet failed to act."

"Then your wish is my command. Come, let us take this discussion somewhere more conducive to progress. I must confess, since my brothers and I first proposed the idea, Erra has been keen to meet you."

Teresa was aghast.

"But I am hardly in a fit state to meet royalty."

"Madam, you should know by now that we never judge a book by its cover. It's what's on the inside that counts. Be glad of that, for your courage will benefit countless others in the future."

The Second's eyes flashed.

Teresa felt a moment's chill, and then found herself somewhere else entirely.

*

A strange twisting sensation gripped Gemini's stomach. Although it wasn't painful, the feeling of being stretched in multiple directions all at once made bile rise in her throat.

I think I'm going to be sick.

A bright flash of light streaked across her vision, followed by the smell of ozone. Forced to divert her eyes, only then did Gemini realize her senses were muddled, for while her balance registered she should be standing upright, she was, in fact, falling slowly toward the floor.

Hey, my legs are descending faster than my chest?

The truth of her situation struck home.

"My plan must have worked. I'm obviously nearer the edge of the gravity field than Nimrod and—"

"Actually, you have me to thank for that."

Surprised, Gemini forgot all about her partner and turned toward the source of the unexpected voice, only to find her muscles were more sluggish than she would have liked.

"Don't worry, the effects will pass as I draw power away from the trap," announced the same mystery person. "Things should be back to normal within a few minutes."

Do I know him? Her gaze fell upon a tall gaunt figure dressed from head to foot in gray combat fatigues. She recognized the face immediately. "Nettesheim? How in the—?"

"Miss Corday. Delighted to make your acquaintance under better circumstances."

"But you're supposed to be locked up in an Omega-class facility undergoing some kind of assessment."

"Just as well I got bored then, really," Nettesheim replied jovially, "since fate insists I play a more active role in current events."

"Active role?"

"Indeed. The last time I spoke with your illustrious leader at the Brass-Steel, I happened to mention how much I like it here. I wasn't kidding. Regardless of what the Sibitti might think, the underworld serves a purpose, or at least it would if interfering busybodies didn't keep poking their noses into things that don't concern them. Don't you agree?"

Gemini attempted to adjust her grip on her knives so she would be in a better position to throw them the first opportunity she got. "I'm sorry: do you want our gratitude or something?"

"On the contrary. You're a bright young lady, so you know as well as I do those idiots I mentioned need putting in their place. What they are doing threatens everyone's security."

"Chopin and Tesla, you mean?"

Gemini's fingers closed about her blades, then froze. For some reason, drowsiness threatened to overwhelm her. Looking toward her foe, she saw an emerald glow emanating from his hands.

"Forgive me," Nettesheim murmured. He strode closer and plucked the weapons from her grasp. "I don't mean to delay your liberty, but I feel I must emphasize something."

Helpless to do anything but listen, Gemini spat, "Such as?"

"I'm not the enemy here. Chopin and Tesla are. Haven't you ever wondered how they've managed to elude the finest hunters and trackers the underverse has ever seen?"

"I leave that to better intellects to fathom."

"You shouldn't. Gemini, your insights are just as valid as the next soul's. Don't be afraid to speak out." He squatted down beside her. "For example, you realized by yourself this snare is based on the manipulation of gravity and, therefore, time. You also worked out a way to free Nimrod before the trap ran its full course. Very clever. Use that ingenuity to understand how Chopin and Tesla are managing to stay one step ahead."

"We already know. They're creating a temporal anomaly somehow."

"You're not listening. I didn't ask if you knew *what* they're doing; I advised you to discern *how* they make their mischief. Once you do, you'll find you can employ their own machinations against them." Nettesheim placed Gemini's daggers on the floor, just out of her reach, and paced to the end of the basement. Then he pointed to his head. "It's all in the mind."

Nettesheim clenched his fist, and Gemini fell the last few inches onto the concrete. Rolling to her feet, she gave herself room to maneuver and prepared to fight. With a sense of dismay, she noted that Nimrod was still marooned within the remains of the bubble.

Dammit, I'll have to do this alone.

"None of us is alone, Miss Corday."

Is he reading my—?

"Yes. But as I said, I'm not your enemy. As events proceed apace, those with the right inclinations need to stand firm together against what's coming."

"And what is coming?"

"Insanity and chaos. Although new to the higher echelons of Hellonian society, you're far from naïve. You know that Chopin and Tesla are just the tip of the iceberg. There are angels and demigods involved, mystics and morons alike. And while each might have a hidden agenda, they are all intent on releasing a plague of woe upon us to achieve their aims."

"And you think you're going to make a difference?"

"I already have."

Something in Nettesheim's voice sang with a profound ring of truth.

"What do you mean?"

"My intervention here has granted you the freedom of choice. A luxury you would not have enjoyed for at least another hour if left to your own devices."

"So? What's your point?"

"My dear lady, the point is that I may have already altered the balance in your favor. As we speak, your leader faces a menace that may forever change things here in the underworld. If I had not acted, you would have remained blissfully unaware of the peril until it was too late. Now, however . . . We shall see."

Nettesheim's form became encompassed within a glittering green radiance and he started to fade from sight.

"Where are you going? I thought you said you would with us?"

"I will. Your fellow Hounds find themselves in a similar predicament. I am keen to extend the same courtesy so they are at liberty to assist you if required."

"You mean, Champ and Yamato are—?"

"Hurry," Nettesheim interjected, "the Reaper needs you within the Palace of Verse and Sighs. Don't waste the opportunity I've extended."

As the mystic disappeared, a loud thump from behind alerted Gemini to the fact that Nimrod had worked free of the trap.

"What the fuck happened?" he groaned.

Gemini rushed to his aid.

"I'll tell you later. Grab your gear; I think Daemon's in trouble."

Chapter 26: *The Palace of Verse and Sighs*

Elizabeth's warning, and the accompanying vision she had somehow triggered, were timely reminders to exercise caution. Therefore, I resorted to the services of an official portal hub to travel incognito to Perish, and then phased across to the Îll-de-Trance region using the lowest resolution matrix I could muster. From there, I first blended with the curling mists and vapor trails always shrouding this region in a halo of thick gloom. Then I allowed myself to drift toward the Palace of Verse and Sighs on the ever-present breeze.

Approaching from the east, I was now only a mile or so from my target. Keen to ensure I remained undetected, I kept my substance as rarified as possible and made a conscious effort to think nothing but gaseous thoughts. Satisfied, I ascended into the clouds to commence a meandering circuit of the encompassing forests.

Dark and forbidding, the tree line fringing the neighboring hills seemed determined to retain the area's secrets. Even at this distance, my scans revealed a menacingly unnatural undertone to them, something Satan had obviously incorporated to discourage unwanted visitors. If that measure failed, I had no doubt the endless demon and reaver patrols would add that final 'fuck off, you're not welcome here' factor that would deter all but the hardiest denizens . . . Or, of course, someone like me.

A series of gardens created a checkerboard pattern about the estate. One in particular drew my attention. As my astral sight zoomed in for a closer look, I came up short.

That walled-in quadrangle? A chill skittered through my distended substance. *It's almost identical to the one from my dream. There's even a troop of stone sentinels arrayed around the outer edge and a Wyrd tree in the middle . . .*

Bloody hell! Have I been here before?

Unsettled, I increased the integrity of my shields, skirted my way to the front of the grounds proper and commenced my final descent. Nothing else rang any alarm bells, so I made a point of noting those aspects of the palace's architecture that had made this place a monument to absolute authority in the world above and a symbol of crushing misery here in hell: such details would help remind me of the gravity of the situation I faced.

The Hall of Battles filled the south wing to my left. A huge gallery of paintings and live exhibits, it was entirely devoted to the glory of our Dark Lord's victories since establishing the underworld as his domain. To the right, the spires of the Royal Theatre dominated. Pandering to Satan's vanities, it staged annual reenactments of his finest engagements for the pleasure of VIDs and other visiting dignitaries. I had never been to a performance but I had heard His Infernal Majesty would sacrifice scores of condemned souls at such events in a merciless homage to authenticity. And directly in front of me awaited my final destination: the Colonnade of Eternal Reflections. Based on the principal and most remarkable feature of the original palace—the Hall of Mirrors—the entire wing was a shrine to the rarest and most precious relics in the whole underverse.

Tonight it would witness my greatest challenge to date: the capture of an angel. And not just any angel, for this creature was an unhinged cherub, as unpredictable as the raging sea and someone who would resort to wanton savagery to achieve his aims.

As more than a hundred thousand subjects awaiting reassignment can attest.

In spite of the extensive use of sheolanite, I could somehow discern the proximity of Grislington's wings through the structure of the building.

And if I can sense them, you can bet your bottom diablo he'll be drawn here like a moth to a flame.

Landing like a sigh within the Royal Courtyard itself, I manifested, but maintained an air of invisibility. Now I was actually here, the weight of what lay ahead pressed heavily on my shoulders.

In my book, something as important and as sensitive as this mission obviously required forethought and a great deal of preparation and planning. I hadn't had time for any of those. It also needed a reliable support system in place, but my Hounds were elsewhere engaged, tying off vital loose ends. Under normal circumstances, I could have turned to any number of Diabolical Enforcement Agencies for assistance. However, the network of spies Chopin and Tesla had cultivated over the years meant I couldn't be sure whom to trust . . . yet. That left me with no option but to go it alone. Alone against a celestially-empowered nut job, Chopin and Tesla, and whatever toys they might bring along to make things as inconvenient for me as possible.

Just another day in hell then. What's not to like?

From the outside, all appeared calm. Most of the windows were shuttered, and while the occasional telltale tracery of light escaped from an opening or cracked frame here and there, I sensed no obvious signs of unlife.

This close in, His Infernal Majesty probably doesn't want any of his riffraff employees sullying his unholy of unholies with their commoner presence. Stuck up or—?

A spike of power, quickly suppressed within the Marbled Courtyard a hundred yards ahead of me, signaled the arrival of someone of significance.

But who? Celestial minion or mundane idiot?

That brief flash transmitted a tumble of contradictory emotions: hope, anger, glee, fear, detachment, anticipation.

Oh, that's Grislington for sure.

With surprising stealth, he moved swiftly into the vestibule to the royal apartments and disappeared from sight.

And he seems to know exactly where he's going.

As I followed, I found it difficult to curb my enthusiasm. At last, I had Grislington in a situation where he wouldn't think of flitting away at the first sign of trouble.

No, he'll be determined to remain here until he's either secured what he came for, or dies trying. Personally, I hope it's the latter.

Recognizing my desire, the tattoos inscribed into my flesh flushed with heat, threatening metamorphosis.

Not yet. Stay calm. Just a little longer.

Leaving the square, I bowled into the Hall of Broken Dreams and spotted a single shaft of radiance spilling from a doorway at the far end of a long passage.

He's heading directly toward the Grand Admissions. I'd better hurry. I can't afford to let him gain too much ground.

With a thought, I increased my pace and reached the main foyer to the gallery like an intruding gust of wind. When I stepped inside, the sight took my breath away.

Although I had never been here before, I had certainly heard of the place, and like everybody else had read numerous magazine articles and seen enough documentaries on National Gehennagraphic to know what to expect. Or so I thought, because the reality of the Colonnade of Eternal Reflections was another thing entirely.

The actual entrance was situated at the northern terminus of the wing and, as its name suggested, led into a huge exhibition of mirrors fixed between a series of starlight marble pilasters that ran the length of the room, all six hundred and sixty-six feet of it. The capitals of each pillar grazed the ceiling and appeared similar to onyx. Each one, inscribed with liquid fire, depicted variations of the all-seeing eye, hexagram, pentagram, and Baphomet, the main state symbols of hell.

Chandeliers hung from the barrel vault above in frozen tiers that made them look like inverted wedding cakes, decorated in frost and dripping with phosphorous icicles. The floor beneath my feet was so highly polished that it appeared as if the scene from above had been transposed into a molten lake of pristine clarity. So pure, so clear was the illusion that were it not for the Corinthian columns ranked along each side of the hall, I might not have realized which way was up.

Before each baluster, gilded bronze plinths featuring telamons and caryatids shimmered, festooned with scented black and scarlet candles. Burning without consumption, they filled the entire gallery with defined pockets of radiance and gloom and the heady scent of incense.

A truly magnificent and opulent spectacle.

Notwithstanding this sumptuousness, pride of place belonged to the shining array along the walls, where thirteen great inner archways cast refracted images back toward their twins, cunningly arranged within an equal number of arcaded windows opposite. Sixty-six giant mirrors spanned the walls; eight hundred and fifty-eight along each side, created a total of one thousand seven hundred and sixteen traps of lethal contradiction. Their substance, designed to reflect the interior contents of the Colonnade, froze Satan's most valued trophies in place within a temporal anomaly: a single moment of forever within which they would neither wither nor die.

And one of them contains Grislington's wings. Speaking of whom . . . ?

Exercising the utmost caution, I cast my astral sight along the length of the hall, only to find my attention refracted away from anything I tried to focus on.

Those mirrors obviously serve a wider function than mere cages. I wonder if the silhouettes they help create are blank spots. And if so, can I use them?

Edging forward, I dropped my cloak of invisibility entirely, in case my attempt at concealment should trigger some particularly nasty reaction. No sooner had I done so than a groaning began. Gentle and resonant, it conveyed a depth of passion clearly designed to wring sympathy from the heart. Fortunately, the *s*-word didn't exist in my dictionary.

But I see now why this place is called the Palace of Verse and Sighs. The theatre obviously caters to one aspect, and here . . .

As if on cue, another moan exuded from a nearby mirror. In it, a member of the Kigali race—a mature specimen judging from the length of his spiked tail and the density of quills dusting his red and black skin—reached out for aid that would never arrive.

On reflex, I looked behind me, expecting to see the source of that image. Of course, nothing was there but an adjacent prism containing a shining jet sword of impressive length.

For some unknown reason, its jewel was missing from the pommel.

That's not right. She won't be able to wo– Oah! An insidious influence tried to drag me in two opposite directions at once. I instinctively phased and punched forward a few feet into the pall cast by a nearby shadow. *Careful, Daemon.*

My knowledge of the security measures within the Colonnade was next to nil. So sensitive was any reference to this place that Satan's henchmen had wiped any mention of it from the Hell Data Net.

Fortunately, thousands of years of my diabolical experience came to the fore.

My best guess? If you do what you're naturally inclined to do and take a peek into one of these mirrors, the traps will activate, mesh to you in some arcane way, and pull you in. My hypothesis presented me with a huge problem. *How the hell am I going to—?*

A flash of movement up ahead caught my eye.

Grislington. And he's nearly halfway there!

Every nerve in my body demanded action. Fighting down that craving, I deferred to caution.

But how did he get so far without tripping additional security measures? I scrutinized the excessive grandeur on display with all its glitz and glamour. Then the next penny dropped. *Because there aren't any. It would defeat the purpose of this place and show that Satan had no confidence in the legend he's built around himself. He's banking on external features and a menacing reputation to keep people away.*

I observed Grislington closely as he skipped from one cocoon of darkness to the next.

The shadows must reduce the opportunity of presenting a viable target. And when he leaves its protection, he's making a conscious effort to stay in the center of the room.

A shiver creased the air immediately behind the angel. He stumbled and began to stagger. The longer it continued, the more I saw how he struggled to arrest his fall. His head snapped up.

I watched, intrigued, as he stared long and hard into the nearest mirror. Its plane flexed, turned fluidic, then rippled like a miniature ocean encapsulated within a gilded frame. Straightening, Grislington dusted himself off, turned his back, and resumed his long slow march toward his goal.

So that's it! His divine essence must counteract the snares somehow. But what caused him to falter? And how am I going to match his character? Think, Daemon. Unless . . . ?

I rechecked the distance between us.

There's only one way to cover that amount of ground so quickly.

Very few denizens of hell were able to wield powers I took for granted. Even Samael and his cronies couldn't match my dexterity with the Bãlefire and God's Grace combined, for I could control both at will and at a moment's notice: finesse they no longer possessed due to the circumstances of their ouster from heaven. I had never understood why I had been cursed with the ability to manipulate celestial energy—or its language, come to that—but I was grateful that I could at this moment, for Grislington was now three quarters of the way toward his goal.

I can't let him progress any further without some form of challenge.

Casting all inhibition away, I summoned that part of my nature most repulsive to me, leaped high into the air, and brought my staff to bear.

"Lan kholyézé lateheno, Tavyeyqa-féenéváh-za Ba-al (By all that is unholy, and in the name of my sacred dark master)."

Not accustomed to such harsh employment, the divine language coursed through my system like an avenging tide. Hearing my cry, Grislington spun on the spot, his neck twisting from side to side as he sought the source of imminent danger. The hiss of his sword clearing its sheath rang loud in my ears.

Light as a feather, I landed before him.

He adjusted instantly, a timely warning.

Our previous encounters aside, I wouldn't make the mistake of rushing in. I had seen the damage he was capable of inflicting when he pretended to be an enforcer. So although he looked about as menacing as a wet fart on a rainy day, I must remember: This creature was an angel, and a cherub to boot. I hadn't yet witnessed everything he was capable of.

And the great thing is, that works both ways.

Mere yards apart, we began to circle, weapons at the ready, weighing the threat the other presented. Forced to compensate for the pull of the surrounding mirrors, we each strove to gain some sort of advantage that would give us an edge.

Eventually, Grislington's lack of discipline got the better of him: "You won't find this as easy as you imagine," he snarled, "for you've never truly tested me. Before my imprisonment, I had existed in the unapproachable light of His throne for an age of days. There are things you know so little about. I will gladly educate yo– Ow!"

He recoiled as the air about him crackled in response to my mental thrust, and a smattering of fizzling fireflies revealed the extent to which I had managed to penetrate his shield. Blushing yellow, it trembled for a good three or four seconds before regaining its unblemished clarity.

He's resilient, all right; my bolt should have taken his head off. But he's way too rusty. In his element or no, countless millennia in a cell won't have done his stamina much good.

I set about using that fact against him.

We clashed, and the reverberation of our meeting set chandeliers swinging as pedestals and statues vibrated. The sound of plasterwork and glass bursting intruded above the steady bite of metal on metal as each clang marked the grueling passage of time.

Minutes chimed slowly by.

He's stronger than he looks too. Good, maybe I'll get to work up a sweat after all.

The familiar feeling of controlled aggression, barely restrained on a short leash, settled over me and I began to enjoy myself, varying the length of my sickle as I aimed blow after blow at different targets. First ankle, then neck; groin and head; knee to chest: I kept sweeping, scything, hacking, and thrusting.

Grislington's blade sang in response, leaving bows of argent brilliance and amber sparks as he whirled to counter my every move, again and again and again.

Just as I thought he might be relaxing into a pattern, the gem on his sword pulsed and I felt an unexpected rush of gravity root me to the spot. A tingle capered along my legs. *Sneaky fucker, is he attempting to open a portal bene–?*

Faster than I thought possible, he was on me, cutting and slashing in an uncontrolled frenzy with the obvious intent of keeping me occupied while the coalescing void did its work.

Oh no you don't.

Relying on my superior bulk, I yanked him toward me by the hair and used his body as a platform to boost myself away. Forced onto a threshold of his own making, Grislington was obliged to protect himself while making haste to close the sprouting booby-trap.

His maneuver gave me an idea.

Channeling all my strength into a hammer strike, I clubbed at the nearest frame and released an overwhelming shockwave of God's Grace directly into the wall. The fixtures cracked and the warded metal shattered. With nothing to hold it, the tremendous weight of the huge looking glass caused it to drop onto the mounting brackets of the mirror below, whereupon it toppled slowly forward onto Grislington.

As it passed, I caught a glimpse of a frozen magma fountain.

Not for much longer . . . This is gonna hurt.

Just in time I skipped away, for a torrent of lava and sulfurous fumes burst through the ruptured event horizon and smothered the floundering angel in a perfect scorching rebuke. As the scalding hot swathe spread across the floor, everything in its path smoldered and blistered, then melted.

Excellent, it should do wonders for his complexion.

Grislington obviously didn't think so, for a silver blade appeared, stabbing up through the rear silkscreen and creating a fretwork of lurid cracks. Its tip blazed like a beacon. From my perspective, it looked as if an unseen hand had reached down from heaven and squeezed, compacting the wreckage into tiny, twinkling fragments. Everything exploded upward and outward as Grislington emerged from the debris, eyes shining with incandescent fury.

Delirium fueled his desperation, for he rode the acidic rubble like a surfer born, and howled as he launched himself at me with wanton abandon, delivering a fusillade of well-aimed cuts that were so swift that I was hard-pressed to keep up.

Toe to toe, we squared off again and began trading an unending flurry of blows. Driving, swinging, chopping and hewing; attack, defense, sally and counter: Our craving to harm one another now dictated our whole world.

Although time passed inexorably, neither of us let up. Not even for a second.

Our rhythm intensified, and the atmosphere buzzed as a static charge coalesced, built, and continued ramping ever higher.

We dared not pause to catch our breath, for our exchanges greased the air with potential; and I knew without a doubt that the first to drop his guard would be the one that died.

I had to admit, I was impressed.

He's lasted far longer than I thought he would. But then a simple truth hit home. *Which I suppose is only natural. Rusty or not, we are employing celestial energy, and having been a cherub for so long, this'll be right up his street.*

That gave me an idea.

I need to change neighborhood.

Inspired, I called forth the Bālefire and allowed its familiar essence to infuse my soul once more. Thus empowered, I advanced down the angel's center line, interspersing direct compound engagements with darting feints along the opposite play of action. Once, twice, three times.

As Grislington tried to find a pattern to settle into, I kept peppering his shields with random bursts of occult lightning. He didn't like it and started to stumble.

Halfway through my next attack, I reversed direction completely and kicked his feet out from under him. Caught off balance, Grislington literally spun head over heels and landed in a heap in front of me. He surged to his feet, but a devastating knee to the chin sent him sprawling into the pool of magma.

My pleasure proved short-lived.

With blinding speed, Grislington righted himself and lashed out.

My arm went numb as it absorbed the impact of a truly stunning riposte, and my tattoos flared in warning.

Unholy shit, he's even faster than I realized! His demonstration was my wakeup call. *Okay, time to show him the meaning of dirty.*

Dropping my shields entirely, I reached out with my telekinesis, grabbed him by the throat and slammed him repeatedly into several mirrors on either side of the hall until his extremities succumbed to the influence of divergent eddies. Only then did I pile-drive him into the floor.

Undeterred, Grislington shook his head clear and returned the compliment, using his arts to douse me in the entire volume of scoria that had spilt from the ruptured mirror. My gambit paid off. Without anything to curtail its automatic function, my armor responded and manifested about my form. Encased in palladinium, I was now protected by the hardest known substance in existence and free to do what I did best. Dispense death.

I stepped back, cast out my senses and took stock of the situation.

Our spat had taken us to the far end of the Colonnade where an elaborate ebony throne claimed prime position atop a set of ornate scalloped steps. Two additional mirrors had been added to the collection and stood in pride of place on either side of His Satanic Majesty's seat of power.

This close, the resonance of the wings set my teeth on edge and my heart racing.

No wonder Grislington's so keen to get his hands on them, they taste . . . they smell . . . I inhaled their tincture again. *Magnificent.*

Grislington was also panting. His visage appeared wild, even rabid, and for some reason he had stopped moving and stared at me. Then his eyes began to glow.

A flare of alarm coursed along my spine as I remembered where I had seen them do that before. *In his cell back at the Black Keep, just before he murdered Straw–*

I ducked as a cogent ribbon of hatred sizzled past my head and impacted on one of the main support columns. The stanchion exploded in a shower of rubble and dust, bringing a slab of the ceiling and two chandeliers with it. Fissures wormed their way along the inner wall and where they passed, more than a dozen mirrors swung free, only to dangle precariously from single hooks too fragile to support such burdens for long.

"Satan's treasures!" I gasped.

Recognizing my alarm, Grislington let loose a withering swarm of laser beams. Some found their mark instantly, shattering pillars and arches alike and creating a tumbling cascade of prismatic splinters and tympanic echoes. Others bounced off the silvered sheen of their targets and ricocheted around the hall until, eventually, they struck something less resilient.

Caught in a no-win situation, I reached out with my mind in an attempt to save as many artifacts as I could. These were part of Satan's own private collection, prized above all others. If they were lost, everyone's heads would roll.

The weight of over a thousand traps and their solid gold surrounds was colossal, and I staggered under the strain of keeping them aloft. The trouble was, such a delay would play straight into Grislington's hands.

Sure enough, no sooner had I started to lower individual casements to the floor than the sound of the angel's running feet distinguished itself amid the bedlam.

I faced a difficult decision.

Fuck it!

Exhaling sharply, I released my grip and winced as hundreds of mirrors crashed onto the hard marble below. The sight of so many twinkling shards spraying into the air at once was hypnotic, as was the following assault on my senses as scores of caged exhibits—many of them unliving—broke free in a cacophony of opposing smells, deafening roars and tumultuous challenges.

Ignoring them all, I spun on the spot, primed my scythe and set off after my prey.

Grislington had already reached the top of the stairway, but instead of rushing to claim his prize, he seemed confused. Standing between the mirrors, he twisted sharply from side to side and appeared to be struggling to reach a decision. Snarling, he cursed, drew his sword, turned to face me, and only then kinked his head in an obvious attempt to distinguish something through the backwash of noise.

An unknown creature roared up the steps behind me, its emanations betraying a lust for confrontation and vengeance after an eternity spent incarcerated. A blast of arcane power roasted it on the spot. For good measure, I sent out a roiling wave of acid fog and noted with satisfaction the resultant cries of dismay that met its issue.

Like I don't have enough distractions already?

As I reached the top of the throne mound, Grislington's countenance flared with hope. Dismissing me entirely, he made a dive for the left-hand mirror.

So what's in the other . . . ?

Bewildered, I glanced right. Suspended in milk-white mist, a wondrous pair of wings hung within an inky-black void. Pearlescent in nature, they called to me with an intimacy that wrenched a sob from my throat and drew tears from my eyes.

Then what the hell is he hoping to—?

Blinking my vision clear, I was stunned to see Grislington turn away from the opposite mirror, a saintly smile becalming his troubled brow and an identical set of pinions under one arm. As they crossed the geodesic threshold of the trap, an effervescent ruffle passed through each layer of feathers and their substance glowed. That radiance spread along Grislington's hand, past his elbow and on toward his body.

"No!"

With no time to think of the consequences, I called forth the full Satanic might of my station. Power flooded into me; and as the Phage took hold, I became encompassed within a midnight nimbus of infinite magnitude. Royal blue and purple streamers sizzled along the edge of my corona, a coronet of scarlet and black flames bloomed about my head, and the glyphs adorning my armor blazed gold. Arabesque flagstones cracked beneath my feet, and those windows that had managed to remain shuttered blew outward.

At the far end of the Colonnade, I noticed a small group of reavers and demons. The first to arrive, they had no doubt been drawn by the sounds of battle and would be calling for whatever aid was available. It mattered not: by the time anyone of import arrived, the main event would be over.

Leaving the escapees to them, I turned to face my foe, stamped forward and unleashed the indescribable potency of Hellfire personified.

Forewarned, Grislington reacted quickly and brandished his sword in his free hand, countering my thrust with one of his own.

Twin beams of iridescent mastery—one blood-red, the other blinding white—lanced out. Slamming together with the force of a nuclear explosion, their meeting released a devastating shockwave that shorted out the dampening field surrounding the palace, shattered the wards, and lifted the roof clean off.

Some form of damage must have also been wrought upon the foundations, for the marble walkway split wide and the ground started to fall away as multiple sinkholes opened up all around us.

I couldn't care less; I only had eyes for my enemy, an enemy who was so close to regaining his means of liberty that he was on the verge of achieving something unheard of: escape from hell.

Something I couldn't allow.

Moments like this are what I was created for.

Up until now, events might have suggested we were evenly matched. But I knew the stalemate for the sham it was.

As I'm about to demonstrate.

Forging ahead, I increased my efforts and poured an obscene amount of energy into my attack. A maelstrom erupted. Ripping chunks from the beleaguered walls and roof tiles of nearby wings, the vortex spiraled in on us and commenced grinding everything to dust. Immune to such mundane interference, I stood unscathed as the runaway conjunction of celestial polar opposites continued unabated. A shimmering nimbus manifested, signifying just how high radiation levels had become.

I took another step and Grislington began to waver. His gaze flicked to the plasma strand and back to me. Grimacing, I squeezed even more avidity into my manifestation and the white end of the ray slowly stained cerise. Then rose. And then red. When it darkened to carmine, it lost coherence and began to shred, spewing out agitated tendrils that thrashed about the room like whips.

Aghast, Grislington spluttered, "How did you . . . ? But I have my wings and can access the very crux of heaven, so . . . ?"

"Maybe, if you were actually wearing them. And if you were, you'd have already dropped the veil and called in your buddies to kick my Satanic ass six ways from Sinday. No, my friend; while you've gained a partial victory, it's a bittersweet reunion, for you can't access their power yet. Bad luck for you, I think."

"But I am a cherub, of the Order of the Throne. You are nothing but—"

I continued my advance in the face of his rising panic.

"This isn't possible," he whined. "I am—"

"You are nothing in this realm. Limited. Finite. I have the lifeblood of the underworld itself to call upon. It runs through my veins, infuses my spirit and makes me one of the strongest creatures in existence."

"Fool! Is that what the Arch Deceiver told you?"

With a roar, I released a meteoric bolt of necromantic vitriol right at him. Traveling along the length of his waning energy ribbon, the efflux careered into the tip of Grislington's sword, oscillated back and forth for a moment, then began to eat its way into the blade's integrity.

Desperation leaked from Grislington's mind like the sweat from his brow. Teeth bared, he clutched his wings to his chest and attempted to rally.

To no avail.

Opening my soul to the vast reservoir of darkness within me, I disgorged an ever increasing torrent of pure unadulterated evil toward him and sealed his fate.

The jewel of his weapon tarnished black, and a keening tone lifted into the air. As the corruption continued to eat its way into the gem's heart, the metal about it faded to gray. Then it bled white, and a ringing scream split the ether. It escalated pitch, went off the scale.

The *Sword of Celestial Arches* vaporized, creating a static backlash that swatted Grislington away and into one of the few columns left standing.

Stunned, I braced myself against a momentary inrush of air and moved to close the distance.

Grief-stricken, Grislington stared in mute horror at the calcified husk of his hand.

"How did you . . . ? What you've done should be impossible?"

Unmoved, I flipped back my cowl and let him gaze into the mask of death.

"This was always your fate, especially after you chose to fuck about after your release."

"But you don't know, do you? We . . . You and I, we're—"

"Save it. Although you've been a royal pain in the ass, you should know by now that you'll never talk your way out of this." Covering my head once more, I stepped back to give myself room and raised my scythe. "Your punishment will serve as a lesson for all infernity. Now take it like a man."

Depressing all five buttons, I absorbed the titanic potential at my disposal and readied myself for the blow that would forever eradicate the creature before me. A name appeared, embellished across the outer veneer of my thoughts, revealing the true identity of my victim.

"Gazárdiel. Your crimes against His Satanic Majesty have been protracted, determined and many. I am therefore authorized by His Dark Highness to obliterate your eternal soul, and erase you from existence. Punishment is to be carried out immediately. Have you any last words?"

"No, wait! Please. There are things I need to tell you. Things about the wings and your true orig–"

For all his dominion, I didn't even notice the moment my blade cut through his flesh. A dull thud followed as his head hit the floor. It rolled to a stop between my feet, eyes wide in shock and disbelief.

"Strange, I somehow expected more . . . ?"

A storm-well gathered about me.

Where the hell did that spring from? Erupting in celestial flame, it was joined by another funnel that punched down from out of the occluding mantle with the brilliance of an oxyacetylene torch. *Shit, wrong realm!*

Like tentacles, each bore spiraled about the other for a moment before entwining into a single, gigantic tornado. Thus augmented, it pulverized the ruined shell of the palace until it had located Grislington's remains and scooped them inside its thundering flume.

Caught in the updraft, I started gyrating with them, round and around, faster and faster. Grislington's body began to shine.

Though I still wore the mantle of the Phage, such was the strength of the buffeting wind that it scrambled my senses. I even had difficulty maintaining any form of valid comprehension. Nonetheless, I was aware of the moment the angel's body flared and vanished; for as it did so, Grislington's essence rushed to imbue me in a frigid resonance of blessed origin.

Oh no, not again . . . Wait a minute . . . Again?

Reality turned elastic, and I found myself free-falling through thick white clouds in a rerun of events from another time and place:

I've been here before . . . although it seems more distinct. So much sharper. How . . . ?

Struggling to break free of the brume, my stomach lurches. I pierce the canopy and majestic sunlight baptizes me in coronal radiance. Wind howls past my face and my insides heave again, but instead of puking, my perspective shifts and I somehow feel myself merge into an old and long forgotten drama.

The plummeting sensation intensifies. Seizing me body and soul, it sends me hurtling to my fate. Nonetheless, I draw comfort from an object grasped tightly in my right hand. I glance to one side and see a huge gold and black sword. It blazes with malice along the keen edges of its midnight sheen and encompasses me within a flaxen scarlet aura that bonds the weapon to my flesh as it inures me against the terrible drop.

The rate of my descent increases. My internal alarm triggers. As I scan the vicinity, something hurtles toward me across the vaulted sky and my sense of danger peaks, for it is plain this intruder would deny me my destiny. Instinctively, I stab out.

Glass chimes against glass and a shower of prismatic light and sparks crisscrosses the heavens with glittering reflections of savage contradiction.

My unknown adversary clamps his hand around my sword wrist. I return the gesture and squeeze as hard as I can. Locked together, we tumble out of control, over and over. Vast ribbons of energy encompass us within a living tau field as we attempt to exterminate each other by sheer force of will.

Our exertions wreak terrible consequences, for parts of us are lost forever. Now conjoined, we act instinctively, each determined to do whatever it takes to retain that spark of identity that will make the difference between life and extinction.

We fade, and a suspended animation rush of impressions overwhelms . . . someone?

I will not die!

One spark dominates, subsuming the other within itself, but at a price.

Metamorphosis.

A kernel of awareness remains, but it is a travesty of nature. Binate, it vacillates between light and dark.

Who am I? Who was I?

What am I? What was I?

Where do I belong?

The weight of eons passing consumes me, and antiquity swallows my memories whole. But the lessons of history remain:

The terrible drop . . .

Pain.

Skin, glowing white-hot from devastating friction . . .

Intense agony.

Primary flight feather torn free by overwhelming drag . . .

Excruciating, prolonged torture.

A vast pit of malevolence rushing up from below . . .

Plunging.

Light receding above . . .

Forever plummeting.

A moment of clarity as the truth of my predicament finally registers.

I've fallen too far!

The endless spiral, down and down.

An overwhelming surge of heat as I pay the price . . .

Depravation.

The silence of eternal midnight . . .

Soul-crushing grief.

The inevitable pressure of all-consuming oblivion . . .

Anguish compounded a thousandfold.

The familiarity of an unexpected voice taunting me from the darkness.

"You are more than you appear to be."

Then why do I feel so emasculated?

"So much more. Do you not realize who you were?"

Who I was?

"What you now are?"

I am alone. Stripped, barren, darkened and taunted.

"Then why tolerate it? It is unnatural."

I deserve it.

"But you are a god!"

Don't be ridiculous, I am nothing. Debased, corrupted, unworthy and tarnished.

"A Titan to rival the likes of Lucifer himself."

That is preposterous. Outrageous. You shouldn't talk like that.

"Why? You are a colossus amongst insects, the Morning Star included. Why shouldn't you release the potential so artfully obscured and claim what could be yours?"

Potential? What are you saying?

"Overthrow the pretender. Why do you think Erra and his auditors were dispatched? Satan is insufficient for the task, but as for you . . ."

Blasphemy!

"Take the throne."

Treason!

"Assume your rightful place as Lord of the Underworld. Have you not personally consigned billions to such a fate? Who better to rule?"

No. Never! I . . . I am . . . ?

Myriad images flickered toward me, each depicting the many realms of hell as they would be under the dominion of my governance. Desolate, inhospitable, and the epitome of pure misery . . .

It was magnificent. I felt emancipated, alive for the first time in millennia.

"This is who you once were," the enticing voice cajoled, "and a portent of what you will surely become if you're brave enough to take that final step."

It was—It was—

"Intoxicating? Your destiny?"

A lie!

After all this time, the very thought of submitting to temptation still repelled me. Fuelled by a sudden burst of unrighteous anger, I trembled on the brink of the Obsidian Rage, a deadly fury as harsh and abominable as all the levels of the netherworld combined. But in my current condition, such a manifestation would have consequences.

You will never use my past against me. Don't ever . . . aargh!

Exquisite agony, the likes of which would usher in chaos and ruination, coursed through me, scourging my soul and burning me clean. Enraptured, I submitted myself to the drop and waited for ultimate blackness to take me. The trouble was, someone seemed determined to delay my transmogrification. Insubstantial voices buzzed about me like wasps, irritating my fragile sensibilities with their incomprehensible babbling.

"Daemon?"

What now?

"Daemon, are you in there?"

Do you seriously think this will confuse me?

A brave challenge, for such were the variant energies fighting for space within my head that I felt sure it would burst at any moment.

"... state of this place. And him. Shoot! Is he even gonna make it? We can't be ..."

"He's got to, he's Daemon Grim."

"You sure, lookin' like that? For fuck's sake, Nimrod, he got hit by fire from heaven. A goddam fewkin' firestorm from—"

"Is nothing. Physically, he's had much worse. Now shut up ... yourself useful. Yamato? Get over here and ... Use the ... you're best suited to manag–"

"... on it. In the meantime, do you think we should get Satan in on this?"

"Yes ... No, wait. Call Strawberry first. If anyone can bring Daemon back, she can. We can worry about ... else squared away. Understoo–?"

Strawberry? I feel like I should know that name.

"And the Boss? He'll sure as hell want a full ... gets here ... update reg–"

"... assured, he'll get one. And he'll fix what's left. Where's Gemini?"

"Over there, nursing her burns."

"... crazy bitch, jumpin' into the cosmic flames like that to pull him out? Didn't anyone think to tell her we ain't immune to ...?"

"... knew all right. She's one of us now and acted without ..."

"Stir-fried crazy, you mean?"

"Hey, Gemini, move your ass and give Champ a hand. We can't find ... the wings. They might have ... destroyed, but can't ... Knowing Chopin and Tesla, we can't ... risk."

"On the wa–"

I couldn't listen anymore. Limitless potential and unbidden memories from the edge of time called to me, and this ceaseless droning merely delayed the inevitable.

Letting go, I breathed a huge sigh of relief and slipped toward the answers to everything.

As I fell, a poignant reminder intruded.

Haven't I done this before?

Chapter 27: No Good Deed

With the utmost deliberation, Nettesheim passed the
northern arch of the Bridge's east tower, walked once around
the central column, and—taking the greatest care to follow
the instructions he had been given regarding the operation
of one of hell's most versatile translocation devices—took
up a position directly opposite the portals arrayed along the
western side.

A mirrored sheen sprang into existence within each
span. Clarifying into shimmering windows, they depicted
a flickering torrent of varying locations from around the
underverse: turbid swamps, frigid forests, arid deserts;
pyramids, hanging gardens, spouting volcanoes; towns;
hamlets; and great cities. All rolled by in rapid succession,
presenting him with a choice seldom extended to those
outside of privileged circles.

Watching intently, Nettesheim refused to rush, instead
letting intuition guide his choice.

He felt a tingling sensation behind his eyes. Within
moments, the Bridge slowed its rambling and seemed to
adapt the character of its offerings.

Is it sensing and anticipating my needs?

Nettesheim soon got his answer, for the tumbling cascade

slowed and eventually stopped on a panorama he knew well.

At six hundred and thirty-six feet tall, the twin gothic spires of Cullogne Cathedral skewered the skyline, making it instantly recognizable from the rest of the sprawling mass spread out on both sides of the River Rhime.

Thank badness the Bridge recognizes the validity of my service. Without its help, I fear even I would be hard-pressed to prepare for what might be coming.

"Destination selected," a metallic, inflectionless voice intoned. "Standby for delivery."

He moved toward the depicted scene and, after a momentary feeling of lightheadedness, found himself transposed across a vast distance. Because he had been concentrating on the towers as he stepped in, Nettesheim discovered himself atop one of the flying buttresses of the cathedral itself. Looking down on the dazzling vapors of the Rhime as they undulated across the city, Nettesheim couldn't help but be enthralled by the results as those mists coated the squares and rooftops in a verglas sheen that tinted everything in glistening pink and cobalt-blue.

He snorted softly. *As pretty as it looks, nothing can hide the fact that this is a dank environment and the perfect setting for the execution squads and kill gangs that roam the streets with nothing better to do than practice their deadly arts on one another . . . and anyone else who strays too close.*

He sighed aloud. "Ah, there's certainly no place like home."

Rendering himself invisible by use of a chameleon shield, Nettesheim then used his arts to lower himself into the throng below, and pondered his next move.

That Grim was able to defeat the angel bodes well for the next phase of the Unveiling. Strength he most certainly has, but now he will need to prove his tenacity and capacity for creative thinking. Only then might he stand a chance of thwarting the menace now looming on the horizon. Even so, there's no guarantee of success, for the nexus indicates a high probability that the very crux of his true nature will be exploited. So how to help?

Magician, occultist, theologian, astrologer, alchemist, physician, legal expert and soldier: Nettesheim had been many things in his life and had continued his quest for knowledge after arriving in hell. Nevertheless, it had been decades since he had last set foot in this city, and an age since he had been so intellectually taxed.

One thing's for certain. For me to be able to predict events with any degree of accuracy, I'll need to gain a deeper insight into the character of the hurdles to be overcome. But where to start? The Master wasn't particularly forthcoming as how best to proceed.

Searching the darkest corners of his memory, Nettesheim considered which of the thirteen high churches of Cullogne might contain the wisdom he sought.

A snippet he had once gleaned—carelessly cast into the hubbub of a bawdy hovel where the participants of a certain conversation were too inebriated to care who might hear—suddenly came back to him.

Ah yes! It is rumored the Church of the Dark Apostate contains a reliquary devoted to those objects seized from Herod and the magi following their betrayal and condemnation. Perhaps I should start my search there?

Safe within his field of obscurity and confident of success, Nettesheim began threading his way through the press without anyone giving him so much as a second glance . . . Or so he thought.

*

Squatting down behind an impressive castellation adorning the highest pinnacle of the Church of the Dark Apostate, Isabella Castile glanced across to her partner in crime and, for the umpteenth time, asked "Anything yet?"

Charles Guiteau, his face pressed firmly to the telescopic thermal imager of his Tartarus T-1000 sniper's rifle, failed to answer immediately. Instead, he seemed content to play the muzzle of his weapon in a slow figure-eight motion across the crowded plaza more than two hundred feet below, before finally croaking, "Still nothing. But he'll be here . . . if your freaky senses haven't suddenly gone haywire and led us on a wild goose chase in pursuit of phantoms."

"Oh, they haven't," she snapped, impatient to be getting on with things that involved slicing and dicing and maiming. "For when it comes to scent, my nose is never wrong."

Guiteau resumed his vigil and lapsed back into silence. With nothing better to do, Isabella adjusted her position and cast her gaze idly across the glitzy façade before them.

Buildings in this part of Cullogne were distinct from the rest of the city in that everything, the elegant town houses and mansions, both palaces (one devoted to a fallen angel and the other reserved for the use of none other than Altos himself) and every commercial premises, uncivic monument, and even the Low Courts of Injustice, combined the most imposing aspects of ancient Roman and Byzantium architecture.

Thick walls, large towers, semicircular arches, sturdy pillars and groined vaults were everywhere; an ostentatious charade that reflected the attitude of local denizens, who thought themselves a breed apart and a cut above everyone else in hell.

Isabella couldn't have cared less. All she wanted to do was cut down to size the upstart who had dared to interfere.

I can't believe how fortunate we were to bag the Hounds in the first place. What a stroke of luck; both teams down and out of action without too much fuss. And then some sneaky, backstabbing do-gooder with an 'I love things the way they are' *complex had to stick his nose in and screw up everything.*

She struggled to contain a knot of growing frustration in the pit of her stomach.

Freed to act before the temporal dilation traps had run their course, the Hounds were able to get to the site of the battle in time to prevent a brain-fried Daemon Grim from permanently losing his sensibilities. Bastard! What a coup that would have been. Chopin and Tesla were fortunate to escape with their prize—and their asses—intact.

Just thinking about their employers caused Isabella's anger to flare. Her cheeks blushed red. Turning away, she made haste to conceal her lack of composure from her partner and contended herself by reflecting on her larger, long-term plans.

We've a score to settle with those two, Guiteau and I, and I would have hated fate to rob me of the opportunity of a little payback. They think they're so clever, with their potions and their toys. All those precious devices they treat like long lost children, imagining that they have us nicely under control. Well, no—

"He's here."

The unexpected warning snapped Isabella from her postulations and into a high state of alert. She checked the mitigator lying on the walkway between them and hissed, "And you're sure this thing will mask our presence from Nettesheim? You've seen how tricky he can be, him and his damnable spells."

Guiteau turned to fix her with a look that plainly communicated his disdain.

"That's what Tesla said it would do."

"And you trust him? You've seen how eager they are to tie off *inconvenient* loose ends."

"If anything, I trust Tesla a lot more than the oily little chit who seems to think he's superior to everyone else."

Unconvinced, Isabella peeped over the rampart and scanned the milling throng below. Although she couldn't see their prey, she could certainly detect his aroma, growing stronger as he approached.

"So where is our mighty mystic?"

Guiteau rechecked his sights.

"Four hundred yards out and closing." He coughed to clear his throat of blood. "What's more, our boy seems happy to stick with a simple invisibility net at the moment. Good news for us. If he'd thought to mask his body heat as well, we'd have had to rely on smell only, which would have made it a little difficult to blow his head off from a distance."

The soft click of a safety catch disengaging signaled Guiteau was keen to progress to the next stage. "So, do you want me to drop him now, or wait until he's closer?"

Isabella considered their options.

"Just cover him for now. If he veers off toward another venue, then by all means, take the shot."

"And if he doesn't?"

"I'd have thought that was obvious. Be honest, wouldn't you prefer the opportunity of voicing your displeasure up close and personal? It carries a sense of karma that smacks of . . . that says . . ."

"Curse your good deeds, and in your face, sucker?" Guiteau offered.

"Why, yes. My sentiments precisely."

*

At more than seven feet tall, the sentinel stood in silence, its stony gaze scrutinizing the Wyrd tree at the center of the quadrangle with a vigilance that would never waver. Coated in the languid breath of the nearby forest, the sculpture's diamond wings and mantle sparkled through all the colors of the rainbow, giving it an ethereal quality that complemented the therapeutic resonance permeating every facet of the garden: from the stonework on the walls and their four iron gates, to the leaves and buds sprouting from every plant and bush. Even the gravel along the pathway exuded a vibrancy that seemed conducive to healing.

But why would that be, especially here at the showpiece of Satan's power? And of the thirteen statues guarding this place, why am I drawn to this one in particular?

I gazed around the rest of the parade and studied each hooded enigma in turn.

They're identical in every way. Eventually, I worked my way back around to my long lost friend. *So why do you haunt my dreams of late? And why is it every time I try to think on such matters, they befuddle my mind?*

I reached out to grasp the engraved jewel mounted into the pommel of the champion's broadsword.

A tremor shook the ground and a familiar hail brushed against my thoughts.

He's coming, Nimrod warned, *we'd appreciate it if you were here by the time he touches down.*

No sooner had I registered the import of Nimrod's message than snow, foul and reeking of decay, began falling from a leaden sky. Soft at first, it soon increased into billowing drifts that swaddled everything in leprous spots of yellow and ash-gray filth.

He's pissed. I'd better move my ass.

I phased, and a heartbeat later manifested on a smoke-blackened throne mound amid a scene of utter devastation. The roof no longer existed, and Satan's advancing ire pattered down unhindered upon broken walls, splintered columns, shattered glass and crushed figurines. Oily vapors ascended from great rents in the floor, and everywhere the stench and stain of a hard-won battle assailed the senses.

My Hounds and Strawberry had gathered together behind one of the few mirrors left intact; the one containing a mystery I dearly wanted answered.

I've gotta ask him about . . . ?

A winged shadow loomed overhead. Soaring like some monstrous serpent-tailed eagle, it led a squadron of similar, smaller creatures in a circuit of the estate before mighty wings tucked in tight. As one they descended, diving through the air like fiery portents of doom. Twelve alighted on the lawns and main courtyards. The largest headed straight for us.

Bugger! He's brought the choir. Not a good sign.

Just before the beast touched down, a golden light pulsed about its outline. It rippled, shrank, and morphed into human form.

His Infernal Majesty stood before us, replete in his favorite CEO guise, although his eyes continued to shine like twin suns. Stilling abruptly, he let the silence weigh heavily between us and surveyed the remains of his prized exhibits. Whenever the heat of his gaze happened to flick my way, the hairs on my skin prickled.

Definitely not a good sign.

"I can't really say I like what you've done with the place, Daemon," began Satan. "You do realize how long it took me to amass this collection, don't you?"

In spite of the flippancy of his words, I knew this was no

time for levity and kept my mouth shut.

Continuing, he muttered as much to himself as to anyone else. "An absolute goddam age. Virtually every one of them is irreplaceable. Thousands upon thousands of years wasted. All those priceless treasures, gone forever." He turned to face me directly. "Do you have nothing to say in your defense?"

I think he'll appreciate me being direct.

Maintaining eye contact, I replied, "Forgive me for saying so, sire, but why should I need to defend myself for doing what I was created to do? After I singlehandedly sent the Sibitti packing in Olde London Town, you said to me, and I quote, 'And now, my Reaper, I'd really like it if you'd put your new enhancements to use, and make haste to rid my kingdom of certain thorns in the flesh who are becoming rather . . . bothersome.' One of those *thorns* was an insane angel"—I gestured to the wreckage around us—"and this is the result."

As Satan regarded me, the stars in his eyes paled, then went out.

Good start.

I used the lull to forge ahead.

"Obviously, I would have preferred not to have wrecked the Colonnade of Eternal Reflections in the process, but you know as well as I do, not only was Grislington completely unhinged but he was a cherub, the same as you were; a cherub who possessed a heaven-forged blade that he was only too willing to use. Look at the carnage he inflicted recently whilst disguised as one of the Seven. No doubt you can recall how difficult it was to capture him in the first place? I nearly found out how wily he can be when he got his hands on his wings—"

The devil's countenance flared. "He managed to get that far, and release them?"

"Indeed. Fortunately, I was on hand to prevent him from accessing their full power."

Satan eyed me suspiciously. "How did you manage that, unaided?"

"By using what you gave me to the full. Potent, Grislington certainly was; however, here in hell his strength was limited. I, on the other hand, have access to dominion that originates in both realms. A shrewd move on your part to empower your prime enforcer thus, for it allows me to maintain an edge." I shrugged. "It's how I managed to defeat the Sibitti too: they cannot stand in the face of such sovereignty."

"I see." Satan fell quiet for a moment. Then: "And what of Chopin and Tesla?"

For some reason, I got the distinct impression that wasn't the actual question he wanted to ask.

What's going on? "As my Hounds have no doubt already reported prior to your arrival, both fugitives were, in fact, the main thrust of our enquiries. By focusing on one thing at a time, we were able to uncover a nest of their informants within the Devil's Children and track them down. Thanks to Gemini's ingenuity, we also determined the location of the fugitives' most recent lair."

"And?"

"From what I have been told, the spies have been consigned for reallocation, where the Undertaker will ensure to extract every useful nuance from their minds. It is my belief that this will lead to other arrests in the near future. Chopin and Tesla themselves managed to elude us." Satan's face fell, so I quickly emphasized, "However, that was not due to negligence. We have now ascertained *how* they've been doing this. Tesla is a scientific genius, and the sneaky swine has incorporated a temporal component into the gadgets they use. Basically, they've been stealing extra hours—days even—and using them to stay one step ahead. I've no doubt that's why we didn't catch sight or sound of them this evening, despite strong intelligence indicating they would definitely be here."

"A temporal component?" Satan looked shocked. "And are you aware exactly how far these devices can be pushed?"

"I'm afraid not. But on a positive note, we are now in possession of a number of transportation orbs and I have your finest experts looking into the matter. Once they unlock the key to accessing the time-travel element, we will be exceptionally vigorous in bringing Chopin and Tesla to injustice and seizing those objects still under their control, as I was hoping to do this evening." I softened my voice. "Sire, if I may suggest, why not make Chopin, Tesla and those items they have stolen the first exhibits in a new collection?"

Satan's eyes narrowed. He pursed his lips.

Fuck me, I think I've done it. He's not going to blow his top.

Then he raised a finger.

"One thing troubles me, Daemon. Perhaps you can help?"

"Anything."

"Though succinct, your explanation was most informative. And while I would have preferred you to have kept my prized seat of power in one piece, I now understand why it lies in ruins. Nonetheless, you mentioned that Grislington reclaimed his wings from the trap?"

"That's correct. Something about his essence caused the geodesic threshold of the glass to become malleable. He pulled them out before my eyes."

"And you're certain he didn't bond to them?"

"I'm no expert, you understand, but I'm positive he wasn't able to restore them to his being. I executed him before that happened."

Satan still looked troubled by something, and once again, his query didn't seem to reflect his real concern. "Most fortunate. Then perhaps you can tell me where they are?"

"I'm sorry?"

"The wings, Daemon. Where are they?"

"I don't know. The last time I saw either pair was just before Grislington got swatted to one side by the backlash from his sword's destruction. I didn't think to—"

"Hang on!" Satan's voice rose by an octave. "You saw both? I mean, are you saying you managed to destroy the *Sword of Celestial Arches*?"

"Yes. It couldn't stand against the Bãlefire. Why?"

Satan's gaze bored into mine, reading me, probing me. *What's really bugging him? And why won't he say?*

When it came, his next question took me completely by surprise: "And at any time during the ruckus, did you lose your new glasses? Were they knocked askew or off your head entirely?"

My glasses? What the bugger have my glasses got to do with anything? "No. I'd assumed the Phage by that stage of the fight, so I was encased in armor."

Another uncomfortable silence ensued. It grew until my Despicable Father decided to let go of whatever was bothering him. Eventually, he took a deep breath. "Hmm. You were telling me about the wings?"

"Er, yes. As I say, Grislington must have dropped them in the explosion. I didn't get a chance to look for them myself as his death caused a bit of a reaction from *upstairs,* and I had my ass handed to me on a plate by a massive electrostatic discharge."

"Yes, I felt that. And, I think, so did everyone else throughout the length and breadth of my realm."

"It surprised the hell out of me too. It was so powerful it

flat-lined my brain activity. I'm thankful one of the Hounds thought to bring Strawberry over to help restore normal functioning; otherwise I'd have been left permanently zombified. Can you imagine it, the Reaper being fit for nothing more than a Cirque du Freak act?"

"That might still happen, unless you get around to explaining why you or your squad didn't think to secure one of the most powerful heavenly totems in existence."

Instantly sober, I looked toward my lead Hound.

"Nimrod, can you assist His Dark Majesty?"

Nimrod stepped forward.

"Alas, no. Upon our arrival, we found you insensible and in need of assistance." He turned toward Satan. "My apologies if we erred, Sire. My natural inclination was to aid your Reaper first. Only after Daemon had been restored did we began a search of the debris to retrieve what items were salvageable."

Shadows congealed about Satan's form. His brows began to glow, and the radiance reminded me of the fire pits of Gehenna. Only then did I notice that his irises had changed into the aspect of fangs. Not a good omen.

He gestured, and Samael and his Fallen cronies materialized about us.

The Hounds and Strawberry glanced at one another and stiffened. I could tell they yearned to draw their weapons, but dared not risk giving offense.

Satan's voice rumbled like lava over hot coals. "This isn't the first time your team has been lax, is it, Daemon?"

"Of course not," I snapped, springing to their defense, "and that isn't surprising, given the nature of the things we deal with. And to be fair, since the conspiracy involving Chopin and Tesla came to light, we've been deluged. The case is snowballing, and the deeper we dig, the more we find.

New technology, ancient artifacts, enhanced denizens. There simply aren't enough of us to handle—"

"I do hope you're not trying to make excuses for your incompetence and hiding behind a wall of ill-conceived sympathy?" Satan's mocking outburst cut me dead. "This is hell. Nothing is fair. You and your team are allowed a great deal of leeway to conduct your affairs without additional interference from me, and yet look what has happened in this past year alone: Champ and Yamato were captured by the Sibitti; your lead Hound was slain by a traitor; and the head Inquisitor got herself assassinated by the rebel angel."

"Sire, listing things in such a way detracts from the acts of valor behind those incidents and the circumstances leading to them. You examined Champ and Yamato yourself after I consigned them to the slab. In the face of horrendous torture, neither broke. They maintained integrity to their oath and brought honor to the Ancient Disorder of Hell Hounds. They should be commended—"

"Commended? For failing me?"

"For remaining loyal. They never—"

"And what about you, my Reaper? Don't forget, you also disappointed me. Despite the most eclectic range of enhancements, you still managed to wind up mutilated beyond all recognition and in need of the most urgent restorative arts I could muster."

"My Lord Satan, you know what I faced that day." I cocked a thumb toward Samael and his white-winged cronies, who seemed to be edging closer. "Do you think any of those with you could have handled the might of the cherub, and the energies unleashed by the Dagger of Damocles *and* the Cup of Tartarus combined?"

"Excuses, Daemon, neat to mollify. I'm not interested in them. You were distracted by petty concerns and shit happened. Results are all that matter to me."

Results? Something about this situation didn't feel right, and Satan had just given me a clue as to what it might be. *Surely it's not about any humiliation he might be feeling. Is it?*

Taking my reticence as an invitation to pursue the matter, Satan continued, "Do you not feel the urge to justify your actions in any way?"

This is too much. "I shouldn't have to. Remember, of all the denizens of hell, I am the only one cursed with honesty. It is also common knowledge that my loyalty to you is beyond question. And really, that serves you well, for your Reaper strikes fear into the hearts of everyone he's sent to harvest. I have no need of gimmicks or tricks. My word and integrity are beyond reproach." I glanced at Samael. "Unlike others close to you. So, if I may say as much, I find it rather insulting that you're insinuating otherwise."

"Oh, I'm not, Daemon. In fact, I'm counting on your loyalty to settle a little matter to my satisfaction in the very near future. After all, actions *do* speak louder than words, yes?"

Where's he going with this? "Yes, but wha . . . ?"

Satan smiled and licked his lips. That simple action filled me with a sense of dread.

If I can just fathom what's really going on, I might be able to steer the course of this charade in the right direction . . . Eh?

Only then did I realize that Samael was still striding toward me, hand on his sword, a look of murderous intent smeared across his visage. I turned to face him.

My jibe about pure service must have stung more than I realized. "I wouldn't, unless you want to be the second angel taken out this day."

My warning stopped him dead. Or perhaps it was the sudden appearance of my scythe in my hands, extended and ready to garner a fresh head.

"You wouldn't dare," he hissed. Nevertheless, he didn't advance farther.

"That's something else that distinguishes us," I taunted. "I don't have to hide behind Satan's skirts. I *do* dare. I'm willing to make the hard decisions that others shy away from. *Do* the things that need to be done. You are nothing more tha–"

"I'm very glad to hear that, Daemon," Satan interrupted, "because I'd like you to make one of those hard decisions for me now. Would you do that? Think of it as a supreme demonstration to the choir of your absolute trust and loyalty to me."

Why would he need me to do such a thing? Then the next penny dropped. *He wants to save face*! I glanced about the shattered shell of his palace and that ugly truth registered more profoundly. *This was his showcase. Here, more than anywhere else, his propaganda promoted the legend of his unassailable sovereignty. Now that it lies in ruins, he needs to restore credibility among those he thinks might represent a threat*. A chill coursed along my spine. *And I bet I know who's expected to pay.*

Satan spotted the flare of concern in my eye and confirmed my suspicions. "You see, I'm of a mind to eradicate your Hell Hounds and make you start over again. A fresh start with a new pack, and all that. I think it would give you the motivation to concentrate your efforts more wisely. Unless, of course, you yourself are willing to save them?"

So, I'm *the threat?*

I decided to face it out and see where this led.

"You want me to volunteer to put my head on a block?"

I shrugged. "Fair enough. I'm the leader of the Hell Hounds and Inquisitors. It's only right I answer for their failings."

"Very noble, Daemon, and I'd expect nothing less from you. But it's not as easy as that. You went to a lot of trouble a few minutes ago to express how your actions reflect on my dominion. Offering up your soul in sacrifice wouldn't achieve that, for it already belongs to me. Instead, I'd prefer you atone for the shortcomings of your department by doing something you'd clearly like to avoid."

All twelve of the Fallen moved closer. As did Satan.

He can't be serious? "Something I'd like to avoid?"

"Yes. I know you're a coldhearted killer in my service. But this . . ." He chuckled, and my entire spine clenched. "Let's just say it'll be something that goes against your natural inclination."

Giving me no time to prepare, Satan stepped outside the closing circle and explained, "With the entire underworld looking into what happened today, I must demonstrate that, as benevolent as I am, I simply can't have the cream of my society—particularly those blessed with additional privileges—acting irresponsibly. Just look at the extent of the damage here. The rank and file expect me to respond swiftly and vigorously. They expect heads to roll: elite heads; heads very much in the public eye. Why, if I fail to act, the more powerful of my subjects—especially those with aspirations beyond their station—will think they can muscle in and challenge my authority. I can't have that, so here's what's going to happen . . ."

Leaving me hanging, Satan suddenly turned and strolled across to his throne where he made a show of dusting the seat with a handkerchief from his breast pocket. Having completed this *essential* task, he draped himself across the stool, and concluded, "In a moment, I'm going to give you a simple command. I expect you to obey that command instantly and without question. Now, what's going to be interesting is the fact that my directive will allow you a certain degree of latitude. I look forward to witnessing *how* you interpret it. Will you extol my sovereignty or not? We're about to see where your heart truly lies."

This cannot be happening.

A flare of alarm coursed through my Hounds. I could tell they were on the verge of arming themselves and fighting back. If they did, they were all dead—or worse. To forestall a catastrophe, I intervened: "Just tell me. *What* do you want me to do?"

Assuming his most dreadful aspect, Satan roared, "A head is nowhere near enough compensation for this debacle. I expect someone to be effaced from existence. Now!"

An edict for true extinction had just been passed, and the resonance of obliteration burned with a sweetness I couldn't deny.

Before I had taken a breath, I raised my weapon and depressed all five studs. Whirling, I gained momentum for my strike, and in completing that maneuver had time for only the briefest glimpse of the faces of my team. Nevertheless, each one brought with it lifetimes of memories.

Sweet Strawberry, a like-minded soul who craved the kill and reveled in suffering; Nimrod, my closest friend and confidant for longer than I could remember; Yamato, always trustworthy and dependable; Champ, as crass and accident prone as the day was long. Of all the Hounds, he had really fucked up badly this past week; and Gemini, the newest member of the pack and the one with the most burgeoning promise.

I am the Reaper. I am death personified, constrained to respond as is my creed.

My blade bit home. As it did so, I opened the vast pit that masqueraded as my soul and reveled in the giddy rush of life essence. Reversing my sickle, I stabbed down onto the severed head, impaling it to the cold marble beneath, and increased the drain. Foul arts bent to my will, preventing the disintegration of the body until I had depleted its vitality and sucked the marrow of its memory dry.

At the end, thunder rent the heavens and the atmosphere sizzled as lightning etched the sky in lurid threats. Before me, my oblation dwindled to nothing.

A palpable shock skittered about the cabal of fallen angels surrounding me, a sentiment echoed by the throb of apprehension escaping those of my team who had survived.

Ignoring everyone else, I spun on the spot to face His Infernal Majesty, planted the heel of my staff to the floor and knelt.

"It is done. I trust you find the value of such an offering sufficient?"

Tap-tap-tap. Tap-tap-tap. Tap-tap-tap.

For long minutes, the devil made no response other than to drum his fingers upon the armrest of his throne.

Tap-tap-tap. Tap-tap-tap. Tap-tap-tap.

I stayed where I was, on my knees. No one made a sound. Even Samael kept his mouth shut.

Tap-tap-tap. Tap-tap-tap. Tap-tap-tap.

"Rarely am I so surprised." Though low, Satan's voice rent the air like a knife. "Would you mind explaining your choice?"

"Call it instinct. You made it plain that the entire underworld will be watching to see how you dispense injustice. How better to respond than by having your Reaper act without mercy? And not merely against one of his own, but against the very best of them? Only by such an inexorable demonstration of brutality did I judge your ire might be assuaged and a sense of balance restored."

Approval pulsed, crackling through the ether—alongside something else.

Fear?

"Do you see, Samael?" Satan crooned. "Did I not say your suspicions were unfounded and my Reaper's ruthlessness would extend even to those closest to him?"

Samael? So he . . . ?

I almost looked up from the floor.

"That you did, sire," mumbled the coward. "That you did."

The terse acknowledgment was offered grudgingly. Nonetheless, it revealed who I would have to watch closely in the future.

Inhaling deeply, I allowed the outer veneer of my mind to turn to ice.

I'll remember this day, you motherfucker. You and I will have an accounting.

Footsteps approached. A pair of highly polished shoes appeared in my peripheral vision.

"Please stand, Daemon." I did as instructed and looked the lord of the underworld square in the face without flinching. Cold. Emotionless. Blank. "Nimrod was your best friend, wasn't he?"

"He was, sire. For the past three . . . no, four thousand years."

"And how do you feel now he's gone forever?"

"Honestly? A little pressured. We're a man down, so it's going to make our job even harder as we enter a crucial stage of the investigation." I indicated the brooding knot of killers clustered behind me. "So, with your leave, I'm keener than ever to get on?"

Satan nodded and waved me away."By all means: go get 'em, tiger."

One gesture brought my team to my side. Addressing them on our unique frequency, I warned, *Let's get the fuck outta here before I do something we all regret.*

As we left, Satan called out, "No good deed ever goes unpunished in my realm, Daemon. So make sure those who deserve it are left in no doubt of your displeasure."

I glanced at Yamato, Champ, Gemini and Strawberry in turn. *Oh I will, don't worry.*

Aloud, I replied, "As you wish, Sire."

Chapter 28: The Lull Before the Storm

With a couple of celebratory glasses of chilled *Démon Bleu Cuvée* to hand, Tesla entered the salon of his new abode to find his partner in crime lost in a world of personal reflection.

Chopin's eyes were wide and staring, and while it looked as if he was surveying the scene from their 11th Avenue apartment, Tesla doubted anything had actually registered.

Culture shock at its worst, I'll bet.

They had lived in Perish for many years, and as the decades dragged by, the Gallic charm of that city with its brooding menace and *joie de la souffrance* had slowly wormed its way beneath their skin. It was crass, it was blunt and yet, Perish possessed a certain style envied by denizens the underworld over. Hell's Kitchen, however, here on the other side of the Frantic Ocean, couldn't have been more different.

Padding across to peer out that same window, Tesla could see why his friend had succumbed to silence. Twenty-four hours a day nose-to-tail traffic, constant noise and fumes, the claustrophobic press of endless ranks of red-brick tenements. Together, it all seemed overly oppressive to say the least. Even the air refused to do its job, only reluctantly succumbing to the ebb and flow of myriad lungs all clamoring for breath at the same time.

And now it's home. He sighed. *But at least it serves its purpose and allows us to disappear whilst remaining in plain sight.*

A scuffle across the road on the corner of 47th and 48th Streets indicated yet another mugging was in process. From the look of it, a young punk was trying to snatch an elderly lady's handbag from off her shoulder. Passersby, well used to such minor inconveniences, adjusted their step so they could part like an unending flow of inhumanity around the temporary obstruction. Needless to say, nobody cared to intervene.

Not that it mattered. Far sprightlier than her blue rinse suggested, this particular senior citizen was putting up more resistance than her fragile demeanor indicated she might, for she was now in the process of using the object of her assailant's desire to batter him soundly around the head.

A dull thudding resonance could be heard above the drone of traffic and soon, a dark stain was spreading across the sidewalk and down into the gutter.

What on earth has she got in there? Tesla mused. *Lead pipes? The proverbial kitchen sink?*

Moments later, the robber's body wavered, then disappeared in a puff of smoke.

Nobody batted an eye. Traffic crawled by without pause, and pedestrians kept their eyes firmly fixed on the back of the person in front of them. The only unliving things that appeared interested in what had transpired were a local flock of hell-pigeons that suddenly swooped en masse from a nearby rooftop to feast on the unexpected bounty.

No class whatsoever. I do hope we—

"Is that for me?"

Chopin's query was unexpected, and Tesla jumped. Recovering quickly, he handed over a flute of champagne and replied, "Indeed it is. I knew we should have celebrated yesterday when we got back, but what with the event itself and the time difference, I was exhausted. Still, better late than never, eh?" He raised his own glass in salute. "To the end that is now in sight."

"To the end," Chopin echoed.

A pleasing *ching* rang through the air and they both took a large swallow.

"And to success," Tesla added, "though it seems we've been unusually blessed with that of late."

"I know exactly what you mean," Chopin agreed, "I can't believe we're actually here. Nor how easy it was. We were at the site of one of Satan's most prestigious monuments. Surrounded by reavers and demons and traps of lethal complexity. Up close and personal with two of the most powerful adversaries in existence. How the hell we didn't get caught, I'll never know."

"Tell me about it. I almost died when we strayed too close to Grislington, and the Dagger of Damocles nearly cancelled out the mitigating effects of his essence. He just missed landing on you. And when he stared into the mirror, well, I thought he was looking straight at us. I'm not ashamed to admit I nearly shit myself."

Chopin chuckled. "Grim will never fathom how he came to our rescue at that moment. Leaping out of the air and yelling blue murder. What a distraction. I must confess, Nikola, I've never been so pleased to see him."

Both men burst out laughing.

"Fortune favors the brave," Tesla murmured. Taking a seat opposite his counterpart, he dared to express something that had concerned him ever since they came back. "Don't get me wrong, Frédéric, I'm grateful that the two were so willing to lay into each other like that, but . . . my word. I never realized just how strong Grim had become. All brava-do aside, we were very fortunate. Our luck can't hold out like that for much longer."

"It's not down to luck, my friend. We were well prepared, well positioned, and it was a textbook snatch-and-grab. In and out before anyone knew we were there. Anyway, it's al-most over now, and he won't be our concern for very much longer."

Tesla caught the subtle reference. "Much longer? Are you going to activate our sleeper agent and—?"

"No, that's not what I meant."

"What then, I thought all we had to do now was wait for the Winter Soulstice?"

Chopin leaned forward in his chair and dropped his voice. "True, but that's a little while away yet and there's something I feel we ought to do in the meantime."

"And what might that be? I do hope it isn't something that will expose us to needless danger."

"Like you, I didn't fail to miss how dominant Grim has become. For all his faults, Grislington was a cherub. That put him beyond the ability of Samael and his cohorts to deal with. Even Satan would have been hard-pressed to handle him alone, especially when you consider Grislington also had one of the most powerful totems in existence to back him up. Yet Grim managed to destroy the angel's weapon without breaking a sweat. It's unnatural. So, I'm thinking we ought to look into that aspect more thoroughly. The *Sword of Uncovered Secrets* can expose the obscurest details. At a price, I know, but in this case, I feel the pain of obtaining the truth may be worth the cost. Forewarned will most definitely be forearmed. Of course, it might also be prudent to err on the side of caution in other ways."

"What other ways?"

"I was thinking we ought to take a chance in going for a couple of soul sapphires."

"Soul sapphires?" Tesla was aghast. "Are you mad? You do know they can only be found in the darkest depths of the largest and most temperamental volcanoes on the Kigali home world?"

"I do."

"And the Kigali are not averse to stomping intruders to death."

"They're not, no."

"Then why take the risk?"

"Think of it as insurance. Like I said, Grim is too influential for his own damned good . . . or ours, come to that. Badness knows what other abilities he might have tucked up his sleeve. I don't want to go to all the bother of putting our long-laid plans into motion only to have them thwarted at the last second. So, think of the gems as our last bit of indemnity. Hopefully, we'll never need them, but if we do—?"

"Then why not simply use our agent? It'd be a superb opportunity to catch him with his pants down and we might not get another chance like this."

Chopin's eyes narrowed. "I must admit, the idea intrigues me the more I think about it." He shuffled forward to the edge of his seat. "Do you think the asset will be up to it?"

"Of course I do, and let me tell you why . . ."

*

In an effort to appease the fragile sensibilities of his guest for the last few days, Erra had been at pains to spruce up his temporary throne room.

The barrow of rotten corpses had been cleared away, and the stench associated with decaying flesh and putrid organs had been completely expunged. Even the insects that had lingered following the destruction of the mound had been excised from existence, so that nothing might present an obstacle to the unprecedented negotiations currently taking place between the mystic and his Seven.

Garlands of poison ivy, red berry, white rootsnake and monkshood now hung between vaulted arches, cunningly intertwined through chains once used to bind hostages. Huge bouquets and baskets of oleander, Amazon lily and sea hibiscus showered down from peacock displays, cunningly arranged to hide those stains that had proven too stubborn to resist the cleansing fires of the Seventh himself. And everywhere, the scent of attar and brimstone combined in a heady battle to dominate the senses.

Surveying the columns and balusters edging his chamber, Erra thought them somewhat plain and lacking in character, and hoped the talks wouldn't drag on.

It doesn't feel like a home from home anymore. The sooner we get this little exercise finished, the sooner I can return to Emeslam's embrace and . . .

A delegation, consisting of all seven of his personified weapons, entered the far end of the vestibule. He could tell immediately by the way they bore themselves they were doing their best not to overawe the much smaller figure walking in their midst. Their manner forced him to acknowledge a simple truth.

This fiasco just might work. The wildfire sparked by the Reaper's latest exploits burns from one end of the underverse to the other . . . As does the plaguing rebuke of Satan's response. That fool of a would-be king insists on doing our work for us. Perhaps I ought to take Grim up on his offer and allow him to demonstrate his tenacity for auditing? By the way he eliminated his foe, and a cherub no less, I'm beginning to think he may have been genuine in his offer to clear the dregs from that level for us. Who would have thought I might even entertain the notion that the Reaper knows what he's talking about? Erra chuckled softly to himself. *Or this tiny creature, come to that?*

The contingent came to a stop near the bottom step, and the Titans parted.

"The saint has agreed to our terms," explained the First by way of introduction, "and while she deplores the barbarity of our methods to date, is willing to overlook such shortcomings in an effort to speed along a resolution to everyone's liking."

Is she indeed? How quaint.

Though still seated, Erra towered over the diminutive woman before him. Peering down, he found her pale complexion, rosy lips and slight form a pleasant change to ruined bodies. An unflinching pair of hazel eyes regarded him studiously.

A sudden impulse spurred Erra to ask an unusual question: "Teresa, how old were you when you died?"

"Sixty-seven, Lord Erra."

"Yet you appear before me looking no more than, what, thirty years old? Why do you think this is?"

The young woman smiled.

"You'd need to ask the devil about that, I'm afraid. His mind tends to work in unfathomable ways . . . as we've all witnessed not these two days past."

"I appreciate what you say. But would you care to venture a guess?"

"In truth? I have always suspected he believes me more of a threat than he lets on. Satan is as Satan does. He went to all that trouble to fool me and make me feel unworthy over so many years that, well, once he'd snared me, what was he going to do with me? A saint in hell is a dangerous thing, for I would be a beacon of hope in the darkness. He no doubt realized this and sought to minimize the damage. What other reason could there be in hiding such a prize away where she couldn't be seen openly?"

"And making you look so innocent?"

"A part of his strategy, I'm sure. I can provide a valuable service to the damned that would otherwise be denied them. But it would take faith on their part to reach out and work for it. Who would they more readily listen to? An elderly prune who looks like she has earned her bent back and wrinkled face, or a sprightly little thing in the bloom of youth?"

Erra delighted at the weight of wisdom in the saint's words and laughed heartily as their import struck home.

Such a timely lesson. Am I myself not guilty of that very same prejudice?

Aloud, he replied, "A cunning ruse, I see, especially when your arts are the very antidote this loveless place needs to overcome the infection of isolation and loneliness that keeps people without hope."

"Precisely. You may see *why* it is a cause so dear to my heart."

"And now our long-term policy has been explained, are you certain you want to assist us?"

"I am, especially if it fosters room for growth and repentance before Satan's subjects are audited."

"Excellent!" Erra beamed. "How soon can you begin?"

"Once I have my rosary, holy cross and the phial containing the blood of Christ, I can begin immediately."

"These articles are necessary to your work?"

"Vital, for the task ahead is long and laborious. It will take weeks to formulate the esoteric template upon which to mount the anagogic formula, and those relics will act as a focusing agent to allow me to complete the task at hand that much quicker."

"Then by all means, we will endeavor to secure those items for you, forthwith."

"Thank you, Lord Erra. From what I am led to believe, they are kept within the strong room at Wormblood Scrubs." Teresa glanced at her imposing companions. "I also have it on good authority that the warden possesses the only cipher. Though, I suspect your most able stalwarts won't find that to be much of a hindrance?"

"Indeed they won't."

Erra chose his next questions carefully, for the matter had caused him concern ever since he had heard of his enforcers' plans to involve the mystic's services.

"If I may ask? Once completed, how far will the impulse you release actually travel and for how long will it retain dominion?"

"From what the Second explained, you need my compulsion to extend across New Hell in its entirety, is that right?"

"That's right, yes."

"Then it's simple. If the Seven are able to do as they assured, and position me at the precise cosmic juncture I require within the Sheolspace continuum during the coming Infernal Equinox, I'll be able to release the sovereignty of the incantation directly into the cords that hold all the circles of New Hell together. Juxtapose, Perish, Dark Cairo, Niflheim; all will be affected. What's more, if my calculations are precise enough, you might even find that compulsion spilling over into older realms too."

"And for how long will your enchantment hold the minions in thrall?"

"Ah, I'm afraid the answer to *that* is far more complicated, for it will depend upon the degree to which individual denizens damned themselves. Human nature is a strange and wondrous thing, Lord Erra. Frightening too, as emotional ambivalence can quickly turn love to hate, especially in those instances where affection is not reciprocated or where people have been denied intimacy for too long. Remember, many are here for what we term 'crimes of passion.' Where such intense feelings and a loss of control were involved, I fear my influence will be reduced to naught but a passing flight of fancy, a diversion to keep them occupied for an hour or two. Nothing more.

"Regardless, I still have faith and believe the vast majority will be moved to express their desires until the conjuration has run its course." Teresa shrugged. "Needless to say, I fear those brave souls who are truly contrite will be few and far between, but at least for them the metamorphosis will be permanent, though ultimately lethal."

A blunt assessment, but in all honesty, one better than I'd dared to hope for.

"Thank you for being candid, Teresa. Then by all means, don't let me delay you any longer. The First will assist you personally in securing everything you need to begin as soon as possible. In the meantime, we are at your service. If there is anything you need to make your stay here and back at Emeslam more comfortable, do not hesitate to let me know."

The First moved to usher the saint away. Nevertheless, Erra could already see a question forming on her lips.

"Yes?"

Teresa nodded toward the multicolored wreaths festooned about the hall. "I was wondering if I could have some of these moved to my room? I know you've gone to a great deal of trouble to make me feel welcome, but I'm sure the last thing you want to see is all this greenery spoiling your man cave? Somehow, it doesn't seem to be . . . *you*. I'd be glad to take them off your hands."

Erra slapped his knee and chortled aloud, a rare sight and sound for one so attuned to misery and mayhem.

"Dear lady, you are a delight and most perceptive. Please, help yourself. Or perhaps it might be better if some of my deacons helped you. Though beautiful, the blooms are toxic to humans. I tell you what, if you commence your labors immediately, the whole lot will be moved to your room and anterior corridors as you work. How does that sound?"

"It sounds like we have a deal."

Turning on her heel, Saint Teresa of Ávila strode from the room, confidence radiating from her in waves and her retinue of demigods gliding along in her wake.

"Second?" Erra called out. "Stay behind, will you."

The Second of the Seven returned to his station before the throne.

"My lord?"

"I have something to discuss that might prove beneficial to our cause, something dangerous. Something only *you* might be capable of securing. Can I rely on your utmost discretion?"

"Of course. How may I assist?"

"The beginning of the end is upon us," Erra began, "and in anticipation of the hurdles we might face, I want you to . . ."

Epilogue

In through the nose, and out through the mouth. In through the nose, and out through the mouth.

Alone at last and safely ensconced within my bedroom at the Black Tower, I repeated that simple mantra over and over in the hope that it would ease the pressure of the thousand concerns crowding in on me all at once.

Who said this crap would work?

Too much had happened over the past three days for me to be able to simply let go, and the iron bulwark of my resolve crumbled in the face of a fresh onslaught of contradictory images and sensations:

Empyrean vistas dominated. In most of them, myriad angels wielding shining swords threatened universal war. Roused to anger, their zeal knew no bounds and the cosmos trembled as it contemplated extinction.

Grislington featured in many of those visions, especially near the end where his face became a battleground of conflicting emotions as he reclaimed his long-lost identity, and victory—along with life itself—was snatched from his grasp at the final moment.

Then fire came from heaven: primal; fervent; ancient; and all-consuming, focused on one individual in particular who dared to push things too far.

Finally, Nimrod appeared: quiet; confident; dependable. Apart from Satan himself, he was my oldest friend here in hell, and my closest confidant.

A spurt of anger coursed through my heart at the bitter consequences of Samael's interference, causing my tattoos to glow hot. An antithetical wave of guilt doused the ardor of my ill-conceived outburst. Shame followed, as did an unhealthy dose of confusion.

What the fuck? I can't think like this, I'm Satan's man, through and through . . . ?

There was no getting round it, though. My confidence had been shaken by what had happened.

Of all the denizens in hell, I can appreciate the need for uncompromising brutality, even if undeserved. Discipline has to be maintained. Through fear or respect, it doesn't matter in a place like this where your own granny would stab you in the back as soon as look at you if it proved to her advantage.

At times, I felt it impossible to understand His Infernal Majesty's reasoning. A rare necessity, true, but something I had been doing more often since the events of only seventy-four hours ago.

This is Nimrod we're talking about, someone who accomplished everything a human could ever wish for in his time on earth: a builder of cities and tyrannical king over millions; one of the most superlative hunters of men ever to exist; an adversary of God himself and a promoter of false worship. If that isn't a prime candidate for the underverse served up on a plate, then I don't know who is. He loved being here and always viewed hell as the playground it is for creatures like us . . . killers. So how does sacrificing him serve my Dark Father's designs? If Satan allowed himself to be maneuvered into a situation where someone's head had to roll, why not dispose of the biggest threat?

No matter how hard I tried, I couldn't get over the fact that we needed Nimrod now more than ever. As usual when I was frustrated, I verbalized my thinking process:

"I may have destroyed one of the greatest hazards to infernal insecurity ever to exist, but in reality, Grislington was merely a bonus. Something extra uncovered during our enquiries into a cancer that's been eating away at the bowels of Hellonian society for decades, perhaps longer?"

That reminder of Chopin and Tesla made me realize how much work I still needed to do.

"Now we're a team member down at one of the most crucial periods of our history. Proscribed artifacts are in play, arcane powers are on the loose, and we still haven't identified the extent of the mole problem. The Sibitti are smarting and no doubt plotting new atrocities and, just lately, all sorts of enhanced individuals are popping up all over the place. Not good! I need everyone motivated, focused and on their toes, not staggering about blindly in the wilderness because we're too hard-pressed to see the bigger picture."

Fortunately, hard-hearted commonsense won the day:

"Like it or not, there's no use crying over spilt milk. What's done is done. Satan will still expect me to achieve results, so we'll all have to buckle down and get on with it."

Pondering what lay ahead of us, I wrestled with the dilemma of how I would best allocate the Hounds.

"There's no way I'm going to split Champ and Yamato. They've been together for more than a century and Champ's far too disruptive to take any changes now, especially as his only viable option is Gemini. The last thing I want is for their affection for each other to blossom into another reason for Satan to demonstrate his displeasure. No, he needs a steadying hand to keep him useful." I sighed. "Which means Gemini is my new right-hand man. I won't be as free to act as I was when—?"

"Unless I factor our unexpected sponsor into play?" This epiphany struck me so suddenly I sat bolt upright.

The more I thought about it, the more credence I gave the notion.

"He's powerful, inspired, possesses off-the-charts ability in areas we don't understand. And he was a soldier too. I wonder how his expertise would be affected if he adopted the mantle of Hell Hound? If it's anything like what happened to Gemini, well . . ."

Myriad new possibilities sprang to mind. Only then did I realize that the spinning vortex of doubt that had plagued me these past three days had frittered away.

Flopping back onto the pillow, I threw my glasses to one side, closed my door and the secondary blinds with TK so it was now as black as midnight, and allowed myself to relax properly for the first time in what seemed like an age.

Yamato will assume the role of pack leader, of course. That's not a problem; he's more than capable and maturity will add . . . round out their skill . . . balance them . . .

Problem solved, I felt drowsy.

I must have dropped off, for it only felt like a second or two later when I became aware of a nearby presence.

Friend or foe?

Remaining completely still, I allowed the steady rhythm of my breathing to continue and cast my perceptions into the gloom. A sizzling concentration of longing and anticipation emanated from inside my en suite bathroom.

Strawberry?

She sensed the subtle nuance of my probe and called out, "Sorry to wake you. I didn't mean to spoil your surprise. But frankly, I'm so turned on I can barely hold it together."

Surprise? Turned on?

My heart beat that little bit faster, and I marshaled all my self-discipline to prevent myself from leaping off the bed there and then. Instead, I made a conscious effort to lie completely still and savored the occasion, waiting for Strawberry to come to me.

To no avail.

I lasted all of two seconds before projecting my farsight toward the doorway.

So, what might this surprise *invol–? Wow!*

A blood-red pool formed about Strawberry's feet as she let her cape fall to the floor. Naked as the day she was born, the woman of my dreams had obviously been enhanced, for her long-dead flesh now glowed with the healthy golden hue of someone who had spent months under a Mediterranean sun. And from what my clairvoyant projection revealed, no bikini lines spoiled the view.

How did she manage that? Has the Undertaker gone soft or something?

The all-over tan complemented her honey blonde hair while accentuating every delicious curve of her body. So faultless was she, it appeared as if the gods had gone to great lengths to form the perfect example of sexuality, only to pour it out before me as an offering to lust.

Astral sight or no, Strawberry looked stunning, and I gorged myself on the sight of her. As I did so, I couldn't help but note how her aura sparked with barely suppressed desire—and something more. Ravenous green eyes locked onto me as she padded like a lioness toward her prey.

A needle of caution burrowed its way into my spine.

"Strawberry, what are you actually doing here?"

"Ah, it seems you've caught me out." Producing a set of gravity shackles from behind her back, she explained, "Everyone has noticed how much stress you've been under, these past few days. You haven't eaten or slept, and you haven't even bothered to recharge yourself in the soothing balm of the Bālefire. It's as if you've lost your motivation." Twirling the cuffs on the ends of her fingers, she announced, "I'm here to remind you that there are things worth unliving for."

I liked the way she was thinking. I really did. But one thing bugged me.

"And what makes you think we'll actually be able to do that? You know how our Dark Father mutated our genes so we aren't able to touch after the . . ."

"After the Isle of Cogs?" Strawberry concluded my line of reasoning, but then expanded it: "This is twelve months later. Not only have you been reverted to human form, but you've been enhanced as well. Everyone's discerned the change in you. Why do you think Satan has been so hard on you lately? You've become someone worthy of respect — a threat, even. He's trying to remind you of your place."

"My place? But I've always known I'm the Reaper and — "

"Yet, consider what you achieved at the Palace of Verse and Sighs. Some of us think you're powerful enough to override even the devil's machinations now. We also suspect that your increased dexterity might extend to physiological and esoteric adaptations. Think of it as the reverse of what you do when you manifest your death touch. Satan is unnerved."

Bloody hell . . . she shouldn't really be talking like this. "And if you're wrong?"

"If I'm wrong, I'll get to spend a few days on Slab A with nothing more than a slapped wrist. C'mon, think about it.

How can His Royal Travesty argue against something that gets his Reaper's mind back on the game?"

By now, Strawberry had reached the bottom of the bed. Her fingernails tapped a steady beat against the smooth metal of the restraints. My senses swirled about them and tasted their character, their potential, before expanding like a lover's caress toward her body: probing, exploring, teasing, savoring. She squealed at my mind's intrusion, and gasped, "For badness sake, what have we got to lose? Just keep your eyes shut and try."

She has a point, I suppose. I grinned. *And now I've got my balls back, I wouldn't want them to turn blue and drop off. Ah fuck it! Why not enjoy a little fun?*

I beckoned, and felt the edge of the mattress compress as Strawberry edged forward to kneel by my feet. Being careful not to touch my skin, she placed the first of the manacles about my ankles. As she did so, I turned inward, reached down into the abyss at the center of my being, and let instinct guide me.

This was Strawberry, my Chief Inquisitor and someone I dared to admit I cared for. She offered no threat to Satan or his realm. And although relationships were frowned upon for the elite, and prohibited for the masses, nothing we contemplated could imperil anything of value. All I must do was make my spirit realize that fact. Stilling the boiling cauldron of wrath that always simmered within me, I took hold of its passion and molded it to my will.

It was far simpler than I had ever imagined it would be. A shimmering well of darkness stretched out to blend with Strawberry's aura, and we became one. She felt it, and a corresponding pulse issued from somewhere deep inside her, where an abiding hunger saturated her soul.

I think she's just as desperate for attention as I am.

Strawberry continued to creep along the duvet without a word. Once she reached my side, I raised my arms above my head to make it easier for her, and allowed her to place the last two bracelets about my wrists. Once finished, she propped herself up on one elbow.

"Ready?" she whispered.

"Ready," I echoed.

The room was still as black as pitch. Nevertheless, my telepathic senses allowed me to watch with infinite clarity as Strawberry tentatively reached out to stroke my arm.

A voltaic charge skittered across my epidermis as we made contact.

"Oh my fucking God," Strawberry blasphemed, "you did it!"

Ornaments and light fitments jingled and furniture juddered in response to a momentary tremor. In the distance, thunder rumbled.

Strawberry's touches grew more frantic. She groaned and swung one leg across my body to straddle me. The urgency of her movements caused me to stiffen instantly. Fire bloomed in my veins.

"Wait," I hissed, "not like this."

"What do you mean, *wait*? We can hold each other, Daemon. We can actually . . ."

"I mean, I don't want to do it as if we're sharing a stolen moment that's only fit for secrecy and shadows. We haven't been together for what, over a year? Let's take our time. Treasure it. Make it last. And as I haven't even allowed myself to think of you this way for fear of being driven mad, you can at least do me the courtesy of waiting one moment while I turn on the lights."

"Okay, but when you're done, you must withdraw your perceptions back inside your skull. I'm going to punish you

for this and make you work for every moment of enjoyment."
A throaty laugh pierced the air. "Let's just say, neither of us
will ever forget it."

I can definitely work with that.

The shackles activated, pinning me to the sheets.

Strawberry placed a soft cloth across my eyes. Her titter-
ing distracted me, and it took a great deal of effort to focus
enough to activate the control.

Now limited to purely mundane sensations, I discerned a
muted radiance worming its way through my blindfold.

Strawberry's giggling got louder, and she began to tease
the silken strands of her hair across my face and shoulders.
If anything, my restricted environment only served to arouse
me further.

And still I didn't move.

"Enough of your games," Strawberry's voice had turned
husky. "Now I have your complete attention, the real entertainment can begin."

Her tone possessed a cruel, dominant edge. Usually, I
liked that, but on this occasion it caused a tiny spark of alarm
to raise its pyrotechnic head in warning.

That didn't sound . . . normal?

Strawberry's movements didn't feel right, either. Unnat-
urally tense, her breathing came in short sharp bursts and reminded me of someone asphyxiating.

My uneasiness intensified.

"Strawberry, are you okay?"

"Don't you worry yourself. I've been waiting for this moment for such a long time; it would be a pity to spoil it now."

Attempting to sit up, I found my movements constrained
by the cuffs and started to writhe against them.

"Switch off the restraints, Strawberry. I've changed my
mind and — "

"Oh, it's too late for that."

Something switched all right, but it wasn't the manacles. One moment Strawberry was there, the timbre of her inner turmoil ringing through loud and clear despite our agreement. Then her mind went blank.

I strained harder, and the Bãlefire surged to the surface, yearning for release.

No. I can't, not against Strawberry.

Making a last-ditch effort to prevent the floodgates from bursting, I pushed my astral sight up and out past the blindfold. That was what she'd been waiting for.

Bathed in sweat, eyes glazed, fangs and talons fully extended, Strawberry sat astride me like a demented rodeo rider, a cruel-looking dagger gripped tightly in both hands.

Where the fuck did that come from?

Then I noticed the blood, and a huge gash in her abdomen.

Did she just gouge her belly?

A shrill buzz emanated from the weapon's core. Completely alien, it hurt my ears and seemed to exert a strange influence over Strawberry's behavior.

"What are you doing? For badness sake, stop while you can."

"I can't help it, baby. I've got to."

"Please . . . stop before it's too late."

She didn't seem to hear me. "Can you imagine any better way out than this? Just the two of us, together at the end, sailing off into oblivion?"

Oblivion? But that's not possible here . . . ?

"Don't . . ." Reacting instinctively, I reached into her mind to compel her. I found nothing there. Changing target, I next attempted to counter the resonance given off by the blade she held. It kept slipping away every time my comprehension latched onto it. "Strawberry, help me. Get a grip for—"

"Get a grip?" She did, but not in the way I wanted. Snarling, Strawberry raised the knife high above her head. "I haven't had a grip on anything since the Black Keep."

The awful truth came crashing home, and I was tormented by a recollection of the first occasion when Strawberry's sanity had been taken captive. Cream's voice still taunted me from the deepest shadows of my memory:

"Fool, you chose the wrong target. Her mind is now obedient to me. She is my *puppet to command, not yours . . ."*

Chopin and Tesla must have found a way to maintain a subtle connection and waited until they thought the time was right. Bastards!

The dagger's tip gleamed as it rushed toward my heart.

I needn't have worried, for my tattoos recognized the imminent danger and triggered a palladinium metamorphosis. Nevertheless, I was also the Reaper, a stone-cold killer, and Satan had dropped enough hints and other cryptic references lately about my newly-restored and somewhat enhanced capabilities . . . Including what might happen if I ever laid my naked gaze upon anyone.

My eyes snapped open.

Faster than reason, swifter than thought, the unadulterated tincture of that death's-head stare roared out, augmented and raging far beyond my wildest dreams.

The cloth about my head might never have existed. So fragile, so insignificant was its substance that it ceased to exist the moment my lashes fluttered against it.

Strawberry Fields, aka Red Riding Hood, Chief Inquisitor of the First Order of Shâitan, however, was something else entirely. As one of the most puissant creatures in existence, her mettle was of the purest quality.

Evidently, my new and improved death's-head stare couldn't give a toss how capable she was, nor what dominion her weapon possessed. Both were obliterated in an instant, creating an overwhelming backwash of unrestrained augury I was eager to subsume.

I opened myself fully and inhaled.

In moments, everything about my lover—her hopes and dreams, trials and tribulations, even her aspirations and memories; every single facet of her existence, in fact—was swallowed and absorbed . . . along with the gravity restraints and her weapon itself.

It's as if I have access to her entire history. I didn't know I could do that.

Then the full devastating weight of Strawberry's annihilation crashed down on me, and I shuddered to my core.

Strangling those feelings until some more suitable time, I leaped from the bed, scooped up my glasses, and allowed Olympian majesty to congeal about me. Then I set about ensuring no other hazards loomed.

Twin laser beams marked the path of my scrutiny. I left no stone unturned—nor item of furniture, come to that—and soon the smell of scorched wood and burnt fabric filled the air.

Light footfalls sounded in the corridor outside. After a momentary pause, the door crashed inward to reveal my new right-hand *man*, daggers in hand.

Good start.

"Gemini, nice to see someone's on the ball."

She took one glance at me and the surrounding damage before gamboling across the floor to take up a position at my back. "We felt the signs of a struggle from down in the dining hall. Champ and Yamato assured me it was just Strawberry up to her usual tricks and getting carried away."

We continued to circle for a moment as I completed my scan.

"But not you?" I probed.

"I'm a woman. I've forgotten more about foreplay and roughhousing than you boys will ever know." She paused to meet my eye. "Fortunately, that gave me a head start when I realized something was off kilter. But not in time to help you, it seems?"

Sure enough, the sound of heavy feet pounding up the stairs reverberated along the hallway.

"The immediate danger is over now," I sighed, not really wanting to explain things further until I knew how far the threat extended. "Once we've swept the entire keep, I'll be in a better position to tell you what happened."

Champ and Yamato chose that moment to come skidding to a halt in the doorway, weapons drawn. After inspecting the interior and taking one look at my face, both had the sense to remain silent.

Nonetheless, Gemini eventually asked the question on everybody's mind:

"Daemon . . . where's Strawberry?"

"I destroyed her. She's gone."

"Gone? As in the little love experiment didn't work and your touch sent her for reassignment?"

"No . . . as in she was a sleeper agent. She attacked me and I reacted instinctively. Now she's obliterated, gone forever."

A palpable chill filled the room in response to my announcement. Everyone appeared suddenly awkward and unsure of what to say or do.

"I see." Gemini did nothing more than briefly touch my arm before stepping away, but in that moment I knew she would make the perfect new teammate. "What do you need us to do?"

A brief flash of piercing jade eyes and a mile-wide smile clouded my vision.

I blinked.

My chest heaved.

Extending my hand, I waited for the reassuring *clang* of metal on metal as my scythe slammed into my palm. Only then could I speak.

"First, I want the Black Tower put on lockdown. Then I want everyone—and I mean everyone; Hounds, Inquisitors, security staff, admin—gathered at the blood bowl down in the main yard." I flexed and my weapon extended, snapping into place with a precision that smacked of unavoidable finality. "We have a problem, an infection that has wormed its way into the very heart of our infernal organization. Starting with you Hounds, I'm going to conduct a few . . . tests. I apologize in advance, because they will be invasive and most certainly painful. But I have no choice: I need to be sure, and you must lead others by your example. Once that's over, you will help me sanitize each and every department until we are sure our despised sanctuary is free from taint."

"And then?" Gemini whispered, her eyes alight with fire.

"And then we'll initiate a hunt the likes of which Satan has never seen. We will tear every corner of the underverse apart. We will be vile, remorseless, brutal and merciless. I swear to you now, the screams of any and all that oppose us—be they gods, Sibitti or Titans—will reach the walls of heaven itself, until we choose to stop or we locate those responsible and wreak bloody injustice upon them."

As I spoke, I simply let go and allowed the raw passion of my rage to push through. Extending my senses out across Olde London Town, I paused to witness the results.

Storm clouds gathered overhead, illuminating again and again with fulgurous intent.

"Are you with me?" I thundered.

As one, three heads fell back to voice their support.

Howling, their baying cadence caused the hell-ravens scattered along the battlements outside to take flight. Throughout the length and breadth of the city, necks craned upward momentarily, and all but the most foolhardy cowered.

Then the rain began, heavy and relentless, like the hand I would shortly wield.

And so it begins.

www.ingramcontent.com/pod-product-compliance
Lightning Source LLC
Chambersburg PA
CBHW032301020726
47495CB00001B/203